W9-CBM-548

ACCLAIM FOR LONDONSTANI

'*Londonstani* is an enthralling book. . . . A bold and vigorous debut.'
—*The Independent on Sunday* (UK)

'Witty and acute. . . . Very distinctive.'
—*The Bookseller*

'[Malkani] forces the reader to question the skin-deep assumptions we make about race.'
—*Sunday Telegraph*

'*Londonstani*—with all its bling, gore, graphic language . . . will get the kids' attention. In a language they understand, innit.'
—*TIME* magazine (Europe)

'Wholly unique—refreshing, new, astounding.'
—*Kirkus Reviews*

'In a linguistic politics redolent of Sam Selvon, Victor Headley and Irvine Welsh, Malkani conveys with élan and expertise, through a sub-urban "desi-dialect," the absurdity of adolescence and the complex self-deceptions of contemporary cultural dynamics in the UK.'
—*The Independent*

'Slangy and sharp.'
—*Arena* magazine

'The novel is kept compelling by Malkani's fine ear for inventive expression.'
—*The Times Literary Supplement*

'*Londonstani* subtly explores the contradictions and complexities of relations within Britain's black and Asian communities. . . . It intends, above all, to show you one thing: that being a young British Asian or African—whether you are Muslim, Hindu or Sikh—is not about having a completely westernised identity and set of aspirations.'

—*New Statesman*

'Electrifying.'

—*Red Magazine*

'Give this book to seventeen-year-olds who think novels are musty entities with no bearing on their lives, and you may well find them responding with huge enthusiasm.'

—*The Guardian*

'Malkani has effectively dropped a sociological bombshell with the potential to blow apart the bland assumptions about "ethnic minorities" so easily made by officially multicultural Britain.'

—*The Times of India*

'A vibrant linguistic mash-up!'

—*Vogue*

LONDONSTANI

GAUTAM MALKANI

HarperCollins*Publishers*Ltd

Published by HarperCollins Publishers Ltd

First Canadian edition

The first chapter appeared in slightly
different form in *Prospect* magazine.

'Back for Good' words and music by Gary
Barlow © 1994 reproduced by permission of
EMI Virgin Ltd.

HarperCollins books may be purchased for
educational, business, or sales promotional
use through our Special Markets
Department.

HarperCollins Publishers Ltd
2 Bloor Street East, 20th Floor
Toronto, Ontario, Canada
M4W 1A8

www.harpercollins.ca

Library and Archives Canada Cataloguing
in Publication

Malkani, Gautam
Londonstani / Gautam Malkani. – 1st
Canadian ed.

ISBN-13: 978-0-00-200815-0
ISBN-10: 0-00-200815-7

I. Title.

PR6113.A45L65 2006 823'.92 C2006-902065-5

RRD 9 8 7 6 5 4 3 2 1

Printed and bound in the United States

Typeset in Minion
by Palimpsest Book Production Limited,
Polmont, Stirlingshire

For my wife, Monica, and in memory of Mum

PART ONE
PAKI

1

— Serve him right he got his muthafuckin face fuck'd, shudn't b callin me a Paki, innit.

After spittin his words out Hardjit stopped for a second, like he expected us to write em down or someshit. Then he sticks in an exclamation mark by kickin the white kid in the face again. — Shudn't b callin us Pakis, innit, u dirrty gora.

Again, punctuation came with a kick, but with his left foot this time so it was more like a semicolon. — Call me or any a ma bredrens a Paki again an I'ma mash u an yo family. In't dat da truth, Pakis?

— Dat's right, Amit, Ravi an I go, — dat be da truth.

The three a us spoke in sync like we belonged to some tutty boy band, the kind who sing the chorus like it's some blonde American cheerleader routine. Hardjit, Hardjit, he's our man, if he can't bruck-up goras, no one can. Ravi then delivers his standard solo routine: — Yeh, blud, safe, innit.

— Hear wat my bredren b sayin, sala kutta? Come out wid dat shit again n I'ma knock u so hard u'll b shittin out yo mouth 4 real, innit, goes Hardjit, with an eloquence an conviction that made me green with envy. Amit always liked to point out that brown people don't actually go green: — We don't go red when we been shamed an we don't go blue when we dead, he'd said to me one time. — We don't even go purple when we been bruised, jus a darker brown. An still goras got da front to call *us* coloured.

It was an old joke but, green or not, I in't shamed to admit I'm

3

envious a Hardjit. Most bredren round Hounslow were jealous a his designer desiness, with his perfectly built body, his perfectly shaped facial hair an his perfectly groomed garms that made it look like he went shopping with P Diddy. Me, I was jealous a his front – what someone like Mr Ashwood'd call a person's linguistic prowess or his debating dexterity or someshit. Hardjit always knew exactly how to tell others that it just weren't right to describe all desi boys as Pakis. Regarding it as some kind a civic duty to educate others in this basic social etiquette, he continued kickin the white kid in the face, each kick carefully planted so he din't get blood on his Nike Air Force Ones (the pair he'd bought even before Nelly released a track bout what wikid trainers they were).

— We ain't bein called no fuckin Paki by u or by any otha gora, u get me? Hardjit goes to the white boy as he squirms an splutters in a puddle on the concrete floor, liftin his head right back into the flight path a Hardjit's Air Force Ones. — U bhanchod b callin us lot Paki one more time an I swear we'll cut'chyu up, innit.

For a minute, the gora's given a time out as Hardjit stops to straighten his silver chain, keepin his metal dog tags hangin neatly in the centre a his black Dolce & Gabbana vest, slightly covering up the &. A little higher an he could've probly clenched the dog tags in the deep groove between his pecs.

— Ki dekh da payeh? U like dis chain I got, white boy? Fuckin five-ounce white gold, innit. Call me a Paki again n I whip yo ass wid it.

— Yeh, blud, safe, innit, Ravi goes, cocking his head upwards. This weren't just cos most desi boys tended to tilt their heads up when they spoke, but also cos Ravi was just five foot five. The bredren was chubby too. Matter a fact, if you swapped Ravi's waxed-back hair with a £5 crew cut an gave him boiled-chicken-coloured skin he could pass for one a them lager-lout football thugs, easy. The kind who say En-ger-land cos they can't pronounce the name a their own country.

The boiled-chicken-coloured boy on the floor in front a us weren't no football hooligan nor no lager lout. He wouldn't want to be one an wouldn't want to look like one either. These days, lager louts had more to fear from us lot than us lot had to fear from them. Honest to God, in pinds like Hounslow an Southall, they feared us even more than they feared black kids. Round some parts, even black kids feared people like us. Especially when people like us were people like Hardjit. Standin there in his designer desi garms, a tiger tattooed on his left shoulder an a Sikh Khanda symbol on his right bicep. He probly could've fit a whole page a Holy Scriptures on his biceps if he wanted to. The guy'd worked every major muscle group, down the gym, every other day since he was fuckin fourteen years old. Since, despite his mum's best efforts, he hit puberty an became a proper desi boy. Even drinks that powdery protein shit they sell down there but she don't care cos he mixes it in with milk.

— How many us bredren u count here? Hardjit goes to the white boy.

— Uuuuurgh.

— Fuckin ansa me, u dirrty gora. Or is it dat yo glasses r so smash'd up u can't count? Shud've gone 2 Specsavers, innit. How many a us bredren b here?

— F-F-F . . .

For a second I thought the gora was gonna say something stupid. Something like F-F-Fuck off perhaps, or maybe even F-F-Fuck you. F-F-Fuckin Paki would've also been inadvisable. Stead he answers Hardjit with a straightforward, — F-F-Four.

— Yeh, blud, safe, goes Ravi. — Gora ain't seein double, innit.

So now it was Ravi's turn to make me jealous with his perfectly timed an perfectly authentic rudeboy front. I still use the word rudeboy cos it's been round for longer. People're always tryin to stick a label on our scene. That's the problem with havin a fuckin scene. First we was rudeboys, then we be Indian niggas, then rajamuffins, then raggastanis, Britasians, fuckin Indobrits. These days we try an use our own word for homeboy an so we just call ourselves desis but I still remember when we were happy with the word rudeboy. Anyway, whatever the fuck we are, Ravi an the others are better at being it than I am. I swear I've watched as much MTV Base an Juggy D videos as they have, but I still can't attain the right level a rudeboy finesse. If I could, I wouldn't be using poncey words like attain an finesse, innit. I'd be sayin I couldn't keep it real or someshit. An if I said it that way, then there'd be no need for me to say it in the first place so I wouldn't say it anyway. After all, it's all bout what you say an how you say it. Your linguistic prowess an debating dexterity (though whatever you do don't say it that way). The sort a shit my old schoolteachers told my parents I lacked an which Mr Ashwood'd even made me practise by watchin ponces read the news on the BBC. Honest to God. Why'd the fuck'd anyone wanna chat like that anyway? Or even *listen* to someone who chatted like that? I respect Mr Ashwood for tryin to help me lose my stammer or whatever kind a speech problem it was I'd got when I was at school. But I'd've wasted less a the man's time if I just sat down with Hardjit in the first place. Let's just say Hardjit'd make a more proper newsreader. An the white boy here was listenin to him.

— Dat's right, goes Hardjit, — we b four a us bredrens here. An out a us four bredrens, none a us got a mum an dad wat actually come from Pakistan, innit. So don't u b tellin any a us Pakis dat we b Pakis like our Paki bredren from Pakistan, u get me.

A little more blood trickled down the gora's face as he screwed up his forehead. He wiped it with his hands, still tryin to stop it from staining the sappy button-down collar a his checkered Ben Sherman shirt.

— It ain't necessary for u 2 b a Pakistani to call a Pakistani a Paki, Hardjit explains, — or for u 2 call any Paki a Paki for dat matter. But u gots 2 b call'd a Paki yourself. U gots 2 b, like, an honorary Paki or someshit. An dat's da rule. Can't be callin someone a Paki less u also call'd a Paki, innit. So if you hear Jas, Amit, Ravi or me callin anyone a Paki, dat don't mean u can call him one also. We b honorary Pakis n u ain't.

— Yeh, blud, safe, goes Ravi.

Don't ask me why the white boy still looked confused. It was the exact same for black people. They could call each other nigger but even us desi bredrens couldn't call them niggers. Or niggaz, if you spell it like that. At least that's how NWA was spelt when their name was spelt out in full. In fact, I figured that if Niggaz With Attitude followed the usual rules a acronyms, it'd be more accurate to use a capital letter, as in Nigga or Paki. I know I should've fuckin known better, but I decided to share this thought with the other guys.

— Yeh, motherfucker, an even when you allowed to call someone a Paki, it be Paki wid a capital P, innit.

— Jas, u khota, Hardjit goes, swivelling round so fast his dog tags would've flown off someone with a thinner neck, — why da fuck u teachin him how 2 spell?

I shrugged, deeply lamenting my lack a rudeboyesque panache.

— Da gora ain't no neo-Nazi graffiti artist n dis ain't no fuckin English lesson, innit.

So then I shut the fuck up an let Hardjit sum up his own lesson.

— A Paki is someone who comes from Pakistan. Us bredrens who don't come from Pakistan can still b call'd Paki by other bredrens if it means we can call dem Paki in return. But u people ain't allow'd 2 join in, u get me?

All a this shit was just academic a course. Firstly, Hardjit's thesis, though it was what Mr Ashwood'd call internally coherent, failed to recognise the universality a the word Nigga compared with the word Paki. De-poncified, this means many Hindus an Sikhs'd spit blood if they ever got linked to anything to do with Pakistan. Indians are just too racist to use the word Paki. Secondly, the white kid couldn't call no one a Paki no more with his mouth all cut up. It was still bleedin in little bursts, thick gobfuls droppin onto the concrete floor like he was slowly puking up blood or someshit. It made me feel like puking up myself (the samosas an a can a Coke we got at the college canteen at break time). The blood trickled differently down his chin than down his cheeks. A closer look showed it was cos he'd got this really short goatee beard that I din't notice before. What's the point in havin a goatee if it's so blond no one can even see it unless your

face is covered in blood? Amit'd always said goras couldn't ever get
their facial hair right. If it weren't too blond, it was too curly or too
bumfluffy or just too gimpy-shaped. One time he said that they
looked like batty boys when they'd got facial hair an baby boys when
they din't. I told him I thought he was being racist. He goes to me
it was the exact same thing as sayin black guys were good at growin
dreadlocks but crap at growin ponytails. Amit probly had the
wikidest facial hair in the whole a Hounslow, better than Hardjit's
even. Thin heavy lines a carefully shaped, short, unstraggly black hair
that from far back looked like it'd been drawn on with a felt-tip pen.
Anyway, even if it was possible for a gora to have ungay facial hair,
the gora in front a us now looked like he'd shaved himself with a
chainsaw.

Hardjit was tellin the gora something else, but I din't hear what.
I'd zoned out during the short silence an tuned into the creaking a
these mini goalposts Hardjit'd hung his Schott bomber jacket over.
You could tell from the creaking that they'd rusted an were meant
to be used inside the school sports hall rather than stuck out here
opposite the dustbin an traffic cone that made up the other goal.

— Ansa me, you dirrty gora, Hardjit goes, before kneeling down
an punchin him in the mouth so that his tongue an lower lip explode
again over the library books he'd tried to use as a shield. Even if the
white kid could say something stead a just gurgling an splutterin
blood, he was wise enough not to.

— Dat's right, the three a us go in boy-band mode again, — ansa
da man or we bruck yo fuckin face.

— Yeh, blud, safe, goes Ravi.

We should've just left the white kid then an got our butts back
to the car. We'd still got some other business to sort out before headin
back to college that afternoon. We were also takin some serious liberties with our luck that none a the teachers'd look out the classroom
windows or step into the playground to pick up litter. They'd ID us
for sure if they did. Not just cos we hung round this school's sixth-
form common room now an then, but also cos up till last June we

were sixth-formers here ourselves. We all fuckin failed, a course, despite all our parents' prayin an payin for private maths tuition. An so now we were down the road at Hounslow College a Higher Education, retakin our fuckin A-levels at the age a fuckin nineteen when we should've been at King's College or the London School a Economics or one a the other desi unis with nice halls a residence in central London.

Teachers or no teachers, fuck it. I had to redeem myself after my gimpy remark bout spellin Paki with a capital P. After all, Ravi had spotted the white kid in the first place an Amit'd helped Hardjit pin him against the brick wall. But me, I hadn't added anything to either the physical or verbal abuse a the gora. To make up for my useless shitness I decided to offer the following, carefully crafted comment:
— Yeh, bredren, knock his fuckin teeth out. Bruck his fuckin face. Kill his fuckin . . . well, his fuckin, you know, him. Kill him.

This was probly a bit over the top but I think I'd got the tone just right an nobody laughed at me. At least I managed to stop short a sayin, Kill the pig, like the kids do in that film *Lord a the Flies*. It's also a book too, but I'm tryin to stop knowin shit like that.

— U hear wot ma bredren Jas b chattin? Hardjit says, welcoming my input. — If u b gettin lippy wid me u b gettin yo'self mashed up. I'll bruck yo face an it'll serve u right, fuckin bhanchod. Shudn't b callin us Pakis, innit.

There weren't much face left to bruck, a course. No way Hardjit could've done that damage with his bare fists. I weren't sure whether he'd used his keys or his Karha. One time, when he sparked Imran I think, Hardjit slid his Karha down from his wrist over his fingers an used it like some badass knuckleduster. Even though he was one a them Sardarjis who don't even wear a turban, Hardjit always wore a Karha round his wrist an something orange to show he was a Sikh. Imran's face was so fucked up back then that we made Hardjit promise never to do that shit again. We weren't even Sikh like him but we told him he shouldn't use his religious stuff that way. Din't matter that he was fightin a Muslim. Din't matter that he was fightin a

Pakistani. His mum an dad got called into school an after dinner rinsed him for being a badmarsh delinquent ruffian who'd abused his religion an his culture. Then again, Imran did call it a bangle so served him right.

My fledgling rudeboy reputation redeemed, I was now ready to get the fuck away from there. But Hardjit weren't. He still needed to deliver his favourite line. An just like one a them chana-daal farts that take half an hour to brew, out it eventually came.

— U dissin ma mum?

The blood on the white kid's face seemed to evaporate just to make it easier for us to see his expression a what-the-fuck? But before he could start screamin denials an protesting his inno-cence, Hardjit delivered his second an third favourite lines, — U cussin ma mum? an the less venacular, — U b disrespectin my mother?

The rest a us knew where all a this was headed an Amit, who'd known Hardjit since the man was happy just being called Harjit, was the best placed to challenge him.

— Come now, bredren, dat's nuff batterings you given him. Da gora din't cuss no one's mum.

— Yeh, Amit, yeh he fuckin did.

— Nah, man, come now, we done good here, let's just allow it, blud.

— Allow him to dis ma mum? Wat da fuck's wrong wid'chyu, pehndu? U turnin into a batty boy wid all a dis let's-make-peace-an-drink-spunk-lassi shit?

— No, I mean allow as in, u know, leave it be, blud. He din't cuss your mum n no fuckin way he ever gonna call no one a Paki no more. Let's just leave it, blud. Let's just allow it n get goin wid our shit, innit.

— Da fuckin gora call'd me a Paki. He cuss'd da colour a my skin n my mama got the same colour skin as me, innit.

None a us dared argue, an Hardjit'd found a reason to kick the white kid in the face again, an again, an again, this time punctuating the rapid-fire beatin with, — U fuckin gora, u cuss'd my mum, an then adding variations like, — U cuss'd my sister an ma bredren. U cuss'd my dad, my uncle Deepak, u cuss'd my aunty Sheetal, my aunty Meera, ma cousins in Leicester, u cuss'd ma grandad in Jalandhar.

Hardjit was so fast with his moves that the white boy had hardly got time to scream before the next impact a the man's foot, fist, elbow. Hardjit's thuds against the gora's body an the gora's head against the concrete playground had a kind a rhythm bout it that you just couldn't block out. Ravi starts cheering as if Ganguly had just scored six runs an there'd be no saving the gora's Ben Sherman shirt now. When it was done, stead a knockin the white kid out, Hardjit straightened himself up, took his Tag Heuer out his pocket an put his keys back in it. He could've done the same damage even if he'd just used his bare fists. He does four different types a martial arts as well as workin every muscle group, like I said, down the gym, every other day. He says it don't really matter how many times you go down the gym, you can't be proper tough less you also have proper fights. It was the same with all his martial arts lessons. There weren't no point learnin them if he din't use them in the street or in the playground at least. His favourite martial art that time was kalaripayat, which in case you don't know was one a the first kindsa martial arts ever to be invented. A big bonus point if you know where it was invented. China? Japan? Tibet? Fuck, no. It's from India, innit. Chinese an Tibetan kung fu came later. People tend to forget this cos the British banned kalaripayat when they took over India. But now Hardjit'd found out bout it he wouldn't let no one forget. He reminded the white kid never to call anyone a Paki again before we all headed across the playground to the gate where Ravi'd parked the Beemer on the zigzag line. We were stridin slowly a course, so as not to look batty. With the gora gone quiet you could now hear screamin from inside the school. It was the usual voices. Four, maybe five different teachers yellin an shoutin at the usual kids for fuckin around in lessons, resulting in more laughter from the back rows followed by more shoutin from the front. From outside, the place sounded more like a mental home than a school. Lookin at where the sounds were coming from I figured no way any a the teachers would've spotted us through a classroom window. Even those that were clean were covered in masking tape cos they'd been broken by cricket balls. The result a special desi spin-bowling probly.

Nobody said jackshit to nobody in case it took the edge off Hardjit's warm-up for the proper fight he'd got lined up for tomorrow. But as the four a us got to the Beemer, Ravi remembered he'd left Hardjit's Schott bomber jacket wrapped round the goalposts in the playground.

— U fuckin gimp, was all Hardjit said. He weren't even referring to me for a change but still I volunteered to go get his jacket, even though it meant a spectacularly gimpy fifty-metre trot to the other side a the playground. Not exactly my most greatest idea seeing as how I'd just spent the last twelve months tryin to get upgraded from my former state a dicklessness.

As I got nearer the goalposts, I watched the white kid wipe his face with his shirt. You hardly ever saw a brown-on-white beatin these days, not round these pinds anyway. It was when all those beatins stopped that Hardjit started hooking up with the Sikh boys who ran Southall whenever they took on the Muslim boys who ran Slough. Hounslow's more a mix a Sikhs, Muslims an Hindus, you see, so the brown-on-browns tended to just be one-on-ones stead a thirty desis fightin side by side. Whenever those one-on-ones were between a Sikh an a Muslim an whenever the Sikh was Hardjit, people'd come from Southall an Slough just to watch his martial arts moves in action. If you don't believe me, wait till the big showdown with Tariq Khan he'd got lined up for tomorrow.

The white kid was now lookin me straight in the eye in a way that made me glad we hadn't made eye contact while he was being beaten. — What, white boy? I said. — Did you expect me to stop them? Do you think I'm some kind a fuckin fool?

— Jas, I didn't call nobody a Paki, he said, coughin. — You know that's the truth.

— I don't know shit, Daniel.

— I didn't even say nothing, Jas. Nobody would ever be so stupid as to mess with you lot any more.

I tried to ignore what he was sayin an the way sayin it had made his lips an tongue start bleedin again. But I couldn't help noddin. Damn right.

— Why didn't you tell them I didn't say anything, Jas? What's happened to you over the last year? the gora says before havin another coughin an splutterin fit. — You've become like one of those gangsta types you used to hate.

Damn right.

— Why didn't you tell them I didn't say anything?

— OK, Daniel, I go, — swear on your mother's life you din't call us Pakis.

— For fuck's sake, Jas, you know my mother's dead.

— So, swear on your mother's life.

— But Jas, she's dead. You came to the funeral.

I picked up the jacket, turned around an jogged back to the car. Hardjit'd been wise to take it off. He'd worn the jacket during other fights but wanted to be careful with it now cos he'd just got the word 'Desi' sewn onto the back. He'd thought bout havin 'Paki' sewn on but his mum'd never let him wear it an, anyway, nobody round here ever, ever used that word.

2

Most desis had either black, blue or silver Beemers, but Ravi's was a purply kind a metallic grey. Lilac, I think he said one time. Yeh. He said lilac was his favourite colour a ladies' underwear an he wanted the outside a the car to match the panties pulled off inside.

— If she b wearin black thongs dey'd still match da dashboard, he'd said, stroking the BMW's bonnet before he took us for our first ever ride in it. — But if dey b dem red panties then she a dirrty ho an I'd bounce her ass out ma car, da bitch.

Greasy sleazebag bullshit merchant or not, you had to hand it to Ravi. His BMW M3 was way phatter than other Beemers you saw round here. Most desi bredren had got the E36 model, but Ravi drove a E46. Slick side gills, wider wheel arches, curved roof an four chrome exhaust pipes stickin out from under the rear skirt. He'd stuck on an even slicker spoiler, alloy hubcaps that kept on spinnin at red traffic lights an matchin lilac windscreen wipers. The inside a the ride was pimped up with rally-car-style seat belts that criss-crossed over your chest, chrome plating over the gearstick an handbrake handles, Sony X-Plod three-way speakers with 220 watts a power an sand-coloured seats that looked lush even though they weren't leather. He'd even got those neon lights fitted under the chassis that lit up the road underneath. But whereas most rudeboys'd got blue neon lights, Ravi's were purple to match the car. Purple weren't an exact match, a course, but he couldn't find lilac neon lights an only people in Prince videos wore purple panties.

— Where we meetin Davinder? Ravi goes, tryin to shout down
the DMX CD being turned up by his left hand an the engine being
revved up by his right foot. — You hear me, blud? Where we meetin
Davinder?

— I already told u, u thick khota: outside Nando's, innit, goes
Hardjit, though without needin to shout cos Ravi eased off with his
hand an foot for him. — I also told'chyu we had 2 call Davinder b4
we left dis place, innit, so any a u chiefs know his mobile?

— Yeh, he got one a them new Sony Ericsson P800s, innit, came
my voice from the back seat, all jumpy like when I used to sit up
front in History lessons an knew the answer to Mr Ashwood's questions. — It's a wikid fone, man, it got a camera, it got a video player,
it got them polyphonic ringtunes, an Java games.

— Jas, u pehndu. I meant his mobile numba. I's gonna fuckin
fone him, innit. Fuckin dickless piece a shit.

— Ah, sorry, man, my bad, I go as I start searchin my fone for
Davinder's number.

— Ras clat, fuckin useless, all a u, Hardjit goes, shakin his head
an doing that suckin the inside a his front teeth thing. Hardjit could
suck his front teeth louder, longer an harder than most people could.
Honest to God, the man could tut like a black brother.

— Davinder got a lesson on Monday so he probly got his fone
on silent, goes Amit. — Dem bhanchod teachers make you turn your
fone off now. Stick it in your bag or sumfink so you can't even flex
it on your desk.

— Amit, I don't give a fuck whether his fone's on silent or stuck
up his butt n set 2 vibrate, Davinder told me 2 call him when we
left da school n we b leavin da fuckin school, innit. So c'mon, u
bunch a chiefs. One a u's gotta b havin his numba.

Amit dialled Davinder's number from his Nokia fone book an
passed his fone up front to Hardjit, all in a single, smooth move,
like a cricket fielder scooping up an throwin the ball in one go.

— Shut da fuck up, dis b business, Hardjit goes to all a us as,
somewhere near Hounslow High Street, Davinder's fone started

ringin, or vibrating, or flashin, or whatever the fuck he'd set it to.

— Kiddaan, man, 'sup, homeboy? . . . Listen, blud, we jus leavin now, innit . . . Some gora got lippy wid us . . . Nah, u know it, blud . . . He ain't got no lips no more, bhanchod . . . U know it, blud, innit . . . A'ight, safe . . . Nah, I call her tonite . . . I got me free minutes on my fone, innit . . . Say wat? . . . Nando's. Safe. Nah, we'll hook up wid'chyu dere . . . We leavin da school right now . . . We got da Beemer, innit . . . A'ight, safe, laters.

Soon as Hardjit hangs up, Amit takes his Nokia 6610 back an starts makin a call beside me. He's being all polite an in't using no swear words or nothin so is clearly chattin to his mum. But he makes sure he don't *look* like he's chattin to his mum, narrowin his eyes, suckin in his cheeks an noddin as he stares out the window. Amit pulled a better fone face than all a us. Tellin some stockbroker or banker to liquidate his portfolio a stocks an, no, he din't give a damn how bad the market is today: just fuckin sell.

— Theekh hai, he goes. — Flour an eggs. Free range. I'll get it, Mama. Alright, Mum, theekh hai.

— I ain't squashin u back there, is it? Hardjit goes to me, his seat pushed all the way back so I was gettin, like, kneecapped.

— Nah, man, I'm cool, I go. — Move the seat further back if you need to. I'm cool.

When you're in the back seat a some pimped-up Beemer it's basically your job to be cool. To just chill, listen to the tunes an stare out the window like some big dumb dog with a big slobbery tongue. DMX pumpin so loud out the sound system you can hardly hear what the other guys're sayin up front. Amit shuffles into the middle a the back seat, leaning forward into that death-if-you-don't-wear-a-seat-belt position my mum was always going on at me bout. But I just stay sittin back. The world going by outside the window tells me that in the olden times, before the airport, Hounslow must've been one a them batty towns where people ponced around on cycles stead a drivin cars. Why else we got such narrow roads? Some a them were so narrow that the trees on each side had got their branches

16

castrated to stop them fightin in the middle. In't no leaves on em either, even in the summer. Talk bout a shitty deal for the trees. Castrated an no pubes. Standin there like giant, upright versions a the dried-up sticks a dogshit that lay at their feet. If I was a cycle-riding, tree-huggin, skint hippie I might've given a shit bout the trees an all the posters pinned to them for some Bollywood film that'd been released two weeks ago, the new Punjabi MC single that came out a month ago or ads for a bhangra gig in Hammersmith that happened a year ago. But I in't, so stead I hope the skint people who work for the local council would just finish the fuckin job an chop em all down. Make room for more billboards, more fuckin road. Only proper-sized roads round here were the Great West Road an London Road, both a them runnin along either side a this part a Hounslow like garden fences to an airport at the back where the garden shed should be (they called it Heathrow cos it's bang in the middle a Hounslow Heath or someshit). Lucky for us there weren't no other cars cruisin down all these side roads squashed between the garden fences. There were hardly any parked cars along the pave-ments either, partly cos the staff car parks at Heathrow were full but mostly cos all a the houses round here had got their front gardens concreted over an turned into driveways. Big wheelie rubbish bins an recycling boxes where the plants, flower beds an garden paths between them used to be. No sign a the other stuff I drew on houses when my playschool teacher moved me up from crayons to colour-ing-in pencils. None a them smokin chimneys an those lollipop-like trees were missin too. Missin, presumed castrated. Some houses had got Om symbols stuck on the wooden front doors behind glass porches, some a them had Khanda Sahibs an others had the Muslim crescent moon. All a them had satellite TV dishes next to the main bedroom window, stuck up there like framed dentists' diploma certificates. If there weren't no symbol on the front door, you could still tell if it was a desi house if there was more than one satellite dish. One for Zee TV an one for Star Plus, probly. You could tell if someone was home cos the daal an subjhi smell would mix in with the airport traffic on the Great West Road. An you could tell if the people at home were friendly if the car parked in the driveway was a car with a friendly face. Honest to God, I in't jokin. That kid in *The Sixth Sense*, he sees dead people all the time – me, I see faces in cars. Maybe this makes me some mad weirdo psycho, but I been seein them ever since I was little. It's like as if the headlights are the eyes, the grill the mouth an the wing mirrors the ears. The faces meant that, back before I got tight with Hardjit's crew, I tended to like smaller cars. Ford Fiestas, Fiat Puntos an all the other crappy hatchbacks my schoolteachers drove. I din't like them in a skint hippie way, though, I liked them cos they'd got friendlier faces. Take this red Nissan Micra that just pulled out behind us. It looked like a little, button-nosed puppy dog. The black Volkswagen Beetle parked in a drive on the left had got big friendly eyes. This was why, back when I was a gimp, I never got why everyone reckoned big flash cars were such big fuckin deals. Sure, flashy Mercedes were smiling cos a their massive grilles, but their faces weren't friendly cos it was more like some smug grin: I'm a fuckin SLK, look at me, you pleb. Aston Martins got mouths like piranha fish, Beemers looked like androids playin fuckin poker an Italian sports cars were even scarier cos they'd got no mouths, no eyes even. I dig sports cars now a course, cos my head in't so stupidly fucked up these days an I try an not see the faces no more. Matter a fact it's the bodies I tend to notice now. Take the body on a Lexus SC430. So sleek an smooth you don't even notice its face. Like Christina Aguilera. The curves on an Audi TT make it J-Lo while the Porsche 911 GTS got a booty like Beyoncé. An it in't just divas: I got the Bentley Continental GT as Snoop Dogg an the Hummer H2 down as 50 Cent.

If Ferrari made a 4x4 SUV, it'd be a Hardjit. A Hardjit SUV would have a big engine grille but it wouldn't be grinnin. It'd be more like that constipated face he makes when he's tensing his body an thinks no one else in the gym is watchin him. When I turned my head back from the window to see if anything was going on up front he was still settling into his seat, winding down the tinted electric window, resting his elbow on the door frame, flashin his Tag Heuer, sovereign ring an karha bracelet. Grabbin the top a the door frame with his left hand, he straightened his shoulder so that his upper arm snapped into place, his tight black D&G vest givin everyone outside an even better view. An just like the empty side roads gave Ravi an excuse to slide down into second gear an do some seriously sharp rudeboy manoeuvres, they gave Hardjit an excuse to grip harder on the door frame an tense his arms up more. The engine an drivetrain connected to his biceps, the brake pads connected to his pecs. Ravi swervin past some random slowcoach Citroën like he was at the arcades playin Daytona USA. Beep beep, get the fuck off the street. Pump pump, we don't slow for no fuckin speed hump. Luckily, Hardjit din't notice me watchin him feel his biceps. Otherwise he'd have rinsed me for being gay or a gora lover, or both. I'd caught him enough times feelin his arms an just generally checkin himself out in mirrors an tinted car windows an somehow he always made me feel like I was the batty boy. Right now he only stopped checkin out his arms when he found some other limbs to check out. Her legs had come into view soon as we'd turned out the side roads an onto the London Road. Whoever she was, she was wearin one a them fuck-me miniskirts an fuck-me-harder knee-high boots. The skirt beige, the boots black. Ravi slowed the fuck down now while Hardjit turned up DMX's 'Ruff Ryders Anthem' with the arm that weren't on display in the door frame. Soon as we'd passed her legs, Amit gives it, — Dat gyal ain't nothin, if yous lot wanna see proper fitness you shoulda seen this bitch I shagged last weekend. Harpinder was her name. Imagine if Aishwarya Rai n Raveena Tandon had a twenty-one-year-old love child.

— Yeh, I bet 'imagine' is the right word seeing as how you probly imagined the whole thing yourself, I shouted from the back seat before I could even remember that I was in the back seat.

— Fuck you, Jas, goes Amit. — Jus cos you in't shagged no one. No one female anyway. An even if you did, the Durex'd probly slip off your pin-sized prick n you'd end up wid butt-ugly kids cos dey'll have your genes.

When everyone's finished crackin up, Amit carries on: — Whereas me, if I had a kid wid dis bitch from last week, it'd b better-lookin than Pharrell, innit. Only there ain't gonna be no kid cos I used protection, innit. Extra large a course, none a dat average-sized shit you get outta da machines. Matter a fact, da size I need is so large I gots to go to a special chemist, you get me.

— Safe, bredren, goes Ravi. — Extra large, innit.

— Yeh, bruv, if I din't use a rubber, she'd probly have twins or triplets or four babies altogether or someshit.

— Yeh, you know it blud.

— I din't even need to chirps her very long. Couple a jokes, dat's all. She weren't easy or nothin, she jus took one look at me n decided we was gonna get in my car, you get me.

— Safe, blud, Ravi gives it again. — Wat's her friends like? I'll bone em.

— Too late, bruv, I already shagged her best friend Mandeep last year. She was all over me. Kept textin me afta, leavin voicemails n dat.

— Wikid, man, you b da dog. Da dirrty dawg.

— Yeh you know it, Ravi. Back when I boned Mandeep I was jus using a large size. Now I need extra large, you get me?

— A'ight, blud, jumbo size, innit. Dat's da way. Shag her, innit, Ravi gives it before Hardjit finally cuts in with: — Yeh n I had a nice dream myself last nite.

— So wat'chyu sayin, desi? goes Amit. — You bein like Jas here n thinkin I makin dis shit up?

— Nah, blud, I sayin I *know* u makin dis shit up.

— Fuck you, man. You think you da only one who's been there, done dat, shagged dat bitch, done dat ho?

— No. I ain't sayin dat cos I don't get wid no bitches n hos.

The two a them carried on like that till we pulled up at a set a red traffic lights. This desi who pulled up in the lane next to us din't even look our way once even though we were givin enuff stares at him an his silver Peugeot 305. You could tell from his long hair, grungy clothes, the poncey novel an newspaper on his dashboard an Coldplay album playin in his car that he was a muthafuckin coconut. So white he was inside his brown skin, he probably talked like those gorafied desis who read the news on TV. Probably even more poncier than the way how I used to talk. An think. Probly.

— U boys see how scared a us dat Paki is? Hardjit shouted over DMX so that the coconut heard him too. — Yah, u Mr Muthafucka, I mean u. I ain't seein any otha Pakis round here, do u?

Still the coconut was too wise to bite, just carryin on lookin straight ahead.

— Tu ki samajda hai? U a Paki jus like me. Even tho u b listenin to U2 or someshit. Are *u 2* scared *2* look at us?

The coconut pretty much answered this question by keepin his eyes fixed on the road ahead. Hardjit then tutted at regular intervals till the lights changed. We let the coconut drive ahead a us, cut into our lane an then turn right towards the Great West Road.

— Ain't dat some muthafuckin coincidence, goes Hardjit. — We goin dat way too.

The Great West Road, which is basically the stretch a the A4 that runs along Hounslow, is a dual carriageway. It's got three lanes in each direction so Ravi had no problem pullin up alongside the coconut the next time we got lucky with a red light.

— Oi, mate, Hardjit gives it, pointing at the coconut's car door as if something was wrong with it.

This time, the coconut bit the bait, openin his door a little an then slammin it shut. Then the khota wound down his window. — Thanks, he goes, — I must've got my seat belt caught in it. Thanks again, mate.

Fool.

— No, Mr Matey, your door was shut just splendidly fine, old boy, Hardjit gives it in his best poncey Angrez accent. — I weren't fuckin pointing at yo fuckin door, u bhanchod. I was pointing at yo fuckin car, innit. I mean, look at it.

— I'm sorry, mate? I don't understand.

— Your car. Ain't u noticed? It's crap. Your car's a piece a crapped-up shit, innit.

— Well, it gets me from A to B, the coconut goes before winding up his window. Fool. Fool fool fool. In't no point winding your window up now, not unless it's soundproof or double-glazed or someshit.

— A to B? Hardjit shouted. — Fuckin batty boy, u sound like a poncey gora. Wat's wrong wid'chyu, sala kutta? *U 2* embarrass'd to b a desi? Embarrass'd a your own culture, huh? Thing is, u is actually an embarrassment to desis. Bet'chyu can't even speak yo mother tongue, innit. I should come over there n cut yo tongue out, u dickless bhanchod. Then Hardjit started tuttin like he was in some fuckin teeth-suckin competition, before givin it, — Look at me when I talk 2 u. Ain't nobody mess wid us. Fuckin R.E.M. playin on yo stereo. Ras clat pehndu. Tell him, Amit.

— Bhanchod coconut, Amit goes after openin his window. — In't your own culture good enuf for you, you fuckin gora lover? Amit felt as passionate bout healin coconuts as Hardjit felt bout healin rednecks who used the word Paki an Ravi felt bout healin lesbians. — Wat da fuck happened wid'chyu you gots to act like a gora for? You think you better than your own kind cos you is so white n you read some poncey books n newspapers? I wipe ma ass wid yo fuckin newspaper.

As if tryin to show us he was as streetwise as those dicks who wear hats to horse races, the stupid idiot fuckin khota fool then wound down his window again an gives it, — Look, mate, I'm not looking for any trouble here. I'm just going about my business.

— Goin bout yo business? Ehh ki hai? Amit goes. — Wat business you got goin? Readin fuckin batty books? Take some advice from me, don't mess wid us. Cos we b da man round here n you b da gora-lovin bhanchod who can't even speak his mother tongue, innit. Wat's wrong wid your own bredren, brown boy? Look at us. We's b havin a nice car, nice tunes, nuff nice designer gear, nuff bling mobile. But no, you wanna b some gora-lovin, dirrty hippie wid fuckin Radiohead playin in your car. Look at ma man Jas here. Learn some lessons from him.

On green we left the coconut in our dust an Hardjit started laughin, givin it, — Bhanchod show'd us some respect. Nuff mutha-fuckin respect.

— I remember back in da day when most desis round here were like dat gimp, goes Amit. — Skinny saps pretendin like they were gora so no one treat'd dem like dey'd just got off da boat from Bombay, innit. But all da gora fuck'd wid dem anyway.

— Yeh, bruv, you know it, I cheered from the back, — that in't being our shit no more.

— U can fuckin talk, Jas. U was da biggest sap in town till we took yo coconut-lovin, faggot ass in.

As we turned off the Great West Road an the coconut disappeared from the rear window I almost felt sorry for him. But I din't. Not any more, anyway, not these days, not a chance. Coconuts like him deserved to have Hardjit an Amit lay into them. It in't as if he had to be such a gorafied bhanchod: God had given him brown skin an so he could be a proper desi if he wanted to. He'd made a choice just like I made a choice when I started kickin about with Hardjit. But the coconut's choice was the wrong choice. In't no desi needin to kiss the white man's butt these days an you definitely don't need to actually act like a gora. Fuckin bhanchod. Din't matter what you called them. Coconuts, Bounty bars, Oreo biscuits or any other fuckin food that was white on the inside. Good desi boys who din't ever cause no trouble. But how many a them'll still be here in Hounslow in ten years' time, workin in Heathrow fuckin airport helpin goras catch planes to places so they could turn their own skin brown? No fuckin way I was gonna be hangin round with them saps no more, with those gimpy glasses I used to wear, my drainpipe trousers an my batty books. Fuck that shit. I looked out the car window again to see if I could see any a them saps. See how far I'd come. Weren't none around though, must've all been in lessons. You could play spot the sap in Hounslow these days just like when we went to

Southall one time to play spot the gora. As Hardjit once said, any desi round here deciding they din't wanna be part a the bredren was a bit like some cat barking with the bitches stead a meowing. Complete fuckin pussy, you get me?

We park up behind Davinder's Johnny Depp on the single yellow line right outside Nando's. He got out soon as he saw us an started pointing at his Cartier watch. — Kiddaan, pehndus? Where u been? We's been waitin half an hour 4 yo asses. Wat da fuck is dis? I a busy man, innit.

The we referred to his mate Jaswinder, this tall, fat guy who was built like Hardjit an who was lockin up Davinder's car. Jaswinder never said much. Probly the only time he'd ever spoke to me was when he told me he was pissed off I'd got the nickname Jas. You can be called Jas too, I'd said. Don't be stupid, he'd said. It's bad enough havin so many desis at school with the same names, it'd be stupid havin two people in the same class with the same fuckin nickname. I din't argue with him, mostly cos Jaswinder at least had an easy surname – Singh. Me, I had one a them extra long surnames that nobody'd ever pronounce proply. All my teachers in all my lessons had always got it wrong when they called out the register an even my mum an dad pronounced it the wrong way. Matter a fact I in't even gonna tell it to you it's so fuckin shameful.

— Safe, blud, ma bad we late, Hardjit goes to Davinder, — but we had some business 2 sort on da way, innit. U know wat it's like, bruv.

— Dat's safe, but jus call me next time cos if I ain't mistaken u got some lucrative business here too, innit.

Davinder smiled as he said that. He was easily the most loaded guy for his age we knew, an he knew it too. Stridin around wearin his Swarovski-studded medallion with the letter D on it – the kind that Usher wears, except his is a U an is made a ice. Even when we was all at school, way back before he'd set up his business dealings, Davinder'd got his own business cards printed. Davinder Singh, AKA – Acquirer a Knowledge an Assets.

Amit joined the others as they started walkin towards Nando's when suddenly Davinder turned round to face the Beemer again, checkin out the engine grille as if he saw faces too.

— Ik minute, I got me one question bout dis ride I been meanin 2 aks u bredrens 4 time now.

— Look, don't b sayin shit bout ma car, man. Da car in't slow, Ravi said. — I din't realise we was in a muthafuckin race.

— Nah, chill, dat shit's history, Davinder said, pointing at the licence plate. — Wat I want'd 2 aks u is who da fuck is K4V1TA?

— It's my mum a course, said Ravi. — Da Beemer belongs to her, innit.

3

The Beemer's closed windows couldn't block the smell a spicy peri-peri chicken. While the other guys were gettin stuck into stuffin their faces inside Nando's, I was stuck in the car with the DMX CD an a copy a some tutty Bollywood magazine for company. I couldn't be around when they did a business deal with Davinder, you see. He'd have problems with it. Problem number one: the cars might get parking tickets if nobody kept watch. Problem number two: the fewer a us that huddled round a rucksack full a Davinder's merchandise, the less attention we'd attract. Problem number three: motherfuckin me.

Davinder'd got beef with me since before our GCSEs. Since right back when we was in year seven an every time he passed me in the school corridors between lessons he'd, like, punch me in the face. I couldn't ever see him coming either cos a all the Nike an Adidas ruck-sacks in my face. Then suddenly one a them rucksacks would turn into a fist. I in't sure there was any specific reason for his beef with me. It was just all the usual things. The things bout me that Hardjit'd told Amit an Ravi to just allow. Things like I was a ponce, I acted an sounded like a batty, I was a skinny wimp, I was embarrassin to have around if ladies came by, I wore crap clothes, I used to have braces on both my upper an lower teeth, I'd read too many books, I walked like a fool, I had this annoyin habit a sniffin all the time, I couldn't usually talk proply an even when I did I couldn't ever say the right thing. Basically I was just generally a khota, like that coconut we'd seen earlier today except I din't even have my own car. Hardjit'd stuck up for me like he always did. One time I heard him say, — Look, Davinder, if I b sayin Jas is safe then da boy is safe, u get me? In the end, Davinder'd said he din't mind that I was part a Hardjit's crew, but if that meant he had to hang around with me too then he'd rather take his merchandise somewhere else. Thing is, if people like Davinder hadn't laid into me so much all the time, Hardjit'd never have started stickin up for me in the first place. An if he'd never stuck up for me, I'd probly never've become part a his crew. At first I figured the only reason he'd started backing me up was so he could act like Shah Rukh Khan in front a all the ladies. The Bollywood hero always takes care a the underdog, you see. Only difference was Hardjit din't like takin no glory for stickin up for me. He din't even like it whenever I thanked him for doing so. I reckon he was basically so freaked out by how gimpy I was that he felt he'd got to cure me. Like those people who are so homophobic that stead a beating gay guys shitless, they actually try an turn em into straight guys.

The first time Hardjit ever backed me up was after I walked into a spare classroom one time. Room 418. We weren't really allowed in 418 cos it'd been vandalised so much, but that meant I could usually be by myself in there at break times. One time, though, I walk in an I find Davinder sittin inside there with his tongue sittin inside some girl's throat. She must've been from Green School, Brentford School or one a the other girls' schools round here. I apologised for the interruption (I was really good at apologising in them days) but couldn't bring myself to leave cos, well, she was fit. An her school blouse was half open. It was one a those plunge bras, with a tiny little bow between the white lace cups, probly underwired an with satin padding along the bottom. Davinder carefully removed his tongue an turned to me. — D'ya wanna watch? Dis is probly da closest a fuckin sap like u'll ever get 2 kissin a lady, he goes as he put his hands on the lace straps to stop her buttoning up her blouse. — So why not pull up a fuckin chair, my friend.

Davinder's words had their desired effect by makin him look tough in front a the girl. She rewarded him by crackin up as if he'd just told the funniest joke in the whole wide world an so he continued:

— Look, let me explain: u put yo tongue inside her mouth like dis. See? U don't kiss her *on* da mouth, u kiss her *in* da mouth. Da tongue knows wat it's doin. But in't no bitch gonna get wid'chyu anyway cos u ugly n u stink.

I wanted to stand up for myself but what do you say to something like that? Do you tell him that actually I in't *that* ugly? That, OK, maybe my hair might've been too thick to style proply, but ever since I'd got it cut short an started stickin L'Oréal wax in it a couple a people had said I looked a little like Justin Timberlake, only skinnier. Before I could even begin, Davinder'd started rinsin me for staring at the girl's still-open blouse until finally I turned to leave havin not said a single fuckin word.

— Check da gimpy way he walks away. A sap like dat'll only ever b kissin himself.

— U gots 2 stick up 4 yo'self, Hardjit said, makin me jump as I shut the classroom door behind me. — Read da situation, man. Davinder's too busy wid his ho 2 hit'chyu.

At first I was worried I was in for more a the same shit an so I tried to walk down the corridor away from him, like as if I was late for lesson or someshit.

— Yo name's Jas, innit? U goes 2 da same German n Science lessons as me, but u sit up front wid all dem spods, innit?

I just gave it one a them polite, shit-scared smiles, showin him all the metalwork on my teeth just in case he din't realise I was smiling. If you don't smile proply at someone at a time like this, you'll get accused a blanking them an then smiling won't even be an option.

— Yeh, man, u da one wid da braces Kavi wired up 2 a six-volt battery, innit? Did dat hurt yo mouth, bruv?

Nobody'd ever called me bruv before cos, well, desis who called people bruv din't want a pussy for a bruv.

— Jus ignore wat peeps like Kavi n Davinder say 2 u. Dey shud save up their aggro 4 Paki bashers, u get me?

— Y . . . y. I er y . . .

Shit, that was my voice. I tried to cough up any gungy spit an that

from the back a my throat so that I could go an say whatever it was
I was gonna decide I was gonna say. There weren't nothin there
though, an so I just sounded like one a them poncey tossers that go
around clearin their throats. Back in them days, the braces on my
teeth weren't the only reason why it was generally a bad idea for me
to try an talk. But I was talkin to Hardjit an Hardjit was sorted. You
can't give up tryin to chat proply when you're chattin to someone
sorted, someone like Hardjit. You'll be thinkin I fancy him now, won't
you? That I really am a batty boy after all? But it in't like that cos I
in't batty. I just wish I was as sorted as Hardjit is, that's all.

— Yeh, I think I know what you mean, Davinder an that, like. I
yer gey . . . Well, you know. In't sure like. Depends what you reckon,
I mean, no, depends, sorry.

Hardjit just looked at me, all confused like I was chattin in fuckin
Scandinavian or someshit. An I was thinkin, What the fuck is wrong
with me? Why say sorry when I weren't? Why the fuckin fuck did
people like me say sorry when we weren't?

— I mean, maybe it don't matter, no more. No, forget it, I agree
now. Like just before. Sorry, yeh, OK. No, really I do, Hardjit, actually forget it, like I really think you're right bout them. Sorry.

God. Why'd you make me have to say something if all I can do
is talk a pile a shit. Stupid tutty shit at whoever it was I was talkin
to. But for some reason I remember Hardjit seemed OK bout me
being a dickless khota. He knew what I meant to say was the three
words, OK, I agree. In fact, if Hardjit thought I was just some sap
beyond help then he'd probly help me, say it for me like how most
people do. Stead a that he just carried on tellin me I should stand
up to Davinder.

Thing is, right, I din't really agree with him anyway but decided
not to try an explain why cos I probly wouldn't be able to cos I'm a
sap who can't talk. Cheers, God. No use blaming God, though. S'pose
I should really thank Him for givin us a mouth. If it was a proper
problem, like a stutter or something like what Dave Gilbert has, or
that problem with saying S's what Spencer (fuckface) has got . . .

Then Hardjit said, — Laters, bruv, an then headed to the library. Honest to God, the library. This may sound like a strange place for someone like Hardjit but there weren't no librarian no more so it was a safe place to go when you din't want to go to lessons. Comfy chairs an that. The teachers din't care. Only the librarian used to give two tosses bout the books an the noise an all the yellow stuffing stuff leaking out the chairs. Even though I din't agree with all a Hardjit's mafia rudeboy shit back then, suddenly I wanted to follow him, wanted to carry on talkin to him. Don't matter that you can't actually talk cos if you hang around with sorted people then other people'll think you're safe yourself. But I din't go after him. Din't want to push my luck, you get me?

Every time when it's important to use this gob a mine I hear my voice, which never normly works proply an so I panic. It's as if there's some other voice a mine givin it, Don't say that, it'll make u look like a gimp. An so I'll go, Yeh, maybe so, but . . . Then I'll realise that the other person, the one I'm s'posed to be talkin to, can hear me. So I'll quickly shut my gob, only to hear the other voice go, You fuckin sap. Now you look like you can't even talk. Which you can't, you stammerin piece a wasted shit. For fuck's sake, just speak up.

Fuck off, leave me alone. I've just got gunge an shit down my throat.

Speak up, boy.

Obviously this voice must know that actually it can't speak up, that it can't talk cos it's me, innit, it's my voice. But it keeps tryin anyway. An then another voice, I reckon that makes it three fuckin voices, will go, Boy? In't no fuckin boy. In't no girl either but in't no fuckin boy.

I just slated the way I was thinkin, same way my mind slates the way I speak. I slated it even before I finished thinkin it never mind sayin it, so I ended up soundin like a dick. An it's like I know in my head an can even tell to you why I talked like a fuckin pehndu. But I couldn't ever say it. Couldn't ever explain it to anyone with my

30

mouth. Couldn't say, No, I in't thick, I just got thinkin bout how wrong what I was sayin was, an then got thinkin bout how I weren't totally right to think that way, but by then it was too late to say what I was gonna say anyway, so now I'm just sayin this instead. OK, I suppose it could make sense. I could've said it to someone an they might even've understood me. But I couldn't really say it cos I'd mess it all up with loads a erms an sorrys an shit. An anyway, it only just makes sense an seeing as how I've probly already made a floppy dick out a myself, then the person I'm chattin to in't exactly gonna listen to me explain why I sound so crap. It don't matter none that this time I'd actually be makin sense. An so you just look like a sap an try to make things better by tryin not to give too big a shit. But I in't a sap. OK? In't a sap, in't fuckin thick. I understand me. Fuck it all, fuckin useless tongue. Probly couldn't even sixty-nine it. An no, I in't a perve for thinkin that. This is just my mind remembering one time when my stupid tongue made me look a total khota in front a Kavi an Deepak an all the other guys in my Science lessons. I din't know what sixty-nine meant, you see. I thought they were chattin bout the bus that goes down Chiswick, the one you take if you go down Brentford. I couldn't even ask for a bloody bus ticket. Obviously I couldn't. You can't pull if you can't fuckin talk, can you? Not unless you're that Hugh fuckin Grant from that movie bout shaadis an funerals an shit. Always sayin sorry an erm an stuff. He still got his dick sucked, din't he? It was on the news. Hugh Grant. Ponce.

Daydreamin is good for you. Better than wankin even, or at least that's what someone told me one time. Actually he weren't really tellin me, why would he? He was tellin someone else an I overheard him. At least my ears work. Unlike my fuckin tongue, my fuckin *Shitesprecher*. That in't even my own word. It's from a German lesson, I think. Or History. Same thing really, same teacher so you get em mixed up. — You're trying harder these days, aren't you, Jas? Carry on like this and I mean it, you'll deserve at least a C in GCSE History . . . If you start having all those problems with it again, I'm always

31

here to help. Not just History problems, you understand, any problems. We care about pupils at this school.

Lookin back, he was probly gay.

Or, again, was it German? We did bout Nazis in both lessons. *Heil.* I wonder if it'd be possible for a guy like me to be a Nazi. I'll daydream that I'm a Nazi. I know it sounds like I'm being a wanker cos they were scum like suicide bombers, killin all them people an that. But were they all wankers? At least they walked an talked proply. An even if you reckoned they walked or dressed stupid, at least nobody'd take the piss outta them. Fuckin saluted them instead. Maybe I'd not talk such piles a shit if I spoke in German. It's like, they don't stammer cos they know what to say. An if they're Nazis then fuck to all those voices criticising the way they think bout the way they talk an all that bollocks. Anyhow, fuck it. Someone made up the word *Shitesprecher*, meanin tongue, when we were doing a lesson on Nazis for History or for German. Mr Ashwood laughed with us even though I don't think he found it funny.

Maybe I should've followed Hardjit to the library. I couldn't go back to Room 418 cos Davinder an that girl were probly still in there an I was so late for lesson I'd get a detention if I showed up now. Should I daydream bout being a Nazi, or doing History bout Nazis when Mr Ashwood was always late himself so never got pissed off if you were? I remember that lesson when he . . . oh, man, no way. You in't gonna bunk off lesson just so you can spend your time daydreamin bout some other lesson, you sad, sad, gimpy sap. I'm such a fuckin pehndu that not only can't I decide what to say but I can't decide what to daydream bout either. You could choose anything. But I reckon daydreamin is like proper dreamin, when you're actually sleepin. You can't sleep less you stop tryin to. Just got to ignore the voices tellin you how tired you are, an those that keep sayin, Get to fuckin sleep or tomorrow you'll be knackered. Shouldn't listen to them voices. Shouldn't think at all. I only got bout twenty minutes left so I shouldn't think at all.

*   *   *

— Why you being so quiet now, Jas? I tell you, sometimes you're just like your father. I'm sorry, Bobby, but my son, he's just like his father.

It's Uncle Bobby, one a Dad's best mates from Ilford who always cracks rude jokes whenever he comes round an who somehow makes Mum an Dad stop tryin to sound so fuckin posh all the time. He's probly come over to see Dad but Dad's still at the office cos Dad's always at the fuckin office.

— Don't worry, let him sulk in the corner, Uncle Bobby goes to Mum. — His salad is tasty today. Nice and meaty. Not like that rabbit's food last week, thank God. These vegetarian children. Bloody gaylords, all of them.

— Jas's not vegetarian, Mum goes, grabbin the corner a her turquoise pashmina shawl before it slips off her shoulder. — His grandmother is, and I'm trying to cut down for this new diet I'm trying. But Jas just doesn't like meat, do you, Jas? That's why usually he doesn't put it inside these healthy salad plates of his. He doesn't even eat my chicken biryani any more, even though I put extra chillies in it just for his sake.

— There's a word for this kind of behaviour: arrogant. That's what you are, Uncle Bobby says to me. — You should be grateful for the food your mama cooks for you. I remember I was bloody grateful to my mother when I was a young boy.

— Oh, don't worry, Bobby, I don't mind. It means I don't have to reheat yesterday's leftovers so I don't have to feel like a bad mother, she goes, lettin out one a her posh laughs that makes her shawl nearly slip off again. Fuckin pashmina shawls. She's got eight a them. She even wears one when she's gardening. She bought them one time when Amit's mum came back from Bombay an turned their living room into Pashmina Shawls 'Я' Us or someshit. After she's finished straightening it again she tries a spoon a my salad. — He's trying to be a healthy young boy, that's all. She makes me feel nauseous. Mum always makes me feel nauseous.

Can you imagine me makin a salad? Fuck that. But sometimes I'd like to, just to be healthy an that, I'd like to like salad. So fuck it, let me have made the salad.

— This, lamb is it? Never had lamb in a salad before but it's not bad, young man. Then he winks at my mum. — Looks like you've got yourself a gaylord chef in the family. It's a bit too spicy for an old man like me, but it's not bad, son.

Fuck off, you wanker, an stop callin me a gaylord. I so wish I could say this out loud. You wanker, please fuck off. I request you to fuck off out our house an cease referring to me as a homosexual, you wanker. I in't your son. I'd rather be your own personal fuckin rent boy than be your fuckin son. Leave my mum alone, she's only laughin along with you cos she'll laugh along with anyone when they're puttin someone down. My tongue may be fucked but my eyes are wide open. I can understand this kind a shit. But I can't tell that to you, or her.

— It's lamb, no? Just want to make sure because I don't eat beef no more, not after all that mad cow business.

Sorry, but I honestly can't talk to you. Maybe I want to. But I can't.

— Jas probably doesn't even know himself, Bobby, he hates meat. Is that why you're not eating your own salad today, Jas? Oh, just forget it. You just sit and sulk. Bobby, let him sit and sulk. He is always sulking. Just like his father, I tell you.

Suddenly in my mind I can hear all those kids at school. Hardjit, Davinder, Amit. That lot who never spoke to me back then. — Fine, sulk even more, they all go in chorus. — Don't answer yo mama, don't chat 2 no one. U jus like yo papa, u jus like yo papa . . . So jus eat yo fuckin food, u useless khota.

— Oh, come on, Uncle Bobby says, tryin to keep my salad in his mouth, — all this sulking is no good. Jas my boy, tell us what happened, was it girls? That would be a big relief, woman. You don't want a gaylord son, so be grateful if he's sulking about girls.

— In't no chance a dat, go the guys in my head again, — pehndu can't even chat to blokes proply. Probly couldn't even kiss a girl.

Probly couldn't even kiss a girl. Take it from da experts, jus open your mouth n da tongue knows wat it's doin. You don't kiss her *on* da mouth, you kiss her *in* da mouth, u get me? Best try it on yo'self tho, innit, best try n lick your own tongue.

— Jas? Girls? Not yet, Bobby, Jas is too young to have a girlfriend, goes my mum. — Jas doesn't go around giving kissies to girls, do you, Jas? He probably doesn't even know how to give kissies.

Before Mum has even finished, Uncle Bobby spits his laughter into his plate an quickly eats it again. — If I didn't know how to kiss, my wife would never –

Then Mum turns back to me again, this time makin that face she always makes when she decides it's time for her to stick up for Dad stead a layin into him all the time. — Now you listen to me Bobby, you stop saying bad things about my son.

Uncle Bobby weren't havin none a it, though, so Mama then turns to me an goes, — Jas, don't leave this all to me, you've got to stand up for yourself and say something. Open your mouth, please? she sighs. — Why can't you open your mouth?

She is right. I should stand up for myself. I shouldn't leave it all to her. But she orders Dad around enough, why can't she just order Uncle Bobby to ease up? An anyway, it'd be pointless for me to tell Uncle Bobby anything cos I can't talk an I can't eat an it hurts so much. What's the point in feelin pain if you can't even tell your mama bout it? An it don't even matter that Mama is now on my side. Don't matter cos it's started bleedin again. An my cheeks swell up with the blood. Fill em up. Oh, ouch. Ow. Mama, Mama, my mouth hurts. Ouch.

At first it had seemed the blood was violently bellyflopping over my bottom lip, like how it all explodes when you start to puke. Gushin out from where it'd been hardest to scissor it, from the middle bit where my *Shitesprecher* had been thickest. Then the blood settled once again, just trickling over my lip an painting my chin an neck a sort a blackish kind a red. So wet it was, my blood. I could feel it all mess up with the bits a ugly, stragglin bumfluff on my face cos

I was tryin to grow a goatee beard. But I could only feel it on my face when I tried to concentrate on something other than the swirling pain inside my mouth an the sound a '*Kiss*' by Prince, which is suddenly blastin outta the oven, fridge an microwave. Think bout the world outside your mouth, I tell myself, think bout your mama's calm, fuckin *Forest Moods* CD. Think bout the drip-drippin a blood from the end a my shirt collar an into my plate a cucumber, tomato an diced up, lean an tender (but otherwise fuckin useless) *Shitesprecher*. Think bout Mama mopping up my blood with her pashmina shawl, dancin to Prince. My own head stirring, draggin though the air. Fuck knows whether I've suddenly gone bald but my head's fuckin freezin, slowly fallin forward so that I in't got no choice but to let my bloody, painted face roll down with it. Down towards my salad. The kitchen table din't seem so massive before. An all the stains on Mum's pink frilly tablecloth move further out, makin space for all a my blood.

— Oh . . . bloody mad boy, bloody fool, Uncle Bobby gives it, desperately spittin out my salad when I finally open my mouth. He jerks up the table, which launches the whole bowl a salad at me, almost as if to help me reach it as my head continues to slump down, slowly dragged by my mama-it's-so-painful mouth. As I meet the bowl halfway my jaw is still locked wide open an meaty bits a my salad enter, kissin me. A proper kiss. In the mouth.

4

— Wat da fuck you been doin, you woman, playin wid yourself? Amit shouts at me as he opens the car door. — Can't you see Davinder's gettin a parkin ticket?

Shit, he was right. How can I have missed the traffic warden when the fucker's standin right in front a me, wearin that yellow jacket that glows in the light an that traffic warden's hat, the kind security guards wear to look like cops. An in case all that in't enough, there's a massive afro oozing out from underneath it. People usually cuss me for being deaf or mute, but not blind.

Davinder an Jaswinder were standin in the traffic warden's face, shoutin him down so loud, people spilled out the newsagent's next door to see, in their own words, what the fuck was goin on 'ere then.

— Thirty fuckin seconds, man, dat's all I wos, goes Davinder. — I got food poisoning, innit. Had 2 vomit in Nando's toilets. Or wudyu prefer it if I threw up in da street? Oolti out on da pavement here where u cud slip on it?

How gandah is that? The traffic warden was as ready to swallow this excuse as he was the stomachful a vomit Davinder went on to describe. My own stomach felt like it could offer the boy some inspiration, that's how much I was dreadin the rinsin I'd just let myself in for. I turned back to face Amit to see whether it'd be a super-rinse with spin cycle or whether he'd just lay into me with a light-wash piss-take. I try an head him off either way by sayin, — Shit, Amit, I'm really, really sorry, man.

37

— Ohw, you'we weally weally sowwy, arwe you?

His Tweety Bird impression again. Bang outta order then, cos I never spoke like that. I never had a problem with my Rs. I never had no stutter an I never even had a lisp, I just had a problem speakin. An I hardly ever have that problem no more anyway. But none a this matters to Amit. I hate the way people bring up your fuck-ups from the past to make your fuck-ups in the present seem even worse. My mum does the exact same shit with my dad. They'll be all luvvy-duvvy n tight but then Dad'll forget something or fuck up some-how an then it's thapparh time. She'll bring up beef she had with him from, like, before I was even born.

— I'm sow weally weally sowwy dat I tawlk n act like a woman tawlkin n actin like a batty boy, goes Amit again. — Wat's da point in sittin in da car if you jus gonna let someone give Davinder a parkin ticket? Fuck's sake, Jas, you give us all nuff grief by being such a sap.

Amit carries on layin into me for being dickless an also for being dickless to someone like Davinder, someone who was the opposite a dickless. So I'm sittin there wonderin whether that means Davinder'd got a big dick while Amit brings up things like how safe Davinder'd been to us all these years, how we'd already kept him waitin that afternoon, what a great customer he'd been, how he'd given us nuff business an even what a bling car he'd got.

— Him n Jaswinder bringin all their crew to Hardjit's fight tomor-row, Amit goes on. — An you pay dem back by bein a sap n lettin em get a fuckin ticket. Fuckin dickless woman. You lucky dat traffic warden in't got round to givin our own Beemer no ticket yet cos Hardjit'd break yo face. Fuck's sake, Jas, why da fuck din't you call us, you sala kutta?

— I, well, I, the traffic warden, I was kind a, I . . . er, I, you know, er, you know . . .

— For fuck's sake, boy, how can anyone argue wid'chyu if you can't fuckin talk?

— Well . . . I . . . I, er . . .

Remember that Fatboy Slim CD? The one that all the goras liked cos it mixed electric guitars with breakbeats. Remember what it was called? *You've Come a Long Way, Baby.*

— I . . . I, er, I did call you guys. I was shoutin for you lot to come.

— Wat's da point in dat? How we meant to hear you holler from da muthafuckin car?

— No, I . . . I, er foned you, man. I was shoutin on the fone.

Rudeboy Rule #1:
My dad always said that you shouldn't ever lie cos you'll have to tell another ten lies to back it up. However, Hardjit'd taught me that if the back-up lies are good enough, then so fuckin what?

How to tell a good lie, though? Especially when sometimes you stammer even when you tellin the truth. Mr Ashwood taught us in History lessons that Hitler thought a good lie was a big lie. — He even had a minister for propaganda, Josef Goebbels. Jas, explain to the rest of the class what propaganda is. However, Hardjit'd taught me that a good lie is a lie with lots a detail in it. That's why, right now, Davinder an Jaswinder were being even more gandah, listing the ingredients a Davinder's imaginary vomit. Rice, daal, aaloo ki subjhi mixed in a base a bhindee an bile. If the back-up lies were detailed enough, then so fuckin what?

— I foned Davinder to warn him, innit, I say to Amit as I carefully reached for the Nokia 3510i in my back pocket an dialled Davinder's number, stealth-style behind my back. Davinder an Jaswinder were frettin so much they probly wouldn't hear the fone ring anyway. A long way indeed, baby. — Trust me, Amit, I din't have time to come in an get you guys cos the traffic warden only just showed up. But I swear I foned Davinder though. Check his fone if you think I just be chattin shit. A hundred bucks says it shows a Missed Call.

Amit walks over to Davinder an does that whole Chinese whispers thing in his ear. Sure enough, Davinder's Sony Ericsson P800 colour display showed a Missed Call from me, prompting Davinder to hold his forehead as if to go, Shit, how could I be such a deaf khota? Amit held his palm out towards me, as if he was givin me blessings, though what he was really going was, Shit, sorry, Jas, my bad. Jaswinder held his own palm out to Davinder, though not in a givin blessings kind a way but stead pretendin like he was gonna give him a thapparh across the face for being deaf. All a them too vexed to check the exact time the Missed Call had been missed. Then there's Hardjit givin me a proud grin as he gets in the car an silences the drama outside by shuttin his door. — U jus call'd Davinder now, din't u, bruv? I always knew u could b nuff smart when u proply tryin.

Davinder's leather rucksack had twenty fones inside it this time. I nearly dropped the thing when Ravi passed it to me, though obviously I din't *look* like I nearly dropped it. Most customers usually give us bout two or three at a time but Davinder normly gave us more'n ten. That was why we bought him some Nando's or kebabs or whatever whenever we did dealings with him. The bredren was our best customer, you see, an if a good desi knows anything, it's how to look after their best customer.

I don't even want to know where Davinder'd got all his merchandise from, but it kept us in business an you can't be a businessman if you in't in business, innit. Our business is reprogramming mobile fones, which basically means unblocking them or unlocking them so that they can be reconfigured. To unlock a fone, you change its security code so that the handset can be used on a different network from the one it was originally bought on. Most people came to us cos they wanted to swap fones with their dad or mum or sister or whoever but keep their own fone numbers an tariffs an stuff. After all, what's the point in your dad havin a blinger fone than you when he probly can't even use the thing proply. So say your dad gets a handset upgrade to some slick Samsung on his Orange network an you want to swap it with your Nokia 6610 that you got on a T-Mobile network. You can't just stick the SIM chip carryin your fone number an tariff an stuff into your dad's new handset. It won't work cos most fones are locked to the network they were originally bought on. To switch networks you gotta unlock the handsets by changin the security code. For some reason, the fone companies din't allow people to have their fones unlocked in proper fone shops. In business-speak, that meant the fone companies had gone an left a gap in the market.

Rudeboy Rule #2:

Havin the blingest mobile fone in the house is a rudeboy's birthright. Not just for style, but also cos fones were invented for rudeboys. They free you from your mum an dad while still allowing your parents to keep tabs on you.

So any time anyone round here wanted to enforce Rudeboy Rule #2 by doing one a these family fone swaps while keepin their own fone number, all they had to do was dial our fone number. Easy. Except for one thing: Davinder may've had a lot a cousins an uncles an aunts an everything, but he din't exactly have twenty relatives all wantin to swap their fones round all at the same time like unwanted mithai boxes being recycled at Diwali.

Customers like Davinder were different to our normal family fone swap customers cos there's more to this business than just switchin fones between different networks. If a fone gets reported missin or stolen or whatever, the fone company blocks it so that it can't be used no more. They do this by deactivating a 14–17 digit code called the IMEI number. To unblock a fone (stead a just unlocking it) you gotta change the IMEI number. This code also makes it easier for the police to trace the thing, so if you ever find or jack some fones an want to use them you first gotta change the codes or find someone who can change them for you. Davinder an his crew had found us. Every couple a weeks we'd hook up with him an he'd give us this black leather rucksack full a fones. Fuck knows how he got them an how he never got caught gettin them. But he got them. An Amit'd got all the software an hardware for changin the IMEI numbers.

Don't get me wrong, we in't wannabe badass gangstas or someshit.

41

We din't jack no fones or sell no jacked fones or nothin. We just provided a service. We're businessmen, innit. Our business dealings with Davinder just meant that he could guarantee to whoever he sold the fones to that they'd work an that they'd never be identified as being jacked. People keep sayin it's becoming illegal or someshit to tamper with a fone's codes, but, let's face it, the cops would only round up all the little dodgy corner shops that offer this service, they'd never get round to little people like us. The feds were such pehndus they thought the little shops *were* the little people.

Rudeboy Rule #3:

My dad always told me to stay outta trouble. However, Hardjit'd told me to stay outta trouble with the police. After all, while the law is for goras, so is Feltham Young Offenders Institute. An while the police may be a bunch a pehndus, so are those who end up in prison.

Only last week we'd helped Amit swap fones with his dad. We did that job for free a course, even though Amit's dad wanted to pay us anyway cos he said he admired our business skills. — Give me invoice minus VAT and I pay you boys cash, he'd said. — No use making taxman richer so he can give to bloody Somali asylum seekers. When we told his dad that we din't have any a that VAT thing going on in the first place he got even more excited. Said he'd send more business our way. So let's face it, we'd be gimps not to play this game. It's what our A-level Economics retake teacher calls the informal economy. There was demand for a service out there an we could supply it. An it was all cash, so why not? Amit had the tools, Ravi had the transport, Hardjit had the contacts an I did what I was asked an din't ask no questions.

Actually I *did* bring something to this gig: market information. As our A-level Economics retake teacher always said, markets can't work proply without information. That's why, before the Internet, they invented pigeons an newspapers. I got my information from my dad. After all, he's a businessman too. He's in the mobile-fone business, though it in't like I'm tryin to copy him or nothin. He's got a warehouse an office near the airport that sells handsets an accessories. He only sells stuff to all them small, independent mobile-fone shops though, cos all the big high street chains have got their own supply networks. Anyway, thanks to all a Dad's catalogues an magazines an leaflets an shit that the fone companies keep givin him, I could provide our own business with all kindsa info bout all the different fones that were on the market already or coming onto the market soon. I in't exactly sure how much a this info we actually needed to do our business dealings, but we figured when you're chattin to customers it's best to sound like you know what the fuck you're chattin bout. All I had to do was ask Dad for all the stuff when he'd finished readin them. Said it was for my Economics coursework. The old man was so happy his son was takin an interest in his shit, thinkin maybe I might even work with him one day. He probly even messed up the bed sheets dreamin bout havin some big family business. Wake the fuck up, I felt like sayin. It might've been like that in your generation, but why'd anyone want to work for their dad nowdays? I mean, what the fuck were you s'posed to do with your own plans? An how the fuck would you ever really know if you were really any good? Only fuckin reason I can see for joining my dad's business is maybe that way I'd get to have a proper converfuckinsation with the man. Matter a fact, stead a gettin me ready to work with my dad, our business was actually competing with him, puttin him outta business. After all, if people round here couldn't come to us to get their fones unlocked they'd probly end up buyin new ones from shops supplied by my dad. Serve him right.

I'd never told my dad bout our unblocking operation. Not just cos he was allergic to conversation an so I never told him much bout anything, but also cos he'd know our fone operation weren't totally, 100 per cent legal. So stead he thought we made all our extra bucks by DJing. The man was probly proud I din't spend Saturdays being another fast-food or supermarket pleb, I guess. Probly proud a the fact that he bought my first record player. That's my dad: the man might not talk much or do much when it comes to me, but when it comes to tellin other people how proud he is a the way I turned out, the man'll open his gob quick time, soakin up the credit like it was fuckin coconut butter.

We did in fact actually do some DJing one time. We used Hardjit's Technic turntable an Amit's Jamo speakers. Ravi was a pretty fly MC, probly cos he talked so much shit all the time anyway. I was crap at all that stuff a course so I just handed out the flyers. We don't do DJing nowdays cos there in't as much bucks in it no more. In business-speak it's called price deflation prompted by oversupply. Too many other desi kids round here set up their own sound systems an there just weren't enough bhangra, RnB gigs an wedding receptions to go round. Back before the market got too crowded you could get four hundred bucks just doing a big shaadi reception in a hotel ballroom near Heathrow. Also, as Ravi kept pointing out, being a DJ meant it was practically your job to flirt with fit, tipsy ladies. But when the usual Saturday-nite shaadi rate fell to, like, two hundred bucks, we decided unblocking mobiles would be better business an so now it was fones for us.

Here's hoping fones don't give you radiation when they're switched off cos otherwise there'll be no grandchildren for my dad to be proud bout. I had to move the rucksack onto my lap when Amit got back inside the Beemer, givin me another silent apology as he did so by tapping his left shoulder with his fist an then givin me a high-five with it. As if that were some kind a signal, Ravi turned the key in the ignition. But before revving, he waited for Hardjit to finish callin out to Davinder an Jaswinder, — Relax, blud, it's all good. Jus let da traffic-wallah do his shit n we'll settle da ticket wid'chyu later, a'ight.

5

I was secretly lookin forward to our Economics lesson today. I guess I hadn't *openly* looked forward to a lesson in years, not since we were back at school an Mr Ashwood showed us *Schindler's List* to help us understand the Second World War.

— I'ma take da short cut back to college, goes Ravi, — othawise we b headed for traffic, innit, Hardj?

— Nah, man, it gettin late an we gots twenty fuckin fones in da bag. Fuck college, let's take em straight 2 my yard.

Rudeboy Rule #4:
According to Hardjit, it don't matter if the proper word for something sounds fuckin ridiculous. If it's the proper word then it's the proper word.

Yard is one a them words. If it was me who was the American hip-hop G or whoever the fuck it was who invented all this proper speak, no way the proper word for house'd be yard. That's the garden, for fuck's sake. I in't feelin the word crib either cos that's what American babies sleep in. Also, I wouldn't decide that the proper word for wikid is heavy. Why they decided that The Shit should mean The Greatest I got no idea, maybe cos bad's always meant good. But more than all a this, if I was the Proper Word Inventor I'd do two things differently. I wouldn't decide that the proper word for a dickless poncey sap is a gay batty boy or that the proper word for women is bitches. That

shit in't right. I know what other poncey words like homophobic an
misogynist mean an I know that shit in't right. But what am I s'posed
to do bout it? If I don't speak proply using the proper words then
these guys'd say I was actin like a batty boy or a woman or a woman
actin like a batty boy. One good thing though: now that I use all these
proper words I'm hardly ever stuck for words. I just chuck in a bit a
proper speak an I sound like I'm talkin proper, talkin like Hardjit. I
just wish I was the Proper Word Inventor so I could pick different
proper words, that's all. But, seeing as how I in't that person, we were
cruisin to Hardjit's yard in Ravi's ride, checkin out the bitches round
the high street. We nod at some bredren we know from Hounslow
Manor School as we turned off the London Road. We pass some G
drivin a red Pharrell Williams with a number plate that says D3S1,
which we figure is meant to mean DESI. We talk bout how you never
see a car like that without a personalised number plate. We turn up
DMX again as we drive up alongside some ladies in a little convertible Justin Timberlake who're waitin to turn into the Treaty Centre
car park. We see some Somali kids makin mischief near some other
car park by the Yates pub. We see Deepak Gill an his crew hangin
outside the car park by Hounslow West tube station an normly we'd've
shouted Kiddaan at them but we din't this time cos he'd got some
beef with Amit's older brother's fiancée's brother-in-law's nephew.
We din't shout Muthfuckin bhanchods either, though, cos Amit's
brother's shaadi was only a few months away an we din't want to
fuck things up for him by causing some complicated, family-related
shit. Ravi slid down from fourth to second an tried to pull away from
the station, partly to make a loud, angry noise at Deepak Gill an
partly to try an overtake this pain-in-the-butt H91 bus in front. But
the oncoming lane in't clear an so we're fuckin stuck. Right behind
the rear end a some fuckin Grampa Simpson when we could be chasing the rear end a some J-Lo or Beyoncé instead.

— Fuckin plebs, Ravi keeps shoutin at the Grampa Simpson in
front. Then, — Oi, you gandah fucker, every time it, like, farts at us.
We couldn't squeeze past it cos the dickless driver din't pull into the

bus stop proply cos there was another bus in front a him. That bus was a H91 as well. Now that we cleaned these streets a saps, coconuts an Paki-bashing skinheads, we gotta do something bout all these buses. Even with a special slip road for them outside Hounslow West tube station, they always managed to cause chaos there. It was the same near Hounslow East tube, Hounslow Central tube, Hounslow railway station an Hounslow bus station (though I in't sure it's fair for us to have beef with buses hangin round at that last one).

The oncoming lane finally clears up, but we still don't overtake the buses in front cos suddenly one a the H91s opens its doors again to let out a bunch a sixth-formers from the Green School. The Green School for Girls, that is. An even more accurate name would be the Green School for Fit Girls. They were upper sixth-formers, meanin they'd binned their dark green school uniforms a couple a years back an were now struttin around in their best casual garms. Good desi girls, though, so no fuck-me clothes. Jeans an jumpers mostly, but with enough Lycra to make you glad it weren't cold enough for coats. Hardjit leaned out the window an did whatever it is that he does so well. I couldn't hear exactly how he was chirpsin them over the CD, but I caught him givin it the line: — Oye oye sohni kurhiyo! The girls did that giggle-disguised-as-a-smile thing an Hardjit was out the door, escorting them to the tube station before you could say, Dude, the station's only five metres away.

— What the fuck's he gonna do? Buy their tube tickets for them? I asked the other guys.

No answer.

— Or does he reckon he's gonna get off with one a them in the photo booth?

Still no answer. So I look at whatever it is Amit an Ravi are busy lookin at. An suddenly I'm thinkin Cheers God for makin us bunk off lesson.

— Phwoar! Gimme some air, goes Ravi as another Green School girl steps off the bus. — Wat da fuck is Samira Ahmed doing ridin on a bus?

— I dunno, man, maybe her Beemer broke down, goes Amit.

— But ridin on a bus wid all dem plebs, man. She is so fit, she should be in my Beemer ridin wid me. Actually, scrap dat, she should be ridin me.

— Or maybe even me, goes a voice that sounds a lot like mine. Shit. I covered my mouth as I realised I'd just said that out loud. I apologise to my mind even before it starts givin me a bollocking, but it's too late to apologise to Amit an Ravi. It weren't my fault though. I mean, just look over there. Just look at Samira Ahmed. She was the reason guys round Hounslow'd bothered learnin how to spell the word Beautiful stead a just writin the word Fit inside their valentine cards. She was beautiful like them models in make-up ads, the ones where they're so fit they don't even look like they're wearin any make-up. Unlike any a the other desi girls that'd got off the bus before her, Samira Ahmed weren't even wearin no jewellery either. That's how fit she was. Honest to God. She made you realise how some desi princesses were lookin more an more like clowns dressed up like Christmas trees with all their bling-bling Tiffany tinsel an Mac masks. It was like as if they were tryin to distract your attention from other shit on their faces, like their noses, mouths an eyes. Like they'd got so hooked on who'd got more bling that they'd forgot what jewellery was originally for, same way some desis keep complaining bout non-spicy food cos they forget the original reason for drowning food in chillies was cos the desis in the pinds were so skint they could only afford off meat an so wanted to hide the taste. In business-speak it's called over-investing in marketing stead a product development, an sometimes overstating the value a your assets as a result. Soon as the customer's focus shifts back to the product again your business is fucked cos the whole demand curve, like, shifts inwards. That's why fizzy soft drinks in't sellin so well no more now that people know they should be drinkin pani an fruit juice stead a all them artificial flavourings an colourings an all that other shit desi princesses slap on their faces. But not Samira Ahmed. No marketing, no make-up, no sodium benzoate, no jewellery, no aspartame an none a that potassium sorbate shit. Multiply her usual fitness by ten the way she was lookin today, dressed in that tight black polo neck that stretched round her chest an that khaki skirt – shiny, soft, slinky. Satin, probly. What is it bout shiny skirts that let you see a lady's curves even better than you'd be able to if she was wearin no skirt, no nothin? All a that Heaven held together by this thin brown leather belt fastened diagonally across Samira's butt an matchin her boots.

— Yeh, right, goes Ravi. — Why'd she go for a skinny gimp like you when she cud wrap dem legs round a stud like me?

But Amit is less willin to just roll with my comment bout wantin Samira to ride me. — Easy now, Jas, he goes. — Ravi here jus b chattin bout how fit she is. Da way you say it, it soundin like you onto her. Samira outta bounds for all a us bredrens an you know it. She Muslim, innit. We best all stick to our own kinds, boy, don't b playin wid fire. An you best not b chattin like dat in front a Hardjit.

Amit had a point a course. If any a us ever got with Samira, her mum an dad'd probly kill her and then try an kill us. That's if our own mums an dads din't kill us first. An then that's if Hardjit din't kill us before they did. Mr Ashwood had taught us bout the bloody partition a India an Pakistan during History lessons. What we din't learn, though, was how some people who weren't even born when it happened or awake during History lessons remembered the bloodshed better than the people who were.

— Relax, Amit, I jus be jokin, innit. I jus be chattin shit, checkin her out same way Ravi is, I go, tryin to sound casual but not managing to sound casual enough. Not nearly casual enough. — But it in't as if she's like a strict Muslim, is it?

— Wat da fuck is wrong wid'chyu? Wat da fuck'd I jus say, Jas? None a us lot should ever b goin there, man. Don't matter whether she strict n dat. Jus don't b fuckin goin there, a'ight.

I figure things can't get any more tense, so I defy him an go there a little more: — Yeh, but I'm just sayin, how strict can she be? I mean, she's a she. How often you hear bout female Islamic fundamentalists?

— Look, she got three brothers an dey well strict. One a dem even belongs to Hizb ut-Tahrir or Al-Muhajiroun or one a dem groups. Dey stricter bout keepin their sister halal than my mum is bout keepin her shit vegetarian so you jus best shut da fuck up before Hardjit gets back.

— I jus sayin she can't be that strict, that's all, I go, — I mean you seen her when she dresses an dances like she the fourth member a Destiny's Child or someshit. Come on, Amit, admit it, surely even you think she's fit.

— No I don't, Jas. An you best calm da fuck down n focus your hormones on your own kind. Anyway, wat da fuck we arguin bout her being Muslim for? Samira Ahmed ain't nuffink special whether she b a Muslim, a Sikh, a Hindu or a mermaid on a beach in fuckin Goa. In fact, my bum is buffer than her.

— Ahh, blud, now you shut yo mouth, goes Ravi. — Jus cos I ain't wantin to get wid her, it don't mean dat girl ain't da fittest lady in da hood. At da end a da day, she did win Miss Hounslow two years in a row, innit.

— Dat's jus cos I din't enter ma ass. Look at her. She a tramp, da lady ain't got no class. She ain't even wearin no jewellery or make-up, man.

— That's cos she don't need none, I go. — Sayin she ain't got no class is like sayin Pamela Anderson's got a flat chest cos she don't wear a Wonderbra.

Just then Hardjit gets back in the Beemer, bringin a smile an the smell a perfume with him. We stop the conversation bout Samira an skip to the next track on the CD.

— Wat'chyu boys been doin? Hardjit asks as he starts struggling with his seat belt again.

— Nothin, I go. — Jus chattin bout business, checkin out da bitches, innit.

Hardjit's yard had a double driveway, big enough to park his dad's Al Pacino an his mother's Mary J Blige, but probly not big enough for a Mary J Blige an the Amitabh Bachchan his dad'd always wanted.

They really needed a driveway cos his yard was right up near where the Great West Road an the Bath Road joined into the road that takes you to Terminal 4 or the road that went straight to Terminals 1, 2 or 3 – the gateway to India just down the A4. Living there, they din't know what was worse – the traffic on the road outside or the traffic in the sky. Either way the double glazing weren't thick enough an they'd had to hook up their living-room TV to two sets a surround-sound speakers. It'd probly be the best TV ever for watchin MTV Base or the B4U desi music channel, only we'd never know cos we never actually went in the living room when we went round. There was always some auntyji in there with Hardjit's mum, you see. Her an a friend gup-shupping bout this bit a gossip or that bit a gossip. Somehow they always managed to sound like those emergency sessions in the Indian parliament you sometimes see on *Star News*.

It was obviously deeply disrespectful if we din't go in an say hello to the auntyjis, but it'd've also been deeply disrespectful to just suddenly barge in unexpected. This time we figured it'd be more disrespectful to go in than it'd be not to. We could hear Hardjit's mum inside talkin importantly, sayin things like Waheguru. So stead, we politely took our trainers off in the porch, whispered the usual jokes bout Ravi's paneer-smellin socks an legged it upstairs, givin it a respectful Hi, Aunty to his mum, an adding another Hi, Aunty for whoever else was in the living room with her. Aunty's freshly cooked subjhi chasing us all the way upstairs, even though Ravi's feet were cheesier than usual an even though she'd shut the kitchen door to stop the smell escaping. Up on the landing, the subjhi mixed with the incense sticks burning in bedroom number one along the long, L-shaped corridor. There weren't no bed in bedroom number one. It was where they kept their copy a the Guru Granth Sahib on a table. They'd hung their pictures a various Sikh Gurus on the land-ing walls outside. They'd even got a couple a pictures a Hindu Gods too. Usually you only get Hindus who'll blend their religion with Sikhism but Hardjit's mum an dad were one a the few Sikh families who blended back.

Bedroom number two: Aunty an Uncle's. Stricly off-limits, although just inside you can see a blown-up photo hangin on the magnolia-painted woodchip wall. It's from when Hardjit's family went to Disneyland with his chacha's family in New Jersey. Hardjit's dad also got another brother living back in Jalandhar, where according to Mr Ashwood the smells are even stronger an the colours even brighter. But Hardjit prefers visiting his cousin in New Jersey cos she's got fitter friends in her desi scene out there. Fitter buddies with fitter bodies who dress like desi versions a Britney Spears – in the video for 'Slave' a course, not 'Hit Me Baby One More Time'. Before you turn the corner to get to bedroom numbers three, four an five, there's a laundry basket on the landing lookin like a milk pan that'd been on the hob too long. Amit takes one look at it an gives it, — Ehh ki hai? Wat's wid all dis gandh, man? You best gets your mum to do your laundry quick time or you'll have to wear da same smelly khachha every day.

— Ain't ma fault, blud. Da washing machine's fuck'd, innit. Dad was tryin 2 do some shit 2 da plumbing n pipes n dat, n suddenly da washin machine, dishwasher n even da fuckin tea-maker all fuck'd up in one go.

— How da fuck's your chai-maker connect'd to da pipes? Ravi asks.

— I dunno. Maybe it ain't. I ain't fuckin Bob da Builder, innit.

— You know wat I'd do if my washin machine, dishwasher or chai-maker broke down? goes Ravi.

— Wat?

— Divorce da bitch, innit.

On the floor by the laundry basket lay a pile a Bollywood magazines. Old issues a *Cineblitz* an *Stardust* mostly, which Hardjit, his parents an his little sister had agreed to keep out on the landing so that they din't fight over who could keep them in their bedroom.

— Nice stash, bruv, goes Ravi, lookin down at them, which was probly difficult for him seeing how he was more used to angling his neck upwards when he was checkin out magazines, — verrry nice stash, he gives it again. — Hope u in't got yo *Playboys* tucked away in da middle a them. Jus imagine yo mama or sister's face next time dey wanna read bout Shah Rukh Khan, innit.

Hardjit sometimes gets pretty vexed bout that kind a shit. Porn, hookers, slutty ladies. Other times he'll be laughin along, actin like a pimp. Honest to God, one minute he's talkin bout how he's gonna get inside some desi girl's lace kachhian an the next minute he's actin as if a girl's gotta be a virgin if she wants to be a proper desi. Fuck knows why sometimes he'll act one way an other times he'll act the other way. Could be he's only OK bout it when it's obvious we're only chattin bullshit or just fantasising or someshit. Problem is, you in't allowed to fantasise bout Bollywood actresses cos he reckons they're s'posed to be all pure an everything. You in't allowed to fantasise bout someone real in case Hardjit thinks you're being serious bout them an you in't allowed to fantasise bout someone famous cos chances are they're a Bollywood actress. You in't allowed to fantasise bout blatant sluts like porn stars cos desi girls in't meant to be into that kind a thing. An you in't allowed to fantasise outside your own race, like when Ravi goes on bout Page Three models, glamour girls an lap dancers. Those kindsa ladies get Hardjit so vexed that when he calls them bitches he don't just mean they're female. But right now Ravi's only fantasising bout fantasising. That's the way Ravi is. Sometimes if you allow him to just carry on, his gandahness can even get funny. Like when he got us kicked outta B&Q in Brentford by actually using one a the toilet bowls in the bathroom showroom.

— Jus imagine it, man, goes Ravi, — imagine if Aunty n Uncle picked up some bedtime Bollywood readin, innit, n out fell some topless gori woman wearin lacy black chuddies n suspenders, innit. Again, Hardjit just let Ravi carry on: — Or maybe jus a black thong, innit. Maybe it'd even help yo mum n dad, you know, get jiggy wid it.

Hardjit shot him a look, but still without sayin nothin or doing nothin or smackin nothin. — Help em make such a rumble in da jungle dat dey break da fuckin bed, innit, Ravi goes, — maybe even yo dad cud stop takin his Viagra.

The boy was well into red rag an bull territory now, as Mr Ashwood used to say. I guess Hardjit must've been too busy thinkin bout something else. Tomorrow's fight, today's fones, yesterday's fuck. If everyone who dissed him was as lucky as Ravi right now, the ER bit a Ealing Hospital wouldn't be so busy all the time. Stead a coming back proply with his fists, Hardjit just gives it, — Yeh n maybe ma dad can give his Viagra 2 u innit cos u clearly needin it, u fuckin sexually frustrated sex maniac.

— Safe, bruv. But I'm da mack already, innit. I only needs Viagra if ma bitch wanna cum forty times a nite steada thirty. An anyway, ma bitch is so fine I ain't needin no *Playboy* magazines to get ma soldier ready for action, you get me.

— Shut da fuck now, Hardjit gives it. — U best jus shut yo dirrty mouth now, Ravi. Dere ain't no fuckin *Playboys* in dere. 'Sup wid'chyu?

— Yeh, you know wat, bruv, you is right, innit. My bad. Now I'ma got to thinkin, you ain't gonna b havin no *Playboys* in here. You's a desi, innit. You's gonna b havin copies a *Asian Babes*! G-strings always look better on some nice Indian butt. At da end a da day, you b wantin yo meat proply cooked not raw, you get me.

Ravi did some more free advertising for *Asian Babes* before adding: — Hey, any a you boys heard bout dat new American porn star who's actually a desi? Dey call her Miss Vagindia. In dis new film she done, right, I heard she wearin nuffink but a bindi. Seriously, no kachhi, no banan, nuffink.

Forget the red rag an bull territory, Ravi may as well have stripped that porn star's red kachhi off himself an waved it in Hardjit's face.

Rudeboy Rule #5:
Bout six months ago Hardjit taught me that you couldn't learn to chat proply if you also din't know when to stop chattin. — U gots 2 know when 2 shut yo mouth, he'd said. — It da same when u stickin yo tongue down a lady's throat, u can't jus go on an on an on, she'll get bored or fuckin choke, innit.

Ravi was the kind a rudeboy who could never stick to Rudeboy Rule # 5. The trouble with rudeboys like Ravi, by which I mean the sheep kind a rudeboy, is they never realise when they're lucky. Stead they think it's some desi skilfulness they got that keeps other people's fists outta their faces. Just watch em next time you're in a nice bar or a club or whatever. They reckon they're being the shit an so they can't help pushin it.

— Hey relax, blud, goes Ravi again. — You know I'd bruck anyone who bought dat *Asian Babes* shit too. I jus mouthin off cos I got me a high sex drive, dat's all, man. I can't help it if I is a wild fuckin beast. Better'n bein a skinny batty bwoy like Jas here, innit. He probly got a stash a gay porn. *Bud Bud Batties* or sumfink, innit. Dat's if there is a mag for batty desis. Wat bout one for lesbian desis, man? If there ain't one a dem then somebody shud start one cos they'd make big bucks. Desi dykes, bindi'd bisexuals n dat, innit. Bring it on, blud.

It was just a punch on the arm an a follow-through elbow in the ribs. An when it was done, Ravi quietly examined his bruises an Hardjit crouched down by the pile a magazines, flickin through them as if to prove there really were no pornos in there. Then he started readin an article bout Hrithik Roshan's daily bodybuilding routine, as if the rest a us weren't even there an as if he hadn't already read it bout ten times already. This might seem rude seeing as how we were guests in his house, but I guess he knew from the new smells runnin up the stairs that his mum'd already started fryin samosas an makin chai for us. — Dat's some fly shit, he whispered bout something he'd just read, givin Hrithik Roshan a high-five on the shoulder with his still-clenched fist as he did so. Then he closed the copy a *Cineblitz*, wiped it with his vest an placed it on top a the pile, leavin the front-cover shot a Hrithik Roshan facing up so that the rest a us could feel skinny, spotty an just generally ugly.

Not being a bunch a desperate fourteen-year-olds, we'd not come over with the ulterior motive a huntin for hidden pornos. We'd come to check something else out. An, as if she'd just heard the commotion on the landing, she an her glorious midriff were out waitin for us, standin round the corner outside bedroom number five, right where she usually did when we came round, dressed in tight, black satin. A desi Catwoman outfit. It was as if her black, shoulderless top had been moulded over the breasts beneath it, so that it weren't even satin but a thick stripe a that body-paint stuff you hear bout, exposing her midriff, bare hips, bronze collarbone an the soft brown flesh above it that connected her shoulder to her neck. Staring at the three a us from the bedroom door, as if to say, Now which one a you boys is gonna be my man?

Ravi strode up to her, placed his hand over her left breast an proceeded to lick her right breast. Slowly at first, but speedin up after bout six strokes. Well, pretend-lick to be precise. He weren't bout to ruin Hardjit's prized poster a Kareena Kapoor by gettin his saliva all over it.

— Fuckin get yo mouth off ma door, u perve, Hardjit said, pullin Ravi away from the poster, — or I'ma glue yo tongue 2 da inside a da door frame n slam dis muthafucka shut. I mean it, Ravi, u best jus ease up on dissin ma shit today b4 I smack u again.

— Safe, bruv, ma bad. But chill, man, I wouldn't really lick yo poster anyway.

— Fuckin tell me 2 chill, Ravi. D'yu know where u is at, bhanchod? In ma mum n dad's house. Not some fuckin perve's sex shop in Soho. We treatin our bitches wid respect, innit.

Amit began to say something, then hesitated, but then had to say it now cos he'd look like a batty boy for stammerin. — Da poster n da door, dey probly already sticky, innit, n I ain't meanin from glue.

Sayin shit like that was Amit's privilege in life. If those words had come outta anyone else's mouth, Hardjit would've smacked them for dissin him, dissin his house, dissin his mum's magazines, dissin the poster he probly got free with one a them magazines an dissin bitches in general. Truth is, we weren't actually dissin nothin. We were appreciating his poster, like how poncey people do when they go to poncey galleries to check out paintings a sunflowers an shit. I know this cos

I seen em do it. We all went to one a them places one time, honest to God, up near Trafalgar Square. Ravi'd wanted to go inside cos he said his mum had suddenly gone all poncey bout famous paintings. She wants some tutty picture a fuckin water lilies, he'd said as we headed straight to the gift shop. We soon managed to get ourselves kicked out by some bitch who wore glasses on the tip a her nose, loads a make-up over her wrinkles an who spoke like she was the Queen's first cousin or someshit. Seems that you in't allowed to say things like Check out da size a her melons, not when you're lookin at a painting which shows a naked woman with big melons. Seems that it in't no defence if you argue that you din't even use the word tits. Also, it don't help if you say, Fuck off, bitch, u jus jealous cos your own melons are saggy wid cobwebs in between them, innit.

Anyway, if you ask me, posters a Bollywood babes are better to look at than them poncey paintings. Matter a fact, I reckon they're better than posters a fit goris like Kate Moss or Caprice or fit kaalis like Beyoncé Knowles or Halle Berry. Indian women (I know I should say bitches stead a women to keep things proper but I'm still workin on it) are different. Bollywood babes are obviously not black or white so in't bootylicious or waifs. They're somewhere in between. Midriffs. Hardjit's dad once explained his theory bout all this when he caught me staring at a picture a Kate Moss in the paper one time. — Jas, my boy. No waste your time with all these skinny kurhiyaan, he'd said. — I'm like uncle to you. As your uncle I tell to you this: If she thin, that means she not eating. She is sick with this anoraks-yar disease. An if she not eat, she not do cooking. So then what's the use is she?

I remember noddin politely, tryin to think a something to say, before Hardjit's dad continued: — See this young kurhi in news-paper, Jas, I say she look like drug addict. I know how these girls are, I tell you. Look at her. I know she not even clean the house. Why she show off her belly button to whole wide world when she not even have belly in first place?

— There's nothin wrong with being slim, Mr Johal, I go. — It doesn't mean she does drugs.

— No, no, young man, nothing wrong with slim. I not say she should look mohti and pregnant. But this girl in newspaper, she starving to death.

Even though Hardjit's dad was chattin some blatant shit bout ladies, at least the man was chattin bout ladies. Only time my own dad ever talks to me bout women is if he's got an important female customer or supplier or whatever. An that's hardly ever seeing as how he mostly does business with businessmen.

— All these kuriyaan they all look like drug addicts, goes Hardjit's dad again, — I know what I'm saying. Delinquent drug addicts. I know what I'm saying. I'm like uncle to you. My father, before he die, he telled to me, you keep your eye on bellies of well-portioned kuriyaan and you get good portions in your own stomach.

I remember I wanted to disagree with Hardjit's dad again, outta respect for Kate Moss an women generally. But Hardjit's mum was standin right beside him givin me two good reasons to hold my tongue. Firstly, she was noddin in agreement with everything he'd just said. Secondly, it would've been disrespectful to her if I disagreed with her husband in front a her.

6

We were huddled in the king-sized bathroom between bedrooms number four an five. Hardjit'd got one a his urges to go shape his facial hair in the big magnifying mirror above the sink. There was always a couple a hairs that the beard trimmer missed an if Hardjit din't pluck em or scissor em they'd totally fuck up the outline a his goatee. It was the same with the lines he'd cut through his left eyebrow like three Adidas stripes. The jacuzzi an shower cubicle in this bathroom had never worked as well as the other two they'd got, not even before his dad's fuck-up with the plumbing. So, depending on which member a his family was lookin into the mirror, this bathroom was only used for shaping, shaving, plucking or waxing facial hair.

I turned my back to the other guys an stared back out across the landing at the Kareena Kapoor poster. I carried on staring at it even as Amit started takin the mick. Stop dreamin, Jas. You couldn't pull a nympho. Fuckin Seema mohti Patel is outta your league. That kind a thing. Still, I carried on staring, thankful that I weren't a gimp into that whole Britpop/R.E.M. scene no more cos if I was I'd probly still be wearin skintight Levi's 501s stead a my baggy Evisu's. Skintight jeans hurt at times like this. Even Hardjit's bedroom-door handle pointed upwards at the poster it shared a door with, though that was probly cos it'd been fixed upside down in another one a his dad's drunken DIY moments.

*   *   *

Rudeboy Rule #6:

Although desi ladies should dress like Bollywood actresses, under no circumstances should desi men try to dress like their male co-stars. Bollywood actors are the only desi men on Planet Earth who're allowed to wear skintight jeans. Watchin em carry it off as they carry the heroine outta the fountain during the soaked, see-through sari scene is just one more reason to sit through more Bollywood movies than you currently do. Must really fuckin hurt em though.

Finally, Amit grabbed my arm, yanking me from Kareena Kapoor's soft arms an then draggin me outta Bollywood altogether. — Kareena Kapoor ain't nothin special, he goes, — none a dem Bollywood bitches is. It all make-up, innit. Even Aishwarya Rai ain't all dat. Jus like I told'chyu boys earlier, I ain't caring how many beauty contests all a dese bitches won. My bum is buffer'n dem.

— Yeh, OK, Amit, we heard it all before, I give it, all pissed off as if my mum had just woken me up from a wet dream before it'd actually become one. — Let me guess, you pulled someone fitter than her last week, right?

Sayin that turned out to be a bad, bad, fuckin bad move on my part cos Amit goes an retaliates by tellin Hardjit how I'd been pervin over Samira Ahmed earlier that day.

— You shoulda seen him, he goes. — Afta we park'd up by Hounslow West, innit. Had his tongue hangin out da car window when she got off da bus.

— Fuck's sake, Jas, goes Hardjit, — I ain't caring how much u fancy a piece a her ass, u stay da fuck away from her. Dat bitch b trouble, u get me?

— Look, man, all I did was tell Amit that she's fit, that's all, bruv.

— No dat ain't all, bruv. How many times I'ma gots 2 tell u she fuckin bad news? Shudn't even b finkin bout her, fuck sayin shit bout her.

— Look, Hardjit, just cos she's Muslim. I in't sayin I wanna marry her, I'm jus sayin she's fit. Wat's wrong with that? You're being racist, man. An anyway, the fact that she's Muslim means it'd be even harder for me to get anywhere with her even if I wanted to, which I don't. So what's the big fuckin deal?

— Muslim ain't got nuffink 2 do wid nuffink, Jas. Everyting u sayin got shit 2 do wid shit. Dere b Sikh n Hindu girls who act like hos n I stay da fuck away from dem too. Bottom line, da bitch is a ho n u best stay clear – less u want me 2 pull out yo tongue wid dese tweezers.

— OK, whatever, man. But it in't right to call her a ho.

— I aksed u 2 shut da fuck up, Jas, I don't wanna hear u sayin shit bout her or shit bout any shit no more, u get me? U seen dat bitch in action when she surround'd by munde? Trust me, I'm da expert. She a muthafuckin ho.

Ravi was even quicker to agree with Hardjit an Amit than he usually was. I should've buckled as well, but that would've contravened my sense a chivalry an shit. An so I carried on standin up for her, carried on defendin her ways. Right up until Hardjit raised his hand as if was gonna give me a thapparh across the face.

Rudeboy Rule #7:
It's Basic Bollywood for Beginners. In situations that involve defending or rescuing a fit lady, you can stand tall with your front intact even if all your crew walk out on you or try an thapparh you. They call it being a hero. An when a lady's got your hormones bubbling like two different types a toilet cleaner mixed together in a jacuzzi, you got no choice but to be a hero.

I'd wanted to get off with Samira since the first time I saw her, but I fell for her proply at Ritu Singh's seventeenth birthday party. Ritu'd only invited me cos I used to help her with her English homework so I'd bought her a book. Her dad'd bought her a VW Golf an she ended up dancin with the keys round her neck before her mum walked up to her an told her she'd ruin her new Swarovski necklace underneath it. Can you imagine havin your mum an dad hangin with all your mates at your seventeenth? Most parents clear the fuck away soon as they've taken all their photos, sung 'Heppi Birday' an then passed round thookafied slices a birthday cake. But not Ritu's. Her mum an dad stayed all the way through, right to the end, makin sure there weren't no troublemakers, ruffians, smokin or underage drinkin. Her dad pretendin like he weren't really checkin out her friends, her mum mingling as if she was only double her daughter's age.

Back then I weren't that tight with people like Hardjit, Amit or Ravi, so I just hung back with the coconuts who were standin around wonderin how come they weren't on the dance floor with all the fit people. Even Ritu's dad was on the dance floor, his blatant wig blatantly slidin outta place. He was dancin bhangra-style to some old-skool hip-hop tune by De La Soul an kept smiling at people who were crackin up at him. Then he kept wiping his thick moustache with his handkerchief an lassoing the sweaty thing around his head until everyone else moved off the floor. Everyone except Samira Ahmed, that is. She never once left the dance floor all the time I was watchin her. An the only time she was dancin without some fit-lookin guy was when she was left on the floor with Ritu's dad. From the way he was lookin at Samira an her tight black dress I knew his wife was gonna pull him away an that was the first an only time I saw Samira Ahmed without other people round her.

September before that we'd both started sixth form, which was the first time I'd had lessons with girls since primary school. Did I ever get the seat next to Samira? Did I fuck. It weren't even as if everyone in the lesson liked her, it's just that those that did really did. At the same time, those that din't really din't. An Hardjit was one a those that din't. Kids back in the sixth form reacted in ways you couldn't predict when it came to Samira Ahmed. Din't matter whether they were Muslim like her, Sikh like Hardjit or Hindu like Amit. Some Muslims, Sikhs an Hindus wanted to shag her, other Muslims, Sikhs an Hindus wanted to smack her. Generally, the more hardcore they were, the more likely that they'd have beef with her. This was odd, seeing as how she mostly hung around with hard-

core desis. Matter a fact, it weren't till I started kickin round with
Hardjit an his crew in upper sixth that I started seeing Samira
Ahmed more an more outside a school. Afternoon bhangra gigs,
Treaty Centre library, Edward's bar in Ealing Broadway, proper desi
events in Hammersmith. First time I ever spoke to her proply was
at this desi gig Hardjit'd taken me to cos all fifteen boys from RDB
were doing a live set. That stands for Rhythm, Dhol an Bass in case
you don't know, they're like the So Solid Crew a desi beats. They'd
just started playin the opening track from *The Lick* an all the guys
charged towards the dance floor. That's when I met her proply. Or
more like she met me. Straight up, started talkin. To me. An honest
to God, what she was sayin had got nothin to do with school or
books or me helpin her with homework. She'd just come off the
dance floor an was sayin she din't like being there when all the rudeboys started jumpin round with their bottles a beer, someone nearly
elbowing someone in the face every ten seconds. She was wearin
tight jeans an a shiny white V-neck top. A capital V. In fact, the V
was so big that the top had to have a white strap across her cleavage so that it looked more like an upside-down A. It was hard to
focus on the words coming out her mouth stead a the letters on
her chest – especially other times when she was wearin one a those
capital U tops or just a B lyin on its back. Even when she was wearin
a closed top, Samira Ahmed was way outta most guys' leagues. She
was probly outta Hardjit's an Amit's leagues an she was definitely
way outta my league. Trust me, I seen proof a this. In fact, I see
proof every day walkin down the street. Guys who're fitter an tonker
an better dressed than me going out with ladies who in't nearly as
fit as Samira. They say all this league system shit was just invented
by insecure people as an excuse for being insecure. Damn fuckin
right I'm insecure. I'm in a lower league than her, innit. By just
accepting this hard fact a life I gradually learnt how to talk to her
without slippin into some X-rated daydream bout her jumpin me
on honeymoon before we even got to the hotel. Pretty soon it weren't
just bout the way she looked an the way I wanted to spend the rest

a my life lookin at her. As well as a fit face, fit body, fit hair, fit way a walkin, fit way a dressin, fit way a smilin, laughin an breathin through her fit mouth, she also had a fit personality. An I mean the word personality in a nice way. Beauty on the inside, inner fitness, that kind a stuff.

You din't need to know Samira well to see her inner fitness cos she'd shove it in everyone's face like it was a Wonderbra. All this ranting an raving that I'd hear in the sixth-form common room, in my dreams an in my daydreams. It weren't the usual bitchin bout other desis or bollocks bout clothes, jewellery, make-up or film stars. Well, not exactly. I mean the last time I'd heard Samira Ahmed go off on one it actually *was* bout make-up. But stead a chattin bout some new shade a brown, she was going off on one bout whether it's right for companies that make make-up an stuff to test their shit on animals. She thinks they should be allowed to, but only in the same way that the stuff is meant to be used by people. So, if a deodorant in't meant to be sprayed in a person's eyes, don't spray it in a monkey's eyes. I in't makin all this up just to big Samira up, she honestly really is into her political shit. An I in't meanin in a poncey, classical-music-an-carpet-slippers way. She even belongs to some group called Amnesty International, where she does someshit to do with women's rights in Pakistan. An the only time I ever heard her bitch bout other people's jewellery was when she went off on one bout Angolan conflict diamonds. An still no flab, no spots, no facial or underarm hair or anything.

Even when she din't have something big to say bout something she'd, like, unload onto you with a machine gun a questions, totally violating all them standard desi-girl rules that said all you should do is smile, look pretty, not get too mohti, do what you're told by your elders an whoever else you're s'posed to respect an maybe learn advanced as well as basic Indian cookin. She just couldn't help breakin all a those rules that required desi girls to check themselves all the time, to check what they say an what they do. So while Hardjit an Amit may not've known what Amnesty International was, never mind havin a problem with Samira Ahmed belongin to it, they still had beef with her inner fitness cos, by breakin some sets a desi-girl rules an generally being the gorgeous way she was, it became too easy for her to break other rules an slip into being the way they din't want any desi sister to be – whether she was Muslim, Sikh or Hindu. Take how Samira joked an chatted with guys bout stuff a good desi girl really shouldn't be jokin an chattin bout. Mrs Ware is such a cow, I overheard her say one time in the sixth-form common room, I hate her lessons. She's always moaning about this and complaining about that. I bet she's the sort of woman who even complains while her husband and her are having sex.

Another time Samira was askin some other guys whether they reckoned VPL was a turn-off or a turn-on, like as if she was doing undercover underwear market research for a thong company. An if a guy told her what star sign he was, she'd tell him if he was good in bed or not, even though her answer usually made the guy decide he din't believe in astrology no more anyway. It was as if she needed guys to flirt with her, especially guys who she obviously din't fancy an who she'd never wanna get with. Like she enjoyed being bounced around naked on the beds inside their heads. Clearly this weren't exactly halal on her part an so it made some people call her a ho.

So there I was that afternoon in Hardjit's house, standin in the bathroom while he shaped his goatee. Defendin Samira once more like it was my duty in life. By the time Hardjit raised his hand to give me a thapparh I figured it was OK to back down cos I'd already made my point. But still Hardjit'd come back, askin me why the fuck I was tryin to be such a hero when she weren't even there to hear me. — Matter a fact, she probly too busy actin like a ho wid her ho friend Ritu Singh right now, innit. Cos make no mistake, bruv, she a ho. Look at her, man, she fuckin dresses like a ho, like a slut in all her slitty miniskirts.

— Yeh, blud, I seen her one time wearin a skirt dat look'd more like a belt, Amit gives it. — An wat's wid her pussyn boots, man? As if any bloke wudn't wanna laugh n chat n shag wid dat.

— Thing is, bruv, she don't even need 2 dress like a ho da way she flirts, Hardjit goes, to Amit now stead a me. — Blokes ain't exactly havin 2 think hard 2 imagine her wearin no boots, no miniskirt n no nuffink. She loves it, man, she a ho.

— No, Hardjit, she's not, I say. — You guys're makin me feel like fuckin Wyclef Jean sayin this again an again an again, but all this stuff you're sayin, it don't make her a ho. For all you know she's still a virgin. She in't no slut an she in't no ho, that in't fair, guys, an you all know it. In fact, Hardjit, you just put your finger on it just now. She's a flirt. She's just an attention-seeker an a flirt. You put your finger right on it.

— I bet I can put ma finger wherever I want 2 wid her. Dat's cos she a ho.

— She's a flirt.

— Ho.

— Flirt.

— She a slut.

— Look, I in't backin down on this. You lot always tellin me to be more assertive an stand up for things I believe in. Well, I'm standin up for her, innit. She's an attention-seeking flirt who likes it when guys flirt with her so she tries to encourage it, that's all.

— Fuck u, Jas, u lairy, lippy little shit, goes Hardjit. — U don't know wat'chyu chattin bout. Let's jus all stick wid our own kinds n chat bout sumfink else cos I'm sick a dis shit, a'ight?

— Fine by me.

Amit's still raging, though, so Hardjit tries to make some jokes, calm things down, by givin it, — I reckon maybe Amit's jus piss'd cos she ain't never flirt'd wid him, innit.

— 'Sup, bhanchod?, goes Amit. — Why you linkin up wid Jas now? Why'd I wanna flirt wid Samira anyway? Even if she was da fittest girl in da world, she still a Muslim. You think I's gonna go out wid a Muslim n let ma dad gimme fifty thapparhs across ma face wid a brick?

— Safe, Amit. But admit it, u did try n chat her up ages ago, goes

Hardjit. — Don't deny it, bruv, cos I was dere when u was actin all smoove wid her n dat.

— Fuck you, man. Dat was years ago. I was jus practisin my technique, innit.

7

All you need to unblock a mobile fone an change its security code is the proper software on your laptop an the proper kind a data cable. But Amit's kit, which he kept in one a them flash aluminium briefcases, also included a money counter an some small weighing scales. He was settin it all up on Hardjit's bed when Hardjit's mum came in the room with her tied-back silver hair an matchin silver tray full a samosas, pakoras, glasses a Coke an cups a chai. Aunty always made sure her samosas weren't as hollow as most aunties made them, her pakoras not too oily, her chai not too masalafied an her Coke not too flat an with slices a lemon an some crushed ice made by their top-a-the-range fridge. We could've done without the red chilli sauce, though, an I'm positive we din't look like we needed frilly pink paper doilies.

— Shukriya, Auntyji, we all said like cheerleaders as she placed the tray on the desk. Each a us then gives it another Shukriya as she handed us a mini-plate an then Shukriya again as she put a dollop a that red napalm in it. Gotta respect your elders, innit.

— Koi gal nahi, Hardjit's mum replied. — You all boys must be verry hungery after college. So much studying, too too hard, I don't know, poor beycharay.

She shook her head in that special way that only aunties can. Not up an down but not side to side either. More like a wobble, a really jiggly wobble meanin either she really meant what she was sayin or she'd got rolls a rasmalai for neck flab. All that noddin an wobbling made her light blue sari rub against itself so hard it sounded like some old-skool DJ scratchin vinyl. Suddenly, the DJ pumped his amp all the way up to ten as Aunty turned to look at all the cables, the weighing scales an money counter scattered around the laptop on the bed.

— Hardjit, beita, vot is this mess?

— Homework, Mama, we need the laptop.

— Haa? Vot lapdog?

— Laptop. I need his laptop . . . Mennu CORM-PEW-TAR di zaruraht hai, Mama. For school project.

— Acha, theekh hai. But please, beita, don't ruffle bedcover. Is made from really real, genuine silk. I got from Aunty Nirmal in Mumbai. Beita, please, why not use desk Papa got for you? Then she started clearin some space on the desk by movin Hardjit's collection a Hugo Boss aftershaves. He actually bought his own stead a just gettin them as recycled gifts from other relatives. There was a bottle a Hugo Man, Hugo Dark Blue, Boss In Motion, Boss Bottled, the original Boss Number One, Hugo Boss Baldessarini an even a limited edition blue ball a Boss In Motion. While she's clanging the bottles together, Hardjit says something to us in Urdu slang so that his mum can't understand. He always said a proper rudeboy shouldn't just know either Hindi or Panjabi to keep shit secret from goras but also a little Urdu slang to keep shit secret from mums an dads. I'm still workin on my Panjabi, though I reckon I already know more than most coconuts do.

— See, there, see more space, Aunty goes. — Now, why not put laptop here? And, beita, phone me downstairs if you bache are still hungery after. I have plenty more pakoras in freezer.

An with that, Aunty left the room before we could say Shukriya again, scratch-scratch-scratchin all the way downstairs back to her important guest. She'd carefully shut Hardjit's door behind her as if she knew we'd got more things to lay out on the bed that she din't want to see. Twenty more things to be precise. Twenty more creases

69

in the silk bedcover. From inside his bedroom, Hardjit's door looked a lot less attractive. He'd stuck the Kareena Kapoor poster on the outside a the door cos his mum normly made him leave it open. Now that the door was closed, the view a Kareena had been replaced by a leather jacket an a pair a stripy pyjama bottoms hangin on a stick-on plastic peg that was shaped like Mickey Mouse's nose. Some num-chuckers were wrapped around the door handle an the Adidas tracksuit top that normly hung over them to stop them rattling had slipped off into that dusty bit a carpet you get behind doors. Along his wall was a Bollywood princess hall a fame. Aishwarya, Raveena, Sushmita, Kareena again, Shilpa, Aishwarya again, an Rani. They were all there. Well, tiny little headshots a them anyway. He'd saved most a the wall space for a full-body shot a Arnold Schwarzenegger wearin just a headband an kachha as Conan the Barbarian an his poster a Bruce Lee's bare torso from *The Big Boss.*

That afternoon, though, the fit Bollywood faces on the walls were nowhere near as gorgeous as the twenty fit fones laid out on the bed. Side by side like Ferraris an Maseratis in the car park a your dreams. There was a Nokia 6610 in there, a Motorola V300, a Sony Ericsson T630, a Nokia 8310 an also a couple a Samsung E700s. Serious merchandise for them days, even for a G like Davinder. Amit got to work on the fones, unblocking them and makin them untraceable. Pluggin them into his laptop like he was some film star deactivating a bomb. Red, blue, green? Just make up your fuckin mind an cut a fuckin wire. That left the rest a us sittin around, Hardjit flipping between MTV Base and the B4U desi music channel. I think bout maybe playin on Hardjit's PlayStation2, but pluggin it into his flat-screen bedroom TV would mean I'd have to disconnect either the DVD player, video player, Sky Plus box or the Scart socket that lets him pump his TV through his hi-fi speakers. Fuck that. Honest to God, it was like Dixons in his bedroom. He'd even sorted himself out with an Apple iMac an a little fridge for his bodybuilding protein shakes. The only reason he needed to go downstairs was to use the hob, washing machine or microwave an even then only if his mum was sick. Matter a fact, all a us lot were pretty sorted in our bedrooms if you counted the Xbox Amit shared with his older brother Arun an which he'd probly get to keep when Arun got married later this year. Ravi's set-up was pretty much the same as Hardjit's an I had my cable TV an Nintendo GameCube. For some a us, the TV an DVD came before the PC an games console, for others it was the other way round. Either way, it started with havin your own fone.

I decide to start checkin out the luvvy-duvvy text messages an any other shit stored on the handsets before they got erased. Sometimes you'd find nuff dirrty texts but mostly it'd be stuff like 'Thnx 4 yr msg' or 'I luv u 2 babe xx'. A couple a weeks back I remember readin one that said 'Susy, reprt 2 my office 2 hv knickers removd', but today's fones all had pretty tame texts. Ravi's sittin beside me, muckin around with one a the new Samsung E700s. It was a fone he already knew well cos he'd got his own E700 by legally upgrading his old Nokia 6310 a few weeks back. Ravi'd got three handsets in total, his others being a Nokia 8310 an a Nokia 7210. All three handsets worked on the same network, but his dad only paid the bill for one a them, the one he seemed to use the most. After the first a the E700s was unblocked, wiped clean an given a new identity, he decided it'd be a very hilariously funny thing to do to hide pornographic pictures in one a the fone's data folders. He made sure they weren't too well hidden, though, so that one day they'd pop up an surprise the fone's new owner or, even better, the new owner's new girlfriend. I guess he sent the pictures from his own E700 to the unblocked one. If he'd just kept his trap shut bout it, it might've been worth all his effort. But no, he had to boast bout it. To me, to Amit an, yes the fuckin thick-as-shit khota, even to Hardjit.

— Bhanchod, Amit goes, laughin an givin Ravi a high-five when he saw the porn he'd hidden in the fone. — We shud stick some whorehouse's fone numba in there as well, store it like a business card. I started laughin too, even though I hadn't actually seen it.

Mostly I just wanted to help Hardjit see the funny side stead a developing his usual allergic reaction to Ravi's pervertedness. Then, as if answering my plea, Hardjit started laughin too. A big Bollywood laughter moment this. Ha ha. Hah hah haha. Hah hahahaha. An just like all them Bollywood laughs, it turned out to be just another classic Hardjit front. Make your foe feel comfortable before makin them uncomfortable, just for effect or someshit. — Show me da fuckin fone, Ravi, or I break yo fuckin face.

— Sorry, Hardj, I closed da folders now, innit. It's jus some pictures, blud. Jus for jokes, man.

— Well den, let's jus open da fuckin folders n let's jus laugh at da jokes, innit.

From their wrestling on Hardjit's floor, it weren't clear which a them actually opened up the pictures. But once they'd been opened one thing was clear. Like a bearded Muslim deciding it'd be a good idea to run up to Tony Blair an innocently ask for his autograph, Ravi'd reckoned it'd be a good idea to use pictures a not just any old porn star, but Miss Vagindia herself. A bearded Muslim wearin combat trousers an a camouflage jacket, barging past the security guards. — Excuse me, Mr Blair, Prime Minister? My name is Osama Hussein. Can please I have your autograph? Just please give me moment, I get pen from my pocket inside jacket.

Ravi's head just missed the edge a the bed an when he chucked the fone at Hardjit it just missed his face. Even louder than the sound a the fone smashin against the wall was Aunty's footsteps coming up the stairs. — Vot is this? Vot is this? she screamed. Man, did she have the rage or what. — Vot is going on? You all boys know I have guest in the house. Why all this tamasha?

— Sorry, Mama, I just got carried away playin around, Hardjit said.

— Carried? By whom?

— Carried away.

— Huh? Vot are you talking, Harjit? Who in whole world can carry you?

— No, not carry *me*, Mama . . . Oh forget it, Mama. It was nothin, I promise. We'll be quiet now.

— Forget? I make you bache pakoras and samosas and you embarrass me in front of my guest with this, this . . . ruffian behaviour. Is this the way I bring you up? Like fighter-cock badmarsh ruffian? And already I tell you, no toys on bed.

Aunty started clearin up the glasses and plates, massaging her spine as she bent over, sayin things like God give me strength an Waheguru. Then she started givin it her usual shit, askin what had gone wrong in the world that young bache like us showed such a lack of respect for their elders.

— Ravi, Jas, your mamas will be ashamed of you if they know what you do in my house. All the time playing the fool in my house. Always. Play the fool. Good, good, verry good. Fail your exams, live on the street. Verry good.

She was doing that wobbly thing with her neck again, her sari makin the scratchin sound as she then pointed her guns, bazookas an thermonuclear missiles at Amit.

— And you! You too, Amit, vot I should tell your mama, huh? That you come to my house, eat my fresh-fried pakoras and act like council estate ruffian from the street?

— Aunty, I din't do nothin. Those two were fightin. I was just sittin here.

— Hahn hahn, ji ji. Sitting on silk bedcover. Wait, I tell your mama.

This weren't just tough talk on Aunty's part cos she was really tight with Amit's mum. She was tight with all our mums, but she an Amit's mum were like sisters. Called each other Bhainji, shared the pickin an droppin from school, wore their best jewellery to each other's satsangs. They'd even tried to convince their husbands to go into business together one time, become one big happy family. Hardjit's mum figured his dad could make better bucks than he already did running nine twenty-four-hour local convenience shops in partnership with two a his cousins. Amit's mum thought her husband could do better than the aeroplane catering business he ran with his brothers in Heston. Things hadn't been the same since they lost the contract with Air India or whatever. In the end, though, both men stayed in their businesses by promising their wives rapid, five-year expansion plans. An now it was Amit's turn to plead with Hardjit's mum – who'd already taken out her mobile as if she was bout to dial his mum. But a course she was only pretendin to dial. How much a this whole Rottweiler routine was just pretend it was hard to tell. That's the way with her. She'd play it as sweet as an angel's fairy godmother but if you pissed her off you were as good as dog's diarrhoea on those silk bedcovers. Fucked: that's what we were.

The only way to dodge Hardjit's mum's nastiness was to never cross her in the first place, which might sound like simple advice but it in't easy to follow cos it's really easy to cross her. It's like as if she's addicted to being offended. All her friends seem to have this same addiction, especially this one hairy-faced auntyji who was always round there complaining bout this shit or that shit. If holdin a grudge was an Olympic sport they'd all have even more gold to decorate their wrinkly bodies with. They'd play it in teams, especially at wedding receptions. You'd see them there, all sittin together with their fake smiles like rows a substitutes on the bench.

Hardjit's mum din't give us all a bollocking for too long though, probly cos she figured the doilies an teacups downstairs were becoming emptier than the ones she was clearin up here. So she picked up the silver tray an, scratch-scratch-scratch, went back down to her guest as quickly as she'd come up in the first place. This time slammin the door so hard that the num-chuckers nearly slipped off the handle. They carried on swinging against the door for the whole three hundred hours it took for someone to say something. It was Ravi. — Shit, we bust'd da fone, he said as he picked the pieces a the smashed-up E700 off the floor.

— Uh, I don't fuckin fink so, Ravi, u da one wat bust da fuckin fone, goes Hardjit, puffing out his chest an clenchin both his fists before rememberin his mother's words bout the noise an backin down again like she was still in the room, holdin a gun to his bollocks or someshit. — Look, Ravi, he said calmly, — u da one who threw it across da room pretendin u was playin fuckin cricket wid it. So u da one wat's gonna find us a new one cos no fuckin way I'ma tell Davinder we broke one a his fones.

— C'mon, bruv, man, how'ma get a new E700?

— Dat's easy enuf, bruv. We just take yours, innit.

— Uh-uh. No way. Ma mum jus upgraded to dis last month. Dey won't give her no more upgrades if we tell dem it got bust so soon.

— Well, I guess u'll jus have 2 find one, innit.

— I know what, why don't we ask Jas to gets one from his dad's warehouse, innit? Da man's bound to have E700s in stock.

Before I can even protest Hardjit comes out with, — Why da fuck shud Jas call on a family favour #4? It ain't his bad, it yo bad so u sort it. Best make it quick time tho, cos we gots 2 give dese fones back 2 Davinder by Friday.

As Ravi stood there with his hands stuffed in his jacket pockets, weighing up his options as if he had any, one a the mobiles on the bed suddenly started ringing. This should've made us jump cos the cops can track em if they're pickin up a signal. But we all knew it was just Ravi's mum callin one a Ravi's Nokias. We knew this for two reasons. Firstly, his parents had one a them old mobile tariffs that was free after seven o'clock an rang on the dot if he weren't back by then. Secondly, we all knew it was his mum cos Ravi'd got different ringtones for different people. She'd want to know why her son weren't back from school yet. Was he shaming her by talkin to short-skirted kuriyaan at the bus garage or had he just been kidnapped?

Amit's parents, who lived three houses down from Ravi, would be gettin all worried too. We usually tried to get home before our dads got back from work so as not to give our mums another excuse to look at the kitchen clock an call us. But what happens when your dad works from home? Ravi's dad had been offerin financial advice from behind an IBM Thinkpad in the living room for as long as I could remember. He made good bucks by it too, an best thing was he din't have to commute in the traffic or sit there on the tube with all them plebs who can't afford a decent car an the even plebier pricks who offer to stand up so that other plebs can sit down.

— Hahn, Mama, Ravi goes into his fone, — detention nahi hai, cricket club vich si . . . Hahn, Mama, OK, I'll tell Amit . . . Hahn, eggs and naan bread from Budgens. OK, Mum, see you, bye. He closed his fone an turned to Amit. — I gots to chip now n yo mum wants you back quick time. Sound to me like it urgent.

— Oh fuck, Amit gives it, — I forgot we got anotha a dem family committee meetings bout ma brother's wedding.

— I give you a lift, blud, goes Ravi. — Also, you gotta get eggs n naan on da way. Jas, lift to da tube station, right?

Before we left, Ravi tried to turn his mum's polyphonic ringtone into a bell he could be saved by. But let's face it, that weren't ever gonna happen with the theme tune to *Jaws*.

— Hardj, man, fuck's sake. How'ma jus find anotha E700, man?

— Not my problem, bruv. Same way Davinder jus found all a dese.

— I thought you said we din't jack fones, man. Dat ain't where we at in da supply chain, you says.

— Yeh, but I ain't ever said we b bowlin muthafuckin fones round like dey b fuckin cricket balls either, did I? Dat means dat 2moro, afta ma fight wid Tariq, u best not even show me yo face till u jack'd us a new E700 or I'ma mash u up like u mash'd up da fone.

It still seemed early cos we'd bunked off college most a the day. That really fucks up your sense a time. Like them nightclubs that hold bhangra gigs at two in the afternoon cos they know it's the only time some desi mums'll let their daughters go out. Not only was it still daylight as we left Hardjit's house, but his little sister had only just arrived back from after-school netball practice. Hardjit's mum was standin in the porch, arms folded, waitin for her. Waitin an watchin as her daughter got her big bag a netball kit from her friend's mum's car boot an said bye, bye an bye to her three netball buddies.

Did seeing all a that human warmth inspire Hardjit's mum to get in on the action an say the same to us? Did it fuck. She was still vexed bout us showin her up in front a her guest. Times like this you're even more grateful for fones. Means you don't have to deal with your mates' parents so much, at least not every time you fone em. It's like I said with Rudeboy Rule #2: you've got your own fone, you call your own shots. Now all they need to invent is that other bit a gear from *Star Trek*, the one that just beams people wherever the fuck they want to go so they don't have to deal with this kind a shit. We could just beam ourselves straight back to our own bedrooms, not even have to deal with our own mums.

You should have seen the face Hardjit's mum made at us as we put on our shoes in the porch. It was the one where she was sayin her ways an standards were so great that even her after-chana-daal farts smelt as sweet as the jalabi an mango pulp she ate for dessert. She was obviously the smell version a deaf or blind cos what the fuck did she know bout what really went on under her nose? What bout the people-pulp made by her own darling son? Would she have made that face if she knew bout all the faces he'd ruined? Or if she knew the truth bout all those days when school or college just happened to finish an afternoon early? Or even bout them daytime bhangra gigs her daughter went to? How could anyone really think gigs in the afternoon made any difference? Daylight robbery is as easy as nite-time robbery for a good-lookin guy who spends enough time fixin his hair an workin out in the gym. Especially when the thing that's being robbed is some snooty mum's daughter's dignity. The blanking Hardjit's mum was givin us as we left his house was even more blatant cos a the way she exaggerated the hello an hug she gave her daughter. She was rewarded by being told she din't need to take the netball kit to wash cos it weren't that dirty. A course, we all still made a point a thankin her again for the pakoras, samosas, chai an Coke. We were rewarded with just enough noddin to ruffle her sari. Scratch-scratch. Gotta respect your elders, innit.

8

It was the morning a Hardjit's big fight an the two a us were kickin bout on the corner a Hounslow High Street an Montague Road. Right outside the Holy Trinity Church. All the other rudeboys hung bout by the bus stop outside WHSmith. All the fit Panjabi girls hung inside the Treaty Centre (where the security guards din't chuck em out cos apparently it in't loitering if you're a fit Panjabi girl). Me, I get the Holy Trinity Church. The place looks more like some school sports hall stead a some church, an in case you're ever hangin outside long enough to wonder why, there's a sign tellin its history.

— Bruv? I go to Hardjit. — Bruv, d'you know the original church got burnt down by two schoolboys in 1943? Hardjit's busy lookin too hard an slick to be hangin round with someone like me. So I try again. — This one here was rebuilt in the 1960s, in the exact same spot.

— No shit, Jas. Does it look like I give a shit? Som'times I's embarrass'd 2 b hangin round wid'chyu. Why da fuck'd I wanna know bout some church's history 4? Do I look like a vicar? U da one wat probly likes choirboys.

I tell him he shouldn't be dissin Christianity, that he should check out his mum during Christmas time. You can tell from the way his eyes kick back that he's considering this for a minute: the way his mum always sends out Christmas cards with a picture a the Nativity on them. How she even puts up a plastic Christmas tree with an angel on the top, right next to the Buddha statue they got in their

79

living room. She told me it's cos she believed all the different Gods are all part a the same crew.

— Look, don't b cussin ma mum, Jas. Least ma mum's got friends to send cards to. I in't jokin wid'chyu, man. U wanna start actin like a coconut then go inside here n start prayin. Betta b prayin dat I don't break yo ass 4 bein a gimp.

Just before a fight was a pretty good time to be gettin down to some serious prayin. Lord, maketh me victorious in battle or whatever. Then again, maybe that's bollocks, maybe God don't cheer people on when they bruck each other. I mean, chanting Om Shanti, Shanti wouldn't exactly make sense right now cos Shanti means peace. Anyway, whatever the Hindu, Christian, Sikh or Muslim Gods thought bout whatever Hardjit intended to do to Tariq's face today, the bredren hadn't come out here to the Holy Trinity Church to say a prayer for victory. He hadn't come here to pray for forgiveness either an I'm pretty sure he din't know what irony was so that also weren't the reason we were hangin round outside a church. We were waitin for Ravi an Amit to show up in the Beemer before we all headed down to Tariq an his crew. Waitin for fuckin ages.

Hardjit kept sayin something bout how, in life, you gotta be a man an scrap a lick with fools now an then. That in't an option, he said. But *why* you fight them is. Today, Hardjit was gonna teach Tariq a lesson or two for going out with a Sikh girl an then tryin to convert her to Islam. That's, like, the desi version a someone fuckin your wife. Sikh bredren're always accusing Muslim guys a tryin to convert their Sikh sisters. Seems that they even got a proper word for it: sisterising. Sometimes the Sikh girls'd start cryin, sayin they'd used brainwashing techniques an that. Sometimes this shit even turned out to be true. Sometimes, though, it was just the girl's way a dumpin some good-lookin Muslim guy she'd been seeing without gettin killed by her community for seeing him in the first place. The desi version a waking up the next morning an thinkin, Oh fuck, I best say he raped me. It's not my fault, he brainwashed me into his religion. I said no, please no, but he forced it into me.

Truth is, none a us knew whether the girl that today's fight was bout was tellin the truth or not. Matter a fact, we din't even know her name. What we did know was that her parents were dyin a shame, her two older brothers had got a restraining order put on them by the feds an all her cousins lived in Birmingham. So it was up to some other Sikh guy to sort things out, an round here that other Sikh guy normly meant Hardjit. Even Hindu kids called on him when they'd got beef to settle. You know how the people a Gotham City've got that Bat signal for whenever they need to call Batman? The home-boys a Hounslow an Southall should have two signals for Hardjit: an Om for when Hindus needed him an a Khanda for when Sikhs needed him. He always used to go on bout how Sikhs an Hindus fought side by side in all them wars. Both got beef with Muslims. Both support India at cricket. Both be listenin to bhangra, even though Sikh bredren clearly dance better to it. He says Sikhs were the warriors a Hinduism one time. Like the SAS but in a religious way too, so more like Jedi Knights. But even though Hardjit said all a this stuff, he din't like the way his mum had hung up pictures a Hindu Gods on their landing at home next to their pictures a Gurus. But then there in't no point tryin to talk to your mum or dad bout religion, innit. They don't know jack bout religion. I seen Hardjit win arguments with his dad by quoting bits a the Guru Granth Sahib that his dad din't even know – like them hardcore Muslim kids who keep tellin their parents what it says in the Koran.

If Hardjit din't like his mum's definition a Sikhism, Amit an his older brother Arun hated their mum's definition a Hinduism. I remember one time we'd all been round their house during one a their mum's high-society satsangs. Snuck a peep round the living-room door a couple a times, watched all the aunties in their pash-mina shawls, sittin on the floor, sayin all the usual prayers, singin all the usual bhajans an singin prayers in the form a bhajans. Those a them with bad back problems or diabetes sat on the leather cowhide sofas, which was just as well cos all this sittin on the floor business usually meant some serious strategic crisis for Amit an Arun's mum.

How to help the oldies stand up on their feet again? How to rearrange the furniture? Where to put the cups a masala tea? They couldn't exactly use their expensive coffee tables with the golden legs cos they'd be too high for those on the floor an'd been moved to the corners a the room for protection anyway. An they couldn't put the cups on the floor in case one spilt an ruined the expensive silk an satin sheets that'd been laid down especially to protect the carpet.

Arun was chattin to me bout it while Amit, Ravi an Hardjit were playin on their Xbox. He was a safe guy, Arun. Two years older than Amit, but smaller an with no facial hair. He could've even been part a the crew but he spent most a his time with this girl he'd got engaged to. He also weren't exactly a proper rudeboy cos he had these boffiny tendencies, but he weren't a coconut either. He always wore jeans, a white T-shirt an a biker jacket made a canvas cos he said it made no sense wearin leather if you din't eat beef. Anyway, while he was dissin the satsang going on downstairs, he told me it'd been even worse in the afternoon, before all his mum's guests arrived. Apparently she'd done so much screamin an shoutin at him, Amit an their dad to tidy the house and wear socks without holes, that Arun reckoned it was amazing she'd still got a voice left for singin bhajans.

A course, everything'd always work out in the end. Maybe it's cos she prayed so hard. There'd be no spillages, no shortages, no shame. She'll've been a won-der-ful hostess, puttin just the right amount a masala in the teapot, serving just enough pakoras an receiving just the right amount a compliments from her guests bout her house an – if she was really in luck – her clothes an jewellery. She could go to bed that nite feelin in her heart an in her soul that both God an her high-society satsang guests had been impressed by how she displayed her devotion to the finest furniture an forks an stuff that her husband's money could buy. Sleepin underneath her silk bedcovers, knowin extra blessings an big-ups would be going out to her tonite cos she'd placed her copy a whatever Hindu holy prayer book they were using on a table from Heal's that matched her golden shawl an earrings stead a some tutty plastic Ikea one like her friend Aunty Narinder did.

I felt really bad standin there noddin while Arun was slaggin off his mum. So I pointed out that all the other aunties were the same. Never mind their best saris an bling, look out the window at the cars parked outside your house, I'd told him. All the satsang guests tryin to reserve their parkin space in Heaven by leavin their last-year's-model hatchback at home an pullin up in their husband's Benz, Beemer or Audi instead. No jokes, I think one a the Holy Scriptures that I haven't read yet says extra big ups would be going out to worshippers who showed up in luxury German saloon cars. Then, as another group a guests arrived late, we suddenly heard, like, black-an-white horror-movie screams from downstairs. Leggin it down to handle some major emergency, we find their mum biggin up another aunty's earrings. — Oahhhh! Wah bai wah! she screamed, — tell me where you got them from. You must tell me where you got them from, they're so, so beautiful.

— Oye, tennu pasand hai, you like? Three carat from Lakha's in Wembley.

Then his mum nodded, as if to say, Verry, verry good, God will reward you for your gold. Back upstairs, I started going on bout artha, which is the Hindu duty to do well for yourself materially. But Arun weren't havin none a it. He said we'd got to go find some-one called Noah who could build a big boat.

If our mums an dads din't know shit bout their own religions, they knew even less bout religious beef. The kind that Hardjit was preparing to settle with Tariq today. You might as well ask your mum an dad bout the beef between the West Coast an East Coast gangsta rappers an see what they tell you (— Beita, it vasn't Biggie's fault, it vas that TwoCartonPacks fellow, I tell you). Fact is, even the feds knew more bout religious beef than our mums an dads did. We had this special assembly at school one time, the headmaster an some fed standin up on the school stage like two world leaders on TV, shakin hands, sayin stuff bout tolerance an callin for what they called a cessation a violence. This was back in the day when things were seriously fucked round here. When all the Muslim kids acted as if they were members a the Wild Apaches or the Chalvey Boys a Slough an all the Sikh kids acted as if they were members a Shere Punjab, which, depending on who you talk to, means either 'Tigers a the Punjab' or 'Lions a the Punjab'. You could tell that the feds understood more than our parents cos every time the Sikhs from Southall stormed Slough, you'd get like a hundred cops in Southall Broadway waitin for the Muslims' revenge attacks. They even sent some a those Sardarji cops with turban helmets. The Jedi Knights a the Met. The feds had got some kind a Asian gang taskforce, I think, just like they had in the old days when Southall was ruled by the Holy Smokes an the Tooti Nungs. Now *those* boys were the hardcore shit. I'm too young to be remembering much bout them, but I do remember that if a desi belonged to the Holy Smokes or Tooti Nungs then everyone'd say the gangsta deserved to be treated with respect. Compared to them, the Shere Punjab an Wild Apaches were more like them batty after-school debating societies or that Duke a Scotland award for ponces that Mr Ashwood wanted me to join. Only difference is the Shere Punjab had a bit a religion thrown in as well, givin you something to pray bout, something to fight bout. That Duke a Scotland dude might've been married to the Queen an everything, but Hardjit wouldn't fight for him. Or his wife. Not when he could fight for God.

Still no sign a Ravi an Amit an so Hardjit fones them. — Where'da fuck u at, man? . . . U was s'posed 2 b at da church half an hour ago . . . Fuck's sake, Ravi, does it look like I give a shit?

I weren't bored enough to ask Hardjit what was holdin them up an I also weren't bored enough to answer my own fone when it started ringing. That's cos the fone's display told me it was Mum. I always reject her calls cos she and Dad make me nauseous. If what she has to say in't enough to piss me off, her fake posh accent will. Her voicemail messages in't so bad, though, cos she chats like she's chattin to a machine an so she don't moan or complain or put you down. — Just to inform you that you forgot your school bag, is the voicemail she leaves me right now. She'd fuckin faint if I told her I din't need my bag cos I'd gone to church stead a college.

Mum'd know exactly which church I was chattin bout. When I was little, back before they pedestrianised this bit a the High Street, I used to wait outside this place while she went into the halal butcher's that used to be near here. That may seem weird seeing as we in't Muslim, but she said the halal butcher's'd got better quality meat than the other butcher's on the High Street. Me, I couldn't stand the smell a chopped an peeled animals no matter how they were killed, so I'd have to stand outside here instead – scared shitless in case some psycho nutter came an chopped *me* up into meat. Mum said I was just being a silly boy cos the church was practically next to Hounslow police station. Honest to God, they're like neighbours. They probly borrowed each other's coffee or someshit. An suddenly I'm thinkin, maybe hangin round outside the Holy Trinity Church weren't one a Hardjit's greatest ideas. Today weren't exactly the best day to attract some fed's attention. But you can guess what he said when I suggested we all hook up somewhere else.

— Jus shut yo ugly face, Jas, n stop bein a pussy, I think were his exact words. — We meetin down here cos we def ain't gonna bump into Tariq or any a his crew here, a'ight.

— Bruv, you're allowed to see him before a fight. It in't like you two gettin married.

— Fuck u, Jas, yeh. Jus shut da fuck up.

Truth is, Hardjit'd just wanted to make sure his entrance to the fight was as dramatic as possible. It's a bit difficult to do that if you accidently bump into your opponent on the way down there. It was the same before we went to a club: he'd rather hook up in some dirty pub full a goras burping beer an playin darts than in some bling bar where all the fine desi girls'd be downing their vodka an cranberries. Today he'd even kept his muscles under wraps in a baggy, long-sleeve Adidas tracksuit top, his firm body a new Audi concept car waitin to be unveiled at the Geneva motor show by Czech super-models wearin nothin but high heels, kachhian an dry-ice mist. Like the curve a the bonnet underneath the drapes, you could only just make out Hardjit's shoulder muscles showin through the tracksuit top. That way, all the other bulges in his chest an arms would look even more bulging when he eventually stripped off into the Versace vest underneath.

He'd chosen the Adidas tracksuit top carefully this morning, standin in front a his full-length mirror an comparing it to his Nike tracksuit top (which din't show his shoulders enough), his tight leather jacket (which showed his pecs too much), a Ted Baker top (which showed too much bicep) an his Schott bomber jacket (which din't show anything). None a them went well with the orange bandanna he'd tied round his head but I din't say jack. I just sat there in his room, pretendin to be readin some Bollywood magazine, tryin not to see the mirror's reflection in his other mirror, thinkin to myself: This must be what high-class hookers are like before they go out on a job. Tryin to wear just enough to take off but not so little that they revealed too much too quickly. Something not too skintight but something that'd still stretch over the right places. Carefully checkin out her bruises, cellulite an abortion scars in her own full-length mirror the same way Hardjit was checkin out his arms an the stretch marks he'd got sculpting them.

He'd been liftin his dumb-bells when I showed up at his house bout nine in the morning, said he wanted to finish a couple more sets. Even his dad came into the room to say, — Juldi chal, young man, hurry up. You boys are going to college not fashion parade. You'll be late for school.

Mind you, Hardjit's dad could hardly talk. He was still wearin a dressin gown an had shaving cream all over his face – that old, nasty, pasty white shit his own dad probly used. Hardjit kept tellin him to use gel but he never listened. Hardjit din't listen either an carried on liftin his dumb-bells even after his dad left for work an his mum headed out to some high-society coffee-morning social-circle thing. The guy always lifted weights before a fight. Sparkin that white boy Daniel yesterday'd made his arms look a little tired an podgy. Workin out for half an hour'd make them more defined. He'd also dehydrated himself on his dad's treadmill beforehand, makin sure he din't down any water afterwards. That was the best way to get maximum definition. There'd be an audience, you see. There'd always be an audience when someone took on Hardjit. An today that audience'd include ladies like Priya, Mona, Seema, Manisha an the other Priya.

There's a reason they're called dumb-bells an not boffin-bells. Before we left his house that morning, Hardjit had taken off the weights an brought the bars with him, shoved them down his trousers or something. I asked him what the fuck he was doing an he gave it, — Wat'dyu fink, u pehndu? Wat'dyu suggest we do if any a Tariq's crew pull any weapons on us? Fight dem back wid fuckin chapples?

I stared to see if the bars were makin any bulges in his trousers.

— Fuckin stop lookin at ma crotch, man.

— But Hardjit, you can't hide them down there. What if someone sees them?

— Relax, blud, not everybody b walkin round checkin out other guys' noonies da way u do, batty boy.

Things got even dumber when Ravi an Amit finally showed up. After Hardjit discreetly hands Ravi the dumb-bell bars to hide inside the Beemer's boot, the bhanchod starts waving the things around like they were fuckin garba sticks for doing dandia dancin with.

— Put dem fuckers in da boot, u khota, Hardjit gives it. — Or I hide dem up yo butt, innit. Why don't u jus stride inside da police station n give em flyers 4 da fight?

— Chill, blud, goes Ravi. — Wat'chyu frettin bout? We next to a church, innit. God will protect us from da feds.

9

The BMX track was right by Hounslow Borough College so should've just been a five-minute drive from the church. You take a left outta Montague Road an then go straight down Hounslow High Street an along the London Road. Only in fact it'd be more like ten cos they pedestrianised the High Street a few years back. How us rudeboys s'posed to cruise down the High Street if there in't no fuckin road to cruise on, eh? Ravi floors it as he backs away from the church, using the police station forecourt to do one a his special *2 Fast 2 Furious* two-point turns.

— Wat'd'fuck's wrong wid'chyu 2day, bwoy? goes Hardjit. — U best not attract no feds 2day, u hear wat I sayin, Ravi? An u best not forget 2 sort us out wid a new Samsung E700, replace da one u brucked last nite, pehndu.

— Relax, blud, Ravi tells Hardjit as he reaches for the CD controls.
— Here, let's drop a tune, chill you out.

The tabla drums from '*Hasdi Hasdi*' by the Panjabi Hit Squad fill the Beemer an start bouncin out the windows onto the road an all the concrete car parks that lie along the back a the High Street. It's just one car park after another round here: grey fields a empty spaces, concrete bollards, those giant bins for shop rubbish, a couple a crap cars an pay-an-display ticket machines bolted onto their posts with extra padlocks. The graffiti on the walls says things like 'Shere Punjab', 'Wild Apaches', 'Boyo Woz Ere', 'Fuck Your Mum' an 'Goods Vehicles and Permit Holders

Only'. Welcome to the London Borough a Hounslow, car park capital a the world. Stuck in the middle a these empty car parks is Hounslow Manor School, where some other safe desis we know used to go.

Hardjit, still pissed off with Ravi, is now also gettin pissed with the cars in front that're obeying all the car park's an school's 'Slow' signs. All a them, drivin like those dickless fucks who're too pussy to drive in bus lanes even during the times that you're allowed to. When we finally leave them behind, we get stuck behind a H28 bus outside Hounslow East tube station. Then we get stuck behind some H32 bus at Hounslow bus station, which is stuck behind another bus tryin to turn into the bus station but can't cos a some H37 bus stuck at some roadworks. Only after that bus clears the road-works can we make a left onto the London Road. Meantime we just sit there, our tabla beats crashing into the windows a the newsagents, halal kebab shops an minicab companies with Special Autumn Airport Fares. Ravi pumps up the sound system an Amit opens his window some more, lettin more tabla beats bounce into the shins an knees belongin to plebs at the bus stops. Even after we clear the roadworks an the buses an shit we still don't head straight to the fight. We wanted to, but you know how it is. Shit happens when you're ridin in a Beemer. It's one a them big, long, metal dicklike rods that attract lightning. If it in't beef it's bredren, an if it in't bredren it's ladies, an if it in't ladies it's the feds or someone's mum on the fone. In this case Amit's mum. She's shoutin so loud into Amit's ear he forgets to pull a proper fone face. It don't matter, though, cos his face gets serious enough on its own. Turns out his mum's even more stressed out than she normly is an wants to know if her beita can pass by a Boots, Superdrug or one a them desi corner chemists with a big green cross. Apparently they sell some stuff that can calm her down, stop her dyin a shame or whatever it is that's makin her die today.

— Theekh hai, Mama, goes Amit when she's finished shoutin. — Ik minute, Mama, can you pass the fone to Arun? . . . Jus because,

Mama. Let me speak to him . . . Because he's my brother an I wanna talk to him.

While Arun is doing whatever it is people do before they finally pick up the fone, Amit tells Ravi to turn back to the High Street cos he's gotta go Boots, innit.

— Hey yo, Arun, Amit finally says into the fone, — Yeh, bro, sounds fuck'd . . . Jus want'd to check n dat, you know . . . You shoulda come wid me, man . . . Safe, safe . . . Don't argue wid her, bro, don't dis her again. But don't listen to her shit either. Dat's da way . . . Nah . . . nah . . . I know, man, it ain't even her time a the month . . . Down da BMX track, innit . . . Nah, we in't there yet, we bout five minutes away . . . Fuckin buses n roadworks n shit, innit. You want anyfink from Boots?

Amit then relaxes his face, closes his Nokia 6610 an turns to see the rest a us givin him a group what-the-fuck-was-all-that-bout? stare. — I jus b chattin to Arun, he says to us. — You know how it is. Complicated family-related shit n dat.

Everyone knows exactly how it is with complicated family-related shit. None a us more than Amit an Arun, what with them being related to their mum an everything.

— So wat's da deal wid yo mum, man, she still ain't likin Arun's lady? Hardjit asks, not even needin to check whether the latest lump a complicated family-related shit had got something to do with Arun's wedding plans an the emergency committee meeting Amit'd got called away to last nite. Amit doesn't answer. He just fiddles with his Nokia while deciding whether or not to discuss the shit in public. You never know when it'll come back on you, you see, get smeared in your face, shoved up your nostrils. Especially seeing how tight their mum is with Hardjit's mum. Complicated family-related shit should just be kept inside, held in your guts, don't matter if it gives you a headache. It's a fact that complicated family-related shit just smells worse if you do it in public. This was one reason why, whenever Arun was hangin round with us an the topic a his pre-wedding marital problems came up, Amit'd try an stop him shittin or oolting it all out. But I guess this time, behind this bus an with all this time an silence to fill now that we in't headin straight to the fight, he decides things are different,

— Nah, man, Mum ain't got no beef wid Reena, goes Amit. — She got beef wid Reena's mum, innit. Says her mum ain't showin her enuf respect or someshit. You know how it is. Mum wants to b treated like she some queen cos she da mother a da groom n dat. An then, yesterday, Reena's mum fones n says dey bought all da champagne cases but would we mind pickin em up from the supplier sometime cos we got a bigger car. Mum got totally menstrual wid Arun. Seems dat when ma sister got married we din't ask da Boy's Side to do jack. We did all the legwork n we treated em wid respect, innit.

— Dat's it, man? You all arguin bout who'll cart da juice?

— C'mon, Rav, you know how it is. It starts wid da champagne but now suddenly Reena's family spit in Mum's face or someshit cos dey in't doin all da work n stuff dat da Girl's Side's s'posed to do. Suddenly she says dey being disrespectful cos dey ain't foned or visited our side enuf times, innit, an now suddenly Reena's dad dresses too scruffily when dey do. Honest to God, Mum's goin round tellin people: When my daughter Anjana got married I did everything for her, but now when my son is getting married we are not getting things in return. Every time Arun argues with Mum bout it, she keeps sayin, But beita, it's the way things are done, it's the way things are done. All da time, all da time, It's the ways things are done. You boys ever heard such a fuck'd-up answer in your life? I mean, imagine if you wrote dat answer in a fuckin exam? An so then Arun asks her for a more proper answer, an she's like, It's the way things are done. I'm like, Mum, you ain't ever free even if Reena's family did fone or come round to visit n, anyway, you keep sayin you wanna get new sofas before they do. Dat ain't da point, she says, it a matter a respect.

— Amit man, how long's Arun been engaged 2 dis lady?

— Dunno, Hardj, it bout eight or nine months since dey did da rokka ceremony.

— Safe. So how long dis shit wid yo mum been goin on?

— Eight or nine months.

— That's a long lump a shit, I say from the back seat.

— Then why'da fuck Arun din't jus keep it all on da sly? goes Hardjit. — Wat's da point a all dis gettin engaged n shit?

— Fuck, man, it in't even like Reena's a gora or a Muslim, I go.

— Imagine what your mum'd be like if she weren't Hindu.

— Yeh, you know it, goes Amit. — Dat's da thing, innit: Mum approves a Reena. Reckons she's a lovely girl. She jus wants more respect from Reena's mum. It well fuck'd, man. I mean, I know we da Boy's Side n everything but dat ain't no reason why Reena's family should get down on their knees n kiss Mum's butt all da time jus cos it's da way things're traditionally done. Fuckin loads a traditions can be wrong, innit. I mean, Mum n Dad din't kill ma sister cos she was born as a girl, did dey? An dat was a tradition one time, dat was da way things were done. Ma mum, man, she actin like dey dissin our religion jus cos dey ain't follow'd all da rules n customs proply. It's proper fuck'd up.

— But at da end a da day, Amit, she a she, innit, goes Hardjit. — An she ain't no Brahmin either. Dey shud at least give u lot a bit more gold, u know, 4 da dowry n dat.

Amit thinks bout this for a moment. His mobile-fone face now lookin more like a crumpled fax, torn between his bredren an his brother. — At da end a da day, Hardj, all me n Arun're sayin is things shudn't be done jus cos dat's da way dey always done, you get me. Anyway, fuck it. It's complicated family-related shit, innit.

We park up as close to Boots as we can, which is on a single yellow line just before the pedestrianised bit, an leg it up the High Street with Hardjit sittin in the car. I don't even volunteer to stay with the Beemer in case I get fucked over by another one a them stealth traffic wardens. Inside, the shop is freezin, like they turned up the AC system to make the place feel extra white. Amit's mum wants some shit called lavender oil an these pills called At Ease to help her sleep. She also wants some Rimmel 007 rose lipstick, the greeny-blue pack a Bodyform (with wings) an some pink Andrex bog roll as they've run out. Amit's, like, dancin around the shop tryin to find everything, too fuckin embarrassed to ask no one. All the time he's sayin something bout Arun's wedding an all their complicated family-related shit an I feel like tellin him maybe he should get some a them Imodium tablets for himself, the ones that stop diarrhoea.

I in't had a wedding in my family yet but I seen this shit drop nuff times during other people's shaadis. The same shit dropped back in summer with Ravi's cousin. The same shit happened with Hardjit's cousins from Bradford. The same shit happened to Davinder's older sister. The same shit even happened with Amit an Arun's older sister, Anjana. Back with Anjana's shaadi the shit was the other way round: the Boy's Side din't actually want to have their butts licked so much, they got embarrassed by it. But I think Amit an Arun's mum really, really wanted to lick them, I guess cos she figured her own butt would get licked nicely when her sons got married. Complicated family-related shit: the chemists should give it its own fuckin aisle.

Most a the shit drops cos people don't get the right balance a respect an duty flowin between the Girl's Side an Boy's Side. Mostly it's gotta flow from the Girl's Side cos she's, like, lower. It's just like tuning one a them old radios, the ones that got knobs an dials. Get it just a little wrong an some loud, angry fuzz'll come from some old auntyji or uncleji or other unemployed member a the family. Straight away, straight outta their mouths like the radio aerial is the fillings in their sensitive teeth or someshit. If it don't happen before the wedding, it'll deffo happen on the day. Someone'll get vexed if they get left out the milni or they in't sittin close enough to the head table. With Ravi's cousin, it was some auntyji from Greenford who reckoned she was, like, the guardian a the family's izzat. That's the Muslim word for a family's honour by the way, but non-Muslims use it too. You pronounce it 'iz-hut', not 'is-at'. Just imagine if someone killed the American president during a high-school shooting on the Fourth a July: that's how big a fuckin deal izzat is.

93

Problem is, nowdays shit can violate someone's izzat even if it in't got jackshit to do with izzat. Little things, like not wearin expensive enough clothes when you go round to visit, or not remembering to say stuff like Goodbye or Thank you twice stead a just once. An you can't do fuck bout it cos you don't actually decide what constitutes izzat unless you're, like, older than forty-five or you in't got a job or something else to do with your life.

— OK, we got everything cept dem pills, Amit goes as he leads me towards the herbal remedies aisle. He looks even more stressed out when he sees that the At Ease tablets in't just chill pills to help people sleep but according to the packet are also the UK's Best-Selling Natural Laxatives. We chuck em in the basket an go get Ravi, who's gone an wandered off to the Ladies' Hair Removal aisle where he's checkin all the pictures a smooth, hairless legs. It reminds Amit to buy some wax strips for his back. Even with all those pictures a naked female flesh, Amit's still going on an on bout his mum.

— I just dunno whether to back her or ma bro sometimes, you know. Arun can b a fuckin tutty-arsed coconut, but she can b a bit unreasonable sometimes too.

— A bit? I go. — Sounds to me like she's fuckin psycho.

— Fuck you, Jas. Disrespect ma mum again n I'll fuckin bruck yo face, I ain't jokin. Even wid all a dis shit going down, I don't even take it when Arun disses our mum. I tell'd him last night, dis ain't no reason to b dissin her. He even dissed her to her face even, I'd've given him a thapparh but da gimp was fuckin cryin.

— Sounds to me like you already decided who you gonna back then, I go.

As we approach the tills Amit's face gets even more stressed out. I look where he's staring an am relieved to realise it in't got nothin to do with his complicated family-related shit. It's got something to do with Sonia Guha.

— Since when da fuck'd she start workin here? he goes.

Sonia Guha's practically engaged to some other rudeboy who's got his own Lexus. But that's never stopped Amit fancying her. Seems that her boyfriend's bucks in't stopped her gettin a part-time job at Boots either. Wearin that white Boots uniform, it in't hard to see why Amit's so into her.

— Shit, man, looks like dat's da only checkout till open, goes Amit.

— But that's good, innit? I go. — You can queue up an chirps her, right?

— Are you fuckin thick, man? I got some batty lavender oil, bog roll, Bodyform, Rimmel rose lipstick n fuckin laxative in here. How da fuck I gonna chirps her? I shudn't even go to da till, she'll laugh in ma face. Shit, she's seen us, he says, waving at her. — Shit, she saw my basket. I can't even put it all back now cos I'll look like a dick.

I look in our basket. He's right except for one thing: the At Ease pills in't in there no more. Ravi's takin them out an is readin the label. — Dudes, he gives it, — I read bout dese pills in some porn mag, I think. Relax, dey in't really laxatives. I mean, dat ain't wat most people use em for. Everyone knows dat.

— Well, we don't, Amit goes. — Wat da fuck are dey then? An why'da fuck you read bout dem in a porno?

— Dey for relaxin, innit. But seems dat dey also wat gay boys use, you know, to make it easier.

Hardjit's foning us now, tellin us to hurry the fuck up, which makes Amit decide that now he definitely can't just dump the Boots basket an go to some desi corner chemist. So he has this idea: he'll fill the whole basket with other stuff, dilute his mum's shit so he'll look less like a dick when we get to Sonia Guha's till. So in it all goes: Dolce & Gabbana cologne; Gillette Mach3 shaving blades; a sexy-lookin chrome shaving brush; FCUK deodorant; Givenchy Rouge aftershave; muscle rub for sporting injuries; bodybuilding protein shakes; some designer hair wax; Boots' own-brand dental floss. But from Amit's face you can tell that somehow it in't enough. So he heads straight for the condoms an grabs a box a 24 Durex Avanti. He says they've got a 64mm width stead a the usual 56mm width. Also they ain't got extra lubricant, which means he generates his own, or rather, some lady's own. You can tell Sonia Guha knows this when we get to the front a the checkout queue an start unloadin everything for her. You can just see it in her eyes. I mean, sure, she's chattin to Amit an laughin at his jokes an lookin at him an all that. But she's lookin at him with these Wow-you-wear-big-condoms eyes. She's so impressed by the condoms an the aftershave an stuff that she don't even notice the lipstick an pink bog roll or the pills. Me, I can't believe Amit's strategy's actually workin. But then suddenly, just as she's pickin up the box a big condoms to put them in the carrier bag, some croaky voice behind us gives it, — Amit, vot is this gandh you buying?

Amit turns an freezes. — Oh, hi, Aunty Narinder. How are you, Aunty?

— Don't you How-are-you me. Vot is this Durex business you buying? Wait till I tell your mama.

— No, Aunty, wait. They ain't for me, Amit goes, as if he's forgotten Sonia Guha's even there. Then there's a pause as he thinks what he can say that'll stop this aunty tellin his mum. — They're for Mama an Papa. I'm doing the shopping for them. See, look, I also buy her Rimmel rose lipstick. I bought the toilet roll, even Bodyform with wings.

But his answer in't enough for her. This auntyji, whoever the fuck she is, then starts inspecting the rest a the shopping. — Ah, this lavender oil, is verry, verry good. Will help you be less anxious about your studies like you were last time. But beita, I already told your mama she shouldn't let you wax with these strips. You should get it done professionally like your mama does. Otherwise you can get bruises. And why take these laxatives? If you feeling constipation just drink prune juice.

Back in the Beemer, speedin back through the car parks, Amit starts up his family-related shit again. It's all that auntyji's fault at the Boots checkout. After basically ruining his life, she'd asked him how the wedding preparations were going, when could she expect her invitation, how was Arun? He'd told her Arun was fine. But seeing as how he don't wanna talk to Hardjit bout Sonia Guha an the shopping, he's now tellin us how, actually, Arun in't so fine. — Shud've seen him last nite, he gives it, — got totally fuck'd up afta da meetin. Downed half ma secret Jack Daniel's while I b tryin to get some sleep, innit. We best stop at an off-licence later, fill up. Da boy shoulda got an arranged marriage, man, I told him at da beginning dis shit ain't worth da hassle, you get me.

An so then we start havin nakhra bout whether Amit's brother would've been better off going for an arranged marriage stead a playin the open market. We figure if it were an arranged marriage, the two sides' parents'd probly already be mates or they'd wanna be mates for business reasons. That'd mean if any complicated family-related shit blew up, they probly'd just deal with it. An if the family-related shit was so fucked that it really did fuck things up, then the bride an groom probly wouldn't give too big a shit anyway cos they probly wouldn't hardly even know each other. They'd just be, like, passengers in the back seat an the car would be driven by their parents. The boy an girl only get to sit in the driver's seat when it comes to the other kinds a marriages. By that I mean love marriages, obviously, but also semi-arranged marriages, guided marriages, encouraged marriages an even misguided marriages, discouraged marriages or whatever other fuckin marriages we can come up with. The only problem is that when the boy an girl in the driver's seat finally get to the exit marked 'Marriage' an start indicating to turn off into it, all a sudden the car grows a no-smoking sign an a meter an everything an changes into a fuckin taxi. Their mums an dads may not have their feet on the pedals or hands on the wheel but they can tell you how to drive, even to stop if they like. They're the customer, the payin passenger.

— Fuck dat shit, goes Ravi from our driver's seat. — Me, I ain't havin any a dat. Fuck all dat arranged shaadi shit, fuck all dat love shaadi shit.

I wanted to tell Ravi he'd be smart to opt for an arranged shaadi cos even with his dad's dough, no way he'd ever pull anyone fit on the open market. But I don't tell him this cos he's still shoutin, even when we reach the BMX track.

— In fact, bredren, I jus decid'd now, innit, right now I jus decid'd. Ain't no kind a shaadi happenin to me, you get me. I'll b a player all ma life. Get off wid as many fit gyals as I want, shag em whenever I want. Fuck dat shit. Arun n Reena gotta b dealin wid all dis shit n all dey wanna do is get married n start shaggin each other, innit. I say fuck all a dis foreplay.

Tariq's crew had already parked their own BMW M3 on the zigzag lines that spring out the zebra crossing. A bright yellow, convertible M3 with extra low suspension. So we stayed in our Beemer for a bit, givin them a chance to check out our badder alloy wheels, bigger spoiler an curvier side gills. They checked us out from the top a the BMX track. Or more like from the top a what used to be the BMX track. Back when I was little there was a small hill there. This whole place was a proper dust track with mud mounds an mud ramps an sharp bends full a even muddier puddles. I never actually BMXed here back then cos Mum wouldn't let me ride by myself an no fuckin way I was riding in here with her. An now that I was old enough to come here without her, nobody used this place for BMXing no more. It's cos a all the grass an weeds an other hairy green shit, growin up to your knees in some parts. Some places it'd grown taller'n I had. Apart from two metal freestyle ramps an a concrete starting stretch, you couldn't hardly tell that there'd ever been a BMX track here cos there was hardly any difference between the track an the overgrown playin field next to it. I in't lyin to you, hairy green shit growin all over the place like Beenie Man's dreadlocks. Mow the fuckin lawn an it could've been the kind a field you'd play cricket in. Stead, some people used it as a place for downing four-packs a Budweiser. Some people used it for lightin up without being spotted by some aunt, uncle or cousin or some friend a some aunt, uncle or cousin. Some people used it to dump non-household waste that the binmen wouldn't take (like burnt-out Ford Capris, for example). Some people used it as a place to hide pornos in the bushes. Some people used it as a place to cop a feel a other bushes. An some people used it as a place to settle their beef. There may not've been a BMX in there for more than five years, but the Hounslow BMX track was still the bike shed a the whole borough.

We strode into the track like a bunch a badass Reservoir Dogs. Me on the left, Amit next to me, Hardjit next to him an Ravi flanking on the right. Badasses. Appearing over the horizon in a fly film with Vin Diesel in it. Fire, foiled feds an fifty burnin baddies behind us. Rescued females in front a us. Fit, fine females, their long hair blowing in the helicopter wind, walkin towards us with their tight skirts an hips ridin in time with our shoulders an the drum machine set to some big pumpin beat in our heads. Not too fast a beat, though, so that we could feel the moment, enjoy the feel a stridin up to Tariq's crew as if we'd already fuckin won. Hardjit set the proper pace. Left. He always set the pace. Right. Otherwise our bobbing up an down would make us look like a bunch a penguins or something. Gangsta penguins, mind you, with shrapnel in their legs from some swim-by shooting or someshit. Left. Right. Or maybe just penguins who really needed a piss.

I counted bout thirty people who'd showed up to see this showdown. All the guys standin up front by the concrete starting stretch a the track, all the girls hangin a bit further back. Like a Diwali firework display in someone's back garden. No sign a the girl who'd started today's fireworks though. Hardjit was checkin the ladies too, makin sure fitness like Priya, Mona an Seema were in the audience. Check, check, check. I looked for Samira Ahmed. Check. It weren't just Muslims an Sikhs who'd showed up. Eddie Bishop was here, this black kid who lived near Brentford an had been tight with Hardjit since before school. He'd even brought some other guys I'd never seen before. Cos that's how big a deal Hardjit was round here: he got desis an black kids kickin round together again, just like it was back when goras still shouted the word Paki an black kids told them to watchit when they did. Wai Qwok-Ho, who was top a

Hardjit's ju-jitsu class, had come down too an brought another Chinese face with him. Respect to Oriental kids, it's their turn now. Those guys are coming the way a black kids an desis, I in't lyin to you. In't nobody messes with em no more, an not just cos they kick ass at Nintendo.

There were other people with fuck all to do with the fight out by the track that afternoon. Random people who worked at random offices, takin random fag breaks to soak up the sunshine. It's what they call an Indian summer. Some random heatwave in the middle a cold September that din't mean get out your T-shirts yet cos tomorrow it'd probly rain again, or snow even. That's London for you. All different kinds a people bringin all their different kinds a weather. Even a group a Somalians who nobody knew had wandered in from the street to see what was going down. You mix Somali kids an desi kids these days, you tend to wish you hadn't. Kid got stabbed one time down by Hounslow West tube. But no bother this afternoon an in this field cos us desis outnumbered the Somalis by four to one. That is if you included Tariq's Muslim crew.

I was appreciating today's hot sun cos it could be my excuse for sweatin like an oily samosa. I started sweatin even more when I realised Samira Ahmed was standin next to Priya, who was somehow suddenly standin next to me. This is what happens when you do that tough-guy penguin walk. You're so focused on whether you're doing it proply, you don't realise that you walk up to the person standin next to Samira Ahmed. Amit an Ravi had taken their walk over to where Davinder was standin. Hardjit an me had stopped back here while he agreed with one a Tariq's crew to wear a tennis sweatband over his Karha. Then he'd strided up to the concrete starting stretch a the track, leavin me standin right here, within smellin distance a Samira Ahmed. She smelt like strawberry soap. She always smelt like strawberry soap. Even when she weren't around I could smell strawberry soap just by lookin at her in the camera-fone pictures from our sixth-form prom.

— So, Jas . . .

Shit. Now Priya'd swapped places with Samira Ahmed, meanin Samira Ahmed was standin next to me. Talkin to me. She was wearin ripped jeans an a tight black blouse with the sleeves rolled up, revealing some sexy-lookin henna tattoo. Mehndi maybe.

— . . . how come you're standing out by the sidelines? We heard the three of you were gonna help Hardjit take on all these guys today, show em how hard you all are.

I'd got a drill for whenever this happened to me. After all, these Samira-talkin-to-me situations had happened more an more since I'd started kickin bout with Hardjit an his crew. That'd lowered the sap signals I used to give off, I guess. The drill was this: every time it happened I tried an stop myself breakin out into a stammerin sweat by thinkin a something else. Dead, rotting animals, slimy aliens, my mum an dad, that kind a shit. Back when it happened in the sixth form, I used to think bout whatever homework essay we'd just been set. Today I started thinkin how weird it was that, even at a time like this, Sikh girls like Priya an Muslim girls like Samira'd got no problem standin next to each other. Like cricket fans who don't care whether India or Pakistan wins so as long as they see some good batting skills.

— Er, well, you know.

Don't start stammerin an talkin like some dickless pussy, you gimp. This is Samira Ahmed an she is talkin to you. Samira Ahmed, the fittest girl in the whole wide London Borough a Hounslow. Talkin to you. Gotta talk back proply when you talkin to someone gorgeous, someone like Samira. Talk like you're as hard as Hardjit.

— Yo, 'sup, Samira? Dey tryin 2 keep dis shit one-on-one, u get me. Like a duel or sumfink, know wat I'm sayin?

That in't bad. That's progress. I need to work on my facial expressions a bit though, an my eyes are still too wide an won't stay still.

— Ah, so you're just a spectator like us girls then?

— Nah . . . I'ma jump in, u know, if dat b necessary, innit. But I figure I'ma stand back here cos if I gets too close I'll b, like, provokin dem n shit, u get me?

— Mmmm. Sounds sensible, she says before doing one a her silent Mmmms with her lips. Samira's silent Mmmms might as well as be silent blow jobs, the way they make me feel. Not that I know what a blow job feels like yet. But if they feel like one a Samira's silent Mmmms then they're worth all the hype.

— I don't actually think I've ever seen you in a fight, Jas.

— Er, well, you know. Cos a privacy n dat, innit. I mean, dat's cos I keeps em private, u know. Restrict'd viewin n dat, u get me. Man to man n dat.

— Well, I'm sure I would've heard if you'd had a fight, though. You know me, I always hear what mischief you boys get up to.

— Well, I in't had 2 teach no one no lesson, innit. Nobody messes wid me.

— Mmmm. You know what I think, Jas? I think that if you got into a fight you'd be just like James Bond or Indiana Jones.

Even though I'm tryin really, really hard to wear a slick facial expression, I can't help but show that I'm thinkin, What the fuck did you mean by that? That I'd need to pull a fuckin gun?

— You know, the way even though guys like James Bond aren't that bulked up, they always take on those seven-foot musclemen or karate experts. It fits with this whole man of mystery you've become. Looks to me like you're starting to bulk up too.

See. I told you. This is exactly what I meant. Exactly precisely what I meant. She flirts with guys even if she don't fancy them. Again, look at her, she's doing another one a them silent Mmmms. I can't even give her her fix a being flirted with back a course cos, well, I'm crap an I can't flirt. I'm completely unable to big her up a little in return an I'm incapable a sayin anything to make her laugh. I'm also in Hardjit's line a sight an potentially in his line a punch an flyin kick so I in't plannin on hangin around being flirted with even if I could flirt back. Too late though. Hardjit walks over to me, grabs my arm an pulls me far away from her.

— I weren't talkin to her, man, I swear, she was talkin to me.

— Talkin wid who?

— Samira, I weren't talkin to her.

— I don't give a shit bout dat right now, Jas. I jus wanna hang back here wid'chyu 4 a while, innit.

— Er, in't you forgettin something, bruv? Like the fight with Tariq? The ruck, man, the fight?

— U clearly been too busy scoping down Samira's blouse. Din't u notice Tariq ain't even here yet?

— Eh?

— He'll b five more minutes. Had 2 go 2 some supermarket wid his mum, innit, help her carry da shopping bags. But hear me, bruv, if he finks dat'll make him look all sensitive n shit in fronta all a dese ladies then I'ma do da same shit. I'ma hang back here wid'chyu, innit.

10

You know you made it on Hounslow's rudeboy circuit when your fights got different classes a viewing stands for different classes a spectators. Like at cricket matches when all them dapper businessmen stand around in suits, downing whisky an sandwiches up in the hospitality boxes. Davinder an Jaswinder an their crew were standin up on a rusty footbridge by the track, with cans a Budweiser an rolls a spliff in their hands an a clear view over everyone else's spiked, shaved or straight-ironed hair. It was basically a smaller version a the kind a footbridge people'd walk over when they wanted to cross a dual carriageway an were too chicken to just run across. Or when they wanted to jump onto a dual carriageway to kill themselves an were too chicken to just slash their wrists. Despite the rust, the footbridge looked like it used to be painted blue. Back when it was blue, spectators'd stand up on it an cheer as the BMXers took off from the concrete starting stretch. Or, if they could cough up a nice juicy chunk a phlegm, they'd thook onto the BMXers' helmets as they crossed the dusty finish line below. You probly wouldn't kill yourself if you jumped off that bridge into the path a some freestyling BMX. Might kill the BMXer if you were as fat as some a Davinder's crew, though. Just a couple a minutes back, they'd been havin jokes an singin this track by the Panjabi Hit Squad called 'Shere Panjabi'. But now that Tariq'd finally shown up they'd started shoutin abuse at him.

— Bullshit u wos helpin yo mum, bhanchod, u wos jus too chicken 2 show yo tutty self, innit, Davinder gave it.

— You wos only late cos you wos so shittin it u probly had the shits innit, goes one a Davinder's mates.

Tariq din't respond. He was busy talkin to Hardjit, squaring up, sayin things like Wassup an discussing the ground rules. No knives, no Karhas, no num-chuckers, no dumb-bell bars, shit like that. He was a big guy, Tariq, not as big as Hardjit a course, but he weren't as good-lookin either so on the whole they both looked just as hard as each other. Tariq's podgy cheeks makin Hardjit's cheekbones look higher than I'd realised before an his green-an-yellow Pakistan cricket top makin Hardjit's orange bandanna more necessary than I'd realised when he'd tied the thing round his head this morning. He was noddin his orange-covered head up an down, like he was listenin to some bangin hip-hop beat, pausing only briefly to rotate his shoulders back an let his Adidas tracksuit top slip off an hang around his elbows, revealing the gorgeous arms beneath it. Bang. Hardjit suddenly flips the tracksuit top off completely an throws the first punch with his right arm, fuck all that ground rules an squaring up shit. Fuck all that only-for-self-defence shit his martial arts instructors instructed him bout. The best form a defence is to get your retaliation in first, or so Hardjit'd told me one time. He'd told me a lot bout fightin, but let's just say I was better at the theory than the practice. Bang. Hardjit gives it a right-hand reverse punch from his hip to Tariq's stomach, with his left foot forward. It's called a reverse punch cos you use opposite hands an feet. Bang. He blends it into a left-hand reverse punch to Tariq's chest, with his right foot forward. Looks to me like today's martial art is gonna be tae kwon do, though Hardjit'd surely mix it up with ju-jitsu, karate an kalari payat later on like he normly did. Anyway, fuck that. Hardjit's openin moves were basic tae kwon do ones he'd taught me the proper Korean names for an'd even taught me to do. A basic reverse punch is called a bandae jurugi. Bang. Now he gives it an upper-elbow strike, or wi palkop terrigi, to Tariq's chin but which misses an hits the right side a his jaw instead. Bang. Now a left-hand obverse punch, what the Koreans call a baro jurugi an which basically looks like a boxing jab, to Tariq's face.

Hardjit takes care not to overextend himself or lose balance before delivering another baro jurugi, but with his right hand this time so it has more power. Count em if you like: that's four plants an no comeback from Tariq. If that's how easy this fightin malarkey is then even I could fuckin do it. I turn to Ravi. — Rav, man, what da fuck's going on? Ravi just shrugs his shoulders an says, — Tariq's a woman, innit. That'll do for me. You don't need in-depth analysis at a time like this. But I swear, if Tariq weren't Muslim I'd be wondering whether he was one a them people who got turned on being beaten around an spanked. You know the kind, the Bring Out the Gimp kind, as Zed says in *Pulp Fiction* before Zed's dead. I don't suggest this out loud though cos I'm afraid I'll get the words sadist an masochist mixed up again like I did at school one time. Anyway, fuck that. Whether Tariq's a masochist or a sadist or is just shit at fightin, he takes a step backwards to sort himself out. Davinder's crew are reachin orgasms bout the first-innings score, stamping their feet, bashing their by-now-empty beer cans on the footbridge, daring the thing to collapse. Even from back here you can smell the alcohol on their breath stronger than the spliff an their overdoses a aftershave, so strong it blocks out the smell a complicated family-related shit that I've been puttin up with all morning. Their stamping gives us a steady tabla beat while their bashing sounds like the dhol drums we take to the cricket to cheer on Mother India. Ding ding ding, takha da ding ding. Anyway, fuck that. The point is the crowd is cheerin, the spectators are going wild, they think this Test Series is all over but Tariq's come back with his take on a mae geri karate kick, a punch an sideways chop that looks a bit batty but sends Hardjit sprawling onto the concrete anyway. Now the other side think it's over. Come on, Tariq, finish him off. Come on, Hardjit, break his face. Come on, Tariq. Come on, Hardjit. Ladies an gentlemen, quiet please. Bang. Another wi palkop terrigi from the main man Hardjit. Seems he never left the match, he just wanted to feel how hard Tariq could knock his shit about. Know your opponent, he'd told me one time, know your foe. Some a Tariq's crew start complaining that the sweatband they'd made Hardjit wear over his Karha has torn an fallen off his wrist. What d'you fuckin expect, boys? The man has forearms bigger'n most people's biceps. Anyway, fuck that. In't no point in Hardjit doing that rolling down his Karha into a knuckleduster thing now cos he in't using clenched forefists no more. He's using knife-hands with open palms, AKA sonkal. Keepin the front a his palms parallel to the ground, like how aunties hold out their hands when they come up to you an say they've known you since you were this tall an, wow, haven't you grown. Really? Well, you always looked like a wrinkly old hag to me. Anyway, fuck that. The sonkal slams into Tariq's left shoulder but Tariq holds his ground. Realising how batty a sonkal can look if your opponent just stands there an takes it, Hardjit twists his wrist forty-five degrees so that his thumb faces the sky. Know what that means? A spearhand strike to Tariq's chest, signalling he's switched from tae kwon do to karate. Bang. In ancient times the spearhand strike, AKA nukite, was one a the favourite hand formations used by the warriors a Okinawa. A course they did much more damage with that shit cos they had tougher fingers than Hardjit. Kept em strong by ramming em into pebbles or sand, stead a some soft, mushy family-related shit. Anyway, fuck that. All a this changin the shape a his fists business means Hardjit still in't broken into a proper rhythm. He'd worked up a fuckin drum n bass beat with Daniel yesterday, his whole body motorised an turbo-charged so if you blinked you'd miss not just the next punch you'd miss the next three. But today is different. Today there's a crowd, meanin he'll be savin up the turbo-charged beats for the grand finale, for now leavin us with the beats coming from the empty beer cans an stamping up on Davinder's footbridge. Ding ding ding, takha da ding ding. Anyway, fuck that. All a sudden, like it's makin sound effects for a Bollywood fight scene, a burnt-out car behind us makes a crashin sound as the springs suspending the left rear wheel finally creak, crack an collapse. A rusty, powdery mist sprays out from underneath the chassis, like an orange version a the dark red blood droplets squirting outta Tariq's mouth after Hardjit uses some kung fu moves with names I don't know to finally drive home his advantage an take the second inning. At this point he normly introduces ju-jitsu but to be honest kung fu patterns are slicker. There in't no throwin with kung fu an so less need for him to grab Tariq's legs or waist or some batty shit like that. Anyway, fuck that. It in't as if anyone can keep a proper tally a the moves or the score anyway. You can't just measure the number a strikes cos some strikes are fours an some strikes are sixes. Not even if you measured how much blood each a them had lost could you keep a proper score, which is just as well cos Hardjit's spillin blood too now. From his cheekbone an his elbow after their connections with Tariq's Puma trainers an the concrete floor. Wet, trickly blood which makes the cuts above his eye an on his cheek look slick. But no matter how slick those cuts look, the nosebleed in't helpin him look fit in front a Priya. He makes up for this by wiping his bloody nose on his vest, which he knows means he has to expose a bit a six-pack in Priya's general direction. Anyway, fuck that. I don't approve a all this violence, a course. I think all fights should be settled in a more Gandhi-fied way. If I'm ever called to fight in a war I'll declare myself one a those pansyist things. Pacifists. Pussyfists. Anyway, fuck that. When it in't me who's gotta fight an stead it's someone like Hardjit, someone who enjoys fightin like nymphomaniacs enjoy fuckin, then fuck it, I'll take violence. Miss Violence, an invisible woman who spreads her virus by jerking off everyone who watches violence, makin Hounslow's BMX track the capital a the infected world right now. Anyway, fuck that. Even if you're a pussy an hate violent films or boxing or wrestling, when you're in a crowd a people watchin it, you get into it. Bang. Hardjit throws another left-arm spearhand. It's the same with a gig you hate. Some grungy heavy metal band. I mean, even though that kind a music's a pile a crap, if you're in a crowd a people at a gig you'll still feel its vibe, you get me? I in't sayin you'll start all that head-bangin shit that goes down, but you'll feel its vibe. Anyway, fuck that. Tariq's come back with a headbutt that gives Hardjit another nosebleed. The kind a headbutt that gives you a headache just watchin it an the kind

a nosebleed that makes you wipe your own nostrils in case nose-
bleeds are, like, contagious or someshit. After gettin his shit tôgether
again, Hardjit comes back by givin it one a his trademark flyin kicks
an then sprays the fuck outta Tariq's face with some machine-gun
fists. But even though Tariq's now lyin on the floor, Hardjit doesn't
knock him for a six to finish him off, cos finishin him off in't part
a the plan. Stead a that, he just stands back again to let Tariq get
back on his feet. Even helps him up, which makes his arms look even
greater cos he uses Tariq's body weight to proply pump up his biceps
an make them shudder an quake. You gotta hand it to Hardjit. I'm
really admiring that desi today, keepin his shit level ever since the
fight began, takin care not to mash Tariq too seriously too quickly.
After all, people'd come a long way to see this. It in't just the way
Hardjit makes sure not to take too many wickets or hit too many
boundaries too quickly, it's the way everyfuckinthing hangs on the
final over an even then you end up needin one run off the final
fuckin ball. Anyway, fuck that. As I'm watchin Hardjit pace himself,
bouncing around like a boxer, takin a few knocks here an there just
for the fuck a it, I get thinkin that this must be why rioting is such
a riot. The feds can't fuckin machine gun you, can they? Just like
Hardjit in the ring, they gots to keep things level. Otherwise they get
accused a police brutality. It's like how Mr Ashwood taught us in
History lessons that Russia an America never nuked each other even
though they were at war. Anyway, fuck that. I should've been on more
riots. I should've joined in what the local papers called Asian
Rampages on Hounslow High Street, drunk on Foster's, an howling
like a werewolf at whatever moon it was Davinder an his crew are
howling at right now. Anyway, fuck that. You think there's an atmosphere at Lord's or the Oval when Sourav Ganguly scores a century
an all the desi fans start jumpin up an down an bangin on their dhol
drums? You should see the atmosphere here an feel the sound a the
crowd an Hardjit's upper body slams vibrating in your own chest.
This is what proper cricket matches are like. More like the Notting
Hill Carnival than fuckin Notts County's Trent Bridge. Hardjit'll be

carryin on with his showman routine for at least another ten minutes so that the crowd get their money's worth. But it's hard to keep things level when Tariq's such a dickless pussy, not even realising he's just being played with. They say anger an aggression in't got no role in martial arts. But they can kiss my chuddies. When people like Tariq don't fight proply it makes you want to beat them even more for being such pussies. If you hit them harder they might fight back. Stupid, fuckin gimps deserve to have the shit beaten outta them anyway. People who don't fight back proply are like people who don't fight at all. They're like desi dads when they stand there takin all kinds a abuse an shit from smelly skinheads, racist bosses an our mums. Anyway, fuck that. People who don't fight are either wimps who can't fight or they're pussyfists who reckon that fightin is wrong or someshit. Either way, they should have their dicks cut off, that's if they weren't so dickless an annoying already. An annoying someone when they're fightin you is a bit like some fit lady flashing too much cleavage at you while you're watchin a porno. Bang. Who the fuck is Samira Ahmed anyway?

The most beautiful girl in the whole a Hounslow, that's who. An if I had to get my ass bundled into a car in front a her, it should've been with blazing sirens an two armed officers tryin to hold me down. Not this crappy little hatchback job here an some fed holdin the door open for me like a fuckin chauffeur. Never mind no sirens, the fuckers had even switched off their engine an used the sloping lane to just roll towards the BMX track, creep up on us, stop us runnin the fuck away. Lucky for us, Hardjit an Tariq had known the drill, shaking hands, tapping each other on the chest an even patting each other on the back so that from a distance it looked like they were huggin. I in't got no problems with Sikh kids an Muslim kids gettin tighter with each other. It'd make it easier for me to fancy Samira an still stay safe with the other guys. But, fuckin huggin? You wouldn't even hold a lady like that, unless you were going out with her, you wanted beef with the guy who was going out with her or she was one a them ladies who liked being hugged by lots a guys.

The problem is, when a Muslim an a Sikh guy decide to make like friends, they really, really make like friends, just to prove that the whole Muslim-Sikh thing don't mean jackshit to them no more. Hardjit even started callin Tariq his brother.

— Officers, u best sort dis place out. Me n ma bruv here jus b practisin some moves innit, n he fell on some broken glass. Cut him up bad, look at him, goes Hardjit. — It dem junkies, man. Always leavin their shit round here 4 us 2 fall on.

One a the feds took his hat off an crouched down to inspect the bloody mess below Tariq's left eye. — You alright, son? That's a nasty injury. You may need some medical attention for that.

— No, sir, don't worry, Tariq says in a fake poncey accent that I figure is his version a actin polite. — I'm alright, well an truly I am.

— OK, lads, goes the other fed, still standin, — you can stop all that now. You might fool my colleague but I wasn't born yesterday.

— Wat'chyu mean, officer?

— What I mean is do me a favour and don't treat me like an idiot. I see an orange bandanna on you, Pakistani cricket colours on your friend here and lots of blood, cuts and bruises in between. Cut the crap, boys. You might as well have told us you both accidently fell down a flight of stairs.

— Oh, so now we can't wear our national colours? U gonna ban us from wearin turbans n headscarves too then?

— You do realise that you parked your vehicle by a police station this morning, sir? Remember, when you were brandishing your weapons around in the air?

— Wot weapons, we ain't got no weapons, Ravi says. — Where d'you see weapons? I can't see no weapons. Anyone see any weapons?

— Yeh, man, don't be coming wid all a dat weapons a mass destruction shit wid us, one a Tariq's crew joins in. — U see, boys, dis b why I i'nt never listen 2 da cops no more. Dere ain't no fuckin WMD here, innit.

It was a shame the feds had snuck up on us stead a coming with their sirens cos then Davinder's crew would've jumped around singin

'Whoop Whoop, Dat's da Sound A Da Police' like they normly do. But I guess most feds were wise to our ways, to the BMX track an to the car parks behind the High Street. A new venue is what we needed. But we couldn't go south cos that was Richmond. Too swanky, too poncey. To the east was Brentford, but that was going the way a Richmond now. To the north it belonged to the Southall desis an all the land to the west had anti-terrorist police cos a Heathrow airport – an those muthas got guns.

Lucky for us, though, only one cop car showed up. One shitty Vauxhall hatchback, two feds. I thought that good-cop-bad-cop shit was just for the movies. Then a third man's voice came from behind me, sayin us lads should be given the benefit a the doubt or someshit. That should've been even more lucky for us, I should've been sayin, Thanks, man. But it was a voice that'd nagged me so much to stay on what it called the straight an narrow that it was a bit shameful to hear it now. Bhanchod, why couldn't you show up earlier when I was holdin my own chattin with Samira?

Mr Ashwood caught on quick an played along. I nearly pissed myself when he said, — They're not troublemakers, as their former teacher I can assure you. They're always practising their dance moves around these parts. Are you familiar with some of the more energetic bhangra routines?

The hero stole the show, man, even the girls were impressed. Old Mr Ashwood? Street? Takin off his jacket, walkin the feds away from us, waving his hands around like he was givin them a fuckin History lesson. Lucky for us, he'd given his jacket to Ravi to hold. Even luckier, inside that jacket was his fone an his fone just happened to be the same Samsung E700 model Ravi'd promised to replace. If jackin a fone to order was this easy, even I could've done it.

— Looks like it our lucky day, boys, Ravi whispered as he slipped the fone into his own jacket.

Vouching for our good characters was one thing, sayin it so loud that even the girls heard it was another. — Absolute little angels, good to the bone, so to speak. If it's real troublemakers you officers want, just come back to the school with me an I'll gladly palm some off onto you.

— Ha ha, very funny, Hardjit goes to Priya an the other giggling girls as they heard Mr Ashwood an decided to make their exit. — Da man jus b chattin bout Jas here.

But the girls carried on giggling. — Oh Hardjit, you're such a goody good little angel boy, said Priya. — Such a good shareef munda, I should introduce you to my mama.

Then she kissed the four a us on our cheeks an said bye before headin towards the gate. So did this girl called Seema, but Samira just nodded, probly cos Tariq an his Muslim crew were still hangin around. I nodded back at her, embarrassed by what Hardjit'd just said bout me, embarrassed also cos for some reason I seemed to be even more outta breath than both him an Tariq.

Lookin over towards Mr Ashwood an the feds, it seemed like the man'd saved our butts. One a the feds even got back in their car an started the engine. The other fed stood around with Mr Ashwood, probly just to make sure we all cleared off. But then Mr Ashwood stopped talkin to him an looked at us as if he was havin second thoughts. He weren't sayin jackshit, not a word, not to us, not to the feds. Like he was now havin third an fourth thoughts. Then he looked back at the feds an back at us. We decided to leave him to all his various thoughts an started shifting away, catch up with the girls. Tariq's crew had already gone, revving their Beemer louder than an aeroplane as they did so. Then Mr Ashwood started walkin towards us. — Er, my jacket, he said softly so that the feds couldn't hear him. — Which I believe is a little lighter. I also believe you boys are heading to school with me now, right? Unless you want me to explain to the police why my jacket now weighs less than when I gave it to you?

||

A man plasters his office walls with pictures a boys. Hundreds a boys. Aged between eleven an sixteen. Even his PC screensaver is a little boy in blue shorts, though maybe that's his son or his nephew. I don't watch the news much no more but from what I do see on the TV, this all looks a bit dodge. The boys are in school uniform, sittin side by side, row upon row, on benches or on chairs or standin up on benches behind the chairs. Some class photos have got messed up by someone pullin some stupid face. Other photos've been messed up cos some dickhead in the front row's tryin to be Michael Jackson, wearin jack-up trousers with white socks, bright white like they've been brushed with that whitening toothpaste you get. Somewhere in those hundreds a boys, Hardjit's lookin slick even though he'd been forced to wear proper black shoes for the photo an I've got my mouth shut tight to hide my tutty braces.

I'd been in Mr Ashwood's office nuff times back when we was all at this school but I'd never noticed all these boys before. An now that I noticed them, I din't know whether the news on TV'd somehow changed the photos on the walls or whether I'd changed and it'd got jackshit to do with TV. One thing I can guarantee though, Mr Ashwood weren't one a them pervert paedophile people. He'd have tried it on with me if he was. Back when he was givin me all them one-on-one pep talks bout clever boffiny shit to help me with my GCSEs.

Right now, Amit was in the comfy chair I used to sit in back then. Hardjit'd bagged the desk chair after elbowin Ravi in the stomach for it. All a this musical chairs business forced Mr Ashwood to sit on his desk with a pile a exercise books an his desk phone balanced on his lap. Meantime me an Ravi stood in the doorway with that dirty whiff a school dinners wafting around. We din't mind standin in the doorway, though. Truth is, Amit might've bagged the comfy chair but he was the most uncomfortable out a all a us. He was tryin to keep his elbows off these splintery stubs where the caretaker'd sawn off the armrests so they could fit the chair in between the desk an a filing cabinet that'd been dented so many times two drawers were stuck open in Amit's face. The bredren looked like he was playin fuckin Twister.

Mr Ashwood's office weren't as cramped as it'd been in his crappy hatchback – which had been so tight that one a the feds had to help us squeeze in – but at least his car had got windows. The windows in his office were mostly covered up by this massive free-standin whiteboard that jutted out behind Amit's head so he had to do another Twister move by leaning forward a little. Mr Ashwood was bent out a shape too, tryin to use the phone in his lap to arrange for a supply teacher to take his next class. He was sayin he'd got some urgent disciplinary matters to attend to. Whoever it was he was talkin to seemed to understand whatever the fuck that was s'posed to mean, though from Mr Ashwood's end it weren't exactly clear whether any supply teachers were actually free. Like there'd be any difference between a supply teacher an no teacher anyway? You'd think Mr Ashwood was just some supply teacher himself the way Hardjit, Amit an Ravi started cussin him behind his back cos a the poncey way he was talkin. But it in't like you could blame em. It's hard not to cuss the way someone chats on the phone if they use a word like blast. But still, I tried not to join in cos Mr Ashwood'd been so safe to me back in the day. I didn't try too hard though cos, well, these guys were safe to me now.

— Sir, you can't b holdin us here all afternoon, Amit goes, soon as Mr Ashwood hung up an turned to face us. — We don't even go to dis tutty school no more, sir.

— Yeh, man, wot da fuck we doin here, c'mon, bredrens, let's chip, Hardjit gives it, standin up to show he meant it. — Laters, sir. In fact, why'ma still callin u sir? Yo name's Thomas, innit? Thomas Ashwood?

— Fine, Harjit. If you'd rather call me Thomas, I don't have a problem with it.

— Yeh, well, I wudn't even give a shit even if u did have a problem wid it, Tom, I ain't callin u sir no more. An talkin bout yo name, seems dat u still can't pronounce my proper name proply. C'mon, bredrens, let's chip.

— You walk out that door, young man, and I'll not hesitate to call the police. I take time out of my afternoon to vouch for your integrity, I put my reputation on the line with the local beat officers, and you repay me by trying to steal my mobile from right under my nose. What kind of bloody fool do you think I am?

The four a us just sat there, listenin to this little desk fan struggle to cool his broom cupboard office. The thing swivelled its neck from side to side, turnin left towards us then right towards Mr Ashwood. Waitin to see who was gonna talk first. It was a crappy, knackered old metal fan an as it slogged from side to side it sounded like it was snoring itself to death. We broke the silence by sniggering one more time at his class photos, although in a way that looked like we were just sniggering at him.

— You boys think this is some kind of joke? Well, fine. Because frankly I don't see why I should waste my time.

— Listen, Tom, u do realise ain't nobody here call'd Frankly, don't'chyu? Hardjit goes, back on his lippy schoolboy form like he'd never even left the place.

— Fine, Harjit, if you're going to make fun of me then why don't I just save everyone's time by getting that policeman's phone number?

— Ain't nobody here call'd Harjit either. It's Hardjit, wid a d.

Mr Ashwood just ignored Hardjit an stead pulled a business card out his cardigan pocket, twirling it in his fingers like it was a rolled-up Rizla he was keepin for a special occasion. Mr Ashwood used to call his whole Rizla and tin tobacco box thing a poor man's smokin pipe. It looked good with the old grandad clothes he wore. I swear he'd been wearin the same maroon cardigan with the same holes in the elbows since we were in year seven. Back then I thought it was kind a cool. Now the man just looked like a tramp.

— Wat's da matter, Tom? U tired a playin cop already? Need 2 call in da real guns? I got news 4 u, man, feds round here ain't even got real guns.

— Well, Harjit, you can ask PC Boyling all about his gun when you speak to him in person.

— R u deaf, man? I said da name's Hardjit. Hardjit, innit. Wid a d in it, innit.

— I've never known it to be spelt that way before.

— Well, now u do, a'ight.

— No, actually I don't. Don't think you can terrorise me like you did all the other teachers here. Don't think you can pen me as one of those teachers who can't pronounce Asian names just because you've decided you prefer it spelt or pronounced a new way. I wasn't born yesterday.

— Nah, man, u ain't listenin, people really call me Hardjit now. Jus check wid ma crew.

— If you check with your parents I think you'll find your name is Harjit. You were quite happy being called Harjit when you attended this school and if I remember rightly your parents were quite happy calling you Harjit. So unless you've changed your name by deed poll, I'll call you Harjit.

The desk fan woke the fuck up now, swivelling faster an faster as if the tennis players it'd been watchin had both come closer to the net.

— And quite frankly, Harjit, you might like to know that PC Boyling seemed familiar with your name too. I'd say they're looking for any excuse to nick you, make an example out of you to stop all the fighting round here. He even asked me to get back to him if you or any of your mates caused any more problems or if I remembered whether any of you lot had ever been involved in any other kind of trouble before. Instead of telling him the truth, I do you boys a favour by suddenly developing amnesia because, quite frankly, I don't believe in all this zero-tolerance malarkey. But on second thoughts, why should I bloody well bother? As if nearly having my mobile stolen and my trust betrayed aren't reasons enough for me to change my mind, then your sniggering and smart-alec remarks certainly are.

— Then call da muthafucka, innit.

— We're really sorry, sir, I finally said, risking an then receiving tuts from the other three.

Mr Ashwood said he appreciated my contribution but he wanted to hear it from what he called my so-called friends. Hardjit sat back down and pulled out a packet a Malboro Lights, clearly not realising that Mr Ashwood's office was the Yes Smoking room a the whole fuckin school. My so-called so-called friends stopped sniggering as Mr Ashwood put the fed's business card away an offered Hardjit a fuckin light.

— You boys tried to steal my mobile. As I recall you've all got mobiles of your own – Lord knows they interrupted my lessons enough times. So am I to assume your enthusiasm for these gizmos is now such that you've decided to join one of those gangs of high-street mobile-phone snatchers? That sounds like pretty organised trouble for a bunch of A-level students. Tell me, why would I want to withhold something like this from the police?

— Actually, Tom, we ain't A-level students, we A-level retake students. Dat means we ain't fuckin kids no more so ease up on talkin 2 us like we was. Seems 2 me like u been workin on some badass, bad-cop routine, Tom. Dat's safe, dat'll keep yo shit level wid some year-seven kids. But u ain't scaring shit here. An as 4 dis organised trouble u chattin bout, u'd b surprised how organised our shit can b when we proply incentivised.

— Incentivised? That's a big word coming from someone who failed A-level English.

— Fuck u, u fuckin four-eyed muthafucka . . . Yeh, dat's right. I call'd u a four-eyed muthafucka. Wat'chyu gonna do bout it? Suspend me? I alwayz want'd 2 say dat 2 yo four-eyed face when we was all at dis place.

— Well, I'm glad you've been able to articulate your disenchantment about me and my spectacles with such depth and such clarity, Hard-jit. I always say a person can't understand how they truly feel about something unless they can articulate their feelings clearly. In fact I was just saying it to one of my year-eight classes this morning. That's the beauty of being literate, I say. But I don't have all day to say it again and frankly if you want to settle some unresolved conflict with me and my spectacles, save it for after one of you explains to me why you tried to steal my mobile phone. Either that or you can explain it to PC Boyling instead. It's your choice.

I'd been waitin for Mr Ashwood to say that. Not the shit bout being able to express yourself, the stuff bout it being our choice. He was just like our mums in that way. Always tellin us what we should do an tellin us we'd be killed by aliens or someshit if we did something else, before adding, But of course it is your choice. Your decision. I am not telling you what to do. Apparently Amit's older brother Arun was getting that exact same shit from their mum right now over his wedding. Beita, I not saying you *have* to have vegetarian-only at sangeet party, she'd said, all I saying is if you don't, then I not eat anything. Not at sangeet, not at saagai, not at shaadi, not at reception. But beita, is your shaadi, not mine, so is up to you, is your choice. I remember even my own mum'd come out with the same shit to me to make me choose Economics stead a Art for A-level. Fine, you do this arty-farty nonsense. It's up to you. Your choice. Do what you want. But don't expect me to hold my head up high in front of all the other ladies when you don't get a job. An then Mum'd go an do the dishes or hoover the carpet again while I stood there like a dick.

Mr Ashwood'd come out with his own mum-style shit during all those pep-talk sessions. He even came out with it when I said I din't need those extra sessions in the first place. He said it was either the extra sessions or I get a grade E or maybe if I was lucky a D. — But it's your choice, Jas, he used to say. Unlike the other teachers he always did me a favour by not even tryin to say my full name, during lessons or during the extra sessions he reckoned I needed. I couldn't fulfil my full potential during lessons, you see. But it'd be my choice. After all, I weren't in trouble, it weren't cos I was rowdy like the rest a them. Stead it was cos I hardly ever said anything at all. In parents' evenings he used to say my problem was I was the polar opposite a them disruptive pupils, whatever the fuck that means. In History class he used to ask me for the answer to questions even if I din't stick my hand up to answer them. In his office, after he finally got me to do those extra sessions, he used to lend me books like he reckoned he was some kind a library. No of course you don't have to read it. But it'll stop you getting a D or an E. It's your choice, Jas. He even used to give me some a them for keeps, like he wanted me to promote him from librarian to bookshop man or someshit. He said it weren't as if there was a proper bookshop round here where I could've bought them for myself. Not on Hounslow High Street or in the Treaty Centre anyway. Today his shelves still seem to be stuffed with the same old History books. The wall next to it stuffed with some framed posters a Martin Luther King and Gandhi.

— Well, what's it to be, boys? Me or PC Boyling? Just make it quick please and stop wasting my time.

— Please don't call the police, sir, I give it like some pussyfied pehndu crybaby. — I mean, it's not necessary to call them. We in't into sellin stolen fones or nothin. We just had to replace another fone just like yours cos Ravi broke it.

— Look, Jas, I admire your attempts to Band-Aid this situation instead of acting like another one of these tough-guy new friends of yours, but surely you don't expect me to believe that? I know I may be a little old and a little out of touch but I'm not completely stupid. If Ravi broke his phone surely he can just claim it back on insurance. We're all sold insurance for these bloody things. Mine costs me £7 a month.

I tried to explain to Mr Ashwood that it weren't Ravi's fone, it was our fone, well, except that it din't belong to us, but, no, sir, we weren't borrowing it either. Mr Ashwood figured I'd just taken him back to square one again an so started checkin his cardigan pockets for the policeman's card. Out came tissues, cough sweets, old lottery tickets. Just like how people pretend to fumble for money when some smelly tramp sittin by a cash machine asks them, — Got any spare change, guv? My dad does the exact same shit before givin me a fiver for the bus or whatever. Even if he's gettin the car keys for Mum, he'll pretend to look for them all over the place to show that gettin them himself is some kind a household chore he shouldn't have to do. But to be fuckin frank, it was too fuckin hot in Mr Ashwood's office for that kind a shit. The only reason we were in there was cos he was clearly never gonna call the police in the first place. We knew it, he knew it. The fuckin desk fan fuckin knew it, an so it cut out.

— No, it was another mate's fone n he'd given it to us to fix it, Amit joined in from the uncomfortable comfy chair.

Mr Ashwood got the fan going again, grabbed its neck an held it nearer his face. A couple a exercise books slipped from his lap onto the floor.

— How can Ravi have broken it if it already needed fixing? You know what, boys, I'm getting a little tired of all this evasion. Come on, answer a straight question with a straight answer.

— We did, man, u jus too thick 2 understand, Hardjit says. — We weren't fixin shit. We was jus reprogramming its IMEI 2 transfer it 2 anotha network, innit.

Hardjit's got this other handy rudeboy rule, you see. The rule says that if you're havin trouble explainin shit to your elders, especially to your parents, just start throwin in even more complicated words an maybe even a bunch a capital letters an they'll just give up tryin to understand. Goras got a similar rule. Except while they blind their parents with science, Hardjit also blinds his with English, innit.

Unfortunately Hardjit's mobile-fone science just bounced off Mr Ashwood's protective goggles.

— Ahh, I see. The penny finally drops, he said, puttin the fan back down on the desk. — I know a thing or two about these IMEI numbers. They're a bit like electronic fingerprints, right? The police gave all us teachers a talk about it last month. I told you I wasn't that old and out of touch. So the mobile was obviously stolen then, and you were just reactivating it?

In the words a Hardjit, we finally fessed up, though more out a relief that Mr Ashwood finally understood what the fuck we were goin on bout rather than cos anyone wanted to cooperate with the man.

— So you're trying to tell me that you tried to steal my mobile so that you could replace another stolen one? I know you boys are always shaking each other's hands and talking in code under your breath, but what is this? The Hounslow mafia or something?

— Yeh, man, nobody mess wid us, we bad muthafuckas, Ravi said, gettin all excited an using the fact that he was standin up as an excuse to adopt one a his gangsta-rap poses. With his neck raised now an givin it another lick-a-shot flick with his right hand, he continues: — Da gangsta, da killa n da dope dealer.

How embarrassing. Brand new creases formed on Mr Ashwood's forehead an in order to smooth these ones out I now had to explain to my old friend that my new friend weren't really speakin but stead was just quoting hardcore rap tracks cos, well, that's what my new friends do sometimes. It was a track by the Westside Connection, Ice Cube's new outfit with Mack 10 an WC. Ice Cube is the Gangsta, WC is the Killer an Mack 10 is the Dope Dealer. Get it? To our surprise Mr Ashwood got it, an showed he was even less old an out a touch by knowin who the fuck Ice Cube was. This left us more impressed with him than he was with us.

— I cannot believe you're sitting there aspiring to be a gangsta rapper at a time like this, Ravi. Because if you want that kind of notoriety, then quite frankly I could fulfil your fantasy by calling the police and having you arrested while they search your houses for stolen phones. Do you realise how serious this is? At the risk of fuelling your obvious homophobia, I've got you boys by the balls, haven't I? So, please, just stop coming over all rap star with me, sunshine.

With that, Mr Ashwood chucked the pile of exercise books on the floor. — I'm just glad that no matter how much I feel let down by New Labour, at least they're still spending money trying to keep boys like you off the streets. Tough on crime, tough on the causes of crime, or so they keep saying. Mind you, what about tough on the causes of disengagement from society? I suspect that's the real problem here, isn't it?

None a us said a word. The guys were tryin to hold in their laughter cos all a us knew it was best not to talk now that Mr Ashwood'd got that excited look in his eyes. If there's one thing everyone remembered bout Mr Ashwood, it was the way the man always got so excited when he was talkin bout the government an politics an the big media dudes an what'd gone wrong with the world an education policies an all that kind a shit. At first, when we were in year seven, everyone'd relax when he got like that cos it'd mean he was sidetracking from whatever the lesson was actually s'posed to be bout. By year nine we'd all realised that even if you wanted him to stop rambling, it was pointless tryin to get him back on track cos he'd just find his way back to politics again. Nope. When old Ashwood got that look in his eyes, best thing was to just let him get on with it. That afternoon lettin him get on with it meant listenin to him go on bout all these politicians that I guess were in the government or someshit cos I'd heard their names a lot. He said that in the last Budget they talked bout spendin more money on sports centres an youth clubs an shit to keep people like us off the streets. He wondered whether that was something we'd sign up to, whether they should get the local council to lobby for funding for Hounslow, maybe get the BMX track rebuilt. Then finally, after about a whole five fuckin minutes of going on an on like some mental nutter, he started to wind down, even crouching down to pick up the exercise books. — Mmmmm, he said as he did so, — they talk about disentangling the causes of crime, but how does one disentangle disengagement when it's already disengaged? I mean, it'd still be disengaged once you'd disentangled it, wouldn't it? I don't suppose you boys have any thoughts on that, do you?

Old friend or not, even I was crackin up now. I mean, how could the man be serious? One minute he's callin us the Hounslow mafia an threatenin to call the police on us. The next minute, he's tryin to get us to join some kind a youth club batty Boy Scouts movement or someshit. Talkin bout disentangling knots an shit.

— Amit, you must be a keen cricketer. Your dad used to coach one of the primary school teams if I remember correctly.

So now we were laughin at Amit as well, askin him if his dad helped him put on his box an whether his box was an extra small size. This made Mr Ashwood finally snap outta his weirdo mental mode.

— Oh, I've had enough of this. How can my question about the potential for a sports centre be answered by jibes about the size of Amit's member?

— Look, man, we ain't goin 2 no youth centre.

— Yeh, even if you lot stick a basketball court in it wid cheerleaders to help us exercise our own – wat'd'he jus call em, boys? – members, goes Ravi. — Check dat shit. I'll sneak in n bone em all so hard before da match till dey can't do their cheerleader moves no more anyway.

Mr Ashwood just sighed. — Ravi, you astonish me. After all my years of putting up with this kind of disgusting misogyny from boys like you, I still can't work out what came first: your dire social values or your dire rap music. I consider myself a very liberal man but if I was in the government then quite frankly even I'd have to think about perhaps banning it.

It was Amit's turn now. — Who da fuck are you to tell us not to listen to rap music, Tom? Ain't nuffink wrong wid our values, man. We got more values'n you, innit.

— Nothing wrong, Amit? Well, you certainly haven't taken after your brother Arun, have you? That boy was one of my star pupils. I'd so hoped you'd prove to be cut from the same cloth, but I suppose these things aren't genetic. If you want to know about values you need look no further than him, Amit. You people, you want nothing to do with school and society, the way you walk around, shaking each other's hands and talking in your mafioso code words.

— Wat's wrong wid dat? We bondin wid our bredren, innit. You only like Arun cos he's got gora values, innit. You bein racist bout us hangin wid our bredren n usin our own language? Our own muthafuckin mother tongue? Dat is racist, man, dat is so fuckin racist.

— No, you don't get it, do you, Ravi? I don't mind you using your mother tongue. In actual fact I've often thought it admirable the way you boys mix up Hindi with Urdu and Punjabi to create your own second-generation tongue. It's the English code words I can't stand. It's ironic, isn't it? The way your use of English makes you lot look like you're some kind of Asian mafia rather than your use of your mother tongue.

— Dat is racist, man. Dat is so fuckin racist, Ravi gives it. — I ain't even sure wot da fuck you jus said, like, but I know dat dat is so fuckin racist.

— Yeh, fuck, goes Amit. — You sayin we mafia guys cos we b hangin wid our own kind. We reportin you for racism, man, you goin down.

— Me a racist? You're the ones throwing your education away because most of us teachers are tainted with the misfortune of being white. Don't think I didn't notice the way you boys used to show more respect to Mr Sharma and never sat next to fellow white students. I wasn't born yesterday. Your idea of diversity seems to be limited to recruiting Jas.

— So wat you sayin, man? goes Ravi. — Sound to me you jus want us to start lickin some butt.

— No, that's not at all what I mean. But having said that, maybe a few steps towards sychophancy wouldn't be a bad thing in your case. I mean, the problem with you boys is you're the polar opposite of sychophantic.

— Sicko what?

— Sycho . . . Oh, forget it. The point is, all this attitude, is it really worth throwing your education away for? I mean, where's your ambition? Your self-respect?

— Fuck's sake, man, goes Hardjit. — U can't chat 2 us bout ambition n self-respect. U might got a bling fone but u drive a crapped-out 1980s Volvo n carry yo books round in a plastic bag, innit. Anyway, wat'chyu callin us racist 4? Fuck's sake, we only stole yo fone, we din't call u honky da way u goras used 2 call us Pakis. An u b callin us n Asian mafia? Fuckin call da feds if u like, we'll get'chyu done 4 racism.

— Look, Hard-jit, nobody's calling anyone racist and nobody's going to call the police. But you boys do have some kind of worrying anti-integration, anti-assimilation ethic going on and quite frankly I don't intend to rest this old body of mine until today's youth culture stops being so divided along ethnic lines. Do you boys have any idea how hard your parents worked and how hard they fought to be accepted by mainstream society? Well, do you? And all for what? So you boys could just throw it all away by acting like hoodlums and by volunteering for segregation?

— Wot da fuck d'yu know bout our parents, man? Ravi goes. — Don't talk to us bout our own parents. So wat if our parents had to suck British butt? Dat was back then. Now it our turn to teach em some muthafuckin self-respect, teach em not to b so fuckin disgustin.

— You see, I find it really very interesting that you feel that way, Ravi.

— Interesting for wat? So you can b some ponce who nobody ever listens to? Why'dyu give a shit bout all dis shit anyway, man?

— I'll tell you why I give a shit, as you put it. I give a shit for the bloody simple reason that it makes it impossible to be a teacher.

Don't you see, all I wanted to do was to turn you boys into great people – future newspaper editors, director-generals of the BBC, Cabinet members, even a prime minister. But how can I do that if you lot want nothing to do with mainstream society? Look at Trevor McDonald. Trevor McDonald is a proponent of integration and as one of the most respected newscasters in the country he should be a role model for all ethnic kids. In fact, I read an interview with him once and he said quite clearly that if you don't want to integrate, why did you come here?

— We din't fuckin come here, innit, goes Ravi, — we was fuckin born here. Anyway, dat man is jus anotha BBC ponce.

— Trevor McDonald?

— Yeh, man. Only Trevor I got time for is Trevor Nelson.

— I sincerely hope you're just feigning your ignorance, Ravi. Trevor McDonald is on ITV, not the BBC. He's a national institution, for crying out loud.

— ITV, BBC. How does dat make him any less poncey? Put him on MTV Base an I'll listen to him.

— Correct me if I'm wrong, Ravi, but isn't this Trevor Nelson fellow a BBC man?

— A'ight, wiseguy, so you know yo shit. So wat? There're loadsa Asians on BBC but Trevor Nelson don't act like a BBC ponce. He ain't a toff.

— Yeh, man, him n Bobby n Nihal n Westwood, innit, goes Amit.

Ravi was not happy with this comparison. — Shut up, bruv, Tim Westwood's a wannabe, man. I hate da way da gora tries to talk like he's a brother.

— Nah, man, I be listenin to him dese days. He's safe. He well safe.

Now it was Hardjit's turn. — Nah, guys, it's like dis. Westwood, yeh, I did used 2 fink he was a sap. But since dat time he got shot he's been gettin mo respect. Respect 2 his shrapnel, innit.

— Well, I suppose I'm glad you boys are at least getting something for your licence fee, Mr Ashwood said as he sat back down on his desk. — In fact, I'm rather enjoying this discussion. Then he smiled like a psycho batty for, like, a whole minute before givin it, — So what I've decided is this, here's what we're going to do. We're going to forget about the police and we're going to forget about you trying to steal my mobile phone. But on the condition you make a regular point to come back so we can discuss these kinds of things at greater length.

— U wot? U do know u can't give us detentions no more, Tom? said Hardjit. — We ain't at dis school no more, rememba? Dat means we don't gots 2 take yo shit no more, man.

— Look, in case you haven't realised, Harjit, I'm trying to cut you boys a deal. And it's really very simple. I'll only forget about the mobile phone if you agree to take my shit, as you so eloquently call it. Just for one hour, once a week for a month. That's all I'm asking. You sit down and let me try and get you boys interested in our mainstream, multicultural society again, in books, plays, politics, public institutions like the BBC. We can even analyse rap lyrics if you like. Just give me a couple of evenings . . . And don't think I'll be talking down to you either, I intend to learn just as much as you will from these sessions. I mean, I for one would like to be clearer about where all this macho nonsense comes from in the first instance. Maybe it has nothing to do with racial tensions, but we can't know unless we talk about it more. I mean, maybe we'll find that deep down you boys just don't believe there's such a thing as society. Maybe the Iron Lady was right all along? After all, we live in a world where television tells us we should be out there gratifying all our desires. How can you boys possibly be expected to square that with feeling positive about school or society, with the bond of marriage even? Or then again, maybe this all just comes down to you not being taught to share your toys with others when you were children? I mean, who knows? Unless we talk about this stuff, who really knows?

The guys all looked at each other with their funniest what-da-fuck faces. You could hear the same thought going through each a their minds: Either this old man is seriously fucked in the head or he really *is* a batty lookin for an after-school fuck. An so they all laughed.

— Nah thanks, Tom, said Amit. — I gets me ma afta-school sessions at da Green School, innit.

They all laughed again.

— Yeh, Tom. We'll jus leave u 2 gratify yo own desires by yo'self, innit. U got a box of tissues in here, right?

They all laughed again, louder this time.

— Did you not hear me when I said the police are looking for any excuse to nick you? I really suggest you try and maintain our new-found spirit of cooperation if you want me to continue bending over backwards for you.

An then they all laughed once more, this time even louder'n before.

— Now what's so funny? Tell me, what's so funny? Mr Ashwood put his goggles back on an thumped his desk. — I don't see what's so funny about me offering to help you guys out here, to pretend all of this didn't even happen to keep you boys out of trouble with the law. Attempted theft is still a crime if I remember correctly.

— No, sorry, sir, it was the way you said bend over.

— Oh, I see, Jas. Homophobia again. You boys think that by constantly insinuating that I'm gay that somehow makes you big men? Well, you know what? You boys could end up in so much trouble you'll end up in jail one day where you can develop your homophobia further. Then he picked up the phone an started dialling the number on the business card.

— Call da fuckin po-lice kuthe da puther. We'll tell em u bein racist, dat u purposely ain't pronouncin my name proply, dat u tryin turn us into white boys n u makin – watd'yu call em? – homosexual advances, man.

I know Hardjit normly knows best. But normly in't always. So I leapt up an slammed the receiver down before Mr Ashwood'd finished dialling.

— Look, we don't think you're gay, sir. But this in't *Good Will Hunting*, that's all. You in't Robin Williams or the Gandhi a Hounslow, sir.

Then, for some reason, Hardjit decided to calm the situation down too: — Tom, it's like dis. Why we gonna b interested in all dis shit when it means jackshit 2 us? Why'd I wanna give a shit bout politics n shit? It don't mean jack.

— It's not irrelevant. Have you watched the news? Are you familiar with the debate around multiculturalism? Asylum policy? US foreign policy? Do you realise that there's a Mother Nature-raping right-wing psychopath in the White House just looking for excuses to fight wars?

— Forget it, man, dis politics shit, it all bout poncey, grey-haired bald people talkin posh n gettin off wid their secretaries, man.

— But you'll never get to change anything if you don't care. You'll get crappy jobs. You'll end up working at the airport like everyone else from this school, loading other people's luggage onto a rotating conveyor belt.

— Wat's fuckin wrong wid dat? Amit said. — I'll work at the airport. I'll b a pilot *Top Gun*-stylee, innit.

— You really want to be a pilot, Amit?

— Yeh, wat? You sayin I can't or sumfink? You sayin I too thick?

— No, quite the opposite. You can. But you've got to get your qualifications and that process starts in the classroom.

— Ah, man, don't come out wid all dat shit wid us, man. Get ready, boys, here he comes wid all dat fuckin Wat'chyu Wanna Be? shit.

— Yeh, we done dis before already, you know. We had all dem meetings wid dem careers advisers.

— You know dat bitch told me I cudn't be a stockbroker cos it weren't a career n only, like, one in a million people or someshit were good enuf to b dat kind a shit. Fuckin I'm one in a fuckin zillion, I told her, innit.

— Yeh, n she jus ignored me when I said I wanted to b n MC. Fuck dat shit, man.

— Well, I'm not aware of a graduate recruitment scheme for MCs and it does take a special sort of person to become a stockbroker. How many people from Hounslow do you know end up as stockbrokers? After asking this question, Mr Ashwood leapt up like some hippie drama teacher weirdo an clapped his hands together. — Eureka! I've got a better idea. If you won't listen to me then at least agree to meet with a former student who actually does work in the City. I suppose that makes him a stockbroker or something. He's Indian, so don't worry. In fact, I think he was the last student I had with any genuine intellectual curiosity at all.

Mr Ashwood carried on daydreaming out loud bout this golden teacher's pet who from the sound a things was obviously top a the coconut tree. Four A's at A-level (which I guess must've meant he'd actually done four A-levels), head boy, captain a the cricket team, all that kind a shit.

— Sanjay was his name, Mr Ashwood went on. — Crikey, it must be, what, eight years ago now. He was the last student from this school, brown, black or white, to get through Oxbridge, I wish I'd thought of this before. Last I heard from him he was earning a packet and had just bought himself a flash sports car – you'd like him. Anyway, he studied Economics at Cambridge. I'm sure I've got his number here somewhere.

— Brother sounds like king a da coconuts to me, goes Amit.

My old an outta touch friend looked confused again, tried to say something, but decided not to. So I decided to help him out.

— Brown on the outside but white on the inside.

— Yes thank you, I know what a coconut is, Jas. I'm just despairing, that's all.

— Dis coconut culdn't have been all dat if you forgot what uni he went to, goes Ravi. — You said before he went to Oxbridge. Now you say da dude went to Cambridge. Make up yo mind, wot fuckin bridge did da coconut go to?

The rest a us laughed so that Mr Ashwood din't think we were all as thick as Ravi, an in the middle a laughin Amit said, — Yeh, OK, fuck it. Let's meet dis coconut. Sounds like a laugh, innit. Anyway, I got enuf shit at home, don't b needin no shit wid da feds too, you get me.

— U hear dat, Mr Ashwood? goes Hardjit. — Sound 2 me like u gots yo'self a deal, we'll meet dis desi.

— Fantastic. Splendid. I'll phone Sanjay this evening and explain the whole situation. Of course, he's such a straight-laced chap he may not want anything to do with keeping the police away from you. But if he does agree, I'll arrange a meeting for as soon as possible so as not to lose what little progress we've made this afternoon. Does that sound acceptable to you boys?

— Safe, man, innit. But tell me sumfink, Tom, how comes u lettin us loose like dis, man?

— Because, Harjit, no matter how much you want to act like bad-to-the-bone tough guys, I refuse to believe that's what you really are. And while I'm explaining my leniency, let me give you boys some advice. Your friend Jas here, although I lament his decision to join your ranks of hoodlums, the fact that you have his loyalty is a credit to you. You would certainly be in a police station right now and they would certainly be searching your bedrooms for stolen mobiles were it not for Jas's cooperation. I know Jas, probably better than any of you do. And I know that despite your attempts to turn him into a racially charged juvenile delinquent, he has the good sense to keep you at least within driving distance of the straight and narrow. Mark my words, you'd be wise to follow his lead more often. Anyway, now I've done my bit, I have a class of pupils who still attend this school to teach.

I was expecting the other guys to rip the piss outta me as we left Mr Ashwood's office. But stead, Hardjit an Amit just started checkin out some other things stuck to his wall. Five photo-copied GCSE History certificates to be precise. One belonged to some guy called Daniel Stone, the others to people called Jeff Gilliam, Leroy Fraser, Sanjay Varma an then me. All five certificates had got one thing in common: their grade. I din't get an E or a D in GCSE History, you see. I got me a muthafuckin A class, innit.

PART TWO
SHER

12

There. That's it. Remember that point right there. Soon as you feel that stretch behind your left thigh an your body weight starts shiftin to your right butt cheek. That's the biting point a this ride. Pop the clutch, slide the leather-covered gearstick, find the biting point. Ride. You're only allowed to stall three times on the actual nite so better get to know the biting point now. That's your target for Friday nite. No more'n three stalls while you're sittin beside her, driving. No more than seven stalls while you're sittin opposite her at the restaurant, chattin. You'd wanted to set a target a zero, but thought to yourself, C'mon, man, be realistic. This is just the fourth time you've driven this thing, which means Friday'll only be the fifth. Your fifth drive, your first date. Maybe you should try an keep some more weight on your left butt cheek, increase the resistance in your leg so you don't come up too fast on the clutch. Ravi'd always said ladies judge how you're gonna handle their bodies by how you handle a car. You figured that was just more a his sleazy bullshit. But still, it was the kind a bullshit that stayed in your head.

The lights go green an again you stall. Muthafucka. Easy on the clutch, you tell yourself. Then the engine screeches cos you forgot to shift back into neutral before turning the key again. The two gora guys who just checked you out as they crossed in front a your bonnet carryin Sainsbury's bags are just lovin this. At least they din't see you nearly crash the way you did during yesterday's run.

137

Keep tellin yourself, you in't a crap driver, you in't a crap driver. You driven Ravi's Beemer one time. You even driven your cousin's Benz round the block, an that's a big ride even if it's only automatic like for Americans who can't drive proply. The car you driven the most is your mum's. Every day when she an Dad went on holiday one time. But now you're finding out there's a slight difference between handlin her 1.4 litre Ford Focus an handlin a Porsche 911 GT3 Type 996.

Sometime before you do this run for real, you still gotta practise it with the music on. You in't even too sure what kind a music this girl is into. You'd figured, get comfortable balancing the Porsche first, leave the tunes till later. When later comes round, pretend the radio in't workin so there's no question bout it, you're the DJ tonite. Play some mixes you got burned. Not another one a them *Best of RnB* or *Best Urban Hits* compilations, a proper bootleg or mash-up mix. If you really gotta play a pre-recorded compilation CD make sure it's a proper desi one, but nothin too hardcore bhangra. Before hittin the play button, read the situation. If she in't impressed or looks like she regrets agreeing to go out with you, put on N*E*R*D's album, *In Search Of.* If she seems relaxed an up for a laugh, whack in *Diamonds an Pearls* by Prince – remember: retro is the way forward. Stick to the title track an tunes like 'Money Don't Matter 2Night'. Skip over tracks like 'Get Off' an 'Cream', even though they're the best ones on the album. If she asks you to play those tracks, then fine, go ahead. It won't be you who's coming onto her.

You take a left just before passing the Natural History Museum on your right. If you carried on straight you'd head towards Hammersmith an could be back in Hounslow in half an hour, cruisin along roads you'd already got figured out. Stead, Sanjay tells you to take this left here before passing the museum. You'd been inside that place one time. Some big posh shaadi, the bride was a cousin a Amit's. It was an arranged shaadi so you had loads a smarty-pants comments bout dinosaur bones an fossils an shit, but you were wise an kept them buried in your head.

You're tryin to focus on your clutch control while also thinkin to yourself, When we pass this place on Friday nite, I'll tell her we should go in there one day, check out the dinosaur skeletons. Be fun. Hopefully she won't think you're being boffiny like that Ross dickhead from fuckin *Friends*. Then suddenly: — Watch the road, Jas, I told you it was One Way round South Ken.

— Fuck, sorry.

— You weren't joking when you said you weren't good at driving in places you don't know.

— Sorry, man, it's just this car, it's hard to get used to.

— How does that prevent you from seeing a One Way sign? I can't believe you passed your test in the first place. Anyway, the whole point of having a Porsche 911 is so you can drive it like a luxury cruiser on busy roads and save the performance sports car manoeuvres for the motorway.

— Look, man, I'm just more used to my mum's car.

— You wanna borrow your mum's Ford Focus automatic, that's fine with me. But after the trouble I went to swinging the insurance to get you covered on this baby . . . you're not even twenty-five yet.

Sanjay could get as vexed as he liked with you for nearly scratching, denting or writing off his Porsche, it still won't bother you. Partly this is cos you're in the driver's seat in a fuckin Porsche. But mostly it's cos he was nowhere near as vexed as your mum got when you first passed your test an couldn't handle her Ford Focus.

— Jas! What the hell are you doing, Jas?

— It's called stalling, Mum. People do it.

— How did you pass the test driving like this?

— Mum, this happened in my test too. This exact same thing. But they still passed me. They din't scream. They just let me get on with it.

Soon after that time you decided she shouldn't be with you when you drove. An soon after that you decided better not to drive full stop, seeing as how if you ever crashed she'd have told you a thousand hundred billion times how not to have. Even back then, after you got your licence, you still din't want your own wheels. You used to think guys like Ravi and Davinder were spoilt havin their own cars just for driving to sixth form an back. Then, after you got tighter with Hardjit an his crew, you realised they weren't spoilt, they were just lucky that's all. An over the past couple a months or whatever, since we've become tight with Sanjay, you've realised that actually them guys in't even especially lucky either. They just in't unlucky.

— It's not about some shallow definition of status, Sanjay'd explained, — it's about being comfortable and, more importantly, about being comfortable being comfortable. If you leave aside all the kids wearing Burberry, too many people in this country still have such ridiculous hang-ups about having nice things. It's a wonder Thatcherism took root here in the first place.

Sanjay knew his shit. You could see why Mr Ashwood wanted you lot to learn things from him. So the way you saw things now, if a brother in't been given his own set a wheels by his twenty-first birthday, then he should be workin out how he's gonna get one himself. An that don't mean he should become a joyrider or someshit, it means he should be thinkin how to make some decent bucks a his own, take responsibility for himself. If you pass your driving test at seventeen like how you're meant to, then your twenty-first is your mum an dad's fourth chance to buy you a car for your birthday or give you one a theirs like how Ravi's mum did. Respect to you now though, Jas. You might not have a ride a your own yet, but at least you'd got enough bucks to afford a taxi to Knightsbridge on Friday nite. The taxi is plan B in case you can't get the hang a this fuckin Porsche. Not one a them skanky Nissan minicabs with an Afghan driver either, cos now you can stretch to a proper, shiny black taxi, the kind that businessmen take from the airport. Could probly stretch to a stretch limo if you wanted to, but that's a bit too pimpish. So the question is simple: do you take her out in a black taxi, in which case you'd be able to sit right next to her an maybe even get off with

her like how you sometimes see couples do. Or would it be better if
you drove her around yourself by borrowing this shiny yellow
Porsche 911 GT3 Type 996 for the evening, in which case you'd look
really slick sliding up an down the gears an shit but you'd also probly
stall a few times an look like a pehndu. You can't even think which
is the best option cos never in your wildest MTV Base dreams did
you reckon you could have this kind a option. Respect to Mr
Ashwood for settin you up with his former golden pupil, tellin him
to look out for you. If it weren't for him you wouldn't be havin this
whole taxi-or-Porsche dilemma in the first place, you'd be wonderin
which sweaty, dirty an delayed tutty tube line to take her on. Sanjay'd
said he'd never let anyone borrow his wheels before an probly never
would again the way you're handlin the thing. But the fact is, you
were handlin the thing. It's a shame you can't tell Ravi or Amit bout
this. It's a shame you can't let Hardjit see you, even when you stall.
But this Porsche is for you an you only. Well, you an a passenger –
which is why you gotta keep the whole thing hush. When Sanjay'd
first offered it, you'd thought, all you need now is a date with Samira
Ahmed so you got a reason to drive it. You din't realise he meant
driving the Porsche could be your reason for gettin a date with her
in the first place.

You try the whole South Kensington–Knightsbridge circuit again,
but this time with the music. *8701*, the third album by Usher, is the
only decent CD you can find in Sanjay's glove compartment (the
guy actually keeps a pair a gloves in there for a laugh, leather driving ones that smell like aftershave). Start with 'U Remind Me', the
track you first heard at his Wembley gig when he ripped off his shirt
onstage an all these girls started chuckin their kachhian at him. You
can feel from the slack in the Porsche's red seat belt that your own
torso really in't big enough for this shit. You even think bout maybe
endin today's driving lesson early so you can spend some time in
the gym. But then you figure, fuck it, the gym can wait till tomorrow. Usher may've had a fly bod as well as fly tunes, but you're sure
he'd rather you sat in the car driving to his tunes than sit on some

lat-pull-down bench tryin to get his build. You ask Sanjay if you can load up some a your own tunes on Friday, someone more skinny maybe. You tell him you've got it all worked out: N*E*R*D or Prince. But at the end a the day, you know you're gonna stick with Usher. You know you can handle the car while listenin to Usher, so why take a risk?

After teachin you how to operate the Porsche's stereo an sat-nav system, Sanjay teaches you how to hold her car door open without lookin like a gimp: stand behind the door an keep both hands on the top a the frame, that way you won't be tempted to do that batty sweeping movement with your right arm, ladies-first-style, like in case she don't know the way out the car. He teaches you how to give her your jacket if she's cold: slowly, not swingin it like you're a bullfighter, cos otherwise something'll fall out your coat pockets, something embarrassin like your bus pass photo. Then he tells you how to stride up to the maître d': confidently but without walkin in front a Samira as you lead the way. He tells you to nod an smile at the maître d' as if you know her, then simply follow Samira with one hand on the middle a her back so she can feel your confidence through your fingertips. Warning: the maître d' will probly be one a the most fittest, snake-hipped ladies you ever saw ever, but don't give her too many stares.

Sometimes, when he's givin you all these tips, Sanjay smiles in a way that reminds you a the way your mum used to look at you when you were practising piano. She was tryin to be encouraging, she said. You hated all them fuckin piano lessons anyway but apparently you din't realise how lucky you were. You see, your mum'd always wanted to learn piano when she was a little girl but her parents couldn't afford the lessons. An just like your mum, Sanjay makes fun a you too. Soon as you start talkin bout Usher he starts singin 'U Got It Bad', that other big track from *8701*. Sometimes he even sings it when Hardjit, Amit an Ravi are around, just to shit you up. You're always shittin yourself that he'll let slip that you're sweet on Samira, that he's advising you how to chirps her, that he's providing transportation for your first date, that, indirectly, he's fuckin catering for that date by makin sure you get the best table at Vagabond's restaurant (normal waiting list for a Friday night: five weeks if you in't famous). But Sanjay keeps things discreet in front a the other guys, just teasin you with all that 'U Got It Bad' shit, saving all the helpful advice for when they weren't around.

By now you reckon you probly spent the entire two years a your adult life collecting advice bout how to pull a fit girl, though you never actually tried any a it out. Not on sober ones, anyway. Even Mr Ashwood told you one time you'd come across as a bit more together if you weren't so scared shitless a gettin knocked back. Told you there weren't no reason to think other guys were more fly than you. Told you to forget what your mum an dad had said one time at parents' evening bout you being too young to be thinkin bout girlies.

Sanjay's main pullin tip is that you should always chat up a girl without her actually realisin you're chattin her up. He says one way to do that is to slip into the conversation the fact that you find some other lady fit. This weren't designed to make the target lady jealous or nothin, it was just to make sure she din't realise you actually fancied her. An if she din't think you fancied her, she wouldn't think you were chirpsin her either. It had to be a completely covert operation. He'd also said that if the lady'd already got a boyfriend you should ask questions bout him. Not questions like What the fuck d'you see in him? Or Where does he live so I can put superglue on his toilet seat an plant gay animal paedophile porn under his mattress? Stead you'd got to sound really interested in him. You'd got to big him up even, so she'd never suspect you'd ever put him down. That way she wouldn't think you were tryin to muscle in an so she'd feel relaxed, like she was in some muscle-rub bubble bath.

— It's all part of the art of being a guy, he'd said to you. — Trust me. You need to have all this shit figured out in your head but you never act like you've got it figured out. It's a basic rule of getting laid: a lady worth sleeping with, whether she's desi or she's a non-desi, won't want to sleep with a guy if she knows he wants to sleep with her.

How to Chat Up Women Without Them Realising You're Trying to Chat Them Up. Sanjay could've written a fuckin book. You figure, he should know. Apparently he'd shagged seven different models, not famous supermodels a course, but still, proper models who'd been on the front covers a magazines like *Asiana, Asian Woman* an this desi version a *FHM* called *Snoop.* Honest to God, in't no lyin to you. You hear bout them guys who keep trophies or someshit for each new conquest. Some guys carve out notches on their bedposts for each lady they lay there. Some guys collect panties stolen from each lady they get to slip em off. Fuckin Sanjay fuckin Varma collected magazines that'd got his ladies on the front cover.

Hardjit's main tip for chirpsin ladies was to talk bout sex in sly an indirect ways: — Jus b chattin bout sex generally, like u wos chattin bout da weather or some fly new tune or someshit, he'd say. — Then da lady'll get sex wid u on her mind widout even realisin it wos u who put it in dere, u get me? Sanjay'd given you this exact same advice, except when *he* explained it he called it talkin bout sex in the abstract.

Amit's strategy had got even more side spin on it. He reckoned if you wanted to pull a girl you should try an pull her best friend first, especially if you din't fancy her best friend. Again, this weren't bout makin the target lady jealous, it just saves you from tryin to impress someone you really fancy. It's much easier to chirps her best friend an yet the target lady still gets to see you in action. Only problem is you might actually have to go out with the best friend for a while an if that happens you're totally fucked cos you've got to show her what a great boyfriend you can be an still find a reason to get yourself dumped. If you dump her, she'll tell her friend you're a bastard. That's why you all rubbished this strategy when Amit first explained it. All a you except Ravi, who said something like, — Ah safe, man. Chirpsin her best mate, innit. You get two shags for da price a one, a'ight safe, put me down for dat.

As for Ravi's own advice? Well, let's just say it was a little more straightforward than the others'. — Ah, fuck all dis plannin n shit, boys, he'd said. — I jus go up to a bitch n shag her, innit. Dat's wat I do.

In the end you ignored everyone. The whole fuckin lot. The problem for you was that the situation with Samira was different. Specifically, the situation was she's Muslim so you needed to get advice bout what you could call cross-cultural chirpsin. An you weren't gonna get no advice bout chattin up a Muslim from Hardjit or any a the others. If he din't actually take out a contract on your ass, Hardjit'd get so psycho bout it he'd fuckin rearrange your face so that in future you'd only be able to chat people up using fuckin sign language. So stead you searched your brain's hard drive under Cross-Cultural Chirpsin an soon you remembered Andy Marsh. People used to call him Randy Marsh. He was this white boy you used to know who had a thing for desi girls. You used to hang around with him back when you liked listenin to Oasis, if you really must bring it up. Anyway, Andy'd invented some rules bout cross-cultural chirpsin an although they were bout a white boy tryin to get with a Sikh or Hindu girl rather than bout you tryin to get with a Muslim, you download the file anyway.

It was a few months back now, long before Mr Ashwood made you hook up with Sanjay. You were sittin at home one day when Hardjit came over an asked you to check the word going round Hounslow that Andy wanted to try it on with this girl called Geeta Ahuja. Hardjit wanted to check the facts, find out which a the various rumours were true. Cos if he weren't psycho enough bout Sikhs or Hindus gettin with Muslims, when it comes to goras gettin with desis it's like you're talkin bout goras gang-bangin his mum. The man just din't have a sense a humour bout mixed couples, even when one time he declared: — Dey can take our food, but dey can never take our women. An so you tried to calm the situation down, take the heat off your old mate Andy even though you in't spoken to him since you stopped being a gimp. — C'mon, Hardj, you go, — Andy's bound to find fit women fit, he's still a guy after all. It in't like we're a breed apart or anything.

— Dat's da whole fuckin point, Jas, we shud fuckin breed apart. Dat gora shud muthafuckin fuck apart from our kind or da gora's gonna get himself fuck'd, u get me?

— OK, Hardj, you'd said, — I hear you, but wat'chyu want me to do bout it?

— Wat da fuck d'yu fink, Jas? Why u actin like a dumb bitch fool 4? I want u 2 chat 2 him, innit, find out how he plannin on movin on desi sistas, u get me?

— But, Hardj, I told you, he won't wanna speak to me, especially bout Geeta. Far as he's concerned I'm now another rudeboy. An anyway, man, how'ma gonna find him or his fone number? I don't even know what he does these days.

— Does it look like I give a shit? Fone a gora, man.

— Hardj, this in't *Who Wants to Be a Millionaire?* I can't just fone a gora.

— If u takin da mick, Jas, I'ma put u n dat gora in da same body bag, u get me?

In fact, to make sure he was being as psycho as he possibly could, Hardjit even stood right there next to you when you finally foned Andy.

— Yo, Andy, remember me? It's Jas, man.

— Hey, howdy, Jas. Long time. How ya doin, mate? I was wondering when you'd call, you're after my old Economics essays, aren't you? I know I promised you them but that was months back and you never rang so I've already given them to Mike. Sorry, mate.

— Er, nope. I forgot all bout that, man. I just wanted to catch up. Well, not catch up. Wanted to ask you something, actually. I know it's a bit outta the blue an that, but . . . how you been?

— Good. Got a job in Ealing Civic Centre. You enjoying the retakes and being a rudeboy and everything? Or d'ya miss us? Sunil and James are really pissed off that you don't talk to us no more cos you've got all your gangsta buddies now.

— They in't gangstas. They're my mates. Tell Sunil he should stop being such a coconut an come over to the brown side. Anyway, look, I know this sounds weird so I'll just come out with it, man: I heard from someone that you got a thing for Geeta. That true?

— Why're you asking?

— Look, I know it's a bit weird me callin —

— Who isn't sweet on Geeta? Everyone's sweet on Geeta. Geeta's fit. And you know what I'm like about Asian birds. I tell you what, I've finally been proved right about them now that everyone seems to fancy that Miss World Bollywood actress.

— You mean Aishwarya Rai?

— That's the one . . . Hang on a minute, Jas, you ain't gonna go repeat all this to your new rudeboy mates, are you? I don't want no trouble.

— Nah, man, course not.

— So then how come you're asking me about Geeta then?

— Cos, well, I'm concerned for you, innit. That's what it is. I'm concerned for you, Andy. You know, playin with fire an that.

— I can't believe you just used the word Innit. You used to make fun of people for saying that, remember? Anyway, thanks for being concerned but you can relax, man. So I fancy Geeta and Aishwarya and any other Asian girl on TV or round Hounslow. So I fancy Priya and I fancy Samira. So what? It ain't gonna happen. They're Asian. I'm white. I ain't stupid. That answer your question?

Hardjit din't believe him an truth is neither did I. One thing bout Andy Marsh: he may've been a gora but he was a gora who looked like Jared Leto.

— You serious, Andy? I'm disappointed in ya, man. You mean to say that after all these years you still in't worked out any techniques for pullin desi women? That you were just full a bullshit all the time?

— Desi?

— Brown Countryman.

— OK, but you promise you won't tell any of your rudeboy mates?

— Course I promise, man. Why'd I do that?

— Well then, I lied to you.

— Eh?

— I'm sorry, I dunno, I'm just being careful. But the truth is, Jazzy Boy, it's already happened! I didn't want to tell you at first and please don't take offence, but I've been all the way with two Asian girls already this year. It ain't just talk no more, mate. I'm serious, I finally made it inside an Indian fortress.

— What did you say?

— Well, you asked, mate. I tell you what, Jas, you're gonna have to teach me what the word ahstai means in English. I mean, I've been assuming it's Hindi for harder but I wanna be sure and, come to think of it, I don't know who else to ask. In fact, Jas, I could use a whole chat-up line in Hindi if you know an easy-to-remember one. At the moment, I find the best one is to tell her that I know she ain't allowed to go out with me cos I'm white.

— You what? How the fuck can that work?

— Trust me, Jazzy Boy. Firstly she thinks I'm direct and that I confront the situation head-on rather than playing games. Secondly, she feels sorry for me cos I start off by accepting I've failed. Thirdly, she wants to prove that actually she's an independent woman and not afraid to be her own person rather than some goody-two-shoes Asian girl. So she actually decides that I do stand a chance with her after all. You'd be surprised how many times it works, mate. I've been perfecting this for years, I should write a guidebook on it. With these easy steps, a white guy like me can become an irresistible forbidden fruit.

— Andy man, you in't being serious?

— Afraid I am, mate. Well, you asked. I guess it's finally my turn to benefit from positive discrimination.

After Andy'd told me some more cross-cultural chirpsin techniques an Hardjit looked satisfied that I'd done my job an that the gora deserved to be chattin up nurses an physiotherapists for the rest a the year, I wind up the fone call. I don't know whether to say Thanks or Cheers like how goras do. So I end up sayin Chanks.

Once I'd remembered Andy's advice for chattin up desi girls, it din't take me long to adapt it for Muslim girls. Next time I saw Samira alone in the Treaty Centre library I walked right up to her an stead a stammerin I just relaxed, thinkin bout the sound a the Porsche's engine, pretendin Sanjay was with me. That don't mean I came across like a complete stud, a course, an obviously I din't actually tell her bout the Porsche – that'd make me look like a smarmy wanker. But knowin that the Porsche was there made it easier to say what I did say.

— Samira?

— Jas? Hey, Jas, how are you?

— Look, Samira, I know you're Muslim an I know I in't Muslim. An I know the other guys'll kill me an then when they're finished your older brothers'll kill me again.

— What? What are you talking about, Jas?

— The thing is, I know I don't stand a chance with you, I was wonderin whether you'd mind if I just chat you up anyway so that you'll agree to go out to dinner with me next Saturday?

Proud a me? You fuckin should be. I practised that line a hundred times in front a my bedroom mirror an a hundred fuckin times in front a the bathroom mirror. Sometimes I practised it as Johnny Depp, sometimes as Pierce Brosnan, sometimes as Brad Pitt. But in the end I went with this cross between Andy Garcia an Shah Rukh Khan cos it just worked for me. Samira came back with a reply that she'd obviously been practising herself, only I figured she probly din't practise her lines in front a the mirror. Probly she practised it in front a all the other guys who'd asked her out.

— Jas, she said after counting bout twenty Jupiter seconds, — do you mind if we make it Friday night instead? It's just that I'm busy on Saturday, busy on my second date with you.

13

Going to Sanjay's flat made you feel like you were at some full-on Indian wedding with chandeliers, champagne an fit, fair-skinned women. An you were the scrawny, dark-skinned waiter with a saag stain on the collar a your tutty BHS shirt. Normly if you see some other desi bredren at a club or in the street or someplace an he's got bling clothes, nice trainers an a nice car, you don't automatically have to be impressed. You always got the option a thinkin they're a total wanker. Even if they got some fit lady with them, you still got other options. One option is to think she's a ho an is only with him for his bucks. The other option is to think they only just got it together that evening an she in't yet found out he's got a chota dick. But with Sanjay, no matter how hard you tried, how much you told yourself he was just some smarmy wanker flashin his cash, you couldn't help feelin like you'd just been asked to go fetch more naan roti by one a those fair-skinned wedding guests who din't even look you in the eye as she spoke.

Pullin up outside his flat after my secret driving lesson, Sanjay tells me he's got some business to deal with this afternoon an do I mind if he don't drop me home this time? Safe, why'd I mind? Knightsbridge tube station an Hyde Park Corner tube station were both round the corner from his place, depending on which corner you went round. Both were on the Piccadilly line, meanin a straight ride back to Hounslow. An anyhow, I'd tubed it up here with a return ticket, I always do every time I go see Sanjay without the other guys.

An that was gettin to be nuff times since we first parked up here in Ravi's Beemer a couple a months back. The four a us spent half an hour driving up an down back then, lookin for a spot to park the Beemer only to be told by the guy at the front desk that Sanjay'd reserved a space for us in an underground car park, right next to the yellow Porsche.

The flat was on the top floor in a converted house on some apparently big-fuckin-deal road called Something Crescent. I call it a house cos it's terraced but actually they're more like mansions. Old-fashioned an posh, five floors high an big enough to be a hotel. Soon as you got to the end a the lobby, though, you realised all this old-fashioned chandelier business was just, like, fuckin fancy dress or someshit. The lift gave it away. Some shiny silver oval just hangin there on a metal pole like a giant mini golf club. Ravi jumped as the doors slid open from floor to ceiling stead a from side to side. It'd got these voice-activated controls an practically the whole a the inside wall was a plasma TV screen showin the new J-Lo video. Staring at her, all four a us geared ourselves up to hate this Sanjay guy, this teacher's pet, this star pupil who went to Cambridge an so probly was a batty coconut who spoke like a ponce. After the lift said Fifth floor, the TV screen slid up an we stepped straight out into the guy's living room. No corridor, no front door. None a that hallway full a shoes, that table loaded with keys, unopened post, pizza delivery leaflets an minicab business cards. None a those pictures a Sikh Gurus, Hindu statues or signs sayin God Bless This House. Straight out into the sofas, coffee tables an what I'd later learn was Bang & Olufsen's latest BeoVision integrated audio-visual system hooked up to seven surround-sound speakers disguised as giant blurry black-an-white photos. The living-room lights coming on with an angry humming sound soon as we walked out the lift – like we'd just stepped somewhere we weren't s'posed to. The lights underneath the glass floor, I mean. Blue lights on either side a three streams a water runnin across the living room, underfuckinneath a glass floor.

— Don't worry, guys, you can walk on it, came a man's voice from the seven pictures around the room. — It's triple-glazed, reinforced aquamarine glass with protective perspex on top. Trust me, you can walk on the water, guys. In fact, there was a woman dancing around in here yesterday wearing Christian Louboutin stilettos and not even a scratch never mind a crack. It's really nothing but a floor-sized fish tank, only I haven't put any fish in it yet. It kind of makes you want to pee though, eh?

The voice seemed surprisingly desified. I mean, don't get me wrong, we'd been right bout this guy soundin like some posh, perfectly poncey, coconut. Worse than my mum's accent. Worse than Ravi's mum even. But there was definitely a bit a Bombay in there too, or Mumbai as Hardjit said whenever he reckoned he was some fuckin Geography teacher.

— I know what you're thinking, that I must think myself some kind of James Bond villain. People have said that to me before when they visit. Actually I got the idea for all this from that *Cribs* show on MTV. Some rap star or other has a floor just like this. I forget his name, but he also had a chair just like this leather Barcelona one I'm sittin on. Over here, guys, up here on the mezzanine.

The steps were made a that same aquamarine glass shit, with blue lights inside them but with no water an no banisters. There weren't no banisters or railings along the edge a the second level either an I din't care how reinforced the glass floor was, surely it'd break if you fell on it from up there. But I guessed this Sanjay guy din't sleepwalk. The second level was his bedroom, you see. A God-sized bed with a black satin quilt, a large mirror, a glass table with a single aftershave bottle on it, the white leather chair he was sittin in an a clothes rail just like they got in shops. There were, like, twenty suits hangin there, all different shades a black. It was the kind a bedroom I wished my mum could see, maybe get some inspiration from. Maybe then she'd stop forcing me to have that hangin *Muppet Show* shoe-tidy thing an that frilly maroon cloth on my bedside table to protect the wood from gettin scratched by my giraffe-shaped readin lamp an the whole, like, duty-free aftershave counter my aunties an cousins had bought me over the years.

One a Sanjay's black suit jackets was hangin on his shoulders over a light-blue V-neck T-shirt. As he stood up his black suit trousers looked more like baggy tracksuit bottoms that fell perfectly over his light blue Puma Mostro trainers. Where d'you manage to find trousers like that? Smart but baggy. Short enough to show off your trainers but without being too jack-up. Not in any a the shops in the Treaty Centre, that's for fuckin sure. For the first time in like two years I was thinkin maybe I should've carried on being Mr Ashwood's teacher's pet. Sanjay'd even got a slick-lookin face in a Ben Affleck kind a way, except with a bigger chin an some slick facial hair. He was the kind a desi who'd have a goatee beard even if havin a goatee beard weren't proper desi style. His thin black line was carefully shaped around his chin an mouth to form a roundish triangle. Not like Darth Vader's mouth though, more the kind a beard Craig David's got has when he's going for his Droopy the Dog look. The hair on his head was gelled back, held in place by some kind a headset with a mouthpiece that cut through his goatee an made it look like a G.

— Welcome to my crib, he said, speakin without the mouthpiece this time so that he sounded a little less related to the lift. Then he spread his arms out like he was bout to hug someone. — Forgive me. My flat's a bit extravagant. What can I say? Normality has always been a bit too plain vanilla for my liking. Anyway, believe me, this place isn't all that, as they say.

Sanjay continued talkin as he walked down the steps. — Firstly, aquamarine glass flooring isn't that expensive these days. There's a global surplus, you see. Secondly, I paid to do this place up out of a discount I got after the architects managed to screw up this particular conversaion. This mezzanine floor isn't supposed to be a bedroom, you see, but my proper bedroom is somehow part of my neighbour's flat thanks to some kind of design flaw. And I can't even take them to court because, strictly speaking, you're not even allowed to convert these properties into apartments. It's listed, you see. Some Saudi sheikh nearly got deported or slagged off in the papers or something for renovating number 24 down the road. Anyway, thirdly, London's pigeons seem to prefer my balcony to Trafalgar Square, and fourthly, the underfloor lighting combined with underfloor heating makes this place unbearable sometimes. That's why I need two of those things. He pointed to this big silver box on wheels standin in the corner with a giant tube stickin out, like R2D2 with a super-long dick. — That's a state-of-the-art portable air-conditioning unit, Sanjay said proudly as if he was on one a them American shopping channels. — Even on maximum power it's practically pin-drop silent. The apartment supposedly has a built-in AC system but it's just not enough to offset the heat. For a million pounds, give or take, you'd expect they could get the climate control right. Anyhow, these portable units were designed by the same creative team behind my Italian coffee-maker and things so at least they don't clash with the flat. I can't believe I had to roll them out of storage again yesterday. I only put them away two weeks ago when it looked like we were in for another ice age. I guess summer's arrived late again. London city, guys. I always warn any of my associates visiting from overseas that this must be the only place on the planet where both Eskimos and South American Indians could feel at home during the same bloody week.

— Yeh, man, Hardjit said, not wantin some yuppie coconut to leave him speechless just cos they'd got a bling flat, — it's really hot 2day.

I weren't sure who noticed him first but suddenly we realised there was this other guy sittin in the corner behind us. Mean face, massive, maybe bigger'n Hardjit even. His head was turned towards the far left wall – a big fuck-off screen onto which another J-Lo video was being projected but with no sound. Even more fuck-off than the plasma TV in the lift, this screen was so massive J-Lo's butt cheeks looked like two warm pillows fluffed up an stuck on the wall. The big guy was slowly squashin to death the leather armchair beneath him, his black leather jacket lookin like it was bout to rip as it stretched across his shoulders. I counted four chains hangin round his neck. Three gold, the other either silver or white gold. Wearin more rings than he'd got fingers, the guy looked like he was either some kind a bodyguard or bouncer. It weren't just his clothes and his short, fat neck, but the bald head above it.

— That there's my man Bobby, said Sanjay. — Some people recognise him when they see him here but you boys won't because you won't even have heard of the nightclubs he keeps clean, never mind been refused entry to them.

Standin level with us on the ground floor as he said this, Sanjay was bout as tall as Bobby was sittin.

— Needless to say Bobby never refuses entry to associates of mine should you ever be stuck in Mayfair at two in the morning with nothing to do. At other times of the day he hangs around here or my office, keeps me company, that kind of thing.

Bobby slowly turned his head towards us, nodded, then turned back to J-Lo.

Ravi looked at Hardjit as if he wanted to say something but settled for my ear instead cos it was closer. — I knew dis coconut'd b a batty, dey both gonna rape us, let's get da fuck outta here, man.

I just ignored Ravi. Sure, this Sanjay guy was a little weird an his Bobby bredren looked a little scary, but so what? I can't explain, but I wanted to get to know Sanjay better. He'd been to Cambridge, right? You hear bout people who go to Oxford an Cambridge an shit. They're allowed to act a little weird, cos they're so smart or someshit. An anyway, now that I'd got over the shock a seeing him, this Bobby guy just looked like a desi version a Shrek, but with a goatee beard an without the stupid ears. Even Hardjit seemed chilled with it all. After the way he'd been cussin Sanjay in the lift, I half expected Hardjit to start puttin him down. To tell him to ease up with all his frontin around in his pimped-up pad, with his yellow Porsche parked up next to his neighbours' Ferraris, Lamborghinis an Bentleys. But Hardjit just stood there, keepin his fists in his pockets. Then, thirty seconds later, he went up to Sanjay to shake hands, introduce himself an maybe prove he was as tall an tonk as any Bobby-the-bouncer. Then Amit introduced himself, followed by Ravi, before Sanjay turned towards me. — And you must be Jas.

The desi Shrek was still sittin there watchin silent music videos while we were all out on Sanjay's balcony.

— I bet you guys are Jack Daniel's men but I'm afraid my bar's only stocked with Johnnie Walker Black Label or Glenfiddich Solera Reserve, said Sanjay. — I recommend the Glenfiddich with Vanilla Coke. The different vanilla tones just crash together perfectly. I adore vanilla. But your choice, what'll it be?

He poured our Bacardi an Cokes over crushed ice made by his limited edition Sub Zero fridge an then I went with him to the kitchen to refill the ice bucket, get some olives, ask him what Cambridge had been like, how he got into Cambridge, what A-level grades he'd needed to get into Cambridge, did he row them boats at Cambridge, that kind a stuff.

— Mr Ashwood wrote my reference then I went for an interview, he said as he handed me the silver bucket. — Then they gave me a four A's offer and then I got four A's. You like these units? Specially designed for these flat conversions by Boffi. Boffi often recommend fridges from the Sub Zero range to complement their designs.

I in't even gonna try an describe Sanjay's kitchen. Not cos it was too painfully slick but cos apart from the fridge, coffee machine, tiled walls an aquamarine worktop, there weren't much else to see. The only non-slick stuff in the kitchen was a stack a empty dishes on the worktop with a Post-it note for his cleaning lady or whoever that said 'Don't put in cupboard – these dishes belong to Mum'. Later on, during the other times I went round there by myself, I found out that everything else in Sanjay's kitchen was hidden. Only he knew which part a the worktop was actually an electric hob, which bit a the worktop slid away if you pushed the right button to reveal a sink an light-sensor-activated taps underneath. Only he knew which block a kitchen tiles slid open the same way to reveal a hidden microwave, washing machine, oven or cabinets behind it. Him an his cleaning lady, I guess. Then again, once we were back out on his balcony I could see exactly what Sanjay'd meant bout the pigeons. He'd stuck thin metal spikes everywhere to stop them landin there, as if his balcony had gone to a Halloween party dressed as Pinhead from *Hellraiser*. Pigeon-proofing he called it. They'd got the same shit in Hounslow – above the entrance to the Treaty Centre, on top a the shop signs on the High Street and I think I even seen some on the Holy Trinity Church. Sanjay's spikes were people-proof too if you leant on the wrong bit a railing or on the back a the chairs. An still the chairs were covered in birdshit, the fresh slimy green oolti type stead a the white, dried-up Tipp-Ex type. We were all happy to stay standin anyway cos it gave us a better view a this blonde lady sunbathing on the balcony across the courtyard. She'd got this swimsuit that basically looked like someone had just painted a thin, silver V-shape on her skin that linked her shoulders to, well, the bottom a the V.

— Tere kaprhe kithe ne? Amit shouts in her direction.

— In ma car where she left em, goes Ravi.

I don't want to seem as pervy, immature or corny as the other guys an so I try an look away before part a my own body becomes pigeon-proof.

— It's called a V-kini, goes Sanjay, — and don't even think about it. She's a Russian oligarch's niece. She'll only go out with you if you're the heir to a global industrial conglomerate and can dine at Firebird five nights a week. Actually her family are originally from Uzbekistan. I met them for the first time last week – her uncle's trying to buy one of the nightclubs I got Bobby a job at.

— U own a nightclub? goes Hardjit. — We thoughts u was like an investment banker or someshit.

— No, I don't own it, I'm advising the club's owners. Sort of like a consultant, only without the spreadsheets, dreary work socials and boring suits. Since you ask, it's owned by a consortium of financiers from Saudi Arabia and Turkmenistan at the moment. But they've had one of those scandals there so they're looking for an exit.

— Safe, goes Hardjit, — u mean like a drugs bust, innit?

— Hmmm . . . Well, more like Eastern European busts if you must know. A damn shame. They doubled the joint's turnover and they hadn't even had surgery. Unlike that specimen across my courtyard, he says, pointin at the silver V woman an then pourin another whisky for himself. — I know she's some distance away but I swear she's gone from a C to a double D since she moved in last year. Anyway, enough enjoying the view from up here. I understand from Mr Ashwood that I'm to somehow inspire you guys to fulfil your true potential, become more racially integrated. He told me he wanted you to realise your inner social consciousness or something. That sound correct?

— Yeh, Mr Ashwood said we could learn from you, innit, Ravi goes, still checkin out the sunbather. — Learn from your success story so dat we do more schoolwork n dat, stay off da street n dat.

— Indeed. He told me all I'd need to do was talk about myself. I have to admit, I did have a good chuckle.

I felt like laughin at him now. I mean, did the desi or did the desi not just say the word chuckle? He may have gone to Cambridge an everything but even back when I was the gimpiest pehndu hangin with the dickless coconuts in Hounslow I never once used the word chuckle. Batty boys chuckle. Ponces chuckle. Proper guys either grin or full-on crack up. None a that chuckle shit.

— Hahahahaha, says Hardjit, fuckin chucklin. Like as if he knew why Sanjay'd started all this chucklin shit in the first place.

Sanjay just looks at Hardjit an says, — I think we should all go back inside now.

*   *   *

The glass coffee table lit up as he put his third whisky on it an gestured at the white sofas next to his desi Shrek mate. Despite lookin like they were made a metal, the sofas melted like large, leather marshmallows soon as we sat our in-awe asses down. I put my half-full glass a Bacardi an Coke next to these framed photos on this side-board beside me. I couldn't make out all the photos from this angle but one or two were obviously his mum an dad. Another was at some family wedding, I guess, cos they were all standin in a mandap behind a bride an groom. Sanjay was even taller than his bald dad. The other photo I could make out was one a Sanjay lookin like a ponce at his graduation. My mum's already saved space on our mantelpiece for my graduation photo. Just a big space, she won't even stick one a her poncey vases there, don't matter that I in't even at uni yet. She's even got a brand new pashmina shawl still in its cellophane wrapping that she's savin for the fuckin ceremony. I don't want my picture on Mum's mantelpiece anyway. It'd make me feel sick. On the other side a Sanjay's photos he'd got this set a old-lookin books an I was tryin to see what books he'd got when I realised they were fuckin fake. One a them plastic DVD holders disguised as books. I'm sure he must've got loads a proper books from when he was at uni, probly stashed in one a his hidden cabinets. Sanjay looked at us diggin the sideboard, diggin the sofas, diggin Bobby's build, diggin the lights an even the cinema screen again on account a the way it was now showin the video for 'Dirrty' by Christina Aguilera.

— I'm sure Mr Ashwood would like me to tell you that this place is all down to my efforts at school, but frankly that would be the biggest load of BS since – what's that song? – 'The Drugs Don't Work'. I mean, perhaps I owe partial thanks to Mr Ashwood for my place at Cambridge, for all the doors it opened for me in the City and for my subsequent banking career. But let's face it, investment banking isn't exactly a profession advocated by do-gooding, aspir-ationally challenged Marxist public sector workers like him. And anyhow, I've moved on since then. I left the bank three years ago this month in fact. Oh how I chuckled when Mr Ashwood asked me to do this because, frankly, the man hasn't a clue what I'm up to nowadays.

— What's that then? I asked. — I mean, what is it that you're up to then? These days, I mean?

— Well, Jas, since you ask, I still arrange finance for deals and I oversee a few other businesses here and there. But it's on my own terms now. I guess you could call me a one-man private equity outfit. I'm hoping to dabble in being a restaurateur later this year. I'm backing a chef who fuses Japanese, Lebanese and traditional kosher food. Apparently it's the only fusion experience London's restaurant scene doesn't offer yet. But enough about myself. Tell me, what did Mr Ashwood lead you boys to expect of me?

— Well, we thought you'd be more like . . . you know. I mean, more a sort a . . . well, you know . . .

— Wat Jas b tryin 2 say is, well, u ain't exactly da Captain Supergeek we all reckon'd u'd b, goes Hardjit.

— Well, I'm glad you boys are impressed.

— Ease up a minute, desi, goes Amit. — Don't b biggin yo'self up n dat. Jus cos you got yo'self some nice shit n a flash restaurant, dat don't make you some fuckin role model. You ain't exactly Eminem for desi brothers, innit.

— Perhaps I don't want to be your role model. That's not why I agreed to meet you. Let me tell you something. You boys need to forget what you think you know about me, forget what Mr Ashwood thinks he knows about me. You're not here because Mr Ashwood thinks you need mentoring. I mean, the man calls me up out of the blue and asks me to somehow transform you boys into assets to society or some such. I was about to make my excuses and hang up but then he tells me a little bit more about you and I think to myself: Sure. I can turn you into assets.

14

Sanjay's business proposal for us was so simple that it din't make no sense. Basically, the man wanted us to carry on gettin fones from people like Davinder, but rather than reprogramming em an charging a fee to Davinder or whoever, Sanjay wanted to buy the fones from us instead. We'd then keep a cut a that cash for ourselves an call it profit. He said this'd mean our old customers would turn into our suppliers, he'd become our customer an everyone'd get megabucks. Yeh, right, my big brown ass, Amit'd said. The problem we'd all got with it was figuring out what the fuck Sanjay wanted all these fones for in the first place. The desi din't even want us to unblock em for him so what the fuck was he gonna do with em?

— I ain't feelin dis, boys, it well dodge, fuckin weirdness from da start, goes Amit again, standin up an steppin away. — Wat'chyu want dem fones for if dey ain't unblocked? You tryin to pimp our business? Tryin to set us up, eh? Bredren, I say we jus allow dis shit, leave dis joker n chip, you get me?

— Hey, boy, relax and sit back down, goes Sanjay. — If I don't want you guys to unblock the handsets for me you should be grateful. After all, it's less work and more money.

Amit stayed standin. — You ain't understandin our dealings, man. If we don't unblock dem da fone companies can shut dem down n da cops'll know dey stolen.

— That's my problem, Amit, not yours. It's simple business, boys.

162

You give me the goods, I'll give you the cash. To be quite honest with you guys, I can't see why you're even hesitating.

Sanjay made a big deal outta that one. Kept puttin it out there like a DJ with a Beyoncé record: Why're you hesitating? I can't believe you're dithering. Why're you worried? This is a once-in-a-lifetime opportunity of a lifetime. Why're you negotiating? The deal's already stacked in your favour. Hardjit nodded now an then but din't say jackshit. What do you say? Smart guys in Hounslow talked like they were machine-gunning you with their tongues. Sanjay here was, like, layin out fuckin landmines. Must've belonged to one a them poncey debating societies. But while Hardjit just listened, Amit stepped back in. He argued that even if Sanjay was right bout the deal, one thing he was wrong bout was he reckoned all our customers were bulk orders like Davinder's. In actual fact, some a them were just people who wanted to switch their SIM cards so they could swap handsets with their dad or whoever. Those fones we'd have to give back. The answer, according to Sanjay, was to wind down the family fone swaps an cultivate more customers like Davinder. He said we should get wise to our Economics lessons an exploit our comparative advantage.

— Wat da fuck makes you fink we wants to b workin for you? goes Amit, we work for ourselves, innit, boys.

— Yeh, man, goes Ravi, — we got our own business goin on, we got enuf bucks to make, we got places to b, we got people to see, we got ladies to entertain. An top a dat we got our A-levels goin on, you get me. I'm wid Amit. Ain't got time for dis shit. Man's probly justa pimp lookin for more rent boys, innit.

— *Retaking* your A-levels, I think is a more accurate description, goes Sanjay. — And don't flatter yourself, Ravi: even if I did have some pimping interests, you're not good-looking enough to be a rent boy, at least not the kind that makes decent money from it. And as I said, I'm already aware of your business operation. I can't imagine you're making decent money from that either if you have to resort to ripping off Mr Ashwood's mobile phone. And that, guys, is what I'm offering you: the chance to make decent money. Indecent, actually. Like I explained, you've already got the operation, the skills and the contacts that I'm looking for. I assume from what Mr Ashwood told me that the bulk of your bulk orders are stolen, correct?

— Nah, man, we don't jack nuffink, goes Hardjit. — We law-abiding, flag-flyin citizens a da state, innit.

— That's not what I asked. Anyway, tell me, how many phones do you boys usually handle a month?

— However many we wants 2, goes Hardjit.

— OK, how many do you usually want to?

— Depends, innit. Twenty, sometimes thirty. Depends if we got a big contract goin on, u get me?

— How many *could* you handle? I mean if you really, really tried?

— Depends, innit. Fifty or sixty if we want'd 2.

— Hmm. How about the two hundred I need?

— Watever, man.

— And exactly how much money do you make, if it isn't too rude to ask?

— Enuf.

— How much is enough?

— Fuck knows . . .

— You don't know? I'm not the tax inspector, Hardjit, I'm a potentially lucrative business partner.

— Depend on da size a da order, man. We give discounts 2 our best customers, innit, like proper businessmen. A'ight then, thirty bucks a fone then.

Sanjay slams his empty whisky glass on the coffee table an leans back in his sofa with his hands on his forehead. — What are you boys? Deaf? I'm offering to pay you 120 pounds for each stolen handset compared to the pocket money you make doing what you do now. I don't even want you to expend your labour unblocking the bloody things, I want them just as they are. And you're sitting here hesitating? Negotiating? It'll be easy money for you if you're as

networked into Hounslow's grey mobile-phone market as Mr
Ashwood suggested you are.

— So wat'chyu get outta dis, man?

— None of your business, Amit.

— You said we partners.

— OK, I get a steady source of supply. Look, why don't I make
it really simple and easy for you: I'll give you 180 pounds per handset, you seal the deal now. Do the maths. But once again, I'm really
disappointed with your hesitation. You guys don't exactly live up
to your reputation as the hard men of Hounslow. I mean, what
have they been doing back there? Putting oestrogen in the local
water supply?

— Jus tell us wat exactly you gonna do wid da fones n maybe we
can talk some business, goes Amit, still standin. — How you gonna
sell dem for more than da people we already do business wid can?
How you gonna sell dem at all if they ain't been unblocked? More
important, how we know we ain't gettin into some deep stinky shit?

— I cannot understand how you've got moral concerns about this
when I'm only asking you to do what you already do. Don't kid yourselves that you're not already on the wrong side of the law. Anyway,
maybe I'm not selling them – maybe I'm collecting them. As I say,
boys, what I do with them is my business. And it's real business,
unlike that bloody SIM card-swapping hobby of yours. I'd have
thought that by now you boys would be growing tired of hanging
around Hounslow pretending to be tough. I'm presenting you with
an opportunity to stop pretending. You should be treating me like
Father Christmas. You say you're businessmen. Well then, forget
about your prices, what about your profits? I mean, what kind of
profits does your existing business model yield anyway?

The others look at me for this one. — Well, it's a volume business, I go. — Tight operational margins an that.

— You what? What about your last order? What were the margins
on your last order?

— Well, I think we actually might've made a loss on that. You know, cos Ravi broke one a the fones so we had to pay this guy Davinder, an we had to pay his parking fine.

— Davinder's our most safe customer, innit, goes Ravi.

— Oh, already foul of the law and what have you got to show for it? A financial loss. And on top of that you pay your customers' parking fines, do you? What's that about then? Goodwill? Come on, boys, where's your self-respect? If you treat this Davinder fellow like a customer, you'll have to kiss his ass. Work with me, make your customers your suppliers and you'll never have to stoop so low. You'll be his customer, he'll kiss your asses.

— Yeah, but then *you'll* be our customer.

— Right, Jas, but I'll be a customer paying you more than six times the market rate for your supply, not charging you for my bloody parking fines. Anyway, I can't park my car illegally for a second. Do you have any idea how much attention a Porsche 911 GT3 Type 996 attracts?

— Look, man, we gots our own nice car, thank you very much, goes Amit. We got our nice gear. We got our business, innit. We appreciate your offer n all a dat, but fact is we don't need yo bucks, man.

Amit realised he weren't speakin for the rest a us when Hardjit held up his palm as if to say, Relax, desi, sit the fuck back down now. The sofas moved like a marshmallow see-saw: soon as Amit sat back down, the desi Shrek guy stood up. All six feet two inches a him, his bad BO suddenly wiping out the smell a Sanjay's aftershave. Even Hardjit sat up more straight for it. But all Bobby did was lean over an hand Sanjay the remote control for the TV cinema thing. — Listen, boss, I gots to go to work, innit. Jamal, he takin some special delivery. Wants me there early today, innit.

Sanjay took the remote an switched from MTV to MTV Base, which meant goodbye 50 Cent an hello Snoop Dogg.

— Yeah, sorry about all these theatrics, Bobby. This is just taking me a lot longer than I expected. Maybe I'll swing by tonight, buy you a drink during your break.

— Jamal says we can't drink on duty no more.

— What, not even pani?

— No. We can drink dat, Sanj. Pani is cool. Or Coke.

— I'm sure it is. Jamal charges more for bottled pani than he does for beer.

— He don't got no beer behind da bar no more. He say beer for da riff-raff only.

After Bobby nodded at us an headed to the lift, it was Sanjay's turn to stand up, stretch his legs a bit, pour another whisky.

— Well, I guess Mr Ashwood was mistaken when he led me to believe you guys were all card-carrying devotees of all that bling-bling urban youth culture. Truth is, you're just wannabes like most kids. Mr Ashwood was right about one thing, though: I *am* the right man to teach you boys a lesson. So allow me to right some wiring in your brains. For all your hesitation and satisfaction with your own lot, you boys aren't exactly left of centre, are you? I mean, never mind your D&G T-shirts, I can tell just from your designer haircuts that you don't listen to Radiohead and campaign against environmental pollution, do you? No. Conspicuous consumption, luxury brands, immediate gratification and nice things are much too important to you, that much at least you guys have already decided. But what you don't realise is that means there's no going back.

I digged the way Sanjay could use words like gratification without soundin dickless. I mean, he sounded like a ponce with his poncey debating-society slickness, an he loved the sound a his own voice, but he din't sound dickless. His argument was that, once you'd made a commitment to what he called the 'urban youth culture scene' an you'd decided that bling an designer gear in't a bad thing, then that's it. You're in. You can't be nearly a virgin, he said, either you are or you aren't.

— The word bling has made it into the *Oxford English Dictionary* precisely because it isn't some passing phase, boys. This lifestyle, these material possessions, this is how you big yourself up, as they say. You will forever be judged and judge yourselves by your luxury consumerist aspirations, your nice stuff. And if you stop trying to big yourself up, others around you will make you look small pretty quickly, believe me. So as a dear friend of mine once said, you can never have enough bling.

— Fuck, man, wat are you? Sindhi?

— How can you disagree with me, Amit? Think about it. To put it crudely, drawing a line and saying that's it, I don't want any more nice stuff, no more bling, is like stopping sex before you reach orgasm. It's like saying, yeah, that feels good, I'm beginning to really feel horny or whatever now, so let's stop and watch *Coronation Street* on TV instead. That's just the way it is.

— Look, man, if you got some sexual problems n dat, maybe you best discuss dem wid someone else, Amit goes, lookin at Ravi an then at me an then at Ravi again.

— Joke away, Amit, but the truth is you don't really have any options, goes Sanjay. — Well, of course you *do* have the option of listening to Radiohead, taking a relatively low-paid job and reading lots of books to make you feel like you've got a wealthy mind or soul or whatever. But if that isn't the path you choose then I'm afraid this is it, guys. It's not greed, it's just the way it is. Believe me, I've thought a lot about this, I used to be Mr Ashwood's favourite dork, remember. But there's no Marxist alternative any more. The fall of communism, the rise of bling. If this urban scene or society you belong to judged you by the number of books you'd read then maybe you could join a library, big yourselves up for free and give Mr Ashwood an orgasm of his own while you're at it. But it doesn't. By the way, Jas, I resent the way you're looking at me right now. I'm offering you 180 pounds per phone and you boys hesitate.

— We ain't sayin we don't want to do some dealings, make some bucks, says Amit. — We jus sayin we ain't needin to make em wid'chyu, innit.

— Look, man, Amit's jus a pussy cos he don't wanna get in 2 trouble wid his mum, u get me, goes Hardjit. — Da rest a us listenin, carry on.

— All I'm saying is that if you really knew how much money you need in this world to avoid being dragged into the cancer-inducing rat race or being a do-gooder doormat with an overdraft and impotence then you wouldn't say no to making money with me or anyone else for that matter. Guys, I know I must be boring you with my lecturing. But you have to appreciate how frustrating this is for me. It's not just about this little mobile-phone deal. It's about the whole of Whitehall and most of the economists in the City. Speaking as both an Economics graduate with an MA from Cambridge and as a former investment banker at an institution responsible for $7.5 billion worth of deals the year before I left, I can safely say nobody in the City or the Treasury has grasped the importance of the urban scene to our most basic assumptions about the economy. So why I expect a couple of rudeboys like you to grasp it, I don't know.

— Wat da fuck? Amit goes again. — Speakin as an A-level Economics retake student at Hounslow College a Higher Education which is responsible for staffing Heathrow airport, I can safely say nobody has grasped da extent to which you's full a bullshit, man. C'mon, bredren, let's chip. We wasted da whole afternoon here, Hardjit, why'da fuck you wanna hear dis banker carry on wanking for?

— You want a lesson in Economics as well as life, Amit? Sanjay says. — OK, A-level Economics students, let me teach you about what I like to call Bling-Bling Economics. Hands up who knows how we measure inflation?

— Look, we in't thick. They measure all the prices a all the goods an services a typical family buys.

— Wat da fuck, Jas? You start'd revising for da mocks already?

— Shut da fuck up, Amit, goes Hardjit.

— Exactly, Jas. Go to the top of the class. Problem is, the government doesn't realise there's no such thing as a typical family any more. I mean, obviously everyone knows that there has never really been a typical family, but the point is it's become more and more so and the more important your urban scene becomes to people, the more that is the case. What was once a niche is quickly becoming a bedrock of mainstream society with more force than any other youth subculture since, well, rock and roll, I suppose.

Even if all his slick talkin turns out to be bullshit, it's good revision. This measure a inflation Sanjay an me were talkin bout, it's basically a basket a goods an services called the RPI, which stands for Retail Price Index. The basket includes shit like cheese an socks an underwear an maybe a couple a cinema tickets an CDs. But the key question we had to ask ourselves, Sanjay said, was which fools decide what's included in this basket?

— Burnt-out, underaspiring, underachieving public sector workers, that's who, was Sanjay's own answer to his own question. — People who used to constitute mainstream society but are fast becoming a niche. It's their kind of basket. And, sure, they hold up their fancy statistical modelling and claim it's a proper average of every family. But that just compounds the problem because the government assumes people aren't trying to be better than the average. Now, maybe that's actually pretty true when you think about some British people, at least before they started wearing Burberry on *EastEnders*. I mean, in other countries they joke about how British people don't want to be better than the next guy because supposedly it's vulgar or something. Only the royal family are allowed to be blinger than the average. And as every statistician will tell you, the average moves slower than a civil servant's clapped-out car. These are the people who decide whether the cost of living is going up, not people like you. Forgive me for going on and on, guys, but we need to give greater statistical weighting to luxury goods items in the RPI. Or better still, what we need are two different retail prices indices for different groups: those who drive hatchbacks and are happy being the average, and those who want more out of their lives. And the key point is, the second group is becoming more important as more and more people subscribe to urban youth culture. Whether that's wrong or right doesn't really matter, that's the way it is. Like I said, boys, this particular subculture's not a passing phase. You can be a hippie or a punk and then one day grow out of being skint and stoned or having ridiculous spiky hair. But you won't one day wake up and say, I know, I want to be less comfortable, less well off, less sexually attractive and less healthy. If you don't like it then you have to ban urban music and MTV Base. And then what would people like David Beckham do off the pitch? And this second RPI, this second group of people who actually want to be someone, their basket of typical goods and services would include a pair of D&G jeans, some bling jewellery, some covers for China White, a pair of new Nikes, maybe even the expenses involved in throwing a wedding reception at the Natural History Museum. Instead of going to the supermarkets or Argos to measure consumer behaviour, those guys from the Treasury should go to Selfridges. They should measure more Starbucks coffee and less Nescafé. The point is, urban people have a very different shopping basket than the rest of the economy and therefore they operate at a much higher level of inflation. Gordon Brown would puke his breakfast into his copy of the *Financial Times* if he knew what this was, but the fact that he doesn't know doesn't mean it isn't true. Poor Mr Brown just doesn't realise that more and more people are developing expensive tastes and those fools at the Treasury won't pick it up until it's too late. This isn't about society becoming more affluent, this is about a subculture that worships affluence becoming mainstream culture.

Sanjay's argument was that more an more people couldn't live in the official economy when more an more people's inflation rates were runnin at double digits. That meant wages, interest rates, investment yields, everything was off. For example, suppose you was workin for a company that din't recognise the gap between the inflation rate in your urban scene an the inflation rate in the official economy, then even if they gave you an annual pay rise a 7 per cent above the official inflation rate, you'd still be an impotent mug takin a fuckin pay cut an probly needin to borrow money from the bank. Apparently Sanjay'd tried a pay cut himself a few years back when he was workin in the City. Slipped down into a five-figure salary bracket hoping his blood pressure would follow in the same direction. Did it fuck. Something must've happened to his blood pressure though cos apparently he couldn't get a hard-on while he was on a five-figure salary. Amit was like, Dude, stop tellin us bout all your sexual problems, but Sanjay just ignored him an said that even if we rejected his proposal, we should at least make sure all our future business decisions were based on this new inflation index. To save our erections if nothin else, he said.

Even if you ask any a us now, we'll still be able to explain Sanjay's theory a Bling-Bling Economics. Ravi told it to his dad (the financial adviser) soon as we got home that evening. Hardjit told his dad too an also nearly gave our Economics teacher a heart attack by coming out with it during a lesson, although our teacher reckoned it was all nonsense. My dad wouldn't be interested in this shit cos even though it was bout business, it'd sound like it was bout school. It'd be like how I tried to chat to him bout the Nazis an Bolsheviks we'd learnt bout in History. I remember Mr Ashwood told me I shouldn't let Dad bother me, said my dad probly just din't want to look stupid. I guess Dad din't mind *me* feelin stupid realisin I'd been talkin to the wall for half-a-fuckin-hour.

So when I got home that day we first met Sanjay, stead a tellin my dad bout his theory a Bling-Bling Economics, I just thought it over an over in my bedroom after hiding my signing-on bonus inside one a Mr Ashwood's old History books. No jokes, Sanjay even gave us a signing-on bonus up front that day. Another word of advice, he'd said, don't ever, ever work for anybody unless they show you some respect by giving you a golden handshake. He said he hoped 60 pounds each would be sufficient but he hadn't had time to go to the cash machine that day. The thing is, when we got into the lift an looked inside the envelopes, he'd actually given us two hundred bucks each. Two hundred bucks. We din't need no fuckin fancy lift, we could've just flown out the fuckin window. But now, two months since we started doing business with him, havin two hundred bucks in your back pocket weren't no big deal. Like Sanjay said, just do the maths. By tapping all our contacts we were turning in a steady supply a fifty jacked fones a week, easy. After payin our suppliers bout ninety bucks a fone an converting our half a the 180 bucks into a monthly salary, we'd get bout twenty grand a month to split between the four a us. That's an annual pay packet a nearly sixty grand each. But a course, cos we spent less time earning it, seeing as we din't need to unblock the fones, it was probly more like ninety grand. Matter a fact, *not* havin two hundred bucks in your back pocket these days was like not actually havin a back pocket cos you were butt naked. You never knew when you'd see a nice pair a trainers, a nice pair a jeans, a nice whatever the fuck else you'd put inside your inflation-measurement basket.

15

When something good happens they say Christmas has come early. But what's it mean when Diwali comes late? With the Hindu pandits deciding the exact date by where the moon is, Diwali's never normly on the same day each year anyway. Normly it's sometime in October, but this year we were already in November an still it weren't for like two more weeks. A lot can happen in two weeks. The only thing I can think, though, is that if things go well tomorrow nite, then by the time Diwali comes round I might've got a girlfriend called Samira Ahmed. That'd be a Diwali resolution worth stickin to. Don't even matter that havin her as my girlfriend on Diwali wouldn't actually mean jack, what with her being Muslim an everything. Cos if she was my girlfriend on Diwali then my prayers'd be, like, Thanks, stead a, like, Please. An if she was my girlfriend on Diwali then I wouldn't feel like some sad lonely loser during all a them Diwali-time events an gigs. Not that we'd be able to go to any a those events as an actual couple a course, cos we'd have to keep it all hush hush. But still, respect to the way Diwali gigs are getting blended with Muslim kids' Eid events these past couple a years. Some say Diwali an Eid are happenin closer together each year cos a the way the moon keeps movin around up there. Same goes for the Sikh celebration for Guru Nanak's birthday. Meanwhile, goras always complaining Christmas keeps startin earlier an earlier. You can see where this is headin, right? I hope Samira can too. You Muslim. Me not. So fuckin what?

Anyhow, first things first. I got two weeks to practise my bhangra

174

moves for all them gigs, two weeks to clean the house (cos, let's face it, Mum an Dad weren't gonna do any a the Diwali dusting), two weeks till I could be stuffin my face with mithai an two weeks before I could take my rakhis off my wrist. Standin in Ravi's house, waitin for him to get ready for the gym an for Hardjit to come out the toilet, it's the takin off my rakhis part that I can't wait for the most. It in't that I'm shamed a them, it's just that Ravi's mum keeps staring at them while she's waitin for her friend to come pick her up for some kitty party coffee morning. — Do make yourself at home, she goes to my wrists stead a to my face. — I'm just popping back upstairs to touch up my make-up. Cut through her posh, poncey accent an it's like she's sayin, Why it is you got more rakhis than my son?

In case you don't know, a rakhi is a special thread your sister ties on your right wrist, meanin you're their brother an you'll always do your duty an protect them, uphold their honour, that kind a thing. Lookin at my wrist now, you'd think I'd got nine sisters stead a none. That's a fuckload a honour to uphold. Thing is, any girl can tie you a rakhi these days, not just your sister. That's how you can end up lookin like some big-bangled desi bride, the ones with red an white toilet rolls round their wrists. Your rakhi-sisters tie the threads in August an according to some families you're meant to wear em till after Diwali. I reckon whoever invented rakhis must've been a well-built bloke cos if they'd got my skinny wrists then no way they'd focus female attention on em right in the middle a short-sleeve season. In return for havin a rakhi tied on your wrist you give your rakhi-sister some cash. That's the deal: thread for cash. I guess maybe it could've been invented by a girl. Sanjay told me he reckoned rakhi represented a sister tax. He was pretty clever in that way. But then, he did give all his rakhi-sisters three hundred bucks each. Like a lot a desi guys I know, Sanjay'd taken off his rakhis long before Diwali anyway. Said he hadn't even left em on for a day. I don't blame him. The colour runs whenever you take a shower an stains your towel an bed sheets an shit. It in't ever just a simple piece a thread either: sometimes it's some big spangly golden cord, sometimes with some itchy, blingy decoration in the middle. Last year, Hardjit's sister tied me a funky bracelet a beads an I thought, safe, I'll wear this till Diwali no sweat. Problem was nobody else realised it was a rakhi, stead they thought I'd become one a them batty boys, the kind who try an look like Peter Andre by wearin beads from Top Man. Amit's sister always tied us one a them scratchy ones an, this year, one a Ravi's first cousins called Anita tied us all some shiny blue an silver thing. Me not havin no sisters or female cousins a my own for tyin rakhis might've saved the other guys some bucks but it also pissed em off big time. You see, the more rakhis you got, the bigger man you are, with loads a ladies under your brotherly protection. Out a the four a us, Amit'd always got the most cos he'd got so many second an third cousins an all their female friends. Maybe you can do in-laws as well, so if I'm really, really lucky then next year Samira's sisters'll tie me too? But I s'pose if I'm really, really unlucky I'll get one from Samira herself, except a course she's Muslim an Muslims don't do rakhis. An suddenly I'm thinkin: if she comes out with any a that sister-brother shit tomorrow nite then she can tie me a rakhi made out a Gillette razor blades, you get me.

If rakhi *is* a sister tax, it'd be what our Economics teacher calls a progressive tax cos the more bucks you got, the more bucks you gotta pay. It weren't that you'd pay more to each rakhi-sister, it's just that you'd have more rakhi-sisters cos you'd have more mates. With the amount a bucks we were makin now, though, I reckoned by next August we'd probly be wearin the most rakhis a any desis in Hounslow. The guy we'd got to beat was the guy ringing Ravi's front door right now. Davinder was wearin so many rakhis on his right wrist, they made the Cartier watch on his left wrist look like it was just some tutty one-ounce silver bracelet. As well as all the usual sisters, cousins, friends an friends' sisters, he'd also got all his business contacts' sisters. An the number a business contacts he'd got had grown thanks to us. Even though we'd got our new dealings with Sanjay, Davinder an his crew were still our biggest customers – sorry, I mean suppliers. We'd asked him to bring his latest batch a fones here cos it gave us more privacy than Nando's or that Lahore kebab place opposite Hounslow bus station. It was too risky doing this shit in public, not with the amount a fones Davinder was now givin us an the amount a Sanjay's cash we gave him in return. Also, seeing as he weren't our customer no more, we din't need to kiss his butt by buyin him lunch no more.

— Kiddaan, blud, wha guanin? Davinder says, givin me a high-five with a clenched fist as I open the front door.

— Kiddaan, man, I go to him, — nothin goin on. Sub theekh?

— Hahn hahn, sub theekh hai.

Then he slaps me on the back in case I din't realise he was being friendly. Davinder was always being friendly to me now. I'm friendly back, tellin him that Hardjit's on the bog, Ravi's upstairs gettin ready an Amit's still on the way here with the cash. Apparently he'd got held up by some family-related shit to do with Arun.

— Dat's safe, Jas, I ain't in no dash, Davinder says as we head into the kitchen. — Where'd u boys go last nite?

— Leicester Square, Piccadilly. Again.

— U boys been goin up West End nuff times dese days. On a Wednesday nite, man.

— In't no choice, this club we went to's got a desi nite on Wednesdays. It's like Brown Wednesdays or someshit. Seems that more an more desi nites are being held at nite these days.

— Yeh, blud, all a sudden even my little sista's allow'd out till midnite. Dad's gettin soft, innit. Where'd'you go? Elysium? Ten Rooms?

— Nah, some new place called SilkyFlava or someshit.

Davinder says he's heard a the place, he's been meanin to check it out, he knows someone who DJs there, an pretty soon all his being friendly business starts gettin really boring. He wants to know where we ate, so I tell him we did the usual Chiquito's in Leicester Square before the club then onion rings in Burger King after. Then he wants to know what music the DJ played (Juggy D, Punjabi MC); what the entry fee was (expensive, fifteen bucks for blokes, free for ladies); what the drinks were like (five bucks a shot); what the dance floor

177

was like (green lights, that vibrating shit); what the bar staff were like (fast, female, fit); what the VIP area was like (fenced off by the dance floor stead a at the back; fit, female waitresses); what the toilets were like (no oolti, an this attendant who straightened your shirt collar after sprayin your favourite cologne); an a course, what the ladies were like (fine).

— I heard dey got nuff fit ladies goin dere, he says again cos he in't happy with my last answer.

— Theekh hai, I say, checkin to make sure the milk I'm drinkin in't already gone off, — theekh hai. But me, I prefer hangin in Knightsbridge an South Ken, innit. Leicester Square's for tourists an geeks in wolf's clothing, you get me?

Then I have to explain to Davinder the whole sheep-wolf-textiles thing but he interrupts me halfway to say, — Nice garms, man, where'd u get em?

— FCUK, I reply. — You?

— Safe. Cecil Gee, innit. But dis shit on yo back is well wikid. An dey say hoods are for . . . like, hoods. I mean, wat da fuck do dey know, innit? Anyway, where u boys headed so early in da morning we gots to do our dealins be4 breakfast 4?

— Gym, I say.

— U wearin dat top 2 da gym, man? U styler, Jazzy Jas, he goes, flashin a smile as if I'd just scored with a lady or something.

Davinder carries on biggin me up while lickin my butt till Hardjit an Ravi finally come downstairs. Just carries the fuck on, like he's being sarcastic, only he in't. You should've heard the man. I'd never realised what a great guy I was.

— Kiddaan, boys, I jus checkin Jas's garms. U let should pirate his style, man, he cud wear dat shit 2 town tonite, stead he b wearin it 2 da gym.

— How u know we goin out tonite? goes Hardjit.

— Cos u boys go out every nite dese days. An Ravi's beige loafers ain't being in da porch. U polishin em, right?

— Wat da fuck, man, u a detective wid da feds or someshit?

178

— Yeh, din't you know? All a dese fones I get 4 u, dey part a dis sting operation I got goin down. I'ma bust u boys, innit . . . Nah, but seriously, blud, where u boys headed tonite? How comes u ain't aksed me 2 tag along?

— It a business ting, innit, goes Hardjit.

— I'm business, man. I'm yo bestest customer.

— U our supplier now, rememba, goes Hardjit.

— Watever, man, I'm busy tonite anyway, innit.

— So wat'chyu aks us 4?

— Look, man, I jus wanna know who'ma doin business wid, innit.

— Same bredren u been doin business wid 4 da past 2 years, man. C'mon on, let's munch Aunty's kebabs while we wait 4 da cash.

Hardjit just din't get it. We'd turned Davinder from customer into supplier an still he wanted to feed him. Two mini-kebabs later we hear a car honk outside. But it in't Amit. It's Ravi's mum's friend come to give her a lift. Aunty legs it downstairs but stead a going out the front door she comes in the kitchen an scoffs half a kebab.

— Mum, din't you hear? Aunty Geeta's here. She just honked, goes Ravi.

— I'm not deaf, son, she says in a voice that's gettin even poncier than my mum's. Ravi's mum always puts on a posh, poncified accent. Ravi's dad talks like that too, it goes with his sergeant major moustache. But his dad's accent is just for business purposes (you need to be more than just *financially* literate, he'd told us one time). He flips back into Bombay mode whenever he gets angry or drunk an that pisses Aunty off big time cos she reckons he sounds Straight off the bloody boat.

— Bye, son, she goes to Ravi before, like, kissin him. — Before you go, Ravi, please leave your membership card for that Bollywood bar on the coffee table.

— Mum, Bar Bollywood is a nightclub in Mayfair. Trust me, it really ain't the kind a place for you n dad to go.

— No, not for me. Aunty Geeta's coming in for some tea afterwards. She phoned me yesterday to say her Gaurav's got a place at

179

LSE, but she didn't believe me when I told her you've joined that new West End Bollywood club. You know what that woman asked me: Are you sure you don't mean the West End boxing club? I'll give her a bloody boxing club, bloody bitch.

— Mum, please.

— What, please? I give all of you kebabs and all I ask of you is one thing.

After Aunty's gone, Hardjit's like, — Dude, why's yo mama always chattin like dem desis on da BBC? An wat'da fuck's Amit longin it out 4? Ain't got all day, u get me.

— Complicated family-related shit, I say, — said it was something to do with Arun's dowry.

— Man, why'da fuck din't dat boy n his bitch jus split n do their shaadi in Vegas? Save all a dese dramas, innit.

— Don't know why they gettin a dowry anyway, I go. — I thought it was, like, a love marriage?

— Must be a smaller dowry cos it's a love marriage, goes Ravi. — Gold n dat. Jus for respect, probly. It's da Girl's Side's duty, innit.

— You won't be sayin that ten years from now if you end up with a daughter.

— Fuck you, Jas, I ain't gonna have no daughter. All my sperms are men, innit. Matter a fact, my sperm cells got bigger dicks then dat chota maggot you got between your legs, you get me.

— Ahem. I think what my son is trying to tell you is the girl's family derive a degree of honour by offering a dowry, says a voice in the doorway. It's Ravi's dad, standin there in some kind a white salwar kameez top, grey pinstripe slacks an black leather chapples. He takes off his Calvin Klein glasses an walks into the kitchen.

— Papa, sorry, we makin too much noise? goes Ravi.

— No. I thought I might join in your discussion, if I may. Just as you've been explaining to me about that desi inflation Economics these past two months, let me tell you how the dowry business works. After the wedding, the bride will come off her father's balance sheet and onto Arun's father's list of liabilities. She is an underperforming asset that brings in no income. The dowry offsets this transfer of liabilities. Then of course there is what we accountants call exceptional charges. You could say these represent a father's final contribution to the bride's pension, perhaps a redundancy package. Think of it like this and the dowry makes sense.

— But, Uncle, I go, — Arun's fiancée isn't redundant, she's a surgeon.

— Ah, but that will change when she has children.

— It sounds to me more like a tax, like a daughter duty or something, I go in a way that would've made Sanjay proud a me. Ravi looks at me like I'm dissin his dad or someshit, but Uncle gets really excited, droppin the gorafied accent to say, — Exactly. This is exactly what it is I'm saying to you. A father's duty to his daughter.

I wanna ask whether a dowry is a regressive tax, seeing as how it's higher for parents with ugly daughters. But I don't. I change the conversation. — Uncle, if a dowry is a daughter tax, does that make a rakhi a sister tax? I figured he should know. After all, ever since leavin his accountancy firm he'd made his bucks by sellin financial advice to help other people avoid payin taxes.

— No, rakhi it is different type of duty, he says, before spendin like a-whole-nother hour talkin bout tax. — But better to pay your sisters and your in-laws. Why to pay the government? For what? So they can dig up the roads and give me traffic jam? So they can pay dole money to lazy people who call my family Pakis when they come into my brother's shop to spend their dole money on beer and cigarettes? They get lung cancer and I pay for their hospital. Bhanchods. NHS? Hah! I work like dog for private health, Indian food is better there. Defence? Bloody fool Americans should pay for it. Education? Fat lump of good it is, our beitas keep failing the A-levels. Anyway, I pay enough taxes. I pay bloody licence fee for bloody BBC and what do I get? Bhanchod Ferreira family on *EastEnders* kissing with white kurhiyaan in the street. I always tell my son, you want me to pay my taxes? I'll pay from your pocket money. I'll pay from your sister's dowry fund. As far as I'm concerned, Jas, we pay our taxes to *Her Majesty's* Inland Revenue. And when I think of it like this, I think of the Crown jewels. And though my son keeps complaining that his mother and I speak like British royalty, you know what the Crown jewels make me think of? India.

After Ravi's dad has made another cup a chai an gone back to his office, Davinder opens his rucksack to show us his latest batch a fones. His supply now accounted for nearly half the fifty or so jacked handsets we'd been pullin in every week since we'd started doing business with Sanjay. That was stead a the usual ten or twenty Davinder used to give us each *month*. An a course these days the more fones he gave us, the less we paid for each a them. Sanjay'd been right bout that too: it'd taken a couple of months, but we'd managed to turn the whole arrangement round so that Davinder'd started givin *us* bulk discounts. It made sense for him cos at the end a day he was still makin more bucks than before, it was just like he'd moved up into a higher rate a income tax or someshit. We'd still get the same 180 bucks per fone from Sanjay, but stead a keepin our cut at ninety bucks, we'd keep, say, 110 bucks for ourselves. That'd leave seventy bucks for suppliers like Davinder stead a the usual ninety. But on twenty fones a week, what the fuck did he care? Other people'd quickly found out bout the kind a cash we were offerin an pretty soon every fone scammer in Hounslow, Southall an Ealing knew they'd get guaranteed safe bucks if they came to us. But truth is, we preferred dealing with all a them through Davinder or one a the other old an trusted contacts we'd got. Hardjit said that'd keep the feds as far away from our shit as they'd always been. Said he trusted Davinder not to get his ass busted cos if he was gonna get busted for handlin jacked fones he'd've got busted years back. Matter a fact, we din't even know who half our new suppliers were cos they'd come through Davinder. That's desi networking for you. If we could only tell Ravi's dad bout this gig, maybe he'd be proud a us. Spreadin wealth through-out the community an all that. Sanjay'd take as many handsets as we could get for him, the only condition was we kept who he was top secret from our suppliers. That's why we weren't inviting Davinder out with us tonite. The rule was we'd never bring anyone with us if we were hookin up with Sanjay. An if we ever had to mention Sanjay's name in front a other people, we'd call him C for customer. That might sound like we're in some tutty 12-rated James Bond film but actually it made good business sense. Never let your suppliers know who your customer is, Hardjit'd said, otherwise they might get together an cut you out. Being a businessman is all bout havin contacts an Sanjay was *our* contact. Davinder'd asked us who our end customer was nuff times but we'd just blanked him. That was the rule. An soon he stopped askin cos the bucks were so good. It was for the exact same reason that we soon stopped askin Sanjay what he was doing with all the fones we got him. But that don't mean we din't still wonder. An I reckon I wondered more than any a the others.

A couple a weeks back, I show up at Sanjay's flat early for my second secret driving lesson. He should've known I'd be early. After all, I'm learnin to drive a fuckin Porsche. The doorman knows me by now so lets me head straight to the underground car park stead a buzzing me up to the flat. When I get down there I walk slowly an softly, not cos I mean to creep up on anyone but cos I don't want to show any disrespect to all the sleepin Aston Martins, Lamborghinis an Ferraris. Some a them are tucked up under those silky, satiny bedcovers you get for sports cars, but others are just lyin there naked, warm, their knees bent at the front-wheel arches, fuckin touchin themselves. Then I see Sanjay standin by some red BMW 6 Coupe with two other blokes. One a them's Bobby, who's lookin even more like some desi Shrek under the car park's greenish strip lighting. The other desi's got greasy black hair, a brown leather jacket, Armani jeans an one a them whining Brummie accents comming outta his overgrown goatee. — They may not be in their original packaging but five hundred more and we'll fill the truck, man, the Brummie says before lookin up, seeing me an then coughin in that way people do. Sanjay puts his hand on the Brummie's shoulder an says something like something from a movie: — Jas, my friend, you're early.

Then the Brummie moves Sanjay's hand an says to him, — You being serious, man? They just kids.

— Trust me, goes Sanjay, — or would you rather just call the deal off?

Kid or not, I'm wise enough to save askin Sanjay what the fuck that was s'posed to mean until after the Brummie an Bobby have driven off in the red Beemer.

— He wasn't talking about you, Jas.

— C'mon, man, I in't thick, you know. That desi said that thing bout just being kids right after he saw me.

— He meant my friends in general. He thinks I'm having some kind of early midlife crisis just because I hang around with people your age. So anyway, how come you're so early?

— C'mon, Sanj, it's me, don't bullshit. Who was he anyway? He was chattin bout the fones, weren't he?

— Yes, he was talking about phones. That's because he's a business associate of mine. But that's really none of your business seeing as he wasn't talking about you.

— C'mon, Sanj, I promise I won't tell the others nothin, it'll be just between you an me. Like borrowing the Porsche.

— Do you still want to borrow my Porsche, Jas? Or do you want to hang around the car park asking me more questions?

Then he smiles as if to say Just don't worry bout it. That was how he was with all a us when we asked him bout his dealings. What d'you do with a jacked fone if it in't unblocked? we asked him. What d'you do if I cancelled our business arrangement because you keep asking too many questions? he'd answer. An then that smile. Soon we'd stopped askin Sanjay what he did with the fones an Davinder'd stopped askin us what we did with them. This supply chain a not askin any questions was completed with us not askin Davinder bout all our new suppliers that came through him. All we did was make him promise we were only gettin fones from bredren like us, nothin too hardcore, none a that gangsta an guns shit you hear bout in places like Brixton. Definitely nothin that the feds could get wise to. Relax, he'd said, it was bredren a cousins an cousins a bredren only. If we din't buy the fones, somebody else'd buy them instead so, really, we'd got nothin to do with nothin being jacked.

Davinder'd told us bout one crew a suppliers who'd run the easiest operation going, jackin fones from ponces with pinstripe suits an briefcases as they came outta Ealing Broadway tube station. Stead a sellin the fone on, they'd call the guy's home (normly stored in his fone's fone book under Home) an say they'd give him the thing back for fifty quid. Those kinds a ponces'd sometimes pay even bigger bucks just to get their fones back cos they couldn't be bothered to build up their fone books again or go through all that feds-an-insurance-forms bullshit. No jokes. Even though they could probly get an even better replacement handset through the insurance, they'd rather pay, like, ransom money for their old one. We have your fone. If you want to see it alive again, bring fifty bucks inside a brown envelope an meet us at Hounslow bus station. If the feds show, the fone gets it. That kind a thing. Anyway, thanks to Davinder spreadin the word, the bredren who operated that ransom gig now just sent the fones to us instead – an we sent em a lot more'n fifty bucks for em. Bredren a cousins an cousins a bredren only, Davinder'd said they were. Maybe a couple a cousins a rakhi-sisters, but that's it.

16

Anabolic steroid abuse can shrink your balls, give you zits an make you shit like a human espresso machine. They reckon it can also make you violent an aggressive, but on the whole it's bad for you an Hardjit knew it was. So that's exactly what he was tellin the manager a the gym.

— I told'chyu man, I ain't never touch'd dat shit. All I take is protein shakes, u get me? Fuckin chocolate flavour protein shakes.

— Of course, sir, but my colleague was only asking if you'd sign a form to that effect.

— Look, chief, ma cash is all good. I earn'd it doin ma business, a'ight. I'm a businessman, a successful businessman cos dat's da way I do ma business, u get me? U lot shud b beggin me 2 b a member a dis place, not aksin me if I ever took no steroids n shit.

— Sir, please keep your voice down. And I'd appreciate it if you'd kindly refrain from swearing. The health club's policy is to take signed assurances from new members when we deem it prudent to do so. With respect, Mr Johal, we're one of the premier health clubs in west London, we can't afford to have our reputation tarnished by any oversights. I'm sure you can understand.

— Well, wid disrespect, Mr James Braithwaite-Watever-da-fuck-yo-name-is, wat me n ma bredren ain't undastandin is why'd a fellow businessman like u'd wanna b hasslin five new customas for, heh? Count us, man: one, two, tree, four, five. We all wants 2 take out dis Gold Star Premier membership package. Dat's, like,

186

four thousand bucks or someshit. We give it 2 u cash upfront if
u want, help you sort out your tax bill, u get me? On a Thursday
mornin, man. Wat da fuck kind a businessman r u, turn down
bucks like dat?

— I'm sorry, Mr Johal, but it's not –

— Or is it jus dat we ain't want'd round ere? Heh? U b wantin
us 2 take our business back 2 da Cranford Fitness Centre where we
used 2 go? Dey ain't got no problem wid us down dere. Is it cos we
Pakis, heh?

At this point Amit starts tellin him to chill, man, be cool, but
Hardjit just tuts. — U finkin us lot jus some bunch a Pakis, innit?
Fuckin call me a Paki.

Then Arun, who's come down with us today an is the fifth guy
Hardjit's talkin bout, lays a hand on his shoulder to say, Hey, Hardj,
listen to my little brother an chill. Arun then looks at me to say, Jas,
you best say something quick time or we can forget about joining
this joint an go back to tutty Cranford instead.

— Er, I think what my friend Hardjit means is we'd really regret
it if we couldn't join up today, I go. — We've come all this way with
our gym kit, the lady on the phone said it'd be no problem. I appreciate my friend is well built but I've known him for years an trust
me, he got his build through sheer dedication, six full meals a day
an a protein milk shake in between each one.

The changing rooms had got, like, twenty separate shower cubicles so there was none a them puddles a verrucafied piss an no
need for any a that pretendin we hadn't just seen each other's
dicks. An I in't meanin those saloon-door toilet cubicles with
dodgy locks, I mean more like cone-shaped fuckin space pods with
sliding doors. There were separate pods to change in an separate
pods to take a shit in. The pods were metallic blue an there was
a blue neon light strip along the drain you took a piss in that
made patterns on the glass screen protecting your knees from
splashback. Every couple a minutes or so, little machines on the
ceiling squirted out puffs a cologne, fillin the changing rooms with

mint an some kind a Moschino musk. Back at the Cranford Fitness Centre you had to, like, spray your deodorant directly up your nostrils to block out that smell a dirty underarms mixed with sweaty, blistery foot-pus.

— Fuckin steroids, man, Hardjit goes before any a us could actually say anything bout how bling the changing rooms were, — who'dat muthafucka fink he is? Ras clat bhanchod muthafuckin tutty piece a shit. Fuckin tell me I takin steroids n dat. Fuckin, u know it, I don't need none a dat shit, man. Fuckin know it, I'm da shit, I shuda show'd him how hard a muthafucka I am, innit.

Hardjit was still sayin shit like, — I'm a muthafuckin hard muthafucka, when Arun put his hand on his shoulder an said, — Hardjit, you really need to chill. Anyway, us desis don't need steroids anyway, we got enough anger and aggression from our families, innit.

Arun din't normly use words like innit. An whenever he did, I weren't sure whether he was makin fun a rudeboys or just tryin to be like us. He always seemed older'n two years older'n the rest a us. Trainee accountant for some company up in London Bridge. Drove a metallic blue Will Smith convertible, which he'd bought with his own bucks cos it in't as if his mum an dad charged him rent. He'd come to work out with us this time cos a his complicated family-related shit, which apparently he'd made even worse this morning by droppin some other shaadi-related shit on his mum without flushing away last nite's shit first. Sounded to me like the same old shit bout his mum not being shown enough respect by his lady's mum. He'd taken the day off work to go drop Reena an her mother at Terminal 3 earlier this morning cos they were going to India to do all their wedding shopping. Reena's trousseau, the wedding invites, gold for the dowry, that kind a shit. But his mum went menstrual when she found out cos Arun never took the day off work when *she* needed to be dropped at the airport. She said Reena an him weren't married yet an so they shouldn't be actin like they were, shouldn't always be spendin time together an that. It weren't respectful for Reena to keep pullin him away. On top a that, he'd been arguing with his mum last nite cos Reena's mum hadn't even gone round to say Bye. Hadn't even asked her what kind a gold they wanted for the dowry. Then apparently when his mother-in-law-to-be did finally fone his mum from the check-in queue earlier today she din't sound respectful enough when sayin shit like Bye an Is there anything your family need from Bombay? Anyway, when Arun was done arguing with his mum after he got back from the airport, Amit'd told him to come down the gym with us, work off his anger. Arun probly figured we'd get him a guest pass for the day or someshit, din't realise his little bro was gonna buy him a full eight-hundred-buck membership package. — Jus think a it as ma wedding present, Amit said as he slammed his locker shut. — Now after you married you can haul your butt down here, work off some steam whenever Reena starts naggin you n shit.

— Dude, thanks. But does that mean I have to give it back if the wedding gets called off? I mean, at the rate Mum's going you never know.

The two a them carried on with all their brotherly-love shit for a bit, but it was obvious Amit din't want Arun droppin another complicated family-related shit right there in the changing rooms. There were private cubicles for that kind a thing an, anyway, listenin to Arun's pre-marital trouble was gettin to be like watchin the same episode a *EastEnders* again an again. So Amit just narrowed his eyes to say, — Relax, bro, ain't nobody callin nothin off, before pushing open the changing-room door. — C'mon, bredren, he said, — let's go work out.

For the first time I can remember, all a us had a reason to go down the gym that day. Hardjit'd have one a his regular sessions liftin free weights. Machines were for pussies, he'd say, cos proply balancing the weight was half the effort. Amit'd be tryin to bulk up using the lat pull-down machines. Fuck balancing free weights, he'd say, if I wanted to practise my balancing skills I'd become a waiter in my uncle's tandoori restaurant. Ravi'd decided he needed to work off some ladoo flab on the treadmill, make room in his belly for tonite. Sanjay wanted to celebrate all the fones we were supplyin him so was takin us all out to one a them big-deal, seriously super-slick bar/club/restaurants he was always chattin bout. As for Arun, well, even though he never normly came to the gym, the way his mum was yellin down the fone at him all the way here, none a us blamed him when he made a beeline straight for the punchbags. Me, I also never normly saw the point in all this Mr Universe shit. Back at the Cranford Fitness Centre I'd just sit there in the stale, airless hall, some cheesy Kylie Minogue tune pumpin out the speakers, soakin up the smell a sweat an hoping for a whiff a Brut or Old Spice whenever the changing-room doors opened. Far as I was concerned, all a this bodybuilding business was the worst bit a being a proper desi rudeboy. At school, me an Sunil (that skinny coconut who I don't chat to no more) used to laugh at the way the sixth-form common room used to be like some fuckin beauty contest, only with everything the wrong way round so that guys wore tight tops to show off the size a their tits to the girls. Sunil used to say it was all the girls' fault for only going for well-built blokes. It din't matter that the flyest guys in the world, guys like Snoop Dogg, Pharrell Williams an even white boy Eminem, were actually pretty pipe-cleanerish. Take Priya. She's the kind a girl who'd knock back Johnny Depp just cos he in't got big pecs. One time, in the common room, she an Samira'd got all the guys to go all-out topless, flashin their chests, six-packs an that big V-shaped muscle that joins some people's hip bones to their crotches. All the girls shoutin an clappin, singin 'You Sexy Thing'. Gettin guys to stand in different poses, givin em marks outta ten, makin fuckin lists. Samira tryin to guess who'd be able to run fastest while liftin her. Like we'd got fuckin lions an sabre-toothed tigers an shit runnin round the streets a Hounslow that guys had to rescue girls from like we were fuckin cavemen. Back at sixth form, I bought into Sunil's line that being tonked up just made guys carry on actin like foolish cavemen an puttin their biceps before their brains. Not one time did it pop into my head that maybe I might be the fool, puttin my brains before my bollocks.

Today shit was different. Today it'd been my fuckin idea we come here in the first place. Seems like a good way to spend some a the bucks we been makin, I'd said. Fuckin newsflash jus in, boys, a good idea from Jas, Hardjit'd said. Fuck him. I so wanted to tell him the truth, tell him I'd be stridin around with Samira Ahmed tomorrow nite an wanted to keep myself firm. An I in't meanin she's some ho an we gonna get naked on our first date or nothin. But what if she brushed past my arm or maybe even held it? Better to work out a day in advance, give your muscle fibres more'n twenty-four hours to grow, in't that what you always say, Hardjit? But a punchbag is a punchbag an my head is my head an it's best not to let Hardjit mix the two up. It in't for my benefit, is what I actually said to him this morning. It's for you guys, innit. Why'd I wanna work out for?

Hardjit'd told me one time that after you hit your target rep for liftin weights, your muscle fibres grow in greater proportion to each extra rep you manage. He also told me that when you're doing a bench press, the trick is to twist your arms back a bit. That way you work your triceps as well as your pecs. You should also squeeze your pecs a little at the top a the lift. Jus clench em togetha, he said, jus like dey yo butt-cheeks n u is in da jailhouse. Incarcerat'd, innit. Dat's da way 2 exploit dese endeavours 4 maximum efficiency, u get me? I din't get him a course. Not when he was talkin like this. Forget the aggro he always worked up just before liftin weights, forget the vest that was cut so low you could see his fuckin nipple hair. The most ridiculous thing bout workin out with Hardjit was suddenly he'd come over like a teacher, using double the number a words normal people normly knew. I asked him why one time an all I got in reply was, U gots 2 get yo'self a voluminous vocabulary 2 proply do dis shit. Honest to God, that's what he said. An so, for a couple a hours, Hardjit'd become a geek. Just like all them weirdos with binoculars standin by the Bath Road watchin planes take off. Just like dicks who watch *Star Trek*. Just like all them geeks on TV an in the papers who talk bout general elections an books an shit. Just like all a them people, gym geeks like Hardjit were full a clever but basically boring shit. The guy'd talk for hours bout the correct way to grip weights, calculate different types a body mass ratios an measure the relative performance a your thyroid an hypothalamus glands.

— Dat's enuf wid da chest muscles, he said as he helped me through one last rep. — We needs 2 work on our brachialis.

The brachialis is stuck between the bone an the biceps. The bigger it gets, the further out it pushes the biceps. In case that weren't far enough though, we then did the biceps curl with a barbell, the preacher curl with an EZ bar, concentration curls with dumb-bells, hammer curls with some other kind a bar, reverse barbell curls an then more preacher curls at a preacher-curl station. Hardjit stroked the hole in a 10kg plate before loadin it onto the bar an I asked him why he had to load another weight on in the first place? Why couldn't I just do more reps with the load I'd already got?

— Cos, bruv, u do it dat way n u'll only work da slow-twitch muscle fibres. If u b wantin growth, u needs 2 work your fast-twitch fibres n dey only come into play if u b liftin heavy weights, u get me? Then Hardjit's arms did that shuddering thing again as he added another 5kg plate to each end a the bar. — For real, blud. Dem fast-twitch fibres ain't jus bigger, dey gots da potential 2 get even mo bigger. In bigger proportion 2 yo effort, man, u get me? Dat's wat I'm talkin bout, blud. Dat's wat I'm talkin bout. Even if u knacker yo'self wid all a dese light weights, da fast-twitch fibres still ain't gonna come out 2 play less u liftin heavy muthas. Dat's jus da way it is, bruv. It a hard fact a life, but it make u hard. Then he'd come out with even more a that poetic shit, sayin desi bredren gots 2 b extra dedicated cos even when we tonked up, our arms still b lookin podgy like dey made outta rubber. Other hand, well-built goras look like dey carved outta marble n black bredrens, dey look like dey made outta steel.

An suddenly he'd become a fuckin nutritionist, monitoring his food intake more obsessively than a diabetic vegan doing a Weight Watchers' diet. It was easy enough for him to pile on the calories, after all, his mum was one a them desi aunts with some kind a secret samosa factory in the basement, cookin him up whatever he wanted, whenever he wanted it.

— I don't hardly ever eat dat high-cholesterol fried shit, he said to me when I mentioned this once. — Not afta ma milk intake n ma egg intake n my egg-milk-shake intake. Which reminds me, Jas, best to drink dem protein shakes b4 da session stead a afta, u hear?

I couldn't be bothered to tell him I'd already drunk one this morning cos he'd given me this same fuckin advice every time we went to the gym. I also couldn't be bothered to tell him the advice I really needed on the protein milk-shake front was how to clean the fuckin glass. No jokes, no matter how much you whisk it, some a the powdery protein crust sticks like cement to the bottom a the glass an it gets even worse if you stick it in the dishwasher. So any muscles you build up doing weights, you knacker out tryin to scrape that shit out the glass. Apparently unflavoured whey protein is s'posed to be better, not just cos it leaves less crust but also cos it's less loaded with other chemicals, sugar an stuff that actually makes it harder to bulk up cos you end up shittin more. That reminds me a this other problem with Hardjit's Golden Rule Number One bout eatin as much as you can as often as you can: it increases the probability a food poisoning. Trust me, I been there, man. Either Hardjit's stomach is as hard on the inside as it looks on the outside, or his mum's food in't ever too dodgy for her darling sona puther beita. She cleans his fuckin milk-shake glasses, that's for sure.

Forty minutes a Hardjit being a brainy, boffiny geek was bout all I could handle. I told him maybe we should think bout leavin this place, we'd got to go out tonite, we din't wanna be knackerin ourselves.

— We ain't all bein wimps like u, he goes, — I'd go 2 my ju-jitsu class dis aftanoon as well if dere wos one, dat's how hard a mutha-fucka I am.

So I headed over to Ravi an Amit who were busy laughin at a couple a obviously gay guys on the chest press machines. But I still couldn't be homophobic enough for them cos a some inner conflict with my conscience or someshit an so then I went over to the cardiovascular area. I sighed as I settled on an exercise bike cos all a that liftin an lowering weights shit was killin me. Times like this I wished doctors could give wimps like me some kind a reverse liposuction. Or at least silicon pectoral implants. Matter a fact, fuck it, why couldn't they just wrap silicone breast implants around our upper arms?

Back in the Cranford Fitness Centre, the cardiovascular area was where all the fit Lycra-leotard-wearin ladies normly hung out. Only problem was the fit ladies were mostly desi an they mostly covered up their leotards with baggy tracksuit bottoms. Here, most a the ladies were locked away in some aerobic-yoga-Pilates-meditation class, leavin me just one lady to zone in on, which I did by staring at her in the massive mirror on the left wall by lookin at its reflection in the right wall. She was stretchin onto a bar like some pole dancer in one a them strip clubs Sanjay's always promising to take me to. She'd got long legs, long, red, wavy hair, green eyes an her white leotard was so tight round her body she may as well've been naked. Suddenly it din't matter no more that I'd spent most a the day checkin out my biceps, Amit's triceps an Hardjit's pecs an nipple hair. Or that I'd been incapable a bench-pressin more'n 30kg an equally incapable a cussin the gay guys. Matter a fact, as the lady walked in front a me I couldn't stop myself wondering. I mean, I heard a sports bras before but I in't ever heard a no sports G-string. I got an even better look at where that sports G-string may or may not have been on this lady's Lycra-buttered butt when she picked an exercise bike right in front a me. She was strugglin cos even with legs like that the seat was a little high for her an stead a just adjusting the bike, she leant a little forward. Pervy pictures an porn films I never even seen before crashed through my mind like music videos designed to kill epileptics. Clench my muscles, Hardjit? Sure. Eat meat straight after workin out? Fine, whatever you say, man. Drink lots a milk shake? No problemo. Fuck anabolic steroids cos a some other side effect they got. A hard muthafucka indeed. Then all a sudden I'm like, What the fuckin fuck are you doing, Jas? After nineteen years you've finally got a date tomorrow night with a girl you fancy an you're sittin here perving like fuckin Ravi at some non-desi lady that you don't even know.

Even though I'd managed to block out the Lycra-leotard lady, I still din't wanna stand around by myself lookin like some skinny pehndu with no mates. So I went over to Arun an started kickin bout on some lat pull-down machine that you could load up with light weights without anyone else noticing they were light. I don't know Arun like I know the other guys so I figured hangin with him was the best way to get some peace an quiet. But was it fuck. Straight away, soon as I sat down, he slid over to the machine next to me an started givin it some shit bout all his pre-wedding marriage problems. No jokes, right there in the gym, sittin on a lat pull-down machine, he started doing another one a his complicated family-related shits for everyone nearby to smell. If things were that fucked up why couldn't he just go see a counsellor or someshit? I just kept noddin, pretendin like I was checkin out the TV screens. But it became obvious I was just pretendin when they started playin some batty boy, skintight-wearing grunge band. When I started sayin the usual things, things like Aw, man, that's too bad, or even Fuck, man, yeh, he started sayin how it was good he could hang about with his brother's mates while Reena was in India. After all, we'd all be at his wedding so he might as well get to know us. An so I just listened to him, inhaling the smell, learnin how all the problems in the whole wide world had got something to do with his pre-wedding shit.

It turned out he couldn't work out too much cos his sherwani an all his other wedding clothes had already been tailor-made to fit perfect. Everything except the English suit he'd wear for the reception, which Reena's parents were going to buy him as part a the dowry – which he objected to but his mum was forcing him to accept. — She keeps tellin me not to let them buy me a cheap suit, he said. — She wants me to ask for a Versace one. She reckons anything lower than Versace would be disrespectful to us. Can you believe that, Jas? I say to her I think it's a stupid custom and I'd rather pay for my own suit. She says it symbolises the fact that I'll be looking after Reena from now on, apparently that's the whole point of a dowry. But the thing is, how does that make sense when Reena can already support herself more than I ever could? So in the end I say, Look, Mum, if I have to take a suit from them then I'm happy with one from River Island or somewhere.

— They got some fly suits in River Island, was my response, — all a those distressed ones with the funky frayed edges.

— That's not the point, Jas. Anyway, how can I wear a frayed suit to my own wedding reception? Mum'll fray my fucking face. She just don't get it. I mean, you know our mum: things she don't agree with, she don't understand. I've tried telling her all this a thousand times since me and Reena did our rokka ceremony. I keep asking her, how is it that every time you tell me to uphold our family honour it somehow involves putting Reena's family out? She says it's not about putting people out, it's about respect. Anyway, Mum's gonna be wearing a Versace dress instead of a sari to show everyone how modern she is so she wants us to match.

When it started lookin like this could be a long shit, I tried to shut him up by tellin him how a dowry is like a daughter tax an maybe he should quit stressin an just let Reena's mum pay it.

— C'mon, Jas, he goes, — you know it ain't that simple. The dowry won't make up for what Mum sees as a lack of respect. But Reena's Side are hardly gonna show her more respect now that she's been dissin them over the dowry. So now I've gotta get My Side to up the respect they show Reena's Side so that Reena's Side will then show them even more respect in return. I guess I could try and tell Mum that Reena's mum said something nice about her, that might work.

Arun realised this meant that, in the end, nobody'd really be respecting anyone, but he said at least everyone's izzat would be upheld an all their butts would be proply kissed. Cos if he couldn't get one side to start kissin the other side's butt long an hard enough soon, the other side, the side whose butt weren't proply kissed, would, like, retaliate before they'd even pulled their kachhian back up. The problem for Arun was how to get His Side to start kissin the Girl's Side's butts when his mum kept actin like she'd been farted at in the face.

When it looked like the shit on Arun's cheeks weren't just gym sweat, I tried to make the dickless fool feel better by sayin, My mum's the exact same. But this din't work cos apparently that's different. Bullshit, I said, they're all the same. Always tryin to control us so that they can live out their dreams through us. It's like they want to have our bodies, like a fuckin fancy dress outfit or someshit. Arun liked the sound a this bullshit an so I carried on. Why d'you think we end up choosing the lifestyle an the career they'd choose if they had our bodies? Why d'you think we end up havin the wedding they'd have if they had our bodies, with the wife they'd choose if they had our bodies? Arun was smiling now an loading on more weights. — Jas, you speak a lot of truth, man, but I don't think my mum would choose to marry Reena. And if I were you, I wouldn't suggest our mum's a lesbian in front of Amit. He'd probably kill you.

— No, I don't mean she'd choose Reena herself. I mean she'd choose her if she was you. It's bout controlling what you do with your body.

— Come to think of it, Mum's even got beef with the food I eat.

— Let me guess. She wants you to become one a them healthy vegetarians, make fuckin salad an shit?

— Nah, man, she wants me to eat meat again.

— I thought you did eat meat.

— I did. But I stopped cos Reena's family are all vegetarians. But Mum says I'm being a wimp cos they're the Girl's Side and so Reena should do what we do, not the other way round.

— Arun, if you've become a vegetarian then what the fuck're you liftin weights for? You probly in't got enough protein intake to feed your fast-twitch fibres.

17

Of all the days in like the last decade, Dad decides to come back
from work early today. I'm in Mum an Dad's bedroom when I hear
him strugglin to get his key in the front door. Then I hear him grunt
at Mum an ask her what she's cooked for dinner. I can't hear her
answer but I can hear her ask why he's home so early. Then it's his
answer I can't hear. I've got the bedroom door shut, you see. The
curtains are closed too, but I figure maybe the windows are open
cos I'm freezin my bollocks off. It don't help that I in't wearin no
clothes. Butt naked but for my new Ted Baker watch. I don't grab
my towel off the bed, though, cos no way Dad'll head up here. Their
bedroom in't exactly his room, you get me. It's painted fuckin pink
for a start. Then there's the flowery bedcover, flowery smell an that
flowery frilly cloth shit Mum's got going on on top a the dressing
table an chest a drawers. An every time he leaves his stuff lyin around
she hides it in its proper place. Meantime she's allowed to dump her
stuff wherever she likes. Fuckin pashmina shawls everywhere in here.
So, stead a coming up the stairs, I can hear Dad head straight to the
living room while Mum heads back to the kitchen. I press my ear
against the door an can hear Dad open his usual can a Carlsberg an
then turn on the TV to check today's cricket scores. I reach for the
towel just in case he decides to come up here an change outta his
suit. But Dad always wears his work clothes at home an so I stay
naked.

They got a full-size mirror in their bedroom so I can check out

198

the results a today's gym session. But that in't why I'm here. I sit on the edge a Mum an Dad's bed to put on my socks. A breeze sneaks through the windows an suddenly I'm feelin like a complete pehndu sittin there wearin nothin but a watch an a pair a socks. So I take off the socks an start again. This time, the white Calvin Klein chuds come on first, then the high-collar chocolate Reiss shirt, the Reiss trousers, an then I'm back sittin on the bed to pull up the socks again. The other guys'll be wearin their best garms for tonite. But I was wearin my second-best garms, save my best garms (my chunky black DKNY top an grey Prada slacks) for tomorrow's date with Samira.

Even before I put my Patrick Cox loafers on an stand up, I get this feelin I'm still gonna look like a pehndu, such a prize fuckin pehndu that I might as well still be sittin there in just my socks. Four words is all I can say: Stupid fuckin useless bitch. I'd got these new Reiss trousers 'shortened' by Mum's tailor-friend in Heston an now I could see why Mum called her a tailor-friend stead a proper friend. Too much fuckin slack in my slacks again, innit. After driving down my thighs, the slacks crash into a pile-up around my shins an then skid outta control across my shoes. Where the fuck was she lookin? How the fuck did she pass her tailoring test? Fair enough, the fact that my legs are narrower than most guys' arms don't exactly help, but it in't as if the tailor-friend din't measure me. Her old an wrinkly hands had brushed past my bollocks as she did so. I shudder again as I look back in the mirror. Then, after takin off the loafers an unbuttoning the shirt I'm just bout to drop my slacks when the door opens.

— Mum! Can't you knock?

— But it's my bedroom.

Then she asks me what the big deal is, it in't as if I'm naked an even if I was, it in't nothin she hasn't seen before. I don't answer, hoping she'll just go to the en suite bathroom or wherever. I can't stand being in the same room as her even when I'm fully clothed. Matter a fact I start gettin that nausea feelin again, the one I always get when she's around. *Go away, Mum, or I'm gonna oolti all over my new Reiss shirt an trousers.*

— I can't find my black shawl. Is it here, son? The house is feeling cold. I want to point out that she's already wearin her grey shawl, the one that matches her hair, an wouldn't she be better off just wearin a jumper or thermals or someshit. But I figure it in't my job to tell her how to dress. *I in't gonna say jackshit more than I got to, Mum, that's my best strategy for dealing with you.*

— How many times have I told you not to put your wet towel on the bed? she says. As she comes closer to me to pick the towel up, I feel like oolting all over it, over her bedcover, over her shawl. *Then I'll stuff em all into your mouth, Mum, so you'll shut the fuck up with your poncey voice an get the fuck away from me.*

— Anyway, dinner's nearly ready. Your father's home early. What are you doing in my bedroom anyway, son?

— I know. I heard him.

— Are you modelling in front of the mirror again?

— I'm tryin on these new trousers, OK? The ones that your friend Sonia altered for me. But she's screwed them up. She's such a dumb bitch fool.

— I've told you before, don't you dare swear in this house. The trousers look fine, darling. Absolutely fine. Dinner's ready.

— Why d'you always say everything's fine when it in't? You sound like you're related to the Queen a England. *It's disgusting. I wanna strangle you with your shawl when you chat like that.* — Look, I'll put the shoes on, Mum, you'll see they in't fine.

As I'm puttin the loafers on, I can't help it. Something bout Mum's ponciness an the way she's sayin everything's absolutely delightfully fine fucks me off big time an I end up havin a proper chat with the woman. I start by stressin bout this stupid Sonia woman an then I start stressin bout how all my life I been dealin with trousers that don't fit proply. It'd started when Mum reckoned she was being supersmart when we went to get my first school uniform. Buy his trousers a few sizes too big, her friends'd told her, then have them taken in an gradually taken out again as he grows. It's cos my trousers were too long one time in year seven that other kids kept callin me a tramp. It's cos my trousers were too jack-up one time that they all noticed the fuckin *Thomas the Tank Engine* socks she made me wear. It's cos my trousers were too long one time that wiping my shoes in a rain puddle din't get rid a this stinky dogshit I'd stepped in one time in sixth form. Then there was that time she made me wear one a Dad's old suits to a family wedding an I looked like the biggest idiot there. I know it in't fair to blame Mum, but you gotta understand how big a deal it is: when your slacks are too jack-up you look totally dickless but when they got too much slack it looks like you got big hard dicks stickin out your shins. Mum clearly don't understand cos she's lookin at me like I'd just fuckin slapped her or someshit.

— Why are you so miserable all the time, son? If you don't like your trousers, alter them yourself. You should be grateful I fixed your school uniform for you, your PE kit too, then I washed it every week, I still wash your clothes, I cook for you, I'm cooking for you now. If you think you're so great, why not do it all yourself?

— I'm sorry, Mum. I don't know what's wrong. It's just that we're going out an I'm gettin stressed. *I don't wanna fight with you, Mum, cos I don't wanna chat to you. Matter a fact I don't even wanna see you. Get the fuck away from me.* I spot her black shawl on the pink cane chair an pass it to her, hoping this'll calm things down, protect me from gettin the nuclear bollocking I guess I deserve, persuade her to stop chattin an leave me alone. But she just grabs it from my hand an says, — What going out?

— You know, with the guys.

— Dinner's ready. I've been in the kitchen since four. Your father's home early, I thought it would be nice if we ate dinner together. You and Harjit and those other boys always eat out these days.

— I told you yesterday I'd be eating out again.

— Again? You ate out yesterday.

— I know, I told you I'd be eating out both days when I told you I'd be eating out yesterday.

— Where are you going?

— I don't know. Mum, I'm gettin late. Ravi'll be here soon.

— I really don't know what's got into you, Jas. You don't tell us where you're going any more. Are you hiding something? Is that why you're hardly ever home? Why you don't want to see us? What is it? Are you doing drugs?

— Oh, don't be crazy, Mum. Course I don't do no drugs. That's ridiculous, I don't even smoke. *Mum, please shut the fuck up with all this bullshit. You know why I'd rather starve or go on a diet a dog's diarrhoea than have dinner with you an Dad. So why we even chattin for?* — Look, Mum, it's a place up town. I don't know the name. It begins with a V, I think. I'll have my mobile on, what difference does it make where we are?

— But you never answer when we call. And these days you're always going out with your friends.

— You didn't complain when I used to go round Hardjit's house every evening. What's the difference if we're going out?

— Because you studied at Harjit's house.

— Oh, yeh. Right.

— If you fail your A-levels again, you'll be destroying your life. And my life. How will I show my face? If you're not doing drugs then what is it? Why are you always angry with us? Always running off, not even answering the phone when we call. I think it's time I got together with Harjit and Amit's mothers again, see what they think you boys are up to, see if they know why my son hates his own home. I must phone them and invite them.

— Look, I in't doing no drugs an I in't got no homework today, Mum. Anyway, I'm nearly twenty years old.

— So? You're living in my house. You can't treat it like a hotel. If you want to come and go as you please, try pass your A-levels first.

Dad eventually hauls his butt upstairs to check out what the fuck's going on. Mum tells him her version, which I guess is the only version that matters. His baggy-eyed face looks like he's in pain, like someone's stuck electrodes into his testicles. But I know that that face an the way he's massaging his bald head really means he can't be bothered with all this hassle. Either way, seeing him makes me feel even sicker an so now I barely have the energy to get vexed. I just need them both to go away.

— Why can't you sit and eat dinner with your mother and father like a normal boy? he goes.

— I can. But sometimes I gotta go out. They're my mates.

Mum then delivers her all-time favourite line, which is Do what you want, before going back downstairs cos she can smell something burning. Once she's gone I know exactly how to make Dad follow. I'll freak him out with one a them conversation things he can't handle. You see, one thing I never understand bout that man: how is it that I hate the way he sulks an how he can't hold a conversation, but at the same time I don't really want to be around him anyway an so it actually helps me when he goes off an sulks? So what I do now is I tell him that he can't tell me to stay home an eat when he in't here for dinner himself most days cos he's so busy with his business. I wouldn't say that in front a Mum a course, cos she'd defend him an it just wouldn't be worth all the drama. But Dad knows what I'm sayin is true an so does his I-got-nothin-else-to-say routine. He just, like, massages his head, squints his baggy eyes an starts sulkin again. He's lookin really upset but I don't care cos, like I said, it's fuckin true. Apart from today, the earliest he ever gets home is 8pm on a Wednesday an that's just to check the midweek National Lottery draw on TV cos all he cares bout is bucks. He's just like Amit's dad in that way, although admittedly Amit's dad even does a quick Om Jai prayer as his lottery slip goes through the machine. Amit's dad's so funny like that, it cracks me up. Matter a fact, whenever he gets Amit to buy the ticket he asks him to say the same prayer. That's what dads do, I guess – obsess bout the lottery. Lottery an business. Business an lottery. The only one a our dads who in't obsessed with buyin a lottery ticket is Hardjit's dad an that's cos he don't play the lottery no more. That man, he cracks me up too. One time he used to lay on at least a tenner a week (their regular numbers plus four Lucky Dips). But bout six or seven months ago, Hardjit's dad told me he'd stopped playin cos he'd decided the lottery was a tax an

if God meant for him to become a millionaire then it'd happen whether
he bought a ticket or not. But even though Uncle din't play no more,
he still watched the draw live on TV to make sure his regular numbers
hadn't come up while he hadn't been playin them. Said he wanted to
make sure he hadn't lost the lottery. That way, when his numbers din't
come up yet again, he could sigh with relief an be a happy husband
for the whole evening. I remember when Hardjit's dad explained all a
this to me, I was like, wow, my dad couldn't even think like that, or at
least if he could he wouldn't be able to explain it to people. Now, Dad's
bout to go back downstairs to finish sulkin, when he looks at me an
says: – You're not doing drugs, are you?

— No. For goodness' sake, I just told Mum, I don't even smoke.

— Your trousers, son, they look funny.

— Yeh, Dad? You in't ever said nothin bout my clothes before. I
think I need a belt but my loops are too narrow.

— No, the trousers fit fine. But are they supposed to be white?
You look like that *Saturday Night Fever* fellow.

The triangular ashtrays are screwed into the fluorescent purple bar,
makin it impossible to pass one a the things to Ravi.

— Dude, they're all stuck, I shout back at him over the Arabic
rap music. — Anyway, man, I don't think you're meant to keep flickin
the ash all the time. It in't a fag.

— Say wat, bruv?

— I said it in't a fag. You in't meant to keep ashing it.

— Da fuck you tellin me hows to smoke dis? Ravi shouts, before
shuffling next to me at the bar so that we don't need to yell over the
music no more.

— You fink I ain't knowin how to smokes a cigar, bwoy?

— I'm just sayin, bruv. I mean, you did *inhale* it a minute ago.

— Hey, Jas, I'm da mack. I smoke dis joint however da fuck I
wants to, you get me? Least I ain't no batty bwoy like you, stickin it
up ma butthole, innit. Jus jokin, blud, jus jokin.

The music might be loud but the bass lines in't bouncin off the walls like they do in some a them tutty Leicester Square clubs – the ones that make your ribcage feel like there's twenty fones set to vibrate an strapped around your chest. An unlike them tutty Leicester Square clubs, you can actually smell ladies' perfume stead a Hugo Boss aftershave. It's as if the purple from the lights smells a perfume. The glow makes Ravi's white Versace shirt an my slacks look, well, purple. He's wearin his new contact lenses tonite, the ones that turn his brown eyes grey. Only now they're a bit purpley too.

Sanjay appears behind us, bobbing his head to the beat as the DJ starts mixin in some French an Arabic remix a some Missy Elliot track.

— They stick them to the bar to stop people stealing them, Sanjay goes. — I know this guy, he's got four of these in his apartment. Collects the things. The guy's lifted ashtrays from every joint in London, don't ask me how. Back at Cambridge he used to be an expert at stealing the silver candlestick holders from Formal Hall. I'm not kidding you guys, his apartment looks like a London restaurant guide. He's got a Quaglino's one on his coffee table, Bluebird on his side table, Zuma on his drinks cabinet, Oxo Tower on his balcony, Isola on his sideboard and then four of these triangle Vagabond ones in his snooker room. The funny thing is, he doesn't even let people smoke in his pad.

Sanjay carries on tellin us bout trendy London ashtrays an I'm tryin really hard to memorise every single word an every single restaurant or bar that he in't already taught me bout before, when Hardjit an Amit stride over.

— Muthafucka, check dis shit out, dat's bigger'n ma mum's car, Amit says, pointing at the chandeliers.

— Yeh, goes Hardjit, — nice.

The DJ's playin another big beat Arabic tune now. That 'Kiss Kiss' one, but blendin it in with some other remix I never heard before but which gets everyone else going. Sanjay, who despite being an Indian knows his Arabic tunes like we know our bhangra, leans over an tells me, — They mix this sample in a lot here. It's from an Amr Diab track called 'Wala Liylah'.

I turn to watch the fluorescent dance floor light up an fill up, spreadin the lilac glow all the way up people's legs. These Arabic tracks, they're so hectic even the goras hit the floor. I hear some posh ponce standin next to me go to the guy standin next to him, — Hamish mate, it's that Middle Eastern song you like. An then the other guy goes, — Oh yeh, Charlie, let's boogie.

But no matter how wikid the music, it can't drown out this other tune that's been playin in my head all evening. It's an old Bollywood song from the Amitabh Bachchan film *Hum* an it's called 'Jooma Chumma De De'. That basically means give me a kiss on Friday. But today's still Thursday.

— So, guys, I trust you're all enjoying our little boys' night out, Sanjay goes to us. — I've been a member of this place for two years now, it never drops off the circuit, not the bar, not the restaurant we just ate in, not the nightclub. That's why its ashtrays are still in demand . . . Hey, she's new, he says as his eyes take in the brunette slinking around behind the bar in some kind a Nehru-collared sleeveless top that shows her midriff above her tight leather hipsters that are either black, brown or maroon – you can't tell which in this light. — Cute bartender, ah?

Now she notices me. I'd been standin at the bar like some dickless pehndu for, like, ten minutes tryin to lock eyes with this woman, waving two rolled-up tenners in the air like everyone else. If she weren't fit like a supermodel I'd've got pissed off.

— Twenty-seven fifty, she says to me, smiling with eyes an lips that match her hipsters. But the smile don't mean she's jokin. It's really £27.50 for my beer an Ravi's Bacardi an Coke.

— I'll get these, Sanjay says, slippin her two twenties while askin, — Amit and Hardjit, what'll you be having?

— Safe, bro, we cool wid dese shots already, see.

— OK . . . No, you keep the change, honey . . . Well, guys, here's to what's turning out to be a very successful business arrangement . . . You don't need an ashtray, Ravi, the carpet's fireproof. Anyway, they lay a new one every month.

*   *   *

I tell this to Samira when I bring her here tomorrow. She laughs at me. — Fireproof? What, in case all these posh Hooray Henrys get too fast with their dance moves? She's bopping a little too quickly herself though as she leans against the bar. It's a different DJ but those same Arabic beats again. Although Samira's a Pakistani Muslim rather than an Arab Muslim, she's well impressed that I know the tune being sampled is a track by someone called Amr Diab. An then she goes, — So are you serious about these things, Jas? as she tries to lift the ashtray off the bar once more.

— Hey, why'd I make this up for? Everybody knows that the chrome triangle is s'posed to be a V, which stands for Vagabond, I explain. — So you're meant to be, like, super-trendy or something if you've got one lyin round your yard.

— Mmmm, not just trendy but *super*-trendy.

— Trendy cos you been to this club, *super*-trendy cos you stolen from it. Did you know some a the Conran places actually started sellin their ashtrays so now no one steals em no more? People'll just think you bought it, so what's the point?

— Jas, how do you know all this stuff? Samira asks, just as some drop-dead gorgeous waitress recognises me from last nite an says, Good to see you again, sir. I weren't sure how long I could keep this up. Feelin like a badass VIP whenever some barwoman or waitress recognised me from the night before, yet prayin none a them actually said something like, Hey, buddy, din't we see you here just last nite? What was that about? Dress rehearsal for the big date? Stead the waitress just smiles at me again after she's done emptying out the ashtray using a mini hand vacuum that's strapped to her palm. Samira smiles back at the waitress, then she smiles at me an asks, — Like, since when did you start hanging round here, Jas?

— Couple years back, I guess.

— Hmmm, she says, now smiling to herself. — Then tell me, what other ashtrays have you stubbed out in?

* * *

Apparently Vagabond's big rival is some club called Tramp, which in't as exclusive an top secret as this place although it was the first to name itself after homeless people. Vagabond nearly lost its licence in the 1980s cos it'd had one too many cocaine busts. They closed the private entertaining rooms an bedrooms in 1998 to keep the feds away for good. A few years later they became the first London club to frisk people for camera phones to make VIP guests feel totally safe. An then they'd had this total redesign, one that made the place look like what you'd get if a space station had unprotected sex with an ovulating Oxbridge hall.

I sit back as Sanjay explains all this to the four a us, soakin up his words like the velvet sofa soaks up my butt-cheeks. The stories, the purple an lilac lights, the chandeliers, the fit ladies trickling into the bar from the restaurant, the fitter ladies who worked at the bar, the even fitter still lady doing her stuff behind the turntables. My fone vibrates a couple a times, which means Mum's tryin to call me, see where we are. But how lucky for my health is this: you in't even allowed to *chat* on your fone in this place. The sofas were so massive if you sat all the way back it'd be like sittin up in bed. Don't ask me how come people's shoes an high heels din't leave scratches an marks. I lean back further, feelin like some kind a Godfather, knowin the other guys had got no idea tonite was all just a coaching session for me. A practice run for tomorrow's first date with a girl they din't even know I'd had the bollocks to ask out in the first place. Stead they just sat there, bobbing their heads to Beyoncé an askin Sanjay everything I wanted to know bout being slick in London but'd been afraid to ask.

— Why dey got dese upside-down lampshades? asks Amit.

— They're not upside-down lampshades, Sanjay answers. — They're fluorescent-trimmed silver champagne buckets. They only light up like that when the temperature gets above eight degrees, which is just right for the vintages they stock here.

— Why dey put carpet in da bar for anyway?

— Makes it feel more like an old living room. Makes the ladies feel comfortable, maybe take off their high heels – which they have to do anyway if they put their feet up on these sofas. They do that and one of the foot-masseur-waitresses will come over, do their stuff and add forty quid to the tab.

The club soon starts to fill up. Apparently Thursday nites are when people who really reckon themselves go out, leaving Friday an Saturday nites for plebs an tourists. Even Hardjit din't know that. While he and the other guys head back towards the bar to chirps the least unobtainable ladies they can see, I hang back on the sofas with Sanjay. Before I can even begin to bring up the subject a tomorrow nite, he's called over one a the VIP women, the ones wearin Gucci suits, clipboards an cleavage, to ask if she'll reserve the corner sofa for tomorrow nite in the name a Jas. How safe was that?

— I always get this corner sofa, I say to Samira tomorrow. — Every time I come here. It's got the best view a the floor an it in't as deep as the others so it's clearly not for lyin back an makin out like those two horny people over there.

She looks over at the miniskirt-tugging tongue-fest I'm pointin at an raises her eyebrows.

— You know what, Samira, I'd like to go over there, tell that couple to get a room. Only as it happens this club closed all its bedrooms an private entertaining rooms back in 1998. Still, someone should tell those two that this in't the kind a place for gettin off like that.

Thanks, Sanjay, nice touch, very nice touch. Make out like you don't expect to actually make out with her: check. Sound confident an unconfident all in the same sentence: check. Mention sexual stuff in an abstract way: check.

— Your friends look like they're enjoying themselves, Sanjay goes to me after he's booked the sofa for tomorrow. He's watchin one a the girls feelin Hardjit's biceps through his dark D&G shirt, the one he'd bought two sizes too small. — I bet you any money Hardjit could take her home tonight.

— To his parents' house? You in't seen his mum. She'd cut his nooni off.

— Still, look at them, they're relaxed, they're having a good time. I don't know why you don't just tell them about Samira.

— Are you trippin? I tell them that an they'd whup my ass, cut off my nooni an cut my tongue out.

— I think you're being a bit overdramatic here, Jas. In fact, you're being exactly the kind of wimp Hardjit an Amit keep calling you.

— It in't just bout me. They'd tell other bredren an pretty soon she'd get her ass whupped too. Might even get killed, man. She got three hardcore brothers.

— Look, Jas, enough of the theatrics. You aren't Leonardo DiCaprio and this isn't *Romeo and Juliet*. Nobody's going to kill anybody or whup anybody's ass, as you so eloquently put it. It's the twenty-first century. Surely people have forgotten all that 1948 stuff.

— That's the problem, man. How can Hardjit've forgot something he weren't even around to remember in the first place?

— So he won't like it that you're taking Samira out for the evening, so good luck to him. Her friends might not like it either. Good luck to them, too. But chill out, Jas, you know you're not doing anything wrong. And don't hide behind this protecting her bullshit. As far as I know there hasn't been an honour killing in London for a long time, that shit's just for the Midlands. Do you want me to tell them for you? Make it like tonight's special announcement or something?

— No fuckin way, man, don't you dare tell em jackshit.

— What're you afraid of? They'll probably congratulate you, buy you a glass of champagne.

— No way, I can guarantee that. Even if they did congratulate me, which they won't, have you seen how much this place charges for a glass a champagne? It says on the cocktail menu, twenty-five bucks. You could buy a whole bottle for that.

— Yeh, but which bottle, kid? Some high-street Moët on special offer? How much do you guys pay for a glass of bubbly in Hounslow? A fiver? It's probably sparkling white wine.

— We don't only go out in Hounslow. We been into London loads a times, we just in't ever spent twenty-five bucks on one drink before, that's all.

— Oh, of course. I forgot how well you rudeboys know your London nightlife. Living it up in Leicester Square with all the tourists, tramps an Traceys.

— Don't be so stuck-up, Jas, me and the girls go to Leicester Square all the time, Samira says tomorrow when I pull out the Tourists, Tramps an Traceys line.

— Yeh, but I'm just sayin, Samira, you know, with the tourists an that.

— There's nothing wrong with going out around Leicester Square. I never realised you could be so snooty, Jas.

Fuck. Bad one, Sanjay. An the worst part is I nearly said the exact same thing to you last nite but that fuckin American friend a yours interrupted us.

— Sanjay, pal, I know I'm late. What can I say? I just can't get enough of the shopping in this city. American clothes might cost less but it sure shows. By the way, is it true you Brits named Bond Street after James Bond?

— Hey, Dinesh, there you are. I was beginning to think you'd stood me up. Here, meet my friend Jas. Jas, meet Dinesh, one of my associates from across the pond.

I shake the American desi's hand just as the DJ cuts to another Arabic mix but with samples a Busta Rhymes. It's an even firmer handshake than Hardjit's. I in't meanin to be racist or nothin, but American desis can be such firm handshakers. An not just with their hands but with everything they say, you know? During the rest a the evening this guy says more than the rest a us put together an mostly it's bout himself. He even looks like a firm handshake, standin there in his chinos, some kind a preppy blue shirt with the top two buttons undone, a white t-shirt showin underneath an

211

brown shoes. A little over six foot with big, bulky shoulders. If it weren't for the Hindu Om ring on his finger, I'd've bet he ate a steak, burger an fries every day a his life.

— Straight in from the Apple today, he says after Sanjay's introduction. — Pleased to meet you, what was your name again? Jas? Nice white pants: you a doctor?

— No, I –

— You in college?

— Yeh.

— Which one? LSE, Cambridge or Oxford? That's normally where we hire our Brits from.

— No, they're universities. I'm at Hounslow College a Higher Education. It's for A-levels, not degrees.

— Never heard of it. Take a guess.

— What?

— What I do. C'mon, man, it's fifty/fifty, I'm an American desi so either I'm in medicine or I'm on Wall Street. Take a guess.

— Doctor?

— Bzzzzzz. Wrong answer. I work on the Street. Trade futures. That's how I met your pal Sanjay here. He's told me all about you guys and your boys' night out tonight. I'm ready to party, you ready to party? I'm ready to party. It's a bit empty though, isn't it? I only counted about seven or eight hot chicks as I walked in here. And what is it with some of their long frumpy dresses? Still, it's only half past eleven. You guys eaten dinner? Wanna eat? You fancy some food? Let's get some food and come back later.

— Well, to tell you the truth, Dinesh, I already fed them in the restaurant here.

— Sanjay, dude, I'm in town for just one night and you want me to eat Oriental fusion? I get that in the Apple. I come to London I want proper Arabic food, let's go to that Lebanese place. You hungry, Jas? Line your stomach for some heavy drinking?

— Well, I guess if you're hungry for Lebanese I s'pose I could probly stomach a shawarma, I say.

— See that, Sanjay? Your child prodigy wants Lebanese too. What's the name of that café place, the one you took me to at four in the morning last time?

— You mean Maroush?

— Maroush, man, Ma-roush. Let's all go to Maroush. You know, whenever we go to one of the Apple's poor excuses for a Lebanese joint I always tell my pals there's this little place in London called Maroush, serves the greatest kebabs in the West.

— Then you'll be glad to know there are about fifteen of them now, goes Sanjay. — It's a silent takeover of London's fast-food market. There's a new one opened in Kensington, there's one in Chelsea now, but the Knightsbridge one near my apartment is the nearest to this place.

— Sold to the man in blue. Say, why don't we stop over at Annabel's on the way back, check out the chicks there?

— What's wrong with Vagabond?

— Vagabond, yeh. Vagabond's great. I mean, look at this place. You seen the women here? It's like the Apple but without the botox. Makes me hungry for real meat first, though. Jas, go get your comrades, tell them to bring those chicks they're with.

After interrupting the other guys' chirpsin efforts an gettin laughed at by the girls cos a my white slacks, I come back an tell Sanjay they don't want to leave cos the girls they're with won't come too. I say it'll just be me coming to this Maroush place but Sanjay in't havin it. — Tell them we'll be back in an hour, they can score then. By then the ladies'll be tipsy, it'll be easier. Remind them that they wouldn't be allowed into this place if it wasn't for me. Dinesh is a good business associate and I wanna show him a good time. Why do you think we're all out tonight?

18

— Why da fuck he do dat for? Why da fuck he make us leave dem ladies behind, bhanchod? Ravi goes again as he parks the Beemer behind the Porsche. Sanjay's got a spare resident's parking permit for Walton Street so we in't gotta find a space on Beauchamp Place.

— Dey was too old 4 yo ass anyway, goes Hardjit.

— Fuck you, man, I shagged older ladies before.

— Bullshit, Ravi, wat older lady u shagged?

— Tere ma, innit! Matter a fact, I fuck'd all a yo mums – except Jas's a course. Anyway, why da fuck Sanjay make us leave dem ladies?

— Yeh n all for fuckin kebabs n lamb sausages or whatever, goes Amit. — Widout dem ladies in our car, we like a sausage factory on wheels.

The guys stop complaining once we're seated in Maroush, scoffing those garlic Lebanese sausages, humous an shawarmas. Don't ask me how he did it, but as we sit down at a table after pushin our way through the takeaway customers, this Dinesh guy somehow persuades these four fit ladies on the next table to join us. He just leans across to their table an does one a them I'm-a-confident-an-great-American-desi routines, puffing a cigar, makin the ladies laugh. Two a them are desis themselves an the other two could be, it's hard to tell under all that make-up an big, shiny jewellery. They're wearin stilettos an fuck-me boots, an one's in a short, black backless dress. One a them all the time pretendin to fiddle with her handbag strap

214

to stop her bra strap showin. One a them with a top so tight she could use a bra. An one a them's wearin a black suit with trousers that've got slits up to her thighs an all you can see under the jacket is cleavage an bronze skin, all the way down to the buttons.

— Oh, you're such a gentleman, the lady in the suit says as Dinesh holds out a chair for her an then helps push her in. Gentleman my ass, I think as he spills some drink on her suit jacket. — It won't stain, he says, — it's just good old H$_2$O. Despite him insisting she'll die a pneumonia if she don't dry her suit jacket proply, the lady keeps refusing to take it off.

— So, ladies, what'll you have? Sanjay gives it, browsing the menu. — The shawarmas are the best. You can get chicken or lamb. Or, better still, let's all get half of each and share. Waiter, we'll have five chicken shawarmas and five lamb ones. And bring us some of that humous stuff, will you, and a plate of those garlic lamb sausages while we're waiting. Wait till you ladies try some sausages and humous.

It's nearly three in the morning by the time Samira an I arrive at Maroush. Her dad had told her to be home by one but she busts her curfews as a matter a principle. An, anyway, we've both got the munchies, you know how it is. Stopping off someplace with the munchies is, like, the desi version a coming inside for a coffee. One a the stubbly-an-stylish Arabic waiters recognises me from the nite before an so he says loudly, — Good see you again, my friend. For you, sir, special table by window.

— I guess I can't get enough a your food, I say back to him.

Thanks, Sanjay. This is perfect. The dinner in Vagabond's restaurant was so bling, the club was so bling. I got all my bling boxes ticked. But this, this is the perfect chill-out zone to end the nite in. A jumped-up, nice-lookin kebab shop full a jumped-up, nice-lookin people. Best a all, it's all halal an Samira thinks that's why I've brought her here. How considerate, eh?

— This is where you come when you've got an executive kebab craving, I tell her. — The queue can get crazy sometimes, especially around two in the morning. Look around, most a the guys here are American investment bankers. But do they go an tell their global fast-food corporation clients bout it? Hell, no. They don't want to give away London's best-kept secret.

She smiles, clearly impressed, but doesn't say jack. She's just checkin everyone out, especially this blonde lady with a fur coat an fit boyfriend. I realise all we've been doing all nite is small talk. Fuckin rehearsed small talk. We're coming to the end a the first date an I din't hardly know her better than I did last week. I know it's probly nerves, she knows it's probly nerves. But before we got to Maroush we could pretend it was just cos a the loud music.

The more I listen to this American desi the more I hate him. Sittin there going on bout his work, his Upper West Side apartment, his fast life, his competitiveness, his effectual level a passive-aggressiveness. Wiping the garlic sauce from his mouth an the sweat from his head as if doing so din't look disgusting. Singin along to the music as if it weren't in Arabic. Worst a all, he in't lettin Sanjay get a word in edgeways, which means I'm gettin no anecdotes bout the place to impress Samira with tomorrow nite. Then when Sanjay goes to the loo, I figure maybe here's my chance to see if this American desi knows what Sanjay does with all the fones we give him but I can't even ask the guy cos he don't even stop to breathe. What is it bout these people? Who the fuck teaches them that it's all bout being big an loud an confident an assertive an proud a their stock portfolio? When Hardjit's American cousins came to London one time they'd, like, cheer whenever they saw their fuckin flag. They weren't coconuts but, no jokes, show em a Stars an Stripes an it's like Tendulkar scored a six. Can you imagine a desi in London gettin excited bout the Union Jack? That shit's just for, like, football hooligans, the royal family an all those dicks who go round singin 'Rule Britannia'. The fucked-up thing is, it turns out this Dinesh guy don't even work for an American bank but a Japanese one. It turns out he got sacked from an American bank. I manage to stop him tellin us this next bit a his life story by quickly askin Sanjay when he gets back from the loo: — Dude, you worked for a big investment bank once, din't you? You never told us why you left?

— Well, truth be told it wasn't that big, Jas, he goes, — it was more of a boutique, we only had about six thousand staff.

— Yeh, bruv, why'd u leave 4? goes Hardjit, leaning forward an rolling up his sleeves.

— Wow, you've got tonked-up arms, goes the lady in the back-less dress.

— U know it, someone gotta protect dese boys, innit.

She laughs politely an then looks back at Sanjay to hear his answer.

— In short, I left because they'd turned me into a whore. Giving them my body, seventeen hours a day, six days a week. The money was nice, but frankly I earn more money now for less work and more importantly I've got control over my social life.

Then one a the maked-up ladies (one who knew more words than OK, Oh really, an Oh yeh) gives it, — Yeh, I read this in a magazine. It's nice to have more time for your social life. It's called a work/life balance. My mate Sangeeta, she doesn't get home in the evening till *seven.*

— No, I don't mean more time, goes Sanjay, — I mean I have more control. Those guys at the bank, they pumped me so full of free booze and instilled such a hectic schedule of social events that I completely lost track of my family and friends. And don't think they don't do it for a reason. Every single Away Weekend or office party they said was designed for team bonding was actually designed to bond you closer to the company by breaking your bonds with your life or your family. That's where the whole thing about sleeping with as many female colleagues as you could came in. An office affair was de rigueur, as they say. If you showed signs of fancying any colleague in a skirt, the boss would actually wink at you and tell you to wait for the next office social. That's where you'd both be administered free alcohol like a pimp administers dope. Well, not me.

Sanjay's speech seemed to put him slightly ahead a Dinesh with the ladies. It totally won me over, an not just cos it was shorter than anything that the American had said all nite.

— I'll drink to that, pal, Dinesh goes as he takes out his Amex card to settle the bill. — But it's not like that at these Japanese houses. I'm telling ya, a beautiful blonde can join your team and your manager, he won't even organise a team dinner. And besides, pal, the money in banking is good. And money, after all, is what we work for.

— Damn right, goes Ravi, — here's 2 da greenback.

Then one a the ladies, the one with the suit an cleavage, asks Dinesh straight up whether he really thinks money is all that. Next she just flutters her eyes as he leaves 100 bucks cash as a tip, recrosses her legs, makes a peace sign by her right ear with a cigarette between her fingers an says, — Well, me, I don't think money's that important personally. I think there's so much more to life like friends and being well educated and going out and meeting people and, you know, education and stuff. For instance, me, I went to the best private school in London.

— Well, my philosophy on that one is simple, goes Dinesh. — The more money you make and the less time you spend making it, the more time you have to get educated and be among your friends. It's like a vite-amin. It gives you vitality. I call it vite-amin M. You guys, let me give you some good advice, he says, turning to the four a us. — Now I don't often give people advice, and when I do, they don't often take it. But let me give it to you boys all the same. Life works best if you're relaxed, impulsive and having fun. I mean, how can you sustain a relationship without those things? How can you keep reminding your sweetheart that life can be as magical as when you first started dating if now and again you can't just up and go see things together that you never knew existed before? Take her someplace where even the supermarkets sell totally different kinds of products. But how can you do those things and be that way if you're always worried about this Amex bill or that Visa bill? I'm not saying you actually need to spend the money, I'm just saying you need to have it so you don't have to think about it all the time. Truth is, money allows you to be fun and to behave impulsively. And believe me, boys, if you can't be fun and impulsive you might as well take out a subscription to the Playboy channel, buy a wrist support and some Kleenex and save yourselves some money, you hear?

— Yuk, that's *disgusting*, says the backless dress lady.

— It's just a bit of guy talk, babe, no offence intended.

Clearly no offence was taken seeing as how the four ladies din't even hesitate bout coming back to Vagabond with us. Sanjay sealed the deal by offerin the ladies tickets to next week's MOBO Awards. One a the ladies then leans over to me an says something bout the MOBO Awards being really amazing an could we also sort them out with tickets for the BrAMAs?

— Er, we'll try, I say, tryin not to sound like a dick. — We'll try.

— What does that mean anyway?

— Erm, well, I'll do my best, innit.

— No, I mean what does BrAMAs mean? What's it stand for?

— British Asian Music Awards.

— And the MOBOs?

— Music of Black Origin . . . You must know that . . . how much've you had to drink?

— What about the Brit Awards?

— I think the Brits just means the Brits. I in't sure it stands for anything.

— No, dummy. I mean can you also get us tickets for the Brits?

I'm remembering those ladies sittin here with us last nite when I realise Samira an I in't said nothin for nearly five minutes. Even after the blonde in the fur coat an her boyfriend have gone.

— Samira, can I ask you something?

— Sure, Jas. You don't need to ask my permission.

— You in't bored, are you?

— Bored? No way. Why?

— You're just . . . quiet.

— Maybe my ears are still ringing from the club. Maybe I like this shawarma. Maybe I'm just being impressed.

I know her ears in't ringing though, cos she's talkin softly.

— So does that mean you're still on for tomorrow nite?

— Tomorrow?

— You know, when I first asked you out an you said you couldn't make Saturday cos you were busy on your second date with me. I mean, I'll never forget that line. I mean, did you mean that? Or was it just, like, a line. Cos if you did then tomorrow's Saturday. But obviously if you din't mean it then that's cool. A course it's cool. I just weren't sure an that. You know how it is.

— Yeh, I did mean that. That's why I said it. Why would I say it if I didn't mean it?

— No, it just, er, it seemed a bit like you were fooling around or something, I weren't sure, you know.

— Relax, Jas. Look, if you're trying to apologise for not having organised another fancy dinner, don't worry, we can just go to the cinema tomorrow.

— No, that in't it. I'll take you out somewhere tomorrow. I just weren't sure why you wanted to have two dates one nite after the other. I mean, for all you knew you might've found me boring or ugly or something after tonite.

— I already knew what you look like, Jas. You're not ugly at all, though you might think about getting your hair cut shorter. Anyway, the truth is I was free both nights, I thought it'd be fun. And maybe I just don't see the point in acting like a teenager and spreading the whole should-I-become-his-girlfriend thing out over two weekends. Also you're not Muslim, Jas, so I'm taking a risk just by testing the waters. Maybe I wanted to spread that risk out over a shorter period of time before deciding whether or not I'm going to plunge right in.

I think bout this for a few minutes, tryin to work out whether that means she fancies me or not. Then I come out with, — You know even a Sikh-on-Sikh or Hindu-on-Hindu relationship can be risky.

— Not exactly the same level of risk, Jas.

— Well, yeh, OK, maybe the girl's dad won't actually want to kill her boyfriend or whatever, but –

— Don't worry, Jas. Firstly, you're not my boyfriend yet. Secondly, even if you were, my dad wouldn't want to kill you.

— He wouldn't?

— He probably wouldn't even have a problem with us going out. He sees himself as some kind of wise old man who's above all that stuff. He'd convince my mum not to mind either.

— So then where's the risk?

— Er, hello? My three brothers. Your three friends. That's six big rudeboys trying to kill you instead of one old dad. I think you could call that a risk, don't you? My brothers have gone to Leicester this week, I told you – otherwise why do you think I'd let you pick me up and drop me from my house?

— OK, fair enough, I say, tryin not to sound scared shitless. — But what I mean is, even a Hindu-on-Hindu relationship can have its problems cos a all those big deals bout traditions an stuff. I mean, for instance, take Amit's older brother, Arun, right. You should see the kind a grief he's been gettin even though he's marrying another Hindu.

Samira still says that in't exactly the same thing, but she wants details all the same. I figure, fuck it, Arun's already told so many people that another can't hurt an, anyway, at least this stuff in't been scripted by Sanjay. I unwrap my shawarma, take a huge gobful an even though I know I'm not s'posed to talk with food in my mouth an I'm even less s'posed to talk bout marriage on a first date, I just can't help myself. I tell her bout the general lack a respect being shown by the Girl's Side to Arun an Amit's mum, I tell her bout the dowry, the fone-call stand-offs, the Versace suit, I tell her how Arun an Reena were always tryin to get both their families to step up the respect they showed to the other family so that the other family

221

would then show them even more respect so that, in the end, I weren't too sure anybody was really respectin anybody. But at least all the traditions were being followed, everyone's izzat was being upheld an all their butts were being kissed proply. Samira starts crackin up at my butt-kissin line. I don't know why, I just know I should follow through. — So basically, whenever one family in't kissed the other family's butt long an hard enough, the side whose butt in't being proply kissed retaliates before they've even pulled their kachhian back up. The tricky part for Arun is to get his side to start kissin her side's butt even though his mum reckons she's been farted at in the face.

— Yuk, that's *disgusting*, Jas.

— Sorry. But it all comes down to this thing called izzat, innit.

— Jas, I know what izzat is. I'm a Muslim, remember. It's our word.

— A course, I say as the humous arrives, — I know that. I'm just sayin how fucked up it's got for them. If you ask me, it's all those desi soap operas on Zee TV. Think how many times they show slow-motion action replays a people lookin angry an offended. Makes desi mothers think all this izzat shit actually matters. I mean, think bout it, Samira, they spend so long watchin that crap no wonder they got to invent big dramas an insults an conflicts in their heads just to make their lives as interesting as the bullshit on TV. An the thing is, all a them soap-opera lines they come out with are probly rehearsed or someshit. That's why I say anyone who agrees to get married according to the traditional desi rule book needs their head exam-ined. It don't matter if you're a Muslim or a non-Muslim or a Sikh or a non-Sikh or a whatever or a non-whatever, you know?

The skimpy backless dress-lady accidently flashes the lace band at the top a her hold-ups as we're helpin the girls into the back a some black taxi. At least I think they're hold-ups cos I don't see no suspender elastic. After closing the taxi door on my view, Sanjay leans to me an says, — Didn't I say you could get some tasty takeaway meat at Maroush? Ah? Didn't I tell you? Then he steps to the driver's window an casually tells him to follow the yellow Porsche.

— An da lilac Beemer, yells Ravi.

I ride with Sanjay in the Porsche this time cos his American friend has decided to accompany the girls in the taxi. What a gentleman. Anyway, guess what: the next day with Samira I don't even stall this car once. Not on the way to Vagabond, not on the way back via Maroush. What really gets to me, though, is she don't even mention it at first. Like it's to be expected I'd just roll up in a fuckin Porsche 911 GT3 Type 996. It'd be different if I was Jay Kay or someone, but I'm just plain old Jas. In the end I have to bring up the subject myself by sayin something prize-deservingly dickless like, I hope you like the car.

— Mmmm, she says, — I wonder who had the balls to lend you this for the night.

— A friend, I say, off guard an confused bout why she in't assumed I'd rented it like I'd planned to tell her. — I borrowed it for the nite cos I wanted to impress you.

— Well, consider me impressed. Not because it's a Porsche of course, but because you tried. Not just with the car, but with the halal meat and the conversation. You're not just another one of those rudeboy hard-ons that you hang around with.

As we pull up outside Vagabond again, Sanjay starts checkin himself in the rear-view mirror. — Now that it's after midnight the juiciest meat in London is in Vagabond, he tells me as he's fixin his hair, straightening his collar, pickin his teeth with someone's business card. — All gone? he asks me with a cheesy grin.

— Nah, man, there's some lamb or someshit stuck on the left there.

— Here?

— No, at the top, by your gum.

Then he takes out some proper dental floss from his coat pocket an starts gettin to work. — I always take care of these. Force of habit. My brother's a dentist, he's got a Lexus.

223

— Well, you got very nice teeth, I go.

— These aren't teeth, my friend. I prefer to call them a thong-removal system. But still, you've got to keep them clean.

The bouncer recognises us from before, likes the look a the ladies we'd pulled at Maroush an so nods his head an lets all ten a us through. They just let you go straight through in a place like that, they din't even stamp our hands or nothin. When me an Samira show up around nine thirty tomorrow he recognises me again an so even lets slip a smile. He don't even mention the fact that Samira's wearin jeans. Probly cos she's so fit.

The purple fluorescent light strokes the maître d's curves even more than my eyes do. Not like all that ultraviolet shit you usually get in clubs, the kind that makes your teeth glow an shows up all your fuckin dandruff.

— Didn't you do GCSE Science, Jas? It's because they're coated with phosphor which contains a mercury vapour, Sanjay explains to me. — When that's bombarded by electrons from the cathode you get light.

— See, that's what I like about you, Jas, Samira says when I explain it to her — You've got a brain. Can you imagine one of your rude-boy friends like Hardjit explaining that?

Even the maître d' is impressed when she overhears me. Says she's worked here three years an always wanted to know. It don't matter that in my eyes Samira is the fittest girl here, that don't make the maître d' or any a the other ladies less fit. An even though I'm on a date with Samira, I don't feel guilty for staring at the maître d's thighs some more. I din't feel guilty for staring at that lady's hold-ups as she got into the taxi last nite or the Lycra-leotard lady in the gym beforehand. This is cos Sanjay'd kept tellin me that the day you stopped lookin at ladies is the day you die. Apparently that's exactly what Al Pacino says in *Scent of a Woman*. But truth is, it weren't that simple. All week I'd been shittin myself, thinkin what if Samira stands me up/knocks me back/dumps me? So I'd invented my very own Rudeboy Rule for these situations: you got to keep lookin cos how can you be expected to believe there's plenty more fish in the sea after you get dumped/knocked back/whatever if you don't keep reminding yourself bout all these fish when you're actually with someone? When the waitress leans over me to hand us our second Mojitos. When this brunette in a green chiffon dress an no apparent underwear hits the dance floor. When her friends take a break from dancin by lyin on the sofa next to ours, moanin as they get their feet massaged. When another lady leans her tight dress against the pillar to my right. I promise myself I won't look at her perfectly shaped legs or butt. To be fair, I keep this promise for thirty seconds before she decides to stand right in front a me. Then, as the line a her thong burns a hole between my eyebrows an down the centre a my nose, I got no choice but to take Samira to the dance floor.

I can't fuckin dance though, can I? Whenever it came to going to clubs with the guys I'd have the exact same problem: I felt like a dick. Other guys manage to move like Justin Timberlake but I just can't help standin there, watchin them an wonderin the same fuckin thing everyfuckintime: what would aliens reckon if they landed next to a nightclub an the first thing they saw was a bunch a people, like, gyrating to music? What the fuck would they think a the human race? Especially those people who dance with really serious faces. An once I start thinkin bout that, that's it for me, I'm fucked, I can't dance for shit. I especially can't dance to Arabic music. All I know is what I learnt last nite when this purple-jewelled belly dancer walked into the club an decided that outta all the loser-lookin guys there, she was gonna make a fool outta me. Hardjit, Amit an Ravi were crackin up an they cracked up even more when I tried to teach her some bhangra moves in return.

She'd got some special bouncer watchin over her so I tried to keep focused on her smile, but I couldn't stop staring at this purple jewel in her belly an soon I started wonderin why this was so horny. I mean, she'd got a great midriff an everything, but she was shakin it like Hardjit's mum wobbles her rasmalai neck flab.

At first we're just doing that keepin a lot a space between us thing, just to loosen up I hope. Samira still holdin a fag an me still holdin a drink. I always figure, if you've got a drink in your hand it don't matter if you can't dance. Maybe she'll think I'm just bopping while I drink stead a drinkin while I bop.

The belly dancer was now bending backwards lower an lower, till I could see underneath her top from below it. An she was shakin it faster than the drum beats, as if she'd got her own drum beat in her head that only she an I could hear. It was like they'd tripled the tempo a the tune they were playin an they were playin pretty hectic London-Arabic beats to begin with. Hardjit an Amit couldn't even keep up with their clappin.

Suddenly Samira's holdin the back a my hip now. I guess this is what they mean by bumpin an grindin. Her jeans rubbing against my trousers. Her knees bending lower an lower but not quite crouching. I look down at her face an can't help lookin right down her top. It's 'Doin It' by LL Cool J, the dance floor is vibrating again, they've got strobe lights coming outta the chandeliers an everything in the room I thought might be maroon is actually dark chocolate brown.

With each shake, the slit in the belly dancer's purple skirt revealed another millimetre a her long bronze leg an seeing as how she was shakin so much it weren't long before I realised the slit actually went up just a little higher than her waist an I was just staring at the peep a black elastic hoping nobody'd realised I weren't just checkin out her belly no more.

Samira's hair is so sweaty now from all that movin around an she stops to take another sip a my drink an light up another cigarette. Her sweat smells better than her perfume so I linger above her as she drinks, movin away only cos I'm scared she might burn my shirt. Shit, I should be lightin that for her. Get with it, man.

She was showin me her back now, an I couldn't understand how a skirt with such a large slit could look so tight from behind. All the time shakin, like she was a mad, crazy woman. There was a tattoo on her back but she was movin so fast an I was so drunk I couldn't make out what it was an before I could try again she'd swivelled around with the side a her bare leg standin in my face like a door. Then she closed the slit, winked at me an moved on to another table.

Samira slides her hands in to the back pockets a her jeans then slides them out again when Beyoncé's 'Crazy in Love' starts playin an she just starts jammin away, doing them Beyoncé moves till I just stop to watch her, feelin like the luckiest guy in the club, if not London, if not the world. It's an Arabic mix a Beyoncé an I can hear people start clappin.

She's wearin a white outfit stead a purple this time, but it's the exact same belly dancer an the slit in her skirt is exactly as high as yesterday's. Only with Samira watchin me I in't so stupid that I'm gonna try an make out the elastic. Don't matter that I turn back to Samira though, the belly dancer grabs my arm, twirls me back to her an practically thrusts the elastic in my face before makin me kneel before her. OK, so she *is* wearin purple.

— I always knew you could dance bhangra, Jas, but I never had you figured as an expert belly dancer.

— Don't be crazy, Samira, I in't no expert belly dancer. I never even tried it before tonite, innit.

— Well, that belly dancer clearly thought you were her designated partner or something. All familiar and cosy. I should've said to her, Oi, he's with me. How can you say you're a crap dancer? Justin Timberlake's got nothing on you, boy.

An then, at the end a the nite, in the car on the way back, the seal a approval I'd been waitin for: — I had a wikid night tonite, Jas . . . I dunno how to say it, but I really like your style, seriously, Jas, I really dig it. I like your garms, I like your moves. Never thought I'd say this, but I like your words too.

— Whoa, steady there. But even if you're so drunk that you oolti when you get home, that's a nice thing to say, means a lot to me. Thanks, Hardjit.

19

When Amit an Arun were little, their dad fixed a basketball net an backboard above their driveway. I guess he couldn't drill into the pebble-dashing or something cos he'd fixed it to this row a bricks above the upstairs window. Whatever the reason, he'd fixed it so high that by the time Amit an Arun were tall enough to actually score, their dad din't play with them no more. It was round bout then that their dad also stopped coaching the school cricket team on weekends. Their mum said it was a waste a his time an, also, she liked to hold her satsangs on Saturday nites an so needed him to sort stuff out round the house. A couple a months back, that stuff nearly included takin the basketball net down cos she said it made their driveway look like Ruffian Council Estate playground. In the end they decided to leave it up there cos things'd look even worse if he damaged the brickwork bringin it down. An anyway, how many a her hunchback friends could actually look all the way up there? Shoot too high and you'd smash the gutter along the roof, that's how high up we're talkin. Too low and you'd hit the bedroom window. Too far to the left an the ball'd hit one a their satellite TV dishes. Too far to the right an it'd hit one a three burglar alarm boxes. That's right: three separate burglar alarm systems for one single house. They'd even got metal bars in the downstairs windows.

All this Maximum Security shit was the main reason we'd decided Amit's bedroom should be our warehouse for stashin all the fones an cash we were now gettin. Also, Amit was so used to his mum

228

going through all his cupboards an drawers an shit that he'd already made a secret hiding place for stuff. One a the full-size Jamo speakers in his room was just an empty box with a grille on the front. The speaker'd blown years back, when he was DJing at someone's eighteenth. Now with the rubber drum taken out, you could fit enough bottles a Jack Daniel's, pre-rolled spliffs an copies a *FHM* to last a whole year. You could've fit three hundred fones inside it if you needed to. Matter a fact you could've probly fit a person inside, if they were skinny enough an din't mind squatting like some Indian village peasant takin a shit.

The alarm sensor in Amit's living room had some kind a chip on its shoulder. Sometimes it'd go off if a bird just shat on the window, like in case it was aiming for his mum's designer sofa or the designer cushions she'd got designed for the sofa. That's why I act like I'm allergic to glass or something as I stand below the basketball net, peeking through the window to see why no one was answering the front door. They'd got a double front door, practically the same as Samira's front door, the one I'd been staring at for, like, ten minutes last nite after she waved goodbye an disappeared through it. There'd been none a that kissin her on the porch shit. Not even one a them Moments – you know, like when people in films nearly kiss on the porch but don't. Maybe it was cos no way she'd kiss on a first date. Maybe it was cos she just din't fancy kissin me. Maybe it's cos I hadn't actually walked her up to her porch – she'd told me not to cos it was so late an she din't wanna take liberties with her dad. She din't even let me get out the car. We could've maybe had a kiss through the car window, I guess, but the Porsche was so low she'd have to kneel on the pavement.

I knock on Amit's front door one more time. Nothin. No one. I press the doorbell again an nearly shit myself as my fone rings.

— Jazzy Jas man, wassup? You ain't dere already, is it?

— Standin right outside your front door, Amit. Where you guys at? In't we s'posed to be sortin the cash?

— Shit, yeh we sorry, bruv. We a little delay'd n ting out here in da West End, you know how it is, man. Blowin some bucks in Selfridges, innit. Ravi got dese wikid Moschino jeans an dere some fine desi ladies in here. We b back in a couple a hours. Dat safe wid'chyu?

I ask him what the hell am I s'posed to do for a couple a hours, but to be fair they had warned me this could happen today. They'd told me to go into town with them, which I hadn't. Then they'd told me to fone them before hookin up with them here, which I also hadn't. I'd said I needed to get my haircut, which I had. So I guess I'd got no choice but to be safe bout it. Safe as fuckin houses, as goras sometimes say.

— Don't fret, bruv, my bro'll let you in, goes Amit.

— Arun in't around, man. I've rung the bell five times. Unless maybe he's takin a dump or something?

— Yes I am, comes a voice from behind me. — I mean, no, I ain't taking a dump, but, yes, I am here. If you're talking to my little bro, tell him to hurry his brown ass up. I gave my set of house keys to Dad this morning and Mum's gone to Feltham to watch that new Salman Khan film with all her kitty party friends. I hope you like fresh airport air.

Amit an Arun have got this special edition LA Lakers Spalding basketball signed by Shaquille O'Neal from when they went to America. But their mum goes ballistic if they bring any a their balls in the house so they keep it outside under an upside-down flower-pot.

— Three-pointer, I say after one a my long shots finally drops in, even though I in't actually sure what the fuck a three-pointer actually is.

— Nice one, Jazzy Jas, goes Arun. — But let's just stick to lay-ups cos otherwise we might hit the window.

A course I in't too sure what the fuck a lay-up is either so I just copy whatever Arun does, except none a mine drop in.

— You ain't too good at sports, are you, Jas? goes Arun, passin me the ball so I can try the last shot again. I just nod but inside I'm thinkin why the fuck in't they invented some computer program that you could just upload into your brain an it'd teach you how to shoot hoops? It'd be like *The Matrix*, where Keanu Reeves just plugs that machine into a porthole in the base a his skull an learns kung fu. I'd watched the film bout three times an still I couldn't figure out whether he could actually do kung fu in the real world or only in that fake *Matrix* virtual-reality world that the computers created to enslave people. Anyway, there in't no machine like that, in't no portholes in the base a my skull, in't no programs to upload an let's just say that this basketball shit, well, it in't cricket. The ball keeps going round an round the rim like it can't make up its mind whether to drop in or out before decidin on out. Each time it drops, it hits a paving stone or doorstep or something an, like a pinball, shoots into Arun's mum's flower beds. Each time we tidy up the flowers we start chattin bout this bollocks an bout that bollocks. Arun tells me I'm really safe, that when the other guys first started hangin round with me he thought I was their charity case or something. But he din't think that no more. I was safe, Jazzy Jas man, really safe.

We chat bout so much stuff I guess I should've seen it coming. Soon as we start chattin bout which Bollywood film his mum's gone to see, Arun's stomach starts churning before ootling out all his pre-wedding marriage problems again. Next thing you know he's just squatting there, takin another complicated family-related shit right there in his mum's flower beds. So I start chattin bout being more into cricket than into basketball. It turns out that some a his complicated family-related shit involves the fact that he's joined Reena's brother's cricket club stead a her brother joining his football club.

— Mum says we're the Boy's Side so they should make the effort to integrate, not me, Arun explains. — I tell Mum, But Reena's bro doesn't even like football whereas me, I like cricket.

So then I start chattin to Arun bout how his dad used to coach cricket at the school. But get this: turns out that his mum's obsessiveness bout not lettin anyone mess with her family's izzat started when one a her friends got the wrong end a the stick an told the whole community that his dad had actually become a PE teacher. By the time Amit failed his A-levels, their dad was so outta touch with the school an the way shit worked that he let his wife lie to her kitty party friends bout his son's grades. Somehow all a this shit was, like, really relevant to Arun's pre-wedding marital problems. I in't lyin: the basketball hoop may as well've been a toilet seat from which Arun could spray his family-related diarrhoea over me. In the end I start fooling around, tryin to spin the basketball on my index finger an laughin when it spins off into my face. But it turns out that I shouldn't piss around when there's some serious, complicated family-related shit going down.

Some desi who lives next door starts blastin some tune out their bedroom window, probly to tell us to shut the fuck up so they can concentrate on their own A-levels or whatever. The tune is 'Signs' by these guys called Badmarsh & Shri. They're part a the desi scene that some gora people like to call the Asian Underground. Arun's really into that kind a stuff stead a proper hardcore bhangra cos he's a semi-coconut. An so I ask him how comes so much a that stuff they call the Asian Underground, desis don't even listen to? I mean, look at Talvin Singh an Nitin Sawhney, it's mostly goras who download it, innit? Not lager-lout yobs, obviously, but goras all the same.

— Jas, you're just like Amit. Just cos some desi tune isn't bhangra, that doesn't mean it isn't a proper desi tune. I keep telling Amit that you boys need to go beyond all that hardcore bhangra, open your minds, break free.

— Dude, you're chattin like we're locked in the Matrix or someshit. So what if we like our bhangra tunes stead a all that poncey gora stuff?

— You only think it's poncey gorafied stuff cos you never make the effort to listen to it. Nitin Sawhney's one of the country's biggest musical geniuses, but you never give your culture a chance.

— Arun, you can hardly talk bout not givin our culture a chance.

You're, like, anti-bhangra with your coconut ways. I mean, look at the skintight Levi's you're wearin right now. Even a skinhead wouldn't think you're a desi lookin like that.

— All I'm saying is you boys should broaden your tastes a bit, Jas, listen to some proper desi beats. It's not exactly difficult: we got something called the BBC in this country, all you have to do is start tuning in to the Bobby and Nihal show on Radio 1. Or at least keep your ears open during our wedding cos that's exactly the kind of stuff me and Reena have chosen for our playlist.

I wait a moment, make sure there in't no family-related shit to follow through with this latest wedding talk. Nothin. I figure he was just lettin out a wedding-related fart an so I relax. Then I ask how comes he already knows the tunes they're gonna play. After all, in't there nearly, like, two more months to go before the big day?

— Yeh, but we met up with the DJ last week, wanted to cross the playlist off our To Do list before Reena and her mum went to Bombay. That is, of course, assuming my mum doesn't cross out all the songs and make them play the soundtrack to *Kuch Kuch Hota Hai* non-stop instead.

An with that, his fart becomes one a them dirty, smelly, sweaty ones. I try an block my ears as well as my nose as he starts going on an on bout his mum an her izzat an how it relates to their playlist as well as the guestlist an the giftlist. I make sure not to catch his eyes, try another one a them lay-up things, miss, turn the rebound into another shot, miss again an then nearly fall over as I try an save his mother's flowers.

— Steady there, Jas, it looks like you're practising your bhangra moves, he says. — I'm not joking, you know. Mum wants to vet the giftlist as well as the playlist. We've already handed it in to John Jewis but she doesn't trust Reena's taste in crockery or something. Thinks she'll have chosen stuff that's too cheap. It's, like, just because Mum didn't choose my wife like she always wanted to, she's trying to make sure she chooses everything else – deciding how Reena should act, how she should talk, what outfit she should wear, what jewellery she should wear, what underwear even. Seriously, Jas, before Reena went to India to buy her trousseau my mum gave her a list of approved sari styles and the name of a wedding underwear boutique. In fact, she'll probably even decide what kachha I wear on the wedding night.

I just give a polite laugh an try another shot at the basket when I'm interrupted by a voice from behind us sayin, — Oh yeh? So tell me, what kachhian you guys wearing then?

Shooting hoops is like being the bowler in a game a cricket or even like ten-pin bowling. If you can't get into your stride after a few tries an you don't want to look like a dickless dick, then you should just stop tryin quick time.

— Nice shot, champ, she says again from the pavement. — You trying to knock down the satellite dish?

— Nah, he's practising his bhangra moves, goes Arun.

— Fuck . . . Samira. What're you doing here?

— Well, I was at a friend's house round the corner, then I saw you out here and I thought, wow, what a coincidence, why don't I just check what time you're picking me up tonight?

— Er. This is Arun, Amit's brother. Arun, this is Samira, my friend.

— Friend, ah? Amit never told me Jazzy Jas boy had got himself a Friend.

— Amit din't tell you anything cos Amit don't know nothin, I go. — Amit shouldn't know nothin. I told the guys I'm busy with relatives from abroad tonite. They believed me too.

— Aha, Arun goes, in a way that means, Relax, dude, I can keep a secret,

— Well, pleased to meet you, Friend.

Samira nods back at Arun before givin me wide eyes an an even wider silent Mmmm that says, Oops, sorry, I didn't realise he was linked to one of the guys, he just looks like a coconut in those skintight jeans.

— Careful a the window, I say as she takes the ball from me.

— Relax. I was netball captain, I'm not gonna smash anyone's window.

— I in't worried bout it smashin, it's triple-glazed cos a the airport. I'm just worried bout you settin off the alarm.

She shoots, she scores. I can smell her strawberryness as she lands.

— So, Jas, what're you doing out here anyway? Getting basketball coaching?

— He in't coachin me nothin, I say. — In fact, I'm here coachin him. Bout his wedding problems, innit.

Arun just looks at me an says, — Gimme the ball, Jas. Let me show you how to shoot some hoops.

Whenever Samira takes a jump shot at the basket, her black, sleeveless T-shirt rides up a bit an shows me her full midriff. In my slow-motion instant replay I can make out her hip bones, which cradle a belly that is so unflabby that, if anything, it curves inwards stead a outwards, like a dinner plate. I decide that maybe her bra in't padded today. For a very happy moment, I think maybe she in't even wearin a bra. Then for another moment I think maybe she is. A course, it don't matter to me one way or another. Maybe padded then.

— I see I'm distracting you, Jas, she goes to me suddenly.

— Nah, nah, you in't.

— Hello, I'm not blind, Jas. I can see where your attention is focused now. I just thought I should be straight and say I know I'm distracting you. But it's OK for you to carry on.

— You what?

— You carry on. I don't mind.

— What, you mean you don't mind?

— That's what I just said, Jas. Go right ahead. You've got a tongue, why don't you use it?

— I'm sorry, Samira, but what're you talkin bout?

— Your advice for Arun. Since I showed up all you've been doing is looking at the basketball. I don't mean to distract you or interrupt you or anything. You carry on helping him with his wedding problems. Pretend I'm not here.

So then I turn to Arun an come out with any old shit like: — Fuck's sake, man, you can't let your parents treat you like a little boy. Stand up for yourself. Be a man.

An then next thing you know, Arun's suddenly started defendin his mum an dad. People do that, I guess.

— All I'm saying is maybe Mum's got a point, he goes. — Traditions survive for a reason after all. Maybe I should just respect it and maybe Reena's Side should show our side some respect. I mean, what the hell do I want to suck up to them for?

The more Arun defends his mum's ways, the more I realise that the woman's some fucked-up Nazi. All this talk bout sides. All this puttin people down cos they don't salute you, cos they're lower than you, cos you're too fuckin retarded to question the system. As I realise all a this, I also realise I can use this situation to help with the Samira situation. Cos, after all, it in't like I got time to rehearse it proply. I don't chat bout Nazis, though, cos that'd sound a bit boffiny. Stead a using Nazis, suddenly I'm fuckin Morpheus from *The Matrix*, tellin Arun to free his mind, fight the system, save mankind. After all, in the film, Neo compares Agent Smith to a member a the Gestapo. So I tell Arun to wake up, smell the masala tea, I say he's accepting a world that imprisons him. I argue that maybe we're meant to challenge traditions, defeat the system that allows our elders to exploit us. All I get is him sayin, — No we ain't, Jas. Stop acting like one of those up-themselves coconuts.

He tells me all weddings get a little fucked up cos a this or that complicated family-related shit. All weddings are a headache. What the fuck kind a answer is that? I tell him. You'd get a headache if you knocked on every door with your forehead, that's why we use our fists or door knockers. Fuckin doorbells even. If we're s'posed to just sit there an put up with headaches, then why the fuck they invent aspirin for? Paracetamol? Ear mufflers? Fuckin masala tea? Arun is clearly wearin ear mufflers himself cos he turns round an tells me traditions are there to be honoured. Those are his exact words, Traditions are there to be honoured. Otherwise, he says, he'd

be doubly dishonoured. — First, cos we're not respecting the
tradition, second, cos Reena's Side aren't respecting our honour.

— What the fuck, man? Did the basketball just hit your head or
something? Be a man, Arun. Course traditions in't there to be
honoured. If all we did was sit around on our butts honouring our
traditions while doing complicated family-related shits, then nothin'd ever get better, would it? Cos nothin'd ever change. There'd be
no equal rights for men an women, no crime committed when a
husband rapes his wife. Fuck's sake, we might as well stop our mums
shoppin in Tesco an get our dads to go hunt wild animals for dinner
instead. After all, it's the tradition, innit?

Samira's lookin right at me now so I look right back at her. *You
like the way I use my tongue, girl? Bet you can't guess where this shit's
coming from?* Arun, on the other hand, still in't impressed.

— C'mon, Jas, he says, — no need to get all dramatic. I'm not
talking about raping anyone or going fox-hunting. I'm just talking
about simple traditions that make desis different to other people.

— Fuck's sake, I go, — doing something cos it's tradition, cos it's
the way things are done, is the shittest reason ever to do something.
It in't even a reason, it's a lame excuse for not havin a proper reason.
Din't it used to be a desi tradition to ritually sacrifice your baby if
it turned out to be a girl? But that don't make that shit right, does
it? *Write that down if you like, Samira, I'll sign it for you later. An
there's loads more where that's coming from.* But now she's listenin to
Arun, who's sayin there's a difference between killin your own baby
an expecting your wife-to-be's parents to show some respect to your
parents. You just don't get it, I say. There's a difference between
expecting them to show *some* respect an *more* respect. The former
is fair enough. The latter, on the other hand, is some fucked-up,
lowlife, retarded, Nazi bullshit. How old are your parents anyway?
Four? That gets Samira lookin back at me now. Lookin, as if to say,
OK, Jas, so tell me, where's all this coming from? I never had you
figured as a revolutionary leader of men. *Ah, but that's because you
can't see the base of my skull. The tiny porthole. Plugging me into the*

mainframe. Uploading the program, the knowledge, the truth into my mind. So that I, Morpheus, can free the minds of others. I'd often wondered whether Morpheus felt like a dick chattin all that revolutionary shit to Neo. Now I know. But still I continue. — Most parents are too narrow-minded an set in their ways to see that all desi wedding traditions just don't make sense thousands a years after they were invented in Indian villages thousands a miles away that probly don't even exist no more. You gotta see through that shit, Arun. You tell me to open my mind an not just be listenin to bhangra, well, how's this shit different? Why can't you tell your parents to open their fuckin minds? All them customs, they're just invented to protect the power a older people cos they'd got the time an power to invent shit to protect their power. An now they spreadin this shit round London cos they're the only ones with the time an power to spread it. An the worst thing is they don't even realise they're doing it cos they're so unable to question the system. *Free your mind, Arun. Free your mind, Samira. Join our struggle, Arun. Samira, join me.* Then I tell him he's livin in a dream world, that the system behind it is the enemy. As long as its traditions exist, we will never be free. But he has to free his own mind before he can try an free his parents'. An even then, his parents might not be ready to be unplugged back into reality. They're so hooked on the system, on their traditions an their dreams, that even if they realise it's a system that binds them they might fight to protect it.

— Jas, what the fuck are you talking about? You sound like that dude from *The Matrix*. Not Neo, the other one. What's his name? Morpheus.

That's right, you perceptive muthafucka, you took your sweet time to spot that one. I've morphed into Morpheus, innit. So you best fuckin watch yourself, desi, and free your muthafuckin mind. Hey, are you listenin to me? Or were you lookin at Samira? Samira, by the way, is still lookin at me. Still listenin to every word I say. Staring at me, more like. Holdin the basketball like it's some baby girl she's offerin for ritual sacrifice in accordance with Outdated Desi Custom

Number 412. The basketball is cryin but Samira's still silent. *You gotta hand it to me, girl, it's pretty slick advice.* Samira Ahmed, lost for words. Still wonderin where all this shit's coming from cos she can't see the plug at the base a my skull. I guess you can't blame her. She doesn't have plugs an portholes. She's pure. She was born in Zion.

— You gotta tell your parents to see through all those traditions, Arun, so that they can see the truth. Take all a this caste shit that's involved. I hear your parents in't big fans a Reena's Side cos they in't Brahmin, right?

— Yeh.

— Wrong.

— What d'you mean, wrong? We're Brahmin, they're not.

— No, my friend, I go, — castes don't exist. It's all bullshit, all in *The Matrix,* all part a some illusion created by people who want power over others. You did History with Mr Ashwood, right? The world's full a categories a people that were just, like, invented randomly. How can someone be Brahmin an someone not be Brahmin if the categories don't really exist in the real world? An they can't exist, can they, cos how can someone be better an more fly than someone else unless they're really better an more fly? If a Brahmin's got a low IQ then he's got a low IQ, don't matter that he's Brahmin. You gotta get your parents to let go a that shit. Free their minds.

Now I look at Samira again, hoping she'll realise the same thing goes for different religions. Her Muslim. Me not. So fuckin what?

— An all a this shit bout the Girl's Side havin to bow down to the Boy's Side all the time, Arun. That's cos back in the day the girl din't have no job an brought no income into the family. But back in the day is as good as back in *The Matrix,* man. You keep tellin me your-self, Reena's a qualified surgeon. Not exactly a liability to take off her parents' balance sheet. So answer me, man, how can any groom's family seriously reckon they deserve special treatment today just cos they the Boy's Side an it's tradition? What kind a stupid, ridiculous piece a narrow-minded, backward-thinkin, bullshit nonsense, fucked-up crap, outdated, retarded, lump-a-ludoo-where-our-brains-should-be, Nazi facist kind a tradition is that? In London, man. In this century. In a country where even the public toilets explicitly define us blokes as Gentlemen.

At this point I figure it's probly best if I ease up a bit. The guys'll be back soon, what the fuck am I doing? I turn to Samira an put my hands out like I want to feel her probly padded breasts. She passes me the basketball. It in't dark yet but the sun's going down. *The guys'll be back soon.* Soon every car that turns into this road starts makin me nervous. Maybe without the basketball to play with she'll get the hint an get the fuck away from here. I should just tell her to go but she's too fuckin fit. Some cars that turn into the road have already got half-beam headlights. Others are still waitin for the street lights to come on. If you ask nicely at Starbucks they'll stir whipped cream into your cappuccino so it becomes the same shade as a latte, only thicker an creamier an for some reason shinier. That's the colour the half-beam headlights make Samira's skin. Maybe they'll be another fifteen minutes.

The problem with Arun is his mind just in't ready to be freed. That happens with some people.

— Sometimes when I'm with Reena it *does* feel like I'm number two, he says. — So maybe Mum's right, maybe I don't have any self-respect or dignity. And if that's the case, then it stands to reason I'm not going to be getting enough respect for my family.

Respect, my ass. Dignity, my dick. — Look, if your mum thinks gettin Reena an her family to big you guys up gives you self-respect an dignity then she don't know the meanin a the words. If you was dignified, you'd put the needs a your wife-to-be first. It's called being a Gentleman an not givin in to all this school-playground gangsta izzat shit.

Samira smiles. She smiled the last time I used the word Gentleman. So I tell Arun that if he were a Gentleman he wouldn't even be thinkin bout whether he was showin too much respect to Reena's family. He wouldn't care if things looked one-sided. That's the whole fuckin point a being a Gentleman. That's why you got Ladies an

Gentlemen, not fuckin Gentleladies an Gentlemen. It wouldn't fuckin work, would it? She'd have to take off *her* jacket too an give it to you. You'd end up just swappin fuckin coats. Swappin shopping bags. Swappin the window seat. Openin doors? Fuckin forget it. An if that means your relatives don't get their butts licked or izzat deficits filled as much as they'd like, then so fuckin what? It's only relative. A course, Arun thinks I said only relatives, which causes all kinds a problems an accusations bout not respectin desi family values an then, right while he's in the middle a this, a car with full-beam head-lights honks behind us an turns into the driveway. Like perfect Gentlemen, we step out the way.

It in't lookin good. Arun's mum is out first, wearin that chapatti flour cement make-up an a blue sequinned kurti top that rattles as she slams the driver's door behind her. His dad gets out the passenger side more slowly, grabs his briefcase from the back seat an asks his wife for the keys so he can lock the car. She don't even notice Samira an me, she just walks straight up to Arun an says she's just heard from her kitty party friends that Reena's mum's second cousin's son is gettin married on Saturday.

— Yeh, I think so, goes Arun, — I mean, I know they've got some kind of wedding in the family, I don't know exactly who though.

— Don't know? Tennu ni pata? Vot kind of man you are? Where our invitation is? Lost in bloody post? Vhy we not invited?

— What? Why should we be invited?

— Don't give me stupid question. Their daughter is becoming our daughter and you give me stupid question. Vot kind of man you are? And today my friends ask me vot I'm wearing on Saturday. Wearing to vot? How shameful this is. I not even know.

— Look, Mum, I'd have told you about the wedding but it just didn't seem important enough to bring up.

— I not care whether you tell me. They should tell me. They should pick up phone. Their daughter is becoming our daughter. They should show us respect. But we not even know they have wedding. Then Aunty looks at her son before shaking her finger in the same direction. — It because of you, Arun. So bloody Westrenised you are, they treat us like we are Angrez loki, she says, before lookin at her husband. — This son of yours is so bloody Westrenised. Where his self-respect is? Always he defends them. All this shame they put on us and still your son defends them.

— Theekh hai, darling. He's *your* son too.

— Oh thanks, Dad, why don't you just give me up for adoption while you're at it.

— You not talk to your papa like this. I told you: too Westrenised. They don't phone us enough and our son he just sits there like a lump.

— To say what, Mum? What do you want them to call and say?

— Just to say Hello, how are you? They should at least ask us how we are. Find out what's happening. Even Reena, she never phone to see how we are and she joining our family, becoming our daughter.

— But they do call now and then. And also, they find out what's happening in our family because they ask me. I tell Reena how everyone is.

— Now and then is nothing. Every two, three days they should call us and show respect.

— So then I shouldn't tell Reena how everyone is?

— No, you tell her. But she should also phone to find out for herself. It's matter of respect.

— But then she'll be lying to you, Mum. I mean, she'll be asking you how you are but she'll already know. It's called deceit, isn't it? Reena's really not the kind of girl who plays those kinds of games. That's one of the reasons why I'm marrying her.

— Beita, stop being Westrenised difficult boy. All we are saying is she should call us. She can also tell us vot's happening in her life. How we can know vot is happening in her life when she can't pick up phone to call us?

— But what's she going to say? Aunty, you've really got to hear the latest Destiny's Child album? If you want to chat to her so much then why don't you phone her?

— Don't be stupid. Such stupidness. She's going to be daughter-in-law. It for her to phone us and show respect.

— Are you serious? You are seriously upset about her not phoning you? I mean, you've seriously even noticed it enough to notice it?

— Vhy you not just tell Reena she should call us? Tell her make the effort?

— I can't tell her that. I'd feel like some primary school kid saying My mummy's better than your mummy and she's not going to be your friend any more because you didn't say hello. I can't admit this kind of stuff is going on, Mum. I've got my self-respect.

Arun's mum just storms into the house an nearly slams the door behind her in her husband's face. He turns round before going in an smiles at Samira an me. — Satsriakaal, Jas, nice to see you again. Please, forgive. Important family business. Complicated.

Then his wife comes to the door again. — Vot you stand outside for? Come inside, Arun. At once. Then she looks at the basketball in the driveway. — First, clean up this mess you've made. Tera bhra kithe hai? Hahn? Where Amit is?

Samira quickly makes her exit, sayin Bye to Arun an askin me to pick her up at seven stead a eight. This gives me just under two hours to go home an get ready, which should be enough but there's so much more stuff to tell Arun. Stuff like: — Mate, that's good. I like the way you stood up for yourself. Now you gotta keep it up an make your mum realise just how psycho she's being.

— I can't call her that, he says as he puts his basketball back under the flowerpot.

— Don't call her a psycho. But, you know, explain this shit to her some more.

— No, what you just heard now, that's it for me. That's as far as I go. I'll just agree with her now and try and get her and Dad an invite to this wedding, even though Reena and her mum aren't even going cos they'll still be in Bombay.

— What the fuck? That's it? I thought you was gonna sort all this shit out once an for all.

— Get real, Jas. You know how it is. She doesn't do different points of view. Anyway, if I tell her she's wrong she'll just tell me she's right. And she's my mum, I have to show her some respect.

— No. Fuck. Respect is one thing, but when people say you should always Respect Your Elders what they're really sayin is you should always agree with them. An how can that not be bullshit? If you gotta agree with them all the time, that must mean they're always right. Come on, man. Always right? Who the fuck is always right? Even the Oracle's prophecies in *The Matrix* in't always right.

— Look, I better go inside before she explodes.

— OK, but just do me a favour an tell your mum that you respect her an you respect what she's sayin. Show her lots a respect. She'll like that. But then say that she brought you up to be a Gentleman an therefore you gotta be a Gentleman, you get me?

As he shuts the front door he swears he'll keep me an Samira a secret an then says thanks for the advice for, like, the tenth time.

— Maybe I should just pop on *The Matrix* DVD an explain it to Mum that way, he says.

— Fuck that, man, there in't enough songs an sari changes in it. It's too realistic for her.

20

All this time I been tryin to find someone else who reckons the last scene in *Devdas* is bollocks an finally I found em. Samira admitted she weren't the biggest Bollywood buff in the world, but she did think all that Shah Rukh Khan droppin down dead business before he can get to Aishwarya Rai's front gate is a bit tutty. It's like they tried to think a the saddest, most unrealistically tragic endin possible just to prove that the film in't got an unrealistic happy endin.

— I mean, what is with that? Samira goes after slowly sipping some more Chinese tea. — I mean, even though Devdas is already at death's door before he sets out to find her, he somehow manages to travel halfway across India but can't make the final twenty metres to her courtyard gate. I mean, *per-lease.*

She takes another sip a Chinese tea an makes a funny shape with her lips that I can hardly see in this corner a the restaurant. Even in the darkness, though, I know her mouth looks more fit tonite than it normly does. You could just tell from listenin to her lift her lips away from the tiny black teacup. Curling off the cup like some new kind a silk cling film, like flesh-coloured hold-ups being rolled down some fit lady's thighs. It's the dark designer lighting that lets me hear an see these things. An it's the dark designer lighting that lets me say things I wouldn't normly have the bollocks to say cos she's just so fuckin fit tonite.

— You know what that symbolises, don't you? I go to her.

— No, what?

— That Devdas is impotent.

She practically spits out her tea.

— I'm serious, I go. — He can't get in through her front gates, get it? He just flops down on the ground. You know, like a limp . . . you know. It in't a broken heart that drives him to drink an kills him, he dies cos he can't, you know, do the deed with her. That's why all the flowers fall onto him from the tree. It's cos the branches, they go limp too.

— Er, yeh, right, Jas, she goes, laughin but without spittin this time. Even her laughter tonite sounds soft an delicate an thin like hold-ups.

— I'm serious.

— Look, I know this isn't very ladylike of me, but the words Fuck off come to mind. I've never heard so much bullshit in my life.

— You can use all the swear words you like, Samira, but I'm being one hundred per cent serious.

— Whatever you say, Jas. You know what, though, I feel like we're in a film ourselves right now.

— What? Just cos Hugh Grant is on the table over in that corner? Film stars need to eat too, you know. I guess some like to eat here.

— No, not because of Hugh Grant. It's because we're talking about a film.

— You what?

— We're talking about a film, Jas. Just watch any film these days and I guarantee you'll see two people sitting in a restaurant or bar or café talking about films. If not about films, then about TV or music. I think it started with those Quentin Tarantino films but now all of them seem to show people talking about films. So all I'm saying is that when you and I were just talking about *Devdas* I felt like we were in a film.

— Fair enough. But that's what people chat bout, innit. Films.

As far as I'm concerned, though, I in't really talkin bout films with her. I'm just followin Sanjay's dating tip that you should talk bout sex indirectly, what he kept callin sex-in-the-abstract. I figure Bollywood symbols for sex are abstract enough. The rain, the train, the tunnel through the mountain. An a course the fuckin fountain. The fact that Bollywood films don't actually contain any real sex scenes doesn't exactly bode well for tonite, though. An, OK, maybe symbols for impotence are a little too abstract, but fuck it, it's only my second date with her an I'm still workin on it, innit. Anyway, if Samira don't like all this abstract indirect shit, she can always try an read my mind now and then. Every time she breathes in would be a good time, when her diaphragm lifts up an her breasts strain the buttons on her black satin blouse. In the dark designer lighting you could even hear her bra elastic stretch. The darkness comes courtesy a Hakkasan, with its slick decor an moody lights. You can't normly get a table in this restaurant on a Saturday nite less you book way in advance. But Sanjay came to the rescue thanks to this other business he's got going on. He calls it a clearing market in restaurant reservations. What he does, he gets one a his people to book tables at all a London's flashiest an hardest-to-reserve restaurants a couple a months in advance. Hakkasan, The Ivy, Le Caprice, Asia de Cuba, The Square, Nobu, Zuma, you name it. The man's got table reservations at all a these places every Friday nite an every Saturday nite, always under different made-up names an numbers. Then, when the weekend comes round, he gives or sells these reservations to people who need a flash table for dinner but who hadn't got their shit together to book however many weeks in advance they should've done. When he does charge people for this service, Sanjay don't charge too much. Forty bucks, tops. Says it's more bout goodwill than makin money, a logical step-up from gettin people on guestlists for all them top nightclubs. Except unlike the nightclub owners, the restaurant owners had no idea this shit was goin on.

As the maître d' had shown us to this table, Samira'd said this Hakkasan place was the funkiest restaurant she'd ever been to. I said I preferred Asia de Cuba, we could go there next week if she liked. Asia de Cuba fits the sex-in-the-abstract strategy even better cos it's in a hotel. Not that I was gonna get us a room or nothin pimpish like that. But the fact that there are bedrooms there means the thought might enter her head, which is good, so long as she don't think the thought enters my head, which is bad.

— Next week then, let's go, I say. — I'll ring Asia de Cuba tomorrow an book a table under the name Jas.

— Why Jas? she goes.

— Er, cos it's my name.

— No, I know. But why not give them your surname? It'd sound a lot better than Mister Jas. I was going to ask you that at the club last night.

— At Vagabond?

— Yeh, the dinner table and the sofa were both booked under the name Jas. It just seemed a little odd when they kept calling you Mister Jas. Why not just give them your surname?

— C'mon, if you had a surname like mine would you give it to people? It's such a long-assed surname an people always pronounce it wrong. You know how it is.

— Fair enough, she goes. — This place is soooo slick. I can't believe Hugh Grant's sitting over there.

I figured the fact that Samira was still raving bout Hakkasan being the coolest place she'd been to could've meant two things: firstly, maybe she din't get out an about as much as I thought she did, or, secondly, maybe I weren't impressing her at all. Maybe she was just being polite. Even earlier on she kept biggin up the car, playin with the wing mirrors, the radio an the cup holder. The thing is, we weren't even in the Porsche. Sanjay'd had to go visit an aunt back in Hounslow so stead we were in my mum's Ford Focus. I'd hidden away Mum's lace-covered tissue box an her flowery AutoAroma air freshener an everything but, still, it weren't exactly a panty-remover on wheels.

Sanjay'd told me to order Chinese tea an this stuff called sake. Then, after our starters (scallop shumai, chive dumpling an prawn toast with seaweed an enoki mushroom) I was s'posed to steer the conversation towards sex-in-the-abstract. I din't manage to steer it from *Devdas* to Bollywood symbolism for sex until we'd nearly done with our mains, though, cos I hit so many dead ends with the other routes. First up I'd figured we're in a Chinese restaurant, I'll try steering to sex-in-the-abstract by chattin bout concubines. We're near Soho, I'll chat bout all them vibrator an porn shops. We're in the same restaurant as Hugh Grant, I'll chat bout Divine Brown. Samira don't bite with any a it. Then, as we finish our stir-fry XO eel roll in yellow bean sauce, she talks bout which Bollywood film her parents have gone to see tonite. I tell her it's one I in't seen yet, one I probly won't see till Amit gets a pirated DVD an even then I probly won't sit through the whole thing. She laughs that silky laugh. Then I tell her that, thinkin bout it, I in't actually sat through a whole Bollywood film since *Devdas*, an that was such a safe film they entered it for some big-deal French film award. They even said it could've won an Oscar. At first I'm such a pehndu that I don't even spot the opportunity to tell Samira my theory bout Devdas's limp dick. Or bout the rain, the train, the fountain an the tunnel through the mountain. I was just tellin her bout how normly I'm like, Bollywood, man, don't even mention it to me. The ladies just watch it for the songs, the saris an the dancin, an the guys just watch em for the stunts, the fit women an the stunt fightin. But there's deeper shit going on in there, Samira, an that's what annoys me.

I still couldn't believe how grown-ups din't ever get it. I mean, look at Arun's mum for instance. It din't matter how many films or how many times people like her saw the same fuckin film, they might as well watch em with the sound switched off. An the fuckin subtitles. There in't no excuse not to get it, I mean it in't like they in't always the same anyway. Always all that happy an dancy shit in the first half. Boy meets Girl; Boy an Girl fall in lurve; Boy an Girl sing an dance; Boy rescues Girl from three baddies with loud, gay laughs; Boy an Girl sing an dance again, but in the rain this time so that Girl can miraculously change sari for the fifteenth time while her make-up miraculously doesn't run or smudge or whatever the fuck it is that make-up does when it gets wet. Then, if you sit through the second half long enough, the films'll always tell you the same shit: that you shouldn't get all hung up about your pride an izzat an that. Boy an Girl are always just bout to live happily ever after but then people in their families with nothin better to do with their time start buttin in an havin problems with it, gettin all hung up bout this shit an that shit. Shit to do with their family honour an prestige. Some grandma, grandad, auntyji or some other unemployed relation. All cos they reckon they in't being shown enough respect. An suddenly Boy an Girl got themselves some big fuckin izzat issue to deal with which ends up fuckin everything up for everyone. In *Devdas* all the izzat shit involves Shah Rukh Khan being a Brahmin an Aishwarya Rai not. Then some sister-in-law makes pretty soon Khan's mum insult Aishwarya Rai's mum or someshit an that's how the dude starts drinkin himself to death (sorry if I just ruined it for you). An that's how Bollywood films say all kinds a important shit bout how fucked up things can get if you get too hung up bout your pride an your izzat an shit. As Mr Carver said one time when he was tryin to tell our A-level English class that *The Canterbury Tales* still mattered, Bollywood offers all kinds of important insights into the tragic dysfunctionalities of sociocultural structures when people confuse the concept of pride with the concept of honour.

— You're joking, goes Samira. — Your English teacher taught you about Bollywood?

— Well, only cos he was tryin to explain all that honour an gentility stuff in *The Canterbury Tales*. More like *The Calcutta Tales* the way he tried to sell it to us.

— Which one did your year do?

— 'The Franklin's'. You?

— 'The Knight's'.

— What pisses me off is this: if even our gora teachers can get it, then how come mums only notice what kind a saris an jewellery all the actresses are wearin?

— You know, I never had you figured as such a big Bollywood expert, Jas.

— Well, I din't used to go for all that deep shit either. I mean, take *Devdas* – I just watched it to see Aishwarya Rai, that's all. Wanted to see if there'd be a soaked-see-through-sari scene, innit. That's symbolic you know. The rain, the fountains. Just like the film's endin, that's symbolic, too. Let me explain –

— Oh no, Jas, don't get me talking about the ending of *Devdas*. I mean, that's got to be the worst ending I ever saw . . .

While it took me ages to steer the Bollywood conversation to sex-in-the-abstract symbolism, at least I din't try an share all my Bollywood theories with Samira's dad when he told us him an her mum were going to the cinema tonite. Truth is I din't really say anything to him, I was so fuckin nervous being in the same room as him. Even more so seeing as how that room was his fuckin living room. I'd parked up round the corner an foned Samira to tell her I was waitin there. I thought she was fuckin jokin when she told me to park in her drive-way an come inside to meet her mum an dad. That shit just don't happen round here. Maybe parents in American TV shows check out who their daughters are dating, but desi daughters don't date. Anyway, I figured me havin to meet her parents probly wouldn't be as fucked off as me havin to introduce her to mine an so I went inside. Samira's dad probly just wanted to make sure we weren't, like, going out or nothin, that we were just mates. Check. Make sure I weren't an axe murderer. Check. Make sure I weren't a non-Muslim.

When the Brad Pitt-lookin Hakkasan waiter brings us the garlic an soya crab claw dish, I decide to distract her by askin her again,

— Samira, I know you said your dad was, like, modern an everything, but I still don't get how come he was so safe with me earlier.

— I told you in the car, Jas, my three brothers are out of town. It's them you need to worry about, not my dad. He can be chilled.

— But I in't Muslim.

— So what did you think, just because you're not Muslim my dad's going to grab a butcher's knife and turn you into halal meat? You've been watching the news or listening to all those Hindu elders too much, Jas.

Then she lets out another one a those soft laughs that means I don't need to worry, she in't offended or nothin. — We're not monsters. Of course my daddy's going to be chilled with you. He's always telling my brothers to stop getting so hung up on whether someone's Muslim or Sikh or Hindu or Christian or whatever. He has this whole speech ready for it, says he's lived in this country long enough and lived in this world long enough to know that we're all brothers. For instance, he says the only battle with Hindustan is on the cricket pitch, and even then he supports India whenever they're not playing Pakistan.

— Yeh, OK, I guess I was just surprised he seemed so safe with me an you being alone together, that's all.

— I didn't tell him we'd be alone. I told him you were picking me up and we were going to Priya's house to do our coursework. And even if I had told him we'd be alone, don't worry – it's all about creating low expectations. Before you arrived I made out like you were a real thug so he was really pretty relieved when he actually saw you.

And just like that I see another chance to drop in more a Sanjay's words. I tell her some shit bout that being exactly what it's like in the City. Everyone's so obsessed with share prices that companies end up settin themselves low expectations an targets so that they can beat em an boost their shares. It's called underpromising an overdelivering, I say to her, soundin like some fly businessman in a Hugo Boss suit. She looks at me for a moment an then gets me all keyed up by sayin she'd do the exact same thing if she ever decided to tell her dad the truth bout us. I couldn't fuckin swallow when she said that. I mean, we were only on our second date. Part a me still weren't even sure she weren't jus playin some big joke on me, some early April Fool's shit, that kind a thing. An now she's talkin like she might stay with me long enough to tell her dad bout us. That low-expectations shit really works. She says to me that if it ever came to tellin her dad, she'd tell him to sit down. He'd say, — What for, I'm no invalid. Then she'd say something like, — No, Dad, please sit down. I've got something to tell you. No, please, you need to be sitting down for this one. Create low expectations, make him worry that maybe she's pregnant or she's secretly got married to a black transsexual gangsta lesbian or someshit. An then, when she tells him she's going out to dinner with a guy like me, he'll be relieved it's just dinner. Apparently she did the exact same thing when she got a tattoo. I told her I din't think this was the same thing as gettin a fuckin tattoo. Then she asked me if I wanted to see it. After wobbling over one a my stammerin fits she pushes me straight into it by askin, — Jas, I was wondering, are you a virgin?

My mind cuts in before I can actually say anything. Things are going well, Jas, it starts sayin to me, so how about just telling her the truth? Fuck off wid dat truth shit, man. Well, I wouldn't talk to me like that if I were you. Remember, Jas, I'm your mind. I'll make you imagine her naked, make it embarrassing for you to stand up after you paid the bill.

— Arun an Reena in't even slept together yet an they're engaged, I say, my mind bursting out with laughter at me, fallin off a fuckin chair underneath its own dark designer lighting up there. But soon as Samira starts talkin again my mind shuts the fuck up.

— Some people say it's not natural to hold out till marriage but I totally disagree with them, she goes. — I mean, other people would argue that just because you don't have sex till marriage, that doesn't mean you can't climax or whatever.

I look at her, not realising my mouth is hangin wide open till some sake nearly spills out.

— What's the matter, Jas? she goes. — Lost your tongue?

By the time I get my shit together again – which is a long fuckin time – she asks me what I think bout her, whether she's a virgin or not. I know how to answer that one. That one's so easy I don't even need to listen to my mind, to Sanjay, to Hardjit or Mr Ashwood. I don't need to fone a friend, I don't need any fuckin lifelines whatsoever. I tell her she's saving herself for the right guy, innit.

— Then how come I hear that your so-called friends keep calling me a ho?

This time my mouth weren't full a sake when it opens, it was full a some fuckin lychee ice-cream sorbet thing. Talkin bout why your bredren call your date a ho probly in't what Sanjay'd meant by sex-in-the-abstract. The ice cream dribbles down my chin an onto my DKNY top. She laughs an tells me I should see my face. Then she takes one a the white linen napkins, leans over the table an wipes it off my face an chest.

— Relax, Jas. I know what people say about me. It doesn't bother me, I mean what do they know, right? But what I *am* wondering is this: how come you want to go out with me when all your friends call me a ho?

She's got me coughin an gurgling ice cream but she in't got me stammerin. — I don't think you're a ho, I say.

— An what if I don't believe you? What if I think you're only interested in me because you think I'm an easy lay?

— Cos maybe *I* don't want to have sex before I'm married.

She finds my bullshit so fuckin hilarious that other people in the restaurant turn to look. After she gets her breath back she still wants to talk bout the way other people keep sayin she's a ho an a slut an all, but luckily she stops accusing me a tryin to test that out. Before I know it, we're havin a deep an meaningful conversation bout how I think it's a good thing that she in't afraid to laugh an joke around with guys, to talk bout sex an stuff an not give a shit what other people say bout it. She calls it Vegetarian Flirting. I in't exactly sure what she means by that, but I'm pretty sure she don't mean it makes you fart. I tell her this to get her to laugh again an then I wait till the deep an meaningful chat gets deep enough before I ask her the big question: Why? Why is it that she likes kickin bout with blokes all the time? Why's she always been so relaxed when it comes to chattin bout sex? Why don't she care that other girls an guys call her a ho?

— Why do *you* think? Do *you* think it's because I'm insecure and

254

need to keep proving to myself that guys find me attractive? Because it seems that's what other people say about me.

— I in't sayin that, I go. — I in't sayin nothin, I got no idea why, that's why I'm askin you.

— Well, let me ask you: why should us girls always have to put up with guys coming on to us? Half the time you don't know whether a guy's treating you like a proper person or whether they just want to get into your knickers. I mean, there have been guys that I trusted as good friends and then a few months later I find out they only talked to me because they fancied me. It's like nothing's ever real and maybe I'm sick of it. So, yeh, if people want to call me a flirt maybe they're right, maybe I am. Maybe I just flirt because if I don't, the guys'll do it to me and I won't know what's real and what's not. But that doesn't mean I'm a ho or a slut. That doesn't mean I sleep with anyone. And as for calling me a tease, most of my male friends are only pretending they're happy just being friends anyway. So who's teasing who? And as for talking about sex, Jas, why shouldn't girls be allowed to talk about sex? That's all guys talk about anyway. I'm just making sure they don't talk about it behind my back. People like Hardjit call me a ho for it because they're scared of girls like me. They know they can't control me. But if I spend my life worrying about whether guys like him call me a ho then I'm letting him treat me like one anyway, aren't I?

She goes on an on, till I think I'm listenin to that Destiny's Child track from *Charlie's Angels.* Turns out that the one person she actually wants to piss off with all her Vegetarian Flirting an tight dresses don't even notice it: her mum. Samira says she's so sick a her mum always treatin her like some kind a fairy princess, always tellin her how she's better lookin an more captivating than all her friends' daughters, that sometimes she'd like to be a slut just to piss off her mum. But she in't a slut, she in't a ho, she's just a Vegetarian Flirt, a free-willed, independent woman. An in one a the most cheesiest moments a my life ever, I promise her right there that I in't the kind a guy who'd ever try an change her, clip her wings, put her in a cage, that kind a shit.

She looks at me, cuttin through the Hakkasan darkness somehow, an goes, — Just checking.

Once again I owe Sanjay big time for supplyin the venue, the VIP treatment an even some a the conversation. It's just as well he din't supply the transport cos you try parkin anything other than a hatchback round Tottenham Court Road on a Saturday. On the way back to the car Samira holds my hand. Luckily I'd parked up towards Goodge Street, which gives me a few blocks to hold her hand some more, make a point a walkin nearest to the roadside, ask her if she's cold, give her my jacket, give some spare change to a tramp, double-check I'd put my fone on silent, steer the conversation back to sex-in-the-abstract. An it in't just me who's doing it: every time we walk past one a them big posh furniture shops she's like, — That looks like a comfortable bed. Even when one a the shop windows we pass has got mannequins spread out across the beds dressed in see-through dressing gowns an black underwear. Black satin maybe, just like the skirt Samira's got on an the blouse she's wearin underneath my jacket. She pulls my arm under my jacket when she sees me shiver. Definitely satin. She don't let my arm out again till we reach the car, when I use it to hold the door open for her. First thing I do when I get in the driver's seat, I adjust the rear-view mirror so I can check out the lychee ice-cream stains on my DKNY top.

— You should be grateful it didn't fall on your lap and stain your trousers, she goes. — Or maybe you wished it did seeing that I wiped it off for you.

— No offence, but I think you've actually rubbed it into my jumper.

— Exactly.

I stare into the mirror some more so I don't have to reply an somehow I can't stop myself doing a quick zit-hunt. All I find is a small shaving cut under my chin.

— What? Samira goes.

— Nothin. Cut myself shaving, that's all.

— I am sooo glad you're clean-shaven. I can't stand all those different styles of goatee beards all the other guys have. It's like the facial hair Olympics. Eeuurgh. No thanks. I'll take your smooth face any day, even if the only reason it's so smooth is because you can't actually grow facial hair.

— Er, what's that s'posed to mean, Samira? Course I can grow facial hair. I could look like a Muslim cleric if I wanted to. No offence. Anyway, I did have facial hair one time.

— I know, I remember. It looked like you had a stick of black furry chewing gum stuck between your lower lip and chin. What was that style called?

— A soul patch.

She continues sayin things like Yuk an Eeuurgh, shuddering as if furry facial hair reminds her a furry spiders on people's faces an I realise that we've gone an got sidetracked off the sex-in-the-abstract thing again. It's OK though, cos by now I'm gettin good at this.

— Yeh, well, you can cuss it all you like, Samira, but I bet I heard worse beard cusses before. Take this one guy, he comes up to me and gives it, You look like you got a vagina on your face. So you know what I said? I go to him, Yeh, well, I like havin muff on my face, innit.

I look at her to check I hadn't crossed the fine line Sanjay'd warned me bout, the one between sex-in-the-abstract an dirty-perviness. I'm OK though, cos she's laughin. Next thing you know she's tellin me that a soul patch actually does look like a certain type a bikini wax, though she can't remember the proper name for it. She's going on an on bout body hair an I'm just sittin there, not even turnin on the engine, thinkin bout what we might or might not do next. The more I think bout it, the more annoyed I get that I can't think a anything original. I mean, you only need to've seen a couple a music videos or late-night films an you've already seen all the ways you can get off with someone. I in't meanin to sound pervy or nothin, but every time I could lean over to her, it reminds me a some RnB video, every place I could put my hand reminds me a some Michael Douglas film an every way I could pimp up Mum's car by droppin scraps a satin, silk an maybe even lace on the floor reminds me a some tutty Channel Five film I've seen. By the time Samira leans over to me I'm still workin out how I can be original when suddenly I swear I see a light flash outside.

— Wait, Samira.

— What is it?

— I thought I saw a camera flash.

— Jas, just because you take me to dinner with Hugh Grant and just because you're some wannabe Bollywood film director, that doesn't mean the paparazzi are after us quite yet, she goes.

— Film director?

— Yeh, with all your rain, your fountains, your tunnels through the mountains, she goes, reachin across the fuckin gearstick now, — you'd make a great film director, Jas, everything *means* something with you. But just relax now. That flash was probably just a speed camera or something. What's the matter? You nervous? You've never done this before, have you?

— Nah, no. Course not. I mean, yeh, course I done it before, no, I in't nervous. Just let me just check the doors are locked an the handbrake's up, just to be sure, I go, wishing that somehow we *had* parked in a tunnel or it was raining outside or something. — Samira, you sure they got speed cameras on this road?

— Yes, Jas. Now shut up and come over here. Speed camera or no speed camera, you don't need to go that slow.

21

From outside their house it sounds like how Mrs Ware's classroom used to sound. Screamin an shoutin an yellin an more fuckin screamin, makin you wonder how come the windows in't cracked yet. With all that screamin I figure this must be a bad time, an whatever Arun'd called me round for half an hour ago could probly wait till after whoever was in there had finished hacking to death whoever it was they were hacking to death. Not that I din't have some idea bout what was going down in there. As well as callin me this morning, Arun had texted me the nite before, sayin: 'Gr8 mums turnd psycho. Nd yur hlp.' My fone had been on silent even after me an Samira left Hakkasan, an when I finally saw the message I texted him back sayin: 'Chill b a man.' I tell myself this advice is probly still the best I could give him right now an so I turn away from the house. But before I can head off back home, the front door flies open an Arun's mum is standin there, holdin the door as if she was tryin to squash monsters an rapists tryin to barge in. — Jas! she screams, like she's now tryin to prevent me from gettin run over by a speedin car. Her screamin scares the fuckin shit outta me. A speedin car drunk-driven by monsters an rapists. — Jas!

I consider pretendin I din't hear her, but you can't fuckin pretend you din't hear that. Even if you'd had your ears scissored off an her boiling fryin-pan oil poured over your eardrums you'd still fuckin hear that.

— Aunty? I say, hardly able to hear my own voice.

— Come inside. At once.

— What's the matter, Aunty? Is everything OK?

— Vot is matter? I'll show you vot matter is, hah, I show you I wipe smile off your mouth. You, bloody badmarsh munda, corrupting my beita, telling him to disrespect his mother. Just because your own mother is good-for-nothing woman with social security benefits, vhy you tell my sons to disrespect me?

— Er, sorry, Aunty . . . I don't know what you're talkin bout.

— Look at you. Shame on you. Not even to defend your own mama. You let me speak gandh about her and not even you defend her. Vot are you? Scum? Shit? Come inside an explain vot it is you telled to Arun.

Now I know I should be attackin her for talkin to me like that. Sanjay, Hardjit, Amit, Arun an Ravi, all a them'd've told me never to take this kind a shit from no one no more. But I can't help myself. Amit is in the doorway too now an he's cryin. With fuckin tears an everything. An so I got no choice but to find out what the fuck is going on in there an what the fuck it's got to do with me.

As I walk in, I start apologising for no reason. God, why'd you make me apologise again? I thought we'd cured all that. Inside their living room it's obvious that yet more complicated family-related shit had somehow erupted. That it'd hit their state-a-the-art three-speed tower fan with auto oscillation an random airflow variation for natural wind effect. There's shattered shit all over the floor, chopped-up shit on the dining table, the smell a diced-up an grated shit coming in from the kitchen an fuckin minced shit staining the sofas. There is broken glass by one a the designer coffee tables, a plant pot that's fallen over an puked-up mud an fertiliser balls all over one a the designer rugs, an a pool a some yellowy liquid on the carpet that you might think was complicated family-related piss if it weren't for the broken whisky bottle lyin next to it. Amit's dad is standin there wearin just one chapple, the other is in his hand lookin like some kind a badass weapon, a fuckin chapple-num-chucker. He's got whisky all over his shirt an his eyebrows stick out at least an inch longer than they'd done yesterday. Arun is sittin on the floor like a baby, his arms around his knees, an he's clearly cryin, fuckin snot dribbling out his nostrils onto his shirt an he's doing these sharp intakes a bubbly-soundin breaths as if he's hyperventilating an drowning all at the same time. It's fuckin disgusting, he looks like a mental patient. A homeless mental patient.

— So tell me, Jas, vot it is you have been telling to my son? his mum asks me again.

— Aunty . . . honestly, I really have no idea what you're talkin bout.

She looks at me, breathes in a less gurgly way, grabs her husband's chapple an waves it in the air like a magic stick. — You bring only trouble to my house. Telling my son to talk to me like mad boy ruffian from the street. To throw away his traditions. To disrespect his mother. Your own mother vill be ashamed of you when I call her.

— Look, Aunty, I don't know what the problem is here. Yes, I had a conversation with Arun yesterday. I told him he should tell you the things he was tellin me bout his wedding. It just seemed that he needed to put his point a view across better so I encouraged him to do so. But I din't tell anyone to show any disrespect to anyone an din't mean to disrespect you or your family, Aunty –

— But vhy you talk? You don't understand such things, so then vhy you telled him such things? Vhy you talk? Vot you know about our proper style of shaadi? Nothing. You not understand nothing, Arun not understand, Amit not understand even, only we understand. We know vot needs to be done, not you boys. You not know our ways. These bloody badmarsh ideas you put into my son's head. Look vot you've done to my house.

— Well, if I don't understand, why don't you try an explain things to me? What's the problem, Aunty?

She looks at Arun, who by now has dried the snotty tears an teary snot from his face an stood up. — Vell? Tell your friend, she says to him.

— Sorry to get you involved, Jas. We just had another argument.

— Vot we argue for? Tell your friend vot it is we argue for. Go on, tell him vot your fiancée has done now.

— Well, you see, Jas, Reena emailed us a picture of the diamond set she's bought for the wedding reception, you see, an, well, Mum didn't like it.

I stand there waitin for the punchline or for some TV crew to jump out the plants that are still standin upright, some cheesy TV host maybe, shoutin, Surprise, Jas, you've been had live on national TV. The plants continue shaking but no TV cameras pop out. So I ask, — Yeh? An?

— Well, it's complicated. But basically it's the set we're buying her. Only she chose it herself to match her dress and also cos she's in Bombay and we ain't. Anyway, the thing is, mate, it's not nearly as nice as the necklace an earrings Mum had told her to get.

— Not as nice? shouts Arun an Amit's mum. — We send her to our designer jeweller in Mumbai, give her open credit, she buys a tiny set that looks like she get from bloody Claire's Accessories on High Street. You need bloody magnifying glass to see the diamonds.

— But Mum, I kept telling you, she isn't big on jewellery. She wants to keep it simple.

— I don't care vot you telled me. I telled to them buy a nice set. Vot vill people think of us when they see? They vill know is our gift. Vot is wrong that her mother wants to make mockery of me? Jas, vot is this I hear you tell Arun that I wearing lots of jewellery because I ashamed of my face? Is that vot it is you said?

— Aunty, I din't even know jewellery was such a big issue in this wedding. I just told him you seemed to think it was more important than perhaps it should be.

— Vot you know? Huh? Vot you know? This diamond set my daughter-in-law vill wear for reception, the whole town vill know is from us. She wears cheap set, everyone vill think we are cheap people. I know vot's going on. I know. Her mother, bloody bitch, has told her to buy cheap set so to shame us. To put shame on our family. And Arun, bastard-bitch, tells me to let her do as she pleases. Attacks me, his mother, all because I vont for things to be done properly. This is how he talks to his mother. Telled to me to go to hell with my traditions. Not even married an already he's, votyoucall, henpecked husband. Helping her parents make mockery of his own mother.

Still nobody, still no camera crews. Not in the hallway, not outside in the driveway.

— Is that it? I can't help asking. — You've gone ballistic over that? Arun, is she serious? Amit, I can't believe your mum's serious.

— Vot, I don't look enough serious, young man?

Amit puts his arm out, tellin his mum to calm down, then looks at me. — Look, Jas, I think you should jus apologise to my mum for fillin my brother's head wid all a dese stupid ideas, innit. Stop tryin to turn him into a coconut.

— Hang on a minute, Amit. He was upset, bottling it all up, I told him to tell your mum. That's all.

— You told him to say to me You fuhcking bitch? Huh? You telled my son to call his mother a Fuhcking bitch? Huh?

— No, Aunty, I did not tell anyone to swear at anyone. If he's angry with you that's not my fault. A minute ago he was sittin on the floor snotting over himself like a tramp drinkin tear gas, so if you've made him mad enough to use the word fuck then that in't my fault. I just told him to stand up for himself. We all know who holds the chapples in this house, maybe Arun thought it was time he tried to be a man. He's s'posed to be gettin married, might do him good to try an be a man. In't that right, Arun?

Suddenly another crash. This time it's a flower vase that Arun's just picked up an thrown across the room, hittin the window which shudders but don't shatter.

— Fucking shut the fuck up, everyfuckingbody, he screams as the sound a the vase smashing continues to vibrate in all their crystal glasses. He's tearin at his hair an lettin all the snot an tears flow again. — What the fucking fuck is wrong with you fucking people? I can't believe we're having this conversation when all I'm trying to do is get fucking married. Mum, of course I'm using the word fuck. I don't need fucking Jas to tell me to use the word fuck, I'd use even worse words if I could, only there aren't any. I'd use the word cunt but you're all so stuck in some Indian village you probably don't even know what the word cunt fucking means. So there's no other fucking word to describe the fucking ridiculousness of what the fuck's going on here, is there? Admit it, Mum, this has got fuck all to do with the diamond set. Truth is everything Reena does is wrong in your eyes cos, face it, you don't like her cos she ain't the same as us. You think her mother's got one up on you just cos she's marrying up. But the thing is, her mother probably didn't even know about all our fucking caste and businesses and bank balances and shit until you went an showed it all off to her. But that ain't even the issue here, is it? The issue is you're just messed up in the head. Just messed in the head and I've had enough of it. How the fuck can you give a fucking shit about all this bollocks you give a shit about? How the fuck can you not just put it all aside, just for my sake? For my fucking wedding. Because this is my fucking wedding we're talking about, not some party political society satsang of yours. I mean, I'm so sorry that my happiness is such an inconvenient headache for you, Mum. Why don't you try banging your head against a fucking wall like I do every time you come out with this fucked-up shit about all your fucking hypersensitive sensitivities? Don't you realise that this wedding is the best thing that's ever happened to me? This is the happiest I've been in years and all you care about is what other people think of you and whether all the right customs are being followed and all the right kinds of respect are being shown to you. Well, you know what, I got a headache too. I wanna cure my headache with a fucking gun, that's how much of a headache you're giving me.

Now their dad steps in, briefly putting his hand on Arun's shoulder an sayin shit like, Calm down, beita, before lookin at his wife, walkin towards her an adding, — And no need to talk to your mother like this. Why you use this fuck word? Is this how we bring you up?

You talk this nonsense language to your mother again, I put red chillies in your mouth, you understand? All the time talking nonsense. Is this what you call showing your elders respect?

— Listen to yourself, Dad. Can you hear what you're saying?

— Of course I can bloody well hear what it is I'm saying.

— No, you clearly can't, Dad. Because otherwise you wouldn't say it, because it doesn't make any fuckin sense.

— You show more respect. I told you, don't talk to us like this. Why you want to hurt your mother for? After all she has done for you.

— See, there you go again. You obviously can't hear what you're saying because if you could you wouldn't say it. You're asking me to show more respect to my elders by not hurting their feelings. You guys are always telling me and Amit to respect our elders by treating them as if they were five years old. To treat them like kids cos they're our elders. Well, it makes no sense and I'm fucking sick of it.

— What nonsense is this you talk, Arun? Jas, what is this now that you've taught my son?

— Uncle, this has nothin to do with me. I never told him that.

Their mother huffs as she picks up the broken vase, then she starts sayin things like Hai Rabba even though they in't Muslim. — Look vot you've done to my vase, she screams after she's calmed down.

Arun says he's sorry, sits down an then Amit goes to the kitchen to make tea for everyone. Everyone, that is, except me. But to be honest, I try an not give a fuck. They keep tellin me that I should stay out their family affairs, well, fine, I'll stay out. Arun's breathing gradually gets smoother an less snotty. Soon it starts soundin like Samira's breathing last night. Obviously she din't, like, moan or nothin. But she was definitely breathing more loudly, more quickly, more slowly, more softly. I could feel it on her chest as well as hear it. An maybe I was just imagining it, but I could swear even her hips were movin in time with her breathing. Not just her hips but that muscle below her midriff, the one that connected to a tendon at the top a her thigh muscles.

When Amit comes back with the cups a chai, everyone just calms themselves down. Just like how goras do in *EastEnders*. Their mum is sittin on the sofa an says something in Punjabi that basically means I don't know why you boys want to kick my husband's turban around in the street. She says this even though they in't Sikh an therefore don't wear turbans. Arun goes back to sniffly, snotty mode, but now manages to reply without cryin, yellin or screamin. — I'm not trying to kick Dad's turban, Mum, don't say that. It's just sometimes I don't understand why we have to follow all these traditions when they obviously cause problems, they don't even really matter and are obviously sometimes wrong. You can't be bothered to even think about whether any of this stuff actually makes sense any more.

— You don't understand, Aunty says to him. — You are too Westrenised. I tell you, this munda of ours is too Westrenised.

— It's *Westernised*, Mum, and no, I don't think I am.

— Then vhy you can't understand she is not doing her duties? I did those duties for your sister Anjana when she got married.

Arun's dad gives his wife an Om Shanti sign with his palm an then turns to Arun. — Son, all these things you don't like, they are our custom. All these things you fight about, is about our traditions. Is our custom that we follow the traditions.

– Yeh, but why, Dad? I mean, just give me a good reason why that's the tradition an I'll stop arguing with you guys all the time.

— I gave to you reason, beita. Is the custom. They're the Girl's Side.

— That's not a reason, Dad. *Why* is that our custom? If you were in a court of law you couldn't justify your actions by saying that that's the custom, that's the way things are done. If you keep saying the reason for everything we're doing is because it's the tradition then surely you're just hiding the fact that there's no proper reason.

— No, son, you are misguided. Tradition is reason for many things in life. Even in Angrez weddings is the tradition for the girl to wear white. These Angrez kurhiyaan can wear pink Hawaiian dress if she like, but no, always they wear white because is their custom.

— Why can't you understand what I'm saying, Dad? There's a reason why they wear white. It means they're pure and even if they aren't really pure they want to look pure. Fair enough, no harm. All I want is the reasons why it's the tradition. Maybe we can start talking instead of arguing. Why should Reena's family treat us like we're royalty or something and show us more respect than we show them? Tell me *why* it's our custom and then we can decide whether it's a custom that's worth following or not.

— OK, I see, son. So you want we don't do anything that's our custom, is this what you want? Not to do things the way the things are done.

— No, Dad. See? You're not listening to me. For fuck's sake, why is that how things are fucking done?

— I told you, don't you swear at me. I'm not bloody fool. I understand what it is you are asking. Your wife, she is the girl. You are the boy. You will do all the hard work and bring in all the money and feed her. That is why they should respect us.

— Dad, how many times do we have to go through this? She earns more than me.

— But what about when you have children? Wait. Then you will see how she will depend on you to work and bring home money. Put food on table.

— Me? She'll get less maternity leave than my company gives paternity leave. And anyway, we'll have a nanny. And even if we don't, what if I want to spend as much time as her bringing up our kids? Then what?

— Beita. Please. Stop talking this nonsense. Our customs are good enough reasons for other people to do things, they are good enough reasons for this family. Listen to your younger brother, even he agree with me about wedding traditions.

— Forget the wedding traditions. Let's think of something totally different. Like, what if I were to ask you why grass is green? Would your answer be because that's the way it's always been? No, you'd say something like it's because of the chlorophyll.

— I told you, enough of this talking nonsense. Stop being such a smart alec, clever clogs. I know what is what. I play cricket on grass. I know why is it green.

— Or why not take cricket, Dad? I mean, why is the batsman out when, say, the ball hits their leg? Is it because that's the tradition? The custom?

— Because it's the rule of the bloody game. LBW, Leg Before Wicket. What is this nonsense you talk?

— No. That's my point, Dad. It's not just because it's the rule. It's because if the batsman's leg wasn't in the way then the ball would hit the stumps and then he'd be out. That's the reason behind the rule.

Then Arun's mum puts down her cup a tea an sits back in the sofa before sayin, — But tell me, smart alec, if the ball it hits stumps, vhy it is the batsman is out then? Is because it's the rule, no? The custom. There's no other reason. Stumps are not living creatures. You not have to save them from being killed by flying cricket ball.

— Yes, darling, says his dad, — this is correct. Tu time na waste kar, beita. I think so what you are saying is all nonsense.

— Oh for goodness' sake. You know that's different. That's not a custom, that's a law. But when Reena's family don't phone you, you act like they've broken the law and tried to kill you.

— You vont to kill me, hah? Is that it? You vont to kill your own mother?

— Oh for fuck's sake, Mum, goes Arun, the tea obviously wearin off now, — for fucking fuck's fucking sake. All I'm saying is that when I ask you why something is done the way it's done, it's completely invalid and totally fucking wrong for you to answer that it's the custom, it's how things are done. If you don't fucking give me the real reason then how can you ever be sure we're doing the right thing? And if we don't try to be sure we're doing the right thing then there's no fucking hope for anyone or anyfuckingthing. I mean, if that's the case for doing things then I might as well walk out the house now, find the nearest pack of Rottweilers or Dobermanns and let them all bite me and gang-rape me to death because there's no fucking point. Right, Jas?

I don't even nod cos I was so lookin forward to hearin what his mum an dad would throw back at that. But suddenly the phone rings. Arun's dad picks it up, shruggin his shoulders at his wife as if to say, Well, it's not *my* fault the phone interrupted your retort.

— Yes, well, Arun is little busy right now, Reena, he shouts into the receiver long-distance-style. — I know is hard to get connection from India, but can you call back later? But then Uncle's face melts. — Oh my dear, oh my God, beiti, I so sorry to hear this.

We all just sit an stare as he passes the cordless phone to Arun, who takes it into the next room an shuts the door. His father wipes the sweat from his head an looks at us.

— Reena's grandfather just had massive heart attack in Brent Cross. He was in W H Smith. They say he might pass away.

I look at Arun's mother, who for a split second looks like she's seen a ghost. That's the fucked-up thing bout complicated family-related shit. People only see sense when it's life or death. This is especially fucked up seeing as how people die all the time in Bollywood films an desi soap operas, but it takes someone dyin or nearly dyin in real life to stop people actin as if they're in some desi soap opera. An even then the whole life an death perspective shit only lasts a few seconds. Matter a fact, after only, like, twenty seconds Aunty's face is back to normal. — If that woman thinks this gives her right to call the shots and delay wedding then she can forget it. All arrangements are made. If he dies there is still nearly two months more. By then the mourning vill be over.

— But darling, it's her grandfather, Uncle says. — It must be up to them if they want to delay. Even if he doesn't die, the wedding insurance covers serious illness. Koi gal nahi.

— Don't you start taking their side. The grandfather is old man, always he was going to have health problems or heart attack. If not before wedding then after. Anyway, always grandparents fall ill, always they die. Your parents died, my parents died. I vill not be made mockery of. First they call the shots, then they don't show me the proper respect, they don't phone me, now they better not think they can delay. In my day, daughters carried on with wedding even if their own father died.

I can't believe what the woman just said an I can't stop myself butting in again. — But Aunty, surely that's cos in those days gettin married was for financial support. So if a girl's dad died that'd be even more reason to get married. But that in't the case no more, not these days.

— Jas, vot did I tell you, huh? I tell you already: vot you boys know about our family matters, huh? Vhy you don't just respect our customs, huh? Now, while my son is on the phone, I'm telling to everybody now, I'm promising to all of you here in the room, if Reena's family wants to delay the wedding just because of this then I don't care, the wedding vill be off. I vill cancel it once and for all. I vill rather I kill myself than let her family carry on making mockery of me.

Just then Arun walks back in the room, puts the phone on the coffee table an hugs his mum. Yes, hugs his mum. — Mama, she's so upset, Arun says as if Reena's sadness is somehow contagious. — She's so upset. He's in intensive care at the moment. The doctors don't know if he'll make it. They're coming straight back from India today.

— Ahh, beita, this very sad, is very tragic, his mum says, patting him on the back.

— Mama, he says, — Reena's mum said they might have to move things back to April or May. I told them whatever they needed, we could get married in September even. What do you think?

PART THREE
DESI

22

Every time someone we know dies they go to Heaven or Hell or get reincarnated via the crematorium in Golders Green. Apparently they've got another one in Mortlake an there are loads a these ovens up in Birmingham an Leicester. But if you live in London, chances are your last stop will be Hoop Lane in Golders Green. An not just for desis either, there's also some big Jewish cemetery on the opposite side a the road from the crematorium. Anyway, whatever, here I am again. Standin in the same car park in what felt like the same fuckin rain they pour on you practically every time you come here. The crematorium sandwich shop behind me. The toilets next to it that even weak-bladdered aunties never use. The BMWs an Mercs parked up alongside knackered-out Nissans an Datsuns. All a them with their in-car sound systems switched off for the day. An then in front a me that tower. They probly meant for it to look like some old-fashioned church tower but it's made a red bricks an if you looked all the way up to the top you knew exactly what it was: a fuckin chimney.

The Holy Trinity Church on Hounslow High Street is like the Magic Kingdom castle in Disneyland compared to this place. Only one time do I remember that chimney not scaring me shitless: during Hardjit's grandma's funeral, when the sunny blue skies made it look like some express elevator to Heaven an when nobody was too gutted that she'd died cos, well, after a while that's just what grandparents do, innit. Times like this though, when it's cold an rainy an shitty, nobody hangin round the car park looks up at the sky. Everyone's just lookin at each other, not knowing whether to cry in each other's arms or catch up with mates they hadn't seen in ages. Tryin to override the smile reflex when shaking hands or sayin things like Kiddaan. Keepin it simple. How's work? How are the kids? That kind a shit. An never, under no circumstances Good to see you or Nice to see you. It's less complicated for any a the immediate family who are waitin in the car park. All they gotta say to people is Thank you for coming, Thank you for coming. Always, always, just Thank you for coming.

The only family member I'd made eye contact with out there had been Reena herself. She was carryin the old Delhi Cricket Club umbrella that had belonged to her grandfather before he finally died. His Brent Cross heart attack had been followed by another two – one a couple a weeks later when he got back home from hospital an one a couple a weeks after that while he was back in hospital. Reena nodded to me but even in my sharp black Kenzo suit an tie I din't feel enough a some badass Reservoir Dog to go over an talk to her or any a the immediate family.

As I switch my fone to silent (outta respect this time stead a to avoid my mum) I realise it's still pretty early an we probly won't be allowed into the hall for at least another fifteen minutes. So I find myself walkin away from everyone, feelin shitty an pathetic as I take shelter from the rain under this covered passageway round the back a the hall. The passageway is basically this arcade lined with bunches a flowers an full-on wreaths that'd been delivered earlier by florists an then carefully laid out on the concrete floor in separate groups for each a today's roastings. First up was some woman called Pauline Hewson who according to one a her wreaths was also known as MUMSY. Then some bloke called Vikram Patel who was obviously into his cricket cos someone had stuck a cricket ball in one a his wreaths. Next was someone called Seema Gulchand whose family an friends din't seem big on flowers. All in all it looked like there were bout fifteen funerals happening here today. I check to see that the bunch a flowers I'd sent had been laid out in the correct group, adjust the plastic film an card so that people'll see more clearly that it's a really big bunch a flowers an it's from me. The wall behind the flowers is lined with memorial plaques, but only for people who'd died years an years ago cos they've run outta space. Matter a fact, the wall is so crowded with memorial plaques it looks like it's been made out the fuckin things. Readin some a them, I'm wonderin why they all seem to be for Angrez loki, why the fuck don't they desify the place a bit? As Amit'd said one time, it's mostly desis who like to finish their lives being cooked all the way through stead a going mouldy like raw chicken.

After checkin out the flowers an plaques, I turn round to look at the grounds opposite the wall. It's a little park full a more flowers an stuff planted in memory a various people who died too late to get a plaque. There are memorial hedges, memorial bushes, memorial trees, an memorial benches but no gravestones cos they don't do gravestones in this place. Like always you want to wander further off into the park but each time you come here you never do in case someone sees you an thinks, Poor beycharay. Some aunt or someone might even follow you in there an hug you when the whole point a wandering off is you want to be left the fuck alone. There should be a fence round that park to make it private. Lots a fences, dividing up the grounds into private cubicles like public toilets.

Even when I get bored staring at the gardens, the flowers an the plaques I don't go back to the car park cos I can see Amit an his mum an there weren't no point in me tryin to deal with them. Amit weren't speakin to me no more, you see. He hadn't spoken to me since that big family showdown in his house over Arun's wedding. Said I'd stepped over the line too many times, meddling in his family business an dissin his mum. Hang on, I'd said to him, it's Arun who's been dissin your mum, not me. It's Arun who keeps throwin vases around an machine-gunning your parents with the word Fuck. But when I told him this, Amit weren't havin none a it. An it weren't just him who was menstrual with me; Hardjit an Ravi din't want to know me now either. Not just cos a all the shit I'd stirred at Amit an Arun's house but cos a the shit I'd stirred up all by myself.

I'd been busted, you see. Spotted by one a Hardjit's cousins with my arm around Samira. It'd been a couple a weeks back. My own fuckin fault. Like a pehndu wantin to get my ass caught I'd taken her for a walk in Lampton Park. Lampton fuckin Park for fuck's sake. That's like some celebrity tryin to escape the paparazzi by going to the fuckin Oscars. I told Hardjit that the hug din't mean nothin, we were just hangin out, innit. It in't as if we'd got off or nothin. We just mates, innit, but that afternoon in Lampton Park shit got emotional an that an so we hugged each other, that's all, Hardjit. It in't as if we'd got off with each other. Matter a fact, we in't ever even kissed. But did any a them believe me? Did they fuck. Even Ravi thought I was full a bullshit. Imagine that – this time six months ago they'd've said I was full a bullshit if I'd said I *had* got off with her.

Worst thing is, I was sort a tellin them the fuckin truth. That day in Lampton Park, all I did was put my arm around her so whoever it was who spotted us an shopped us couldn't possibly have seen us do any a the other stuff we'd done together in other places. The stuff we'd done in the back a my mum's Ford Focus on our second date, for example. The stuff we did inside Sanjay's Porsche on our fifth date. The stuff we did on the bonnet a Sanjay's Porsche on our tenth date. The reason I din't do more than put my arm around her that time in Lampton Park was cos she was in the middle a tellin me I had to ease off being so clingy, otherwise she might think bout maybe dumping me one a these days. It's a bit difficult to get off with some- one while they're tellin you that you've become too clingy. Too possessive. Too in-my-face. Too right, I'd thought: too scared fuckin shitless that one a these days'd be today. It's OK though, she reas- sured me, it weren't that day yet – that day might never ever come, she'd said. Then I put my arm around her for a bit. Then I removed it, just in case it felt too clingy. But according to the other guys, even if I *was* tellin the truth bout me an Samira just huggin in Lampton Park, I must've blatantly been tryin to get off with her when we got

busted an that meant I must've blatantly been a fuckin bastard trai-
tor who deserved to get the shit kicked outta him. They said that as
word had got round Hounslow bout me an her an Lampton Park,
nobody else believed we'd just been huggin either. Hardjit said I'd
fucked up his reputation so bad that I should think bout doing my
retakes at some other college cos if I stayed round there he'd have
to settle things. It was a matter a respect, you see. You just don't do
whatever it was I'd done to your bredrens. Especially seeing how
much they'd done for me, how they'd taken me on as part a their
crew, even when other people had laughed at them for hangin round
with a guy like me.

Now Hardjit was being rinsed by people like Tariq an all the other
Muslim guys in Hounslow, Southall an Slough that he'd beaten shitless over the years for goin out with Sikh girls. Aparently Tariq had
even taken the mike at some party an started MCing bout it, tellin
all the Muslim brothers in da house to grab a Sikh boy's sista, Cos
Hardjit's crew chirpsed a Muslim an word is he kissed her. Or
someshit like that. An then on top a shit like that, Hardjit'd had to
deal with all the desis who'd stopped supplyin us fones cos they
thought I'd crossed the line. Crossed what fuckin line? I know for a
fact that Hardjit's dad an Ravi's dad an Amit's dad, they all did business with Muslims. Business is business. Bucks is bucks. An I in't
even Muslim, I just 'hugged' a Muslim. But even Davinder weren't
givin us no fones no more. He'd always told Hardjit I was a liability an I guess this was his last straw. His mate Jaswinder – the one
who'd always hated me in school for gettin the nickname Jas before
he did – had even been foned by other random Sikh bredren askin
if he was the Jas who'd married a Muslim.

Hardjit'd been tryin to limit the damage to our business by tellin
people like Davinder an Jaswinder that I weren't one a his crew no
more. He'd given my address to people like Tariq an even to Samira's
brothers. He'd given em my dad's warehouse address too. In fact,
any time any business contact or Muslim crew asked him what the
fuck the score was between his mate Jas an Samira Ahmed, he'd give

em my address an tell em I weren't his bredren or his business partner no more so they could do whatever the fuck they wanted to me
an there'd be no comeback from him. Business is business, innit.
Turns out Samira's brothers had even foned him an offered him a
business deal a their own: a one-off partnership arrangement to
mash me up proper. Hardjit'd said No thanks, he, Amit an Ravi
planned to surprise me someday after today's funeral. Might be the
day a the funeral, might be any day that week, might even wait till
next week. He'd told Samira's brothers that he'd got extra beef with
me – what with me messin with Amit an Arun's complicated family-
related shit. An so basically the three a them wanted to beat Samira's
three brothers to beatin me. What's more, Sanjay's startin to get
fucked off with me too cos the scandal's hit our supply a fones. He's
sayin if I don't sort things out on the fone front soon, he's got three
associates who'll happily beat the shit outta me. The more shit I got
into, the more I got to thinkin maybe I'd been wrong to go out with
Samira, maybe I'd fucked with dharma.

Hangin around the crematorium now, thinkin sad, funeral-type
shit, I'm wonderin whether, if that day with Samira does come, will
I end up here? Roasted an replaced by a wreath or a plaque or a
fuckin park bench? Call it feelin sorry for myself if you like, but I'm
at a funeral, my mates have dumped me, my first an most gorgeous
girlfriend ever has given me a verbal warning that she might dump
me an practically put me on, like, fuckin probation. There are three
different crews who want to mash me up. I'm allowed to feel fuckin
sorry for myself. In't nobody gonna do jackshit at a funeral though,
so that's OK. An tomorrow, the day after, next week – let them fuckin
try. I'll fight back, innit. Can't let my self-respect go, can I? Otherwise
might as well cut my dick off, give this place one more sausage to
fry. I'll even fight back if Samira tries to dump me. That's right, if
that day ever comes, I promise myself I'll fight back. A course I'm
possessive, I'll tell her. You'd be possessive too if you pulled someone like you. You win the lottery, you're gonna want to hang onto
your ticket. What the fuck's wrong with that? How the fuck does that

make me irritating or insecure? In fact, if that day does come, I won't even consider killin myself or any a the other things you're s'posed to do if you get dumped, like forgettin how to shave an going to strip clubs. There's plenty more fish in the sea, right? More importantly, over the past six months I'd found out London was a fuckin aquarium where even ugly guys could go fishing. I'd spotted fishes swimming by even while I'd been gettin off with you, Samira. In fact, if you really want to know the truth, walkin back into the crematorium car park I can't help myself checkin out one a Reena's fit cousins.

The funeral before ours ends, all its people leave the service hall by the back door an we're finally let in through the front door. As we enter, we can hear people from the previous funeral cryin as they walk through the arcade a wreaths an plaques. Reena in't allowed to stand up onstage with the coffin. Only the male mourners are allowed near it. Fuck knows what that's all bout – maybe women cry too much to do these things. Takin her place in the front row instead, Reena suddenly starts howling like a baby. She just keeps breaking down an fallin onto her mum. It's so fucked up that, even though I don't really know her, it makes me want to go up an hug her or someshit. Stead I stand way at the back a the hall, well away from Amit, Hardjit an Ravi.

Inside, the hall is the same as always. Wooden benches that'd make my old school assembly ones feel like fuckin velvet sofas. More memorial plaques on the walls. A couple a statues. It reminds me a Ravi's grandad's funeral. That funeral had reminded me a Amit's grandma's a year before. An that one had reminded me a my own grandad's funeral when I was fifteen an had to go up onstage an read a fuckin poem. Whenever you're in that hall, sittin on those benches, every funeral just blends into all the others you been to at Golders Green. You're always so busy remembering the last funeral you went to there that you don't really finish experiencing the funeral you're actually at till you've remembered it at the next one you go to. It's like there's some fuckin bereavement time lag going on in there. I can hear sniffles from two years ago, recognise speeches from earlier this year, see faces from a few weeks back.

The speeches just go on an on, people cryin all the time so you can barely hear the speeches anyway. I have to bite my tongue till it bleeds or someshit just to stay the fuck awake. But the thing is, you actually *want* the speeches to go on an on cos you know that when they stop that's when the coffin conveyor belt starts an then it's time to say goodbye. Again. You want the speeches an the music an the cold air to never end. Or at least you want them to fuck up somehow. Anything so that they don't press the button on the podium that starts the conveyor belt. It in't even actually a conveyor belt, it's this set a rollers that the coffin glides on. But when you're standin in the back row it looks like the coffin's on a conveyor belt. Like it'll beep after passin over a fuckin barcode scanner, the first in a queue a coffins at the checkout. Fuckin disrespect, man. You want the button to break or the rollers to jam. Cos no way this should be so fuckin smooth. There's a person in there, innit. This shouldn't run smoothly cos it in't fuckin smooth cos they're fuckin dead. The speeches should get delayed, the songs an bhajans should get stuck. There're, what – fifteen funerals a day in this place? No fuckin way ours is gonna go so smoothly that the pandit don't even remember it a couple a months from now. There is one thing that's different though: the track they play when all the speeches, poems an prayers end an we start shufflin out the back door. Stead a some bhajan or something, one a the kids in the family has decided to dedicate 'I'll Be Missing You', that tune Puff Daddy an Faith Evans recorded bout Biggie Smalls.

Three more women start brand new cryin as we all spill out the back door into the arcade a wreaths. I guess the three women suddenly realised it's all over an if they in't got it out by now they'd better do so quick time. Cryin an shiverin in the queue, waitin to hug the immediate family an say how sorry they all are. All a them, always the same thing: I'm sorry. I'm sorry. Thank you for coming. Thank you for coming. What the fuck else is there to say? The immediate family always lines up at the end a the arcade an people back in the queue are always too quiet to block out the cryin an the I'm sorrys up front. Today there's way too many I'm sorrys to get through an it's too fuckin cold to be standin out here, people's tears makin even colder lines down their faces an their cold snot gettin mixed up with their cryin snot. I hang back a bit, not cos I got a problem with other people's snot but cos I'm still tryin to keep my distance from Amit an Arun's mum. She's busy anyway, standin up front with her husband, comforting someone who's cryin. That someone then thanks her stead the other way round. Lookin at her lapping it all up, there's just enough anger left in me to think, she's the one who should be sorry. She's the one who'd said Reena's family had brought nothin but shame on her own family or someshit like that. Someshit straight outta some desi soap opera. Matter a fact, for a woman who'd said Reena's family, friends an loved ones could all go to Hell for all she cared, Arun's mum is doing a pretty good job a lookin all cut up. She'd said that shit right after sayin she'd never forgive Arun for spittin in her face. That's right: the dude gave his mum one big juicy thooka from the back a his throat after their last big family showdown. From what I could tell, she'd forgiven him a little more than he'd forgiven himself an a lot more than Amit'd forgiven me.

Reena is now howlin even louder. She keeps askin her mum, Why? Why, Mama, why? It was only three weeks ago we'd all been in this exact same place an she'd been howlin over her grandfather's death. Only back then she weren't askin Why, Mama, why? all the time. Back then she knew exactly why: cardiac arrest. Technically, she knew why we were here today too: aspirin overdose. But she din't know why he'd done it an so she was howlin even more. Whatever his reason, Reena's howlin was understandable. After all, Arun had practically been her husband. The dude hadn't even left a note or whatever else you're s'posed to do. The official line was that he'd definitely meant to kill himself – he'd taken a whole pack. But how could anyone really be sure? How did they know he weren't just tryin to get rid a some headache, ease his backache or soothe the tummy ache caused by all a that complicated family-related shit?

23

My stomach weren't the only one that'd been rumblin all through the funeral service. I guess not many people had bothered with breakfast, what with Arun's cremation being at 10am an with his mum's pakoras an samosas scheduled to be on tap at their house after. The difference between all the other rumbles an the ones comin from me was that not only had I skipped breakfast, I also hadn't eaten jackshit for breakfast yesterday, jackshit for lunch yesterday or jackshit for dinner. As I left Golders Green I was so starved I probly couldn't eat jackshit even if I tried. What the fuck is with that, anyway? Your stomach makin you feel too sick to eat if you let yourself get too hungry. It's as if your stomach suddenly says, Fine, don't feed me then, I don't want no food now anyway, fuck off. How fuckin childish is that? It feels a bit like all that nausea shit I get when I gotta be around Mum or Dad. Anyhow, I'd got a good reason for why I hadn't eaten fuck all since yesterday. I hadn't fuckin slept since yesterday, innit. Matter a fact, I don't reckon I'd had more than three hours' sleep or a proper meal since Arun topped himself last week. Too fuckin tired to eat, too fuckin hungry to sleep. I din't even have the energy to oolti up all that empty-stomach acid out so it was just hangin there in my throat. Makes you wonder how the fuck do people do all a them religious fasts? I heard someplace that when you do a fast your body's s'posed to start digesting its own fat. I'm so skinny my body probly finished with my fat days ago, worked its way through other organs like my liver an my dick an was now digesting my brain.

There'd be none a Aunty's pakoras an samosas for me today. Let's just say I wouldn't exactly be welcome at the house this afternoon when I weren't even welcome to the funeral. Amit's mum'd already slapped me an screamed tears an snot across my face when I went round their house the day Arun'd been found dead in his bed. Then, just yesterday, Hardjit'd foned me to say I best stay the fuck away from today's service, told me that after everything that'd happened it'd be better if they din't see my fuckin face ever the fuck again. Soon as I'd defied him by showin up this morning he shot me one a them stares, the Wild West ones that go: Well, You Sure Gotta Lotta Nerve Showin Your Face Round Here, Mister. According to the guys, after gettin myself busted with Samira, the way I'd interfered in Arun's life (by which I guess they meant his death) had been the final straw. For the first couple a days, I'd figured they were just blaming me for what'd happened to Arun cos they couldn't deal with it. They'd calm the fuck down in a day or two. After all, if they'd really thought I was responsible then they'd've beaten me shitless already, innit. Probly even sent me to Arun so I could apologise to him in person. But a week is a long time after someone dies an still the other guys hadn't even started calming the fuck down. Din't matter how many times I tried to talk sense into them, how many times I foned them, texted them or emailed them. I'd even sent Amit a proper letter – you know, like with a stamp. But did any a that shit help? Did it fuck. As far as the other guys were concerned, even if I weren't to blame for Arun's death, the straw before that could've always been the final straw.

I din't feel lucky at the time, but I guess I'd been pretty fuckin jammy that me an Samira were just huggin when we got busted that time in Lampton Park. It meant that as far as the Samira situation went, the only thing Hardjit an the other guys had got on me was what the feds call criminal intent. But as I started dialling her fone number on the tube back from Golders Green, I intended to do more than hug. So what if Samira'd told me I'd been gettin too clingy? It wouldn't be considered too clingy to call her right now, for fuck's sake. She was my girlfriend, we'd both landed in a fuckload a trouble an I'd just been to a friend's funeral whose brother reckoned was my fuckin fault. Anyway, she'd told me to call her after, tell her how it went, maybe hook up for lunch. Might even be able to eat something if I was sittin someplace with Samira. Back when we were at sixth form I couldn't eat jackshit when she was around cos she'd make my stomach decide to go ride some rollercoaster in Disneyland. Now my stomach was ridin the tube with me, from Golders Green station back to Hounslow East after changing at King's Cross. The tube might've been for plebs but it was nice to be sittin in a carriage with em. When I first tried foning Samira – soon as I got a signal when we went overground at Hammersmith – I figured she was probly still in lessons and had stuck her mobile on silent. Then I foned her again when I got to Hounslow East station. Still no answer. Then I foned her while I was waitin at the bus garage. Same. Then again from the 235 bus when I got nearer Busch Corner. Fuck knows how many times I'd called her an why she weren't answering when it'd been her idea we hook up. Said she din't have no lessons in the afternoon an she reckoned I'd need some company after the funeral. Good call. She'd also said she might grab lunch with a few mates if for some reason I din't get in touch. But I *was* gettin in touch. I'm tryin to fuckin call you, Samira, where the fuck you at? A porno starts playin up there, only this time I weren't in it with her. Her fone'd do ten rings each time before it cut to her voicemail, an in my mind I could hear her laughin with all those other, more fun people she'd grabbed lunch with. It was as if her mobile had rung *me* by accident, the way they do sometimes, an I could listen in on whatever she was doing. Most times that happens you just hear tube tracks, the car radio, nothin. When Samira's mobile calls you by accident she's jokin an laughin an havin fun. Even though I'm too fuckin tired to eat an too fuckin hungry to sleep, I weren't too messed up to work out that by the time she finally answered her fone, on the sixth ring the tenth time I'd called her, she'd let it ring ninety-six times.

— But I just told you, Samira, I been tryin to get through for the past hour but you din't answer your fone, I said again when she asked me how come I took so long to call.

— Oops, sorry, I guess I couldn't hear it ring before. We're all sitting here in the canteen and these guys are cracking me up.

— I thought we were gonna meet for lunch?

— Yeh, we can still meet. So long as I don't have to even see any more food, I'm so stuffed and we've been cracking up so much my stomach hurts.

— OK then. I mean, I in't hungry anyway. It in't raining no more so we can go to the usual place OK?

— Sure, you head down there but give me ten more minutes. How was Arun's funeral?

Samira'd got distracted by something going on wherever she was before I could tell her it'd been wikid. That we'd all been crackin up an laughin an havin fun. Then she'd started giggling at something or someone, then she said See ya to me, then she hung up.

The usual place was down by the river near Syon Park. No other kids went that way cos it was a half a mile walk, you had to go past Isleworth cemetery to get there, an anyway, who the fuck wants to be hangin round by the fuckin river? Nothin to laugh at there – less you like watchin ducks slaloming beer cans an gettin stuck in sewage. Still, Samira'd probly find a lot more to laugh at if she went down there with her other, more fun people than when she went down there with me. They'd probly make jokes bout how ducks fuck or something. Why don't Donald wear trousers, that kind a thing. None a this would've actually mattered so much if all those more fun people were female people. But let's face it, it'd probly been another sausage factory in her canteen today. Guys hangin round Samira and Priya like they were two porno DVDs in a video shop full a U-rated Disney films. I used to joke bout all a this with her. An whenever she din't believe that I was just jokin, she'd go she din't care if people thought she was a flirt cos people who said that din't know the difference between flirting an Vegetarian Flirting. She'd also give it the whole I'm Insecure thing and then this I'm A Strong, Free-Spirited

Independent Woman routine followed by the Mum Treats Me Like A Fairy Princess So I Act Like A Ho story.

Me, I'd keep givin it the whole thing bout how she shouldn't ever stop being so free-spirited, how I'd never try an change her, get jealous or clip her wings. After all, that's the way she was. That's all she did. But times like this I couldn't help thinkin, why the fuck did she have to have more fun when she did it? She had so much fun with other guys, she probly din't even think she was being a flirt. She probly thought she was just havin fun, havin jokes with guys who made her laugh, lots a whom also happened to fancy the size 8 La Senza pants off her, lots a whom also happened to be well built and, well, fit. Even my self-defence trick weren't workin now, the one where I check out other fit ladies to remind me that they exist. I mean, there's a limit to how much checkin you can do when you're walkin past a cemetery on the way back from a crematorium. If I bought into Hardjit's martial arts theory I'd get my self-defence in first by actually pullin one a the fit women I'd checked here an there these past couple a months. Yeh, right. An if I bought into Sanjay's business theory I'd just draw up a contract with some break-up penalties to stop Samira discussin any merger plans with other potential partners. Yeh, right. Like what fuckin penalties? Threaten to tell everyone that we'd got off with each other as well as hugged? Or even lie an tell em we'd done more than got off with each other? If there was one thing I'd learnt from everyone's various theories bout women, it was that it'd be a waste a time and just generally a bad idea for me to complain bout her ways an bout her not answering her fone. Best thing I can do when her gorgeousness shows up, stridin past the cemetery fence like some catwalk queen, is to just listen to whatever she wants to go on bout. Yeh, right.

— Why haven't you shaved yet? she says, not even takin my unhairy hand.

— What?

— Why haven't you shaved? That must be, what, a week's growth on your face now?

— Five days. What's that got to do with anything?

— It makes you look ugly. It makes you look like a paedophile psycho cult leader.

— I already told you on Saturday, I in't shavin cos a Arun. Everyone's been growin a beard, that's the Hindu custom. When someone dies, you don't shave until after the cremation.

— It *is* after the cremation.

— I know, but I came straight to see you, innit. That's why I'm still wearin this black suit. If I'd known you were busy maybe I'd've gone to the barber's or something. Anyway, what does it matter, I'll shave when I get home.

— Why's it that they don't shave again?

— I told you. It's cos before the cremation, the dead person's spirit is s'posed to be hangin round on earth. Might even come an hang around with you, hug you, bless you, whatever. So you can't handle sharp things like razor blades cos you might hurt the spirit with them. You also can't hold needles, pins, scissors. Nothin.

Samira checks out some Lexus that speeds down the road an gives it, — Well, couldn't you shave with one a those razors that have grilles over the blades? You know, the ones you can't cut yourself with. That way you won't cut Arun's spirit or ghost or whatever. What about paper? Are you allowed to handle paper? Cos what if you give the spirit a paper cut?

— Samira, are you takin the piss?

— No I'm not, Jas. If I was taking the piss I'd say your beard is so ugly you'd probably cut Arun's spirit by cracking every mirror you look into.

— What? Why're you being like this? Don't take the piss. It's the custom. Someone died. What're you meant to do if you don't follow the custom?

— OK, Jas. Maybe I'm just trying to cheer you up. You're so moody . . . You're upset cos I didn't hear my phone, right?

— No. I'm upset cos you in't takin nothin seriously. I mean, Arun died. I just been to his funeral.

— I know, and like I said, I'm just trying to cheer you up.

— I don't want to fuckin cheer up. I don't want to have fuckin fun. I just been to a funeral. An anyway, forget the fuckin funeral, we need to talk bout your brothers. Did you know Hardjit's given them my address? He's even given them my dad's warehouse address for some reason. They gonna beat me shitless an you worried bout my facial hair. This time tomorrow I might not even have fuckin facial hair cos I might not have a fuckin face.

— Relax. As far as my brothers are concerned you're just another guy who fancies me, that's all. I told them that you proclaimed your undying love for me in Lampton Park and I knocked you back with a gentle hug so as not to break your heart too much. Pretty clever, huh? I don't understand why you're being such a scaredy-cat wimp about all this.

— Yeh, well, I guess you got it all figured, what with you being so used to guys tryin to pull you all the time.

— What's the matter with you, Jas? I'm trying to make things better, cheer you up. And when was the last time you ate? Your breath stinks of stomach acid.

— Well, I was s'posed to have lunch with you but you were too busy laughin with all your fun friends to even pick up your fone.

Shit, now you've done it. Dumbass, gimpy, dickless fuck. Even if you don't have a row with her, you'll sound like a whinging batty boy. Luckily she says she'll let that one go, seeing as how I'm upset after the funeral an everything. Thing is, though, she don't let it go, does she. I've clipped her wings. Might as well have raped her right there in the cemetery, what with her being a free spirit and everything. We get through two minutes a silence, holdin hands even, but then she lets go an comes out with, — Jas, we might have passed the two-month mark but we're not married. I don't need your permission to hang out with other people. Anyway, the truth is, Jas, you don't really mean other people, do you? What you really mean is other guys, right? Be honest. If I was just having lunch with the girls then you wouldn't care, would you? Admit it, inside you're just

289

another typical desi guy who doesn't like his girlfriend spending time with other guys.

— I din't say that. I in't ever stopped you hangin out with guys. I just meant that we'd agreed we'd meet and we'd agreed I'd fone an you should've at least listened out for your fone. Even if it was to tell me you were too busy.

— It was really noisy in the canteen, Jas. What do you want me to do? Wait for your call in the library?

— Oh . . . I'm sorry. It's just that I'm starvin, that's all. Too fuckin tired to eat, too fuckin hungry to sleep. I'm being a total idiot, I'm sorry. Actually, no, what the fuck am I sayin, Samira, I in't. Sorry, that is. I *am* starvin, I *in't* sorry. I mean what the fuck, *you* should've fuckin called *me* . . . The problem in't bout whether you could hear your fone, it's bout your priorities being a little, you know, wrong.

She waits for that one to land on the ground. Wrong. It's as if she watches the word run outta fuel or whatever before it starts nose-diving to the pavement. Only it doesn't. Cos I don't let it. Cos it's fuckin true. Cos it's even politer than the truth. Wrong. More like totally fucked in the head by a strap-on dildo with pump-action chainsaw attachment. Don't let her accuse you a being like a typical desi guy. Fight back. Say you're sorry. Do whatever the fuck a typi-cal desi guy'd never do. But first, let the lady speak first.

— What do you mean, my priorities are wrong?

— Just that they're, you know, fucked in the head, Samira. You're puttin havin jokes with people before takin my fone call. It's got nothin to do with them being guys. You could've been with your girls, you could've been with your family, you could've even been with Zahid for all I care.

Zahid was Samira's badminton buddy. The one she'd been friends with since they were little. The one her parents had always teased her bout one day gettin married to. I'd never had a problem with Zahid but she'd always reckoned I did. I wonder why? Could it've been cos she kept going on bout what a great athlete he was? How big his pecs were? How she never answered her fone whenever they were playin badminton?

— See, I knew you don't like it when I play badminton with Zahid, she gives it, like she's caught me with the pile a porno mags I'd always told her I din't own. — You always deny it but it's true, you do have a problem with it. I've been playing badminton with Zahid for years. I've got a right to play with him whenever I want. And I've got a right to go for coffee with him after if we're having a good time. You, you're just like another typical, straight-off-the-boat desi. You don't like your girlfriend having a life of her own.

— No. No, I don't mind.

— Don't lie to me, Jas. I fucking hate it when guys lie.

— I in't lyin. I don't mind you havin a life a your own or hangin out with other guys. But Zahid fancies the pants off you, it's different, innit.

— Why's it different, Jas? How's it different? So what if Zahid does find me attractive? So what? Lots of guys do. You knew that before we started going out together. What do you want me to do? Learn to be ugly?

— No. It in't like that, Samira. It in't like that. Just listen to the fuckin situation and stop being so blind to what you're fuckin doing. If he fancies you, it means every time you're together he's tryin to impress you an he's hoping you might fancy him back, right? I mean, it's fuckin obvious. It's fuckin natural. I'd be that way if I was him. So there he is playin badminton to show you a good, fun time an everything, an all the time he's just tryin to get his own shuttlecock inside you.

I probly deserve the slap she gives me then. Not for what I said, but for comin out with such a shit line to say it with. A course metaphors matter jackshit to Samira. Matter a fact, she's just another girl version a rudeboys. I can see that now. She probly only does all her human rights activism bullshit just to pretend that she in't, like, a fuckin rudegirl or someshit. A rudegirl who's just fuckin slapped me in the fuckin face.

— Ow. Fuckin slap me for? Face it, Samira, you just can't deal with what's what. I'll fuckin say it again. He's just tryin to get his own shuttlecock inside you, there in't no fuckin doubt bout it. An what do you do? You let him take tiny steps towards his ultimate goal just cos he happens to be more fun than me an better at badminton than me. You put his fuckin fantasy before my fuckin fone calls. An all cos you're so obsessed with being your own independent woman. So, yeh, I'm sick a this shit. An if it in't fuckin Zahid it's that Saqib guy. Was he crackin you up in the canteen too? What were you lot eatin? Bananas?

Before fuckin off back towards the school, Samira tells me that, for the record, neither a them guys were in the canteen today. We haven't even made it to the fuckin river this time an, frankly, I don't give a shit. Even her cute butt looks ugly as it disappears up Park Road towards Busch Corner. Too fuckin perfect. Too on display in that tight skirt. Yuk. Makes me wanna oolti all a that fuckin stomach acid out my mouth, nose an ears. It's fuckin true what I'd said to you, Samira. You're such a little Miss Independent Free Spirit, it's easier for you to keep sayin I'm just like all them typical desis who wanna control you an shit. It means you in't gotta deal with how fuckin spoilt an selfish you been. I know my hungry stomach's eaten most a my brain an everything an I know my mind's gone an decided it don't even agree with me again, but you know what I reckon? I reckon you flirt cos you're spoilt. It in't cos you're insecure or cos you're free-spirited or cos your mum suffocates you or any a that shit. It's cos you think the whole world revolves round you.

I read one time (when I was a dick who read all the time) that when babies get to two or three years old, they're s'posed to slowly figure out that the world in't actually all bout them. That their mum, their dad, their brother, their sister or whoever, they're all independent people. They're all their own main characters. When you're a little baby, you reckon other people are just there cos they're, like, part a your story. Like some Fisher Price toys you got. But that cute piece a ass walkin away from me there, she's nineteen years old, an still she in't reached that stage where you realise the world in't all bout you. She's still walkin away from shit like it's just a toy that don't entertain her no more. Well, if she wants to go an play badminton an have fun then she can fuck off.

The shittiest part a this shit is you in't accidently discovered you could have more fun with all those other people, Samira, you just decided to, that's all. So, technically, you din't even miss my calls, you fuckin chose to ignore em cos you decided to have your fun. I mean, what the fuck, Samira? A course Zahid an Saqib an whoever else you had lunch with are more capable a being more fun an more entertaining. That's what they do with you. They in't tryin to build nothin with you, they in't plannin on going through life with you, on defendin you from your own brothers. They in't thinkin bout how'ma gonna make my friends an family accept this situation? How'ma gonna make *her* friends an family accept this? How'ma gonna look after her in ten years' time when I can't even pass my fuckin A-levels? They jus wanna have fun with you. If all you wanna do is have fun with someone then you're probly gonna have fun with them, innit. Well, I got news for you, tight-skirted-perfect-Samira-with-the-perfect-butt, you don't get to have the better man around in ten, twenty, thirty, forty years' time when you really need a better man, not less you take him now. That's just the way the world works. Cos he in't gonna hang around while you have your fun. He'll just get with someone else, someone who in't a fuckin four-year-old spoilt little emotionally retarded princess with a silver spoon up her ass who one day's gonna be a very lonely dumb bitch who reckons she's really clever and free-spirited. An if you try an get back with him, well, he won't take you back cos he'll be with someone else who appreciates him proply, innit. Yeh, right. No, he won't. Yes, he will. No, he won't be with someone else, yes, he will take you back. Yes, he fuckin will, you dickless sap, I'll take you back, Samira, please come back. Whatever I said, whatever I done, I din't mean it, I just want you back for good. Want you back, want you back, said I want you back for good. What the fuck I gone an done? — Samira, I call out like we're both lost in some fuckin forest film set. — Samira. She can't hear me for shit cos she's already reached the London Road. I grab my fone an call her.

— See, I'm answering your phone call, Jas. You happy now? I heard my phone, saw your name and picked it up. Actually thanks for reminding me, I better delete your name from my handset.

— Look, Samira, I'm sorry I snapped. It's just with the funeral an everything. I'm knackered an I'm starvin.

— Don't try and blame the funeral, Jas, you've been acting like this for weeks. The only reason I picked the phone up now was cos somehow I knew you'd try and blame the funeral and all the big dramas that've happened to you and I want you to know that it's got nothing to do with that. Underneath you're just another straight-off-the-boat possessive desi guy and you've become really boring as well. If my brothers ever ask me about you I'll say there's nothing between us because from now on that'll be the truth.

So that was that. Drink the fuck up through your final drinkin straws. By the time I gave up tryin to call her back, I'd wandered into Isleworth cemetery, tryin to read the gravestones to stop my mind givin me another bollocking, to stop it singin fuckin Take That songs in my ear from inside my fuckin ear. To stop it thinkin anyfuckinthing at all. John Peters died at the age a 82. He was a much-loved father an grandfather who fought for his country. Selina Wilson died aged 45, a much-loved mother, may you rest in peace. Madge Harvey died aged 50, she will always be remembered. Most a the gravestones were just like the plaques in the crematorium, only bigger an obviously not hung up on some fuckin overcrowded wall. An honourable defender a the nation and beloved husband, here lies Barney Noble, who died aged 67. Always caring for the sick, here lies Sheila Bonfield, may you be looked after now, aged 70. Too fuckin tired to eat, too fuckin hungry to sleep, too fuckin dumped by his first an only girl-friend to give a shit. Here lies Jas. My surname too fuckin long an too fuckin shameful to fit on my own fuckin gravestone.

24

I expected Sanjay to do some kind a Come In, I've Been Expecting
You routine. Stead, as I stepped into his living room an triggered the
underfloor lighting, he just carried on watchin TV. Sittin there with
a black silk dressing gown over a white shirt an baggy black trousers,
a glass a Scotch in one hand an a remote control in the other.

— You seen this episode? he asked after a minute that felt more
like thirty, his eyes not even movin from the screen as he spoke. —
It's the one where Tony Soprano first goes to see a shrink. Pour yourself a drink, my friend, it's nearly over.

Bobby the desi Shrek was standin by Sanjay's bar, lookin through
me at the TV, then lookin at me, then steppin out the way so that
I could get to the whisky bottles. A bouncer wherever the fuck he
went. For the first time since I'd known him I was glad Bobby hardly
ever talked. I din't feel like chattin to him an I din't even feel like
chattin to Sanjay. I'd just gone there to face the music an that. Be a
man. See what the fuck I could do bout there being no fones to give
him at the end a the week. I could've come here tomorrow but tomorrow's Thursday an the week ended the day after. I could've come
here tomorrow but Samira'd just dumped me an I wanted to do
something that din't involve going home, havin to see Mum an Dad
an then havin to pretend everything was OK. I could've come here
tomorrow, but who the fuck knows what's gonna happen tomorrow?

The rain had started up again by the time I'd got off the tube at

Hyde Park Corner so my Kenzo funeral suit an hair were still damp, still matchin my dickless, gimpified eyes. Part a me'd just wanted to come here to hear Sanjay tell me to chill, everything'd be cool, we'd find a solution. Part a me'd just wanted to get on the tube, get with the plebs, go for a ride. Both parts a me ended up here, standin in Sanjay's flat, waitin for *The* fuckin *Sopranos* to finish, before Bobby looked at me an nodded at one a the empty sofas. Fine, whatever. Both parts a me sat the fuck down.

— So what's the matter, Jas? Sanjay says, turning down the TV volume but leavin his eyes fixed on the DVD's 'select a scene' screen.
— You don't come round no more, you don't call, you don't text, you don't email. Too busy with your lady, eh? Courtesy of yours truly of course – don't ever forget it.
— Huh?
— Pardon?
— Huh?
He turns his head from the screen now. — Don't speak to me like that, Jas. You sound like a farmyard animal. If by Huh you mean Pardon or Excuse me, then please say Pardon or Excuse me. Not Huh.
— Pardon?
— What I said was your lady is courtesy of yours truly and don't you forget it. She might be contented with your mum's Ford Focus now but, remember, it was my Porsche you first rode in. In my book that means you owe me.
I wipe some rain from my eyebrows an then from my eyes, not knowin whether I should've been smiling at him or correcting him or even lookin at him at all. *The Sopranos* DVD boxset box is lyin out on the coffee table in front a me, upstairs on the mezzanine floor his bed is still unmade an to my right there's a milk carton cluttering up his kitchen. The water under the floor has finally got fish in it, blue ones, swimming the fuck away from the underfloor, underwater lights an into what looks like a maze. There's still a drop a whisky in my glass an for the first time since Sanjay'd got me drink-

ing this stuff I in't clinking the ice cubes to make the last drop weaker but bigger. I'm just lettin the fuckers melt in their own sweet time. Pretty soon the drop's gone.

— But so what if you owe me, right? Sanjay carries on. — A lot of people owe people. Only, the way I see it, the problem with most Indian businessmen is they don't chase their bad debts hard enough. They lend money to friends and to friends' relatives and to self-styled religious or community leaders and then they don't have the heart to go chop off someone's fingers when the money isn't paid back. But I'll tell you what, here's a deal I'm prepared to cut you: whatever you owe me for helping you pull Samira I'll write off as a bad debt.

Some fucker inside me tells me I should give Sanjay the newsflash that Samira an I'd just split up, keep him up to date, save him from wasting time. But that same fucker inside me tells me that if I do that then it'd make it even more true an I'd probly start fuckin cryin again. Howlin like a baby in fact. So I just tell Sanjay all bout Arun, how I'd had to deal with my mate's suicide an how his mum, his brother an my crew all thought it was my fault. That's why I been so busy, man, that's why I in't called or nothin. I'd been to the funeral this morning, that's why I'm dressed up like a Reservoir Dog.

— Have you finished talking, Jas? Good. Because there's a bigger bad debt you owe me, correct? I mean, that's why you've come here two days before you're due to hand over the next batch of phones, correct? By my calculation I'm awaiting a minimum of two hundred handsets for this month, which would take us to nearly a thousand handsets since we started doing business four months ago. Correct?

— Yeh, I go, even though I don't know where I go next. — Yeh, well, yeh.

— Well?

— Well, there's, like, a problem, yeh.

— I know very bloody well there's a problem, Jas. You don't think Hardjit hasn't been keeping me up to date with this month's progress? Just like he does every month, in fact. That's right, every month. Well, I have to talk business with *someone* while you're off trying to get inside Samira's panties. Anyway, I understand from Hardjit that this problem is now so bad that he, Amit and Ravi want out of our arrangement. I told him this isn't some subscription to a porn channel, you can't just cancel it because your parents are back from holiday. Like I said, I don't make a habit of writing off bad debts, and that includes relieving business partners of their supply obligations. But the thing is, I'm not a total bastard. In fact, I have some sympathy for those guys. They already told me about Amit's brother, poor fellow. But you? Well, you're a different kettle of fish, as they say. How could you be so stupid, Jas? I mean, how? After all the support I've given you. Needless to say I concur with Hardjit that the supply shortage is your fault. That means I hold you accountable. So all I'm asking you to do is get me the mobiles you owe me. No more. After everything I've done for you, I can't say fairer than that, can I?

This was like playin cards an I knew it. Try not to let your face show him what's in your head. Fuckin definitely don't let it show him the oolti in your stomach. An don't let it say anything like, What the fuck d'you mean you been talkin to Hardjit all a these months? Keep your face fuckin still, let your tongue do all the talkin – that's what it's there for.

— Look, Sanjay, I hear what you sayin. An I wanna help you out, innit. I mean, I admit this shit's my fault an I wanna, you know, I wanna make it up to you, man. I mean, that's why I come here, innit.

— You're damn right you want to make it up to me, Jas. You'll make it up to me by making up the shortfall of two hundred handsets.

— But that's just it. I mean, two hundred fones in two days, man. I just can't do that, Sanj. It was Hardjit an Amit, they had all the contacts, all the supliers.

Sanjay just sat there an din't say jackshit. Din't even nod or smile. The exact same shit that my dad does, except with dad it's cos he's either sulkin or he just in't got shit to say.

— Look, Sanj, I reckon I could probly get you bout twenty more fones if I had a couple more days. But two hundred in two days, man . . . C'mon. I mean, what do you need them for anyway? I know, I know, you can't tell me. But I mean, is it really that important you get them now? Can't it, you know, wait a bit? It was the other guys who had all the contacts.

— What are you trying to say, Jas? That you're incapable of fulfilling your business obligations?

— What? Well . . . yeh.

— Well, yeh, you should've bloody thought of that before you burnt your bridges with the other guys, shouldn't you? Why the hell did you have to go and stick your dick into Amit's family affairs, Jas? Not to mention that matter of you sticking your dick in other places you shouldn't have. By the way, I hope you wiped my car seats afterwards.

I take like a whole fuckin minute to work out what the fuck he means, before givin it, — You what? Samira? But it was you who was tellin me to pull her in the first place, man. You fuckin helped me.

— Yeh, and like I said, don't you forget it. But *you* were the one who kept saying how important it was to keep your little affair a secret. Not only do you fail to do that, you let your secret out while at the same time interfering in one of your business partner's family affairs. Now not even your own partners will forgive you enough to do business with you, never mind your suppliers. And to be quite honest I don't blame them. I mean, I won't go so far as Amit and accuse you of killing his brother, but you gave that poor fellow the temperament so you might as well have given him a gun. At least that way you'd have saved his mother from having to wipe that nasty overdose-vomit from her dead son's blue lips while you were off somewhere planting your own lips somewhere on Samira.

— But c'mon, man, you were the one who told me to go out with her. You encouraged me. What the fuck did you fuckin expect?

— So I did. I suppose that means you *are* capable of doing things

I tell you to. By the way, you didn't answer my question about the car seats.

— I din't do that. We din't do that.

— You din't do what?

— We din't . . . you know, that. Not in the car, not anywhere else.

— That?

— Have fuckin sex. Ever. Not even close. She's saving herself for marriage, innit, so you in't got to worry bout your car seats.

— Let me guess, that's what you told Hardjit and the others, right? That all the two of you did was hug and kiss?

— I told em all we did was hug. That's all we got busted for anyway.

— That's also no doubt what she told her brothers. You realise that's probably the only reason you're still in one piece. You're a disgrace, Jas. You went out with that girl for how many weeks? Nearly two months? And you didn't have sex. And the other guys, they believe you?

— That's the truth, man. I in't lyin. We din't do nothin, we just got off with each other, that's all.

— Got off?

— Snogged. Got off, you know. Fuckin hugged an kissed, man. She's saving herself for marriage, innit. What the fuck is this anyway?

— Of course that's all you did. I know that's all you did. You're so pathetic you'd probably go limp if she let you do any more. But unfortunately for you, Jas, you went all the way with her. To fourth base, as they say – at least that's the impression one gets from these pictures I have here. Bobby, pour our friend another drink.

Sanjay picked up an envelope from underneath the DVD box an gave it to me in one hand while Bobby put another glass a whisky in the other. Inside the envelope, a bunch a photos. Not those tutty paper ones you print off – thick ones like postcards. Me an Samira coming outta Vagabond on our first date, huggin an laughin; sharing a shawarma in Maroush; gettin off in my mum's Ford Focus on our second date; gettin off in the Porsche on another date; huggin by the river in Isleworth; kissin in some restaurant in Chiswick; gettin off on the Porsche bonnet in an underground car park; gettin off by the airport where sad, sappy plane spotters usually hang out; gettin off in Richmond Park. Everything we'd done, our whole fuckin story rammed into my stomach where memories go to squat when your mind kicks em out. But memory's a tricky fucker. It's tricky even when you in't so hungry an tired that you could collapse an die. Lookin through the photos again, I could swear some were wrong. Well, not wrong exactly, but they weren't exactly how I remembered it either – in my mind or in my stomach. I flicked through them one more time just to be sure an saw my hands touchin things they'd never ever touched when we were in that underground car park. I saw knickers that she'd never even let me see under her skirt, now pulled off an left lyin on the grass beside us in Richmond Park.

— What the fuck have you done, man? I asked him. — We never did that. I mean, we did, but not like that.

— You like it? I got so bored with the same old anodyne hugging and snogging and getting off you guys kept getting up to. So me and Bobby here, we bought the latest photo-manipulation software and had a bit of fun. Touched up the pictures a little so you could touch her up a little. Just tweaks here and there, nothing too drastic of course. See here, this one in the car park: we've moved the hem of her skirt a little higher, moved your hands up a little further and, see that, we've airbrushed out her bra. And look at this one, look on the dashboard, can you see that pack of Durex condoms? That was a last-minute addition. Here, look closely, they're extra small size. Inspired, don't you think?

— What the fuck you doing, man? I go, soothing my stomach with the neat whisky Bobby'd given me. The stuff slid down my throat like some warm honey an lemon cold remedy, stickin my body to the sofa.

— I'm fulfilling your fantasies, Jas. I'm giving you photographic proof that you did everything you wanted to with Samira. I told you that you had a lot to thank me for. It even looks like you're no longer a virgin – congratulations. Though of course I'm not sure your three friends and her three brothers will feel so celebratory when they receive copies of these and find out you lied to them. Truth is, it looks to me like you managed the Kama Sutra with her without even taking your clothes off. What do you say, eh?

— I don't . . . what?

— Basically, Jas, the deal is this: I've got a plan for how you can make up your supply shortfall. Tonight. I'm not waiting till the end of the bloody week. And if you don't go ahead with my plan, Bobby's sending these photos out by first-class post. And if you go ahead with the plan and you fail, he's sending them out by second-class post. And if you even think about going to the police or anything stupid like that, he's gonna deliver them by hand. And you thought you were in trouble when you got here. You don't know what trouble is, you dumb fool. We won't just send copies of these prints to Hardjit and to Samira's brothers. We've got the addresses of her father's business, his business partner's home, her brothers' mosque, their friends.

— But we din't do any a this stuff, Sanjay.

— Fine, tell them all when they come looking for you. To be honest, I can't believe you didn't spot Bobby snapping you. I mean, he's not exactly an inconspicuous fellow, is he? In fact, he was quite concerned that maybe you saw him the first night you made out in that Ford Focus of yours. See here how the flash bulb reflects off the windscreen. Anyway, after then he stopped using the flash – but I guess you were a little too busy that night to notice, eh?

— We did notice, I go, as if it made any fuckin difference now anyway. — We thought it was a speed camera. You know, for the oncoming lane.

— Speed camera? Speed camera?

When he'd finished doing more a his vampire-from-Bombay laugh I asked him why he'd done all this, why the fuck he'd taken the photos for?

302

— Security, Jas, security. It's not my fault, I'm just a creditor. I want the mobile phones you owe me. All two hundred. I need them. Two days. It might sound like a lot to ask, but it's a lot for you to ask me to just write off your debt. But don't worry, I like you, Jas. So, as I said, I've drawn up plans to help you meet your commitments. By the way, should you decline and force me to send these pictures out, do you want me to change any of the positions the two of you lovebirds used? I mean, I tried to have her go down on you but the manipulation wasn't subtle enough, the shadows were all wrong. You could tell she was faking it.

I should've been angry. I should've hit the fuckin skylight. Stead all I could think was how it'd've been to have actually done all that stuff with Samira. I could almost hear the noise she'd make if I really did dare put my hand there, really did squeeze there, I could smell that shampoo from her hair turn to sweat, see for myself how her muscles led to tendons. Sanjay told me if I went ahead with his plan he'd destroy the photos, I'd have nothin to worry bout. Fuck that, I wanted to tell him. If I go ahead with the plan you in't destroyin jackshit: you givin the photos to me, innit. Let me see her whenever I want, the way she stretches, the way her muscles lead to tendons. Let me see us. Especially the picture on the Porsche bonnet. Cos I could've actually done that. I mean, sure, she might've been saving herself for marriage an I respected that. But the thing is, I could've been the guy she married one day. Now she'll go an marry some other guy instead an he'll get to do all that. He'll get to be *me* in those fuckin photos.

— OK, I go, — wat'chyu want me to do?

25

Sanjay starts watchin *The* fuckin *Sopranos* DVD *again*. I'm leaning forward in the sofa, waitin to hear his big master plan for how I could make up the shortfall in fones but he's just sittin there, skipping between scenes, checkin the subtitles, before fast-forwarding through the credits an givin it, — OK, Bobby, this batch is good too.

After fuckin around with the DVD a bit more, Sanjay finally switches off the TV/cinema system, turns to look at me again an says, — Rob your father's warehouse. Tonight.

After doing my usual stammerin routine an spittin some a my Scotch out, I ask him for like the fifth time that afternoon what the fuck he's talkin bout?

— It's a perfect solution. Easy for you, easy for me. I don't know why you boys didn't think of it before. I discussed it with Hardjit yesterday. He said it sounded fair. In fact my suggestion yielded an interesting anecdote from him. Apparently when Ravi broke a Samsung E700 you boys were unblocking over the summer, you all deemed that it was his responsibility to replace it. So you made him steal one and the stupid fool tried to steal one from Mr Ashwood. That started the chain of events that led to us getting acquainted, right? So, Jas, how fitting it is that you find yourself in a similar predicament, multiplied by two hundred to befit your elevated, Porsche-driving status in the world. You know, it's funny, Hardjit never struck me as capable of recognising life's little ironies. He was really impressed with the amount of research I'd done into your father. But hey, I guess so much of it is luck. I mean, can you imagine my luck back in September when we all met for the first time? With a surname like yours I knew you must be related to your father. I mean, what are the chances?

— I never told you my surname. I never tell anyone my fuckin surname.

— You didn't have to. Mr Ashwood mentioned it. That's why I agreed to meet you guys. I spend my whole life dealing with one son of a bitch after another and then suddenly I get presented with the son of a business opportunity. You see, I've developed an interest in your father's mobile-phone business. Do you realise that his is one of the few independent mobile-phone warehouses left these days? Most of the others are owned by the big handset manufacturers or network operators or retail chains. It's become such a professional industry. But your dad, he's one of the last corner shops left in a world of supermarkets and Sainsbury's Locals and Tesco Metros. It was perfect. Exactly what I'd been looking for.

I don't wait till I figure out what the fuck Sanjay's gettin at. I just tell him that I can't. There must be some other way. For fuck's sake, I can't rip off my own dad. So Sanjay asks me if I'd rather rip off someplace I don't know, someplace I don't already have the keys to, someplace with a guard dog that doesn't know not to bite bollocks that smell like mine. I offer to give him the cash instead, askin one more time how the fuck did he expect me to steal from my dad. I'd get the cash somehow. People always get the cash somehow. Twenty grand? I don't think so. Anyway, Sanjay says he wants fones, not cash. Says he's already got bloody cash. So next I offer to buy him the fuckin fones. After all, I could probly get em at cost price through my dad or someshit. But Sanjay says they had to be stolen, remember.

— But it's my dad's warehouse, I go again, — my dad's.

— So what? Wise up, Jas, and stop giving me all this sentimental dad crap. More than four months I've known you. During all that time I've never once heard you mention your dad. Not one time, my friend. You know what that tells me? That I've been the best dad you ever had, better than Mr Ashwood or Hardjit or any other poor fellow you've nominated along the way. I mean, think about what I've done for you. I teach you how to drive my car, I teach you short cuts around London that would make a cabby jealous, I help you court that Samira chick of yours, I show you how to dress desi-sharp instead of like those other hooded rudeboys. Shall I go on?

I say nothin.

— I make you part of my business, I teach you how to stand up for yourself when the other guys put you down, I even teach you how to shave with oil and exfoliant instead of that cheap foam.

— Look, I agree you've done a lot for me, Sanj. An I wanna make this up to you, I'm gonna make it up to you. I just don't reckon it'd be right for me to rip off my own dad.

— Oh, please. Why is that then? Because you *love* him? Because you *respect* him?

— No. Well, yeh. He's my dad, man.

Sanjay gets up an takes his Bombay-baddie laugh all the way to the kitchen, where the echo turns it into his Bombay-vampire laugh. I hear him drop some ice in his Scotch, an when he comes back, he heads straight towards the sideboard next to me, the one with all his framed photos from his graduation, his family weddings an others that show him partying around with various fit-lookin friends a his. Then he reaches for the least fit picture there. An old desi man with a bald head an double chin. He's smiling at the camera from underneath a fat, jet-black, oily moustache, a blue hankerchief hangin too far out his top pocket. Sanjay takes the photo out the frame an then pulls out a lighter he must've just got from the kitchen. Before the flames reach his fingers, he chucks the photo into this giant metal vase thing on the floor.

— This, Jas, is what I think about all your respect-your-father nonsense – Bobby, cover the smoke alarm. You've got a lot to learn, young man. You think your father has any respect for you? Do you?

306

Let me tell you something about my father, the guy now smoking inside my vase. See if it sounds familiar. The man expected me to always respect him but he only had to respect me when I came good. Boosted his prestige or whatever. My beita's got four A's in the A-level, my beita he studied at Cambridge, my beita he did this, my beita he did that. Always showing off about me all the time when the truth is the man had fuck all to do with any of it. Spent all his time in the office, the archetypal Indian businessman. Knew nothing about me that wasn't on my CV. I don't mind him not having anything to do with it, really I don't. But what I *do* mind is him showing off. It means his recognition is dependent upon the extent to which I boost his prestige. So the minute I do something that means he can't show off about me any more, he turns off his respect and goodwill like the bloody hosepipe for cleaning his precious car. It's another one of those rules nobody warns you about. Do something that detracts from a desi dad's prestige and watch how he'll drop you like a hot samosa filled with maggots and shit. My dad dropped me when he discovered I was shagging this gori secretary at the office. Well, more precisely, when the family of a girl I was supposed to be having this arranged marriage with accidently found out I'd been shagging a gori secretary. It was my own fault, I suppose. I really should've labelled my home videos better – it was my *secretary's* twenty-first birthday my prospective mother-in-law borrowed, not mine. And let's just say I gave that girl a better time in my flat than the satsang Mum gave me for my twenty-first. I label my videos and DVDs properly now, of course. You should have seen the family fireworks, Jas. Mum was so angry and ashamed I guess Dad felt he didn't have a choice. But he did. And the only reason I put that photo on this sideboard here was so I could fuck gori girls in front of it.

As Sanjay says all this, he starts stroking the sideboard as if it's a sports car or someshit, before gettin vexed when he finds a scratch.
— Shit, look at this – three and a half thousand pounds' worth of B&B Italia sideboard and it's scuffed. And all because no matter how naked they get, they never take off their jewellery and high heels and

what have you. It's just as well I burnt that photo. In fact, I'm glad I finally did. Every time I looked at his face I remembered all the other times he proved his goodwill was conditional. When I turned up late to one of Mum's satsangs in jeans, when I forgot to shave for some community wedding, when some aunty saw me smoking near Hounslow bus garage, always he'd take his cue from Mum and start throwing his toys out his pram, claiming he wasn't being showed the respect a father deserves from his son. You know what, Jas? He used to be upset that I paid more attention to career advice from Mr Ashwood. I mean, Mr Ashwood – the only man who helped me get into Cambridge in the first place and who visited me umpteen times while I was up there. Of course I was going to listen to him. Dad thinking he had all these rights over me, telling me how he'd done the school run every morning, cleaned up my vomit when I was sick one time, taught me to shave – albeit with some stupid paste. That's their bloody job, it doesn't make them royalty. It's just one big con, Jas. And look at you, acting like a fool because you've been conned into all this respect-your-father bullshit. I mean, why do you think your three buddies are always so full of hot air? And unlike you and me, they didn't have someone like Mr Ashwood. So let's have none of these ridiculous moral qualms about stealing from your father. And like I said earlier, there are no operational qualms. I mean, how hard can it be? You won't even have to break in, you've got the bloody keys.

When the vase on the floor stops smokin, Bobby takes his fat palm off the fire-alarm sensor, empties the ash into a bin in the bathroom an chucks the empty photo frame in after it. The smashing glass hurts my head an suddenly I'm realising Scotch an smoke don't go down well on a hungry, tired, headachy stomach. I just wanna fall asleep an not have to deal with this shit till I wake up tomorrow. But Sanjay's speeches always keep me awake. That an one final question still knockin at my head. Don't ask me how I work up the balls to ask him – maybe it's cos I'm still wearin my slick black suit.

— Tell me why then?

— What do you mean, why? Because you owe me two hundred mobiles, Jas, that's why.

— No, Sanjay. Why is it that I can't just buy em, I mean?

— Look, stop suggesting that you buy the bloody things. I just told you they have to be stolen. I told you boys right at the beginning and I've told you countless times since. I want bona fide stolen mobiles. No exceptions.

— Yeh, but tell me why. Why won't new fones work for you?

Sanjay holds his face like he's bout to start screamin or someshit. But he doesn't. He just sits there, massaging his head, breathing. Till in the end my empty stomach somehow throws up another idea an so I give it, — OK, Sanjay, don't tell me. I got a better idea. What if I buy new fones an then you can steal em from me? I mean, that way they'd be stolen –

— No, Jas, no, Jas, you don't understand, do you? I just told you . . . Oh, fuck it, fine then. You're so stupid and this is so frustrating that I have neither the time nor the energy. The fact is I need stolen mobiles because it's in my interests to create the impression that I'm dealing in stolen mobiles. I need enough to fill a truck. One thousand stolen mobiles, piled high. And that's where you boys came in. I have other sources of stolen mobiles of course, but for some reason – call it a lapse in judgement – I've let myself become a bit dependent on your supply. Don't look so confused, Jas.

Sanjay then walks over to the dining table an straightens the collar a his black suit jacket that's hangin on a chair. — Why do I have the feeling you're going to ask me Why again? Why would I want someone to think I was into stolen mobiles? Well, just think about it for a minute, you're meant to be smart – that's what Mr Ashwood kept telling me anyway. Actually, for the record that's the difference between you and me. We may both be blessed with intelligence but you're incapable of working this out without my help. Think about why you openly admitted to Hardjit that you and Samira had hugged. Because in actual fact you did a whole lot more, didn't you? OK, maybe you didn't do as much as my pictures suggest, but you certainly did more than just hug her. Well, me too. My business is about a lot more than stolen mobiles, but if I ever get stopped by Customs & Excise officers it'll be in my interests to show them that I'm only into stolen mobiles. That way they'll just hand me over to the police. Happy now?

My face says no before I do. An so I ask him why the fuck he'd want to be reported to the feds for?

— For a supposedly smart boy you're even more ignorant than I thought, aren't you? When it comes to enterprises such as mine, Customs officers have more powers than the police. A lot more. They can dig deeper into your affairs, prosecute you for offences you didn't even know you were committing. They need a lower degree of proof to exercise these powers, too. An easier way to think about it is like this: the police may be there for when you steal from others, but Customs & Excise and the Inland Revenue step in when you steal from the British government. You see, Jas, I've run into a little bit of trouble with one of my real business operations. Or at least I might have. Either way, I don't want to take any risks – that's not how I operate. What this real business actually is need not concern you for the moment. What matters is that about five months ago I was tipped off that someone had grassed me up and put my operations on the radar of Her Majesty's Customs & Excise. Well, one of my trucks at least. I was informed some months ago that Customs officers are planning to raid that vehicle just before the end of the financial year. I suppose they want to let me rack up as much profit as I can so that when it comes to compiling their annual report in March they can maximise the amount of money they can say they've recovered. That means they'll be swooping on my truck sometime now. That's where you boys came in. I want to fill that truck with stolen mobiles so that if worse comes to the worst and I do get caught, it'll look like I'm just another small-time crook trucking stolen phones to Eastern Europe or wherever. I need your phones to turn the truck they know about into a decoy. That way they won't bother wasting their time with me or look for any other trucks. They'll just hand me over to the police. If I can convince them that my stock is bona fide stolen, they won't go after my real business. Now do you understand why I'm smarter than you? Why I'm even smarter than Mr Ashwood had me figured? I don't suppose at this stage it really matters if you know what this real operation I'm referring to involves. In fact, you might learn a thing or two about the way the world works. So, time to learn how I make the bulk of my money. Truckloads of brand new mobile phones, that's how. Ten trucks to be precise – though like I said, I'm informed Customs only has the identity of one of them, the one I want to fill with your supply. Anyway, these brand new mobiles of mine, they never end up anywhere. They just stay inside the back of the trucks and warehouses while my drivers drive them around the European Union, importing them, exporting them, importing them again. They're never actually sold to an end customer. Just a chain of mostly dummy companies across the EU that I spend my days setting up and closing down and setting up again under different names. You follow?

I keep noddin. After all, I'm an A-level Economics student. But Sanjay sees right through it.

— Don't look so confused, Jas – you should understand this, what with you being clever. The good old European Common Market. It means VAT is only payable to the tax authorities when goods are actually sold to end customers in a domestic market instead of being imported and exported between them. So what I do with my chain of companies is this: I use one of my companies, let's call it Company A, to buy the mobiles VAT-free from a company in another European Union country, then I sell them on to another one of my companies in Britain at prices that include VAT. Then I close Company A down before handing that VAT over to the government. Of course the company that bought the mobiles from Company A now has a VAT invoice. So when that company conveniently decides to export the mobiles to another EU state rather than sell them to an end customer in the UK, it can reclaim that VAT back from the Treasury here. And so the phones in my trucks go round and round, clocking up phoney VAT rebates for me. Phoney, get it? Anyway, it's not rocket science. In fact, it's quite a common scam, they call it VAT carousel fraud. I like to think of it as the mother of all tax dodges. It used to be done with gold bullions, then microchips and now mobile phones. Anything small and valuable where there's a thriving grey market to insert your companies into. You see, mobile-phone supply imbalances mean surplus handsets are always being redistributed around the world. It's like a clearing mechanism for the industry. But it's also fertile ground for VAT fraud thanks to its high turnover, huge volumes and rapid transactions. And you want to know how to make serious money from it, Jas? Don't just rip off the tax authorities, rip off other mobile-phone companies as well by inserting them into your chain without them even realising. That way, at the point in the chain when they pay you prices inclusive of VAT, they're injecting new money into your chain rather than just one of your companies paying it to another of your companies. So not only do you end up with a VAT rebate from the government, you end up with an actual VAT payment from some naive mobile-phone company that you never pass on. Do you realise how much money you can make just driving ten trucks of mobiles around the EU for years and years, each time claiming nearly a fifth of their value back in cash? It's a no-brainer, Jas.

After spendin months tellin me he'd never tell me any a this shit, Sanjay gets so excited by what he's sayin an by how fuckin clever he is, that he's walkin up an down, makin weird movements with his hands the way Mr Ashwood used to do when he got all orgasmic bout History an Politics. I'm wonderin how he got into it. I mean, this probly in't the kind a thing they teach you at Cambridge. For some reason I raise my right arm slightly when I ask him, — What the fuck are you, Sanjay? Some kind a big boss man or are you in on this by yourself?

— I just told you a moment ago this is a widespread scam. As it happens I work in conjunction with others. Some friends in Birmingham mostly. It's just like a regular desi family business we've got going. I know people who've become multimillionaires doing this.

And it's not just the money. It's such a laugh inserting legitimate companies into the chain – they have no idea that they're buying and selling to companies controlled by the same guy. They just keep paying you money for nothing. All you have to do is find them, cultivate some kind of supply contract and they just snap into place in your chain. That's how I knew about your father's company. I've been trying to stick him into one of my chains for ages. How poetic then that now I can have your father's stock stolen to order to help keep customs off my back. Imagine their surprise when they raid my truck and find it full of stolen phones. I mean, you can't exactly perpetrate VAT fraud on obviously stolen goods, can you? I mean, let's say they prosecute me – it'd be like Al Capone being prosecuted for swearing instead of for tax evasion. Anyway, I'm not a fool. Even if my truck is stopped, it's highly unlikely I'll end up being prosecuted because I've arranged it so that the trucking firm takes the fall. Like I said, I don't take risks. But let's just say for some reason I *do* get fingered, it'll just be a police matter and the police don't have the powers and links with overseas tax authorities to track down all my operations and assets. Worst-case scenario, I'll probably be out in two years maximum with most of my wealth intact. It's not their fault, poor civil servants, they just don't have the resources to deal with this scam.

When he's finished showin off how smart he is, I decide it's probly best not to ask him if these Customs officers are the same customs guys you in't s'posed to stare at when you walk through the green Nothing To Declare channel in Heathrow airport. Stead, I tell him that if he knows they're after him, why the fuck don't he just park his trucks up for a year? I mean, it in't like he in't got the money to just sit an chill for a bit. Seems that he can't stop, though. If his whole chain of companies went dead all at once then Customs would know for sure. Seems that whoever those guys were, they'd been getting wiser and wiser to this VAT carousel shit. He even hands me a newspaper article to prove his point: 'Customs & Excise are cracking down on organised crime groups moving truckloads of mobile-phone handsets around Europe to claim false value added tax refunds.' But the article then goes on to say something bout legit companies gettin shafted cos they accidently find themselves in these carousel chains. Seems that loads a legit mobile-phone traders have even had their bank accounts closed when they din't realise they were caught up in a 'tainted' supply chain.

— You realise what that means, Jas? goes Sanjay. — Your father might not be inserted into my chain but I have my contacts. I know he's inserted into several others without him even realising it. I can accidently arrange for customs to find out too. First he won't be able to claim back the VAT he's owed. Then the banks won't touch him with a stick ever again. Then the Inland Revenue will start looking at all his other tax affairs – for example, how come on paper he only pays one of his co-managers a salary of less than ten grand a year? Your dad will be ruined. In fact, by stealing two hundred phones from him tonight you'll probably help your old man because he can mount a compensatory insurance claim. Like my own father always said, if you can't rip off the taxman, then rip off the insurance companies. So if you must insist on respecting your father, Jas, then you must at least know the score. Either your dad gets investigated by insurance companies or by Customs & Excise officers. I know who I'd rather not have breathing down my neck – that's why I've gone to all this trouble with you boys. Anyway, Jas, I'm getting a little bored of twisting your skinny little arm. I can't even believe I've needed to. I mean, what have you got to lose? Even if your dad catches you tonight, he's hardly going to press charges against you, is he? So really, what have you got to lose? Your dad's respect? The only thing you've got to lose is your beloved Samira because she will surely dump you if I circulate these doctored photos. Can you imagine life in a world where you had a lady like that and then she dumped you? How shameful would that be?

It takes me a whole five minutes to stand up, Sanjay switchin the DVD back on again as I do so, an I swear I can see images a Tony Soprano butt-fuckin my dad with me dressed up like some random TV presenter with a microphone, dippin crisps in dogshit before eatin them. Crunch, crunch, crunch. I just stand there an stare at

The Sopranos, Sanjay an Bobby laughin at me. My eyes have gone all fuckin rainy again an I can't answer when Sanjay asks me why cos I honestly in't sure whether it's cos a Samira, cos a him an Bobby, cos a Tony Soprano butt-fuckin my dad or whether it's cos I can actually taste shitty crisps mixed with empty stomach acid. I just fuckin cry, snot streamin onto my top lip like those aunties at the funeral this morning. Then I rush to his toilet to let the shitty, crispy stomach acid ejaculate out my throat. In't nothin there though, so I'm standin over the fuckin designer toilet, violently pukin but with jackshit coming out. Just a few drops a Scotch an stomach acid that look like some kind a yellow paste that stretches from my mouth into the toilet bowl. Milky honey burning my throat like the first time my dad let me try Scotch. I was nine years old an it was his fortieth birthday. I feel a little a that same burning honey shit in the back a my nose an so I sniff hard to stop it coming out my nostrils. The smell a burnt photo hits my sinuses an I look at what's left a Sanjay's dad in the bin beside me. Then I reach into the ash an smashed photo frame an aaawh fuck, fuck, fuck, I cut my right hand on the broken glass. As if his dad had fuckin bit me. I don't wash it though cos I don't want to stain Sanjay's hand towel. Stead, I stick my hand in my pocket, get the fuck out the toilet an head straight for the front door so as not to get blood on Sanjay's floor. But the fuckin thing is locked an it won't fuckin open an I'm fuckin stuck there, leaning against the door in case I fall over or someshit.

— Nice to see you're so eager, Jas, Sanjay says, still laughin. — I'm glad I could persuade you. I knew I could be persuasive. Bobby here wanted to help me influence your decision-making, he'd even called these two old schoolfriends of his from Southall to give him a hand. Lucky for you I assured him my methods of persuasion would work. Don't get me wrong, though, their methods are effective too. In fact, I wouldn't even know that Customs were after me if it hadn't been for Bobby and his two friends getting to work on the trader who grassed me up. You should see Bobby and them in action. In fact, you still might if you screw up tonight. My own trio of big heavies, it's just like being a Bollywood baddie. Well, I say big, but one of them's as short as your mate Ravi. I think he's some kind of professional hooligan in his spare time. But what he lacks in height he more than makes up for in sheer psychoticness. Unluckily for the trader who grassed me. Telling me exactly what he'd told Customs was the last thing he ever said. You know why?

I don't even nod this time, I just kind a retch a little more a that invisible puke. Just tell me an shut the fuck up, Sanjay, I think to myself. I need to get outta here. It's fuckin boiling in here. I can't even take my suit jacket off cos I gotta keep my bloody hand jammed in my pocket, all the time hoping it don't show through my black trousers.

— Don't be so anxious, Jas, we didn't kill him or anything. We just played a few games. You know the story of William Tell? Where he puts an apple on someone's head and shoots it with an arrow?

He waits for me to turn my retching into a nod, the blood in my pocket now soaking against my right thigh, warm, like when you wake up after a wet dream.

— Well, Bobby and his boys like to play a little variation on that scene. But in true desi style, they used a gulab jamun with this trader instead of an apple because, well, I guess we're just a sweet bunch of fellows in that way. And just so that this trader could taste how sweet we are, we put the gulab jamu on his tongue instead of on top of his head. Boy, did he stick his tongue out far. Imagine how happy his wife would have been if she'd known just how far he could extend his tongue when he really put his mind to it. She'll never know now because these heavies of mine, they're a bit unconventional. Instead of a bow and arrow they used ordinary knives.

26

Mum keeps all our spare sets a keys in her top drawer, underneath the lumps an clumps a white an beige M&S granny-style knickers. You should've seen them: I'd be less embarrassed if I looked in there an found out she wore leather thongs. I rummage through them with my left hand cos my right hand's still bleedin a bit from when I slashed it in Sanjay's bathroom bin. Dad's spare warehouse keys are right at the bottom, bunched together with the spare house keys we give to our cousins whenever we go on holiday so they can deal with any false burglar alarms, overwater our plants an overfeed our tropical fish. I take the keys, an old suitcase, a rucksack an a pair a Mum's knickers. No danger a her walkin in on me groping her underwear cos she's downstairs watchin some soap opera on TV with Dad. Still, I make sure to keep my bloody hand from staining the drawer handles, the frilly flowery cloth on top, the light switch, the pink, woodchip walls an the stair banisters. Anyway, no time to describe my fuckin house. Bye, Mum, bye, Dad, I'm going out, innit. No time for any a that What, at this time? shit.

My poor parents. They just took it from me. An the more they just took it when I took liberties, the more liberties I took. It'd stay the same as long as we never spoke bout it proply, so looked like I'd be takin liberties for a fuckin long time. Just like everyone else's dickless dad, my dad was basically too woman to ever bring it up, an Mum wouldn't bring it up cos she wouldn't go over Dad's head. Me, I was the only one who could start chattin bout this stinky shit. An

317

I weren't bout to do that. Gotta respect your elders, innit. Not just the stinky shit to do with Sanjay an the fones, I mean the whole stick a stinky shit, from the first push to the plop or satisfying splash. Hardjit, the fights, the daytime bhangra gigs, Amit, unblocking the fones, the fights, Ravi, bunking off school, bunking off college, bunking off the fuckin A-level exams, the fights, the hospitalisations, the fights. I mean, what the fuck would I say? Mama, Papa, I got something very important to tell you. Please sit down. No, please, you need to be sittin down for what I'm bout to bring up. I, well, er, I, uhm, stammer, stammer, I just wanted to tell you that I don't muthafuckin stammer no more. I don't borrow books from the library no more, we just go there to check out fit girls from the Green School. I don't listen to batty rock bands who wear skintight jeans no more. This calculator bulge in my shirt pocket? Pack a Malboro Lights. Two packs. The bulge underneath the bulge in my pocket? Newly sculpted pecs. Tupac's. An those parents' evenings you used to love so much? They in't ever gonna be the highlight a your year again. In't gonna be bout school teachers like Mr Ashwood lining up to lick your probly-old-an-hairy butts no more to congratulate you on what a fuckin fine job you done with me. Stead they gonna be bout college teachers stressin over my attendance record, my unfinished homework an the lip I give the teacher during lessons, innit. Tough shit. Tough, stinky shit. Maybe this shit's all your own fault anyway. Tough family-related shit. Cos, let's face it, you din't really do a fuckin fine job with me, you get me? D'you muthafuckin get me? Your fuckin fault. Gotta go now, don't wait up. Watch some more soap operas. Lick your own butts. Bye.

Unless a course you guys feel like stayin up to talk bout this shit? The full shit: the fights, the bhangra gigs, the fones, the fights, the bunking, the fights. Samira, Hardjit, Sanjay, Samira, Arun, Samira. The Porsche, Sanjay's flat, Vagabond. The warehouse I gotta go to now. Dad's warehouse, the one with fitter merchandise in it than that legendary Southall whorehouse Ravi used to chat bout. Maybe then we could all stay up an have our own big family showdown,

Arun-an-his-mum style. Forget your fuckin TV programme, we can have our own big drama, our own version a that big soap-opera showdown where everyone in your family suddenly decides to just oolti shit out. One giant explosion a long-retained, complicated family-related shit. An I in't meanin the usual How dare you speak to your mama that way? You are no longer my son, I am no longer your father, your mother, who is no longer your mother, is no longer my wife. Say sorry right now, go to your room, get out of my house, get out of my shop. Fuck, no. I mean the big Bollywood soap-opera showdown where they oolti everything out. Everyfuckinthing. Especially your dad. He'll still come out with all the usual Don't you dare speak to your mama that way stuff that dads always come out with. But then he'll go on to actually argue an explain his point. He'll say complicated family-related shit that so's complicated no one would ever say it in real life. Shit like, Son, I agree your mama is being a paranoid control freak military dictator but I still have my own reason for being overprotective and not wanting you to go out so late tonight. I'd just feel too guilty if anything happened to you. You must understand that I already have enough guilt bearing down on me because of the way I used to make my own mama cry when I was about your age and I accidently killed our sacred village goat and then she died an I think maybe it's emotional guilt that's caus-ing my heart disease rather than all these oily pakoras I keep eating so just do me a fucking favour and stay in tonight. Or something like that. An finally, fuckin finally, you can watch your dad kick some ass stead a just sulkin.

I'm halfway down the London Road now, an even with the empty suitcase an rucksack I got with me, I'm gonna do it in fifteen fuckin minutes. There in't many cars around, which is weird seeing how hard it's raining. An Afghan minicab driver in some tutty Nissan pulls over beside me. — Hey, mista, you vhant taxi? Huh? You vhant taxicab? I don't even look at the probly batty, kerb-crawling fucker, I just keep going, the rain splashin all down my shoes, soakin my socks, soakin the panties wrapped round my bloody right hand. You see, the reason I took a pair a Mum's knickers was to use it as a bandage for where I cut myself. They'd already got bloodstains on em anyway.

It's darker an damper outside than I thought it'd be an my head hurts even more from a daydream I had where I was back in Sanjay's flat an Bobby actually boxed me. I can still feel him grabbin me in a headlock. I can still feel him slammin his fist down on my forehead. An now I can feel some Nazi Rottweiler high on acid fuckin me in the hole that Bobby's fist made in my skull. I want to take some more aspirin for it, but don't cos I'm scared shitless a the shit that happened to Arun. The packet said don't take more than eight tablets in any twenty-four hours. Don't matter that the Rottweiler is barking in my ear at the same time as he's fuckin me, I must not take more than eight aspirins, I must not take more than eight aspirins. Arun, Arun, wherever you are. You stupid fuck. No more'n eight, you stupid fuckin dickless pehndu. While you're kickin it in Heaven or wherever with grapes an harps or whatever, everyone down here reckons it's my fault. I told you to quote Morpheus from *The Matrix*. Stead a that, your dumb ass decided to quote me. Do me a favour, dude, you owe me that much. If you're in Heaven, can you at least turn off the rain? I paid 500 bucks for this black Kenzo suit an I feel like I'm covered in wet, snotty tissue. A course, if you took them pills on purpose an you're therefore in the other place, don't worry. Save me a spot by the fire, I'll dry off when I get there.

Arun doesn't answer me, what with him being dead an the rain being too fuckin loud for me to hear his ghost. But he's here enough for me to not take no more Extra Strong Pain Relief aspirin tonite. To be sure I in't tempted later on, I pull the packet a waxy-white pills out my jacket pocket, kiss it a fond farewell an chuck it in a puddle. I can already hear the kid who'll probly find em tomorrow. Mummy, Mummy, I no feel well. I find box of white sweeties in the street, ate them all up and now I no feel well. I'm sorry, Mummy, please don't take my Barney the Dinosaur away. I no feel well, Mummy. Mummy, Mummy, ow, I no feel well.

Soon my suit gets even soggier cos each time some car whizzes past it splashes me. Only one car slows the fuck down as it passes me, a grey BMW M3. Or is it lilac? It speeds up after passin me so I can't tell. Hardjit an the others could've been coming from my house. They could've headed over there to tell me to come outside, let them beat the shit outta me in the rain like we're in some muthafuckin Bollywood film. Now they're searchin the streets a Hounslow tryin the fuck to find my ass. If that's you, stay the fuck away from me. Stay the fuck away from me tonite, I'ma take care a business. The Beemer turns left into a side street an the red, rainy glow from its tail lights goes out. It could've been grey. No one else walkin or standin out on the street, not at this time, not without an open car door to get into. Then a little further up, as I pass another side street, these three guys step out the road – two a them walkin tall cos they got them parka anoraks on, the other one a them walkin tall cos he's fuckin tall, fuckin six foot two, as big as Hardjit, as big as Bobby. Even under the anorak hoods you can tell they all got beards. Muslim maybe. Minding their own business maybe. Not doing no one no harm. Then, thud, thud, thud, they get in a car too, start the engine an stay there. If that's you, Samira's brothers, stay the fuck away from me. I said, stay the fuck away from me, Samira's brothers. I treated your sister with respect. I swear, I treated your sister with respect. Another car passes me by, some red BMW 6 Coupe. Three guys inside, the guy driving is bald an massive, six foot two maybe. Bobby, if that's you an your Southall crew, stay the fuck away from me. I'm doing Sanjay's job tonite. I know I'm a little late but my hand wouldn't stop bleedin an I'm doing it now. So stay the fuck away from me, let me do our business in peace. Another car to my right now, driven by three people with fuzzy, long hair. Their laughter cackling in the rain, broomsticks stickin out the car boot. Witches. Stay the fuck away from me. One a them's really tall, six foot two. Wearin a leather bra an thong set, with a matchin whip.

You could've been a supermodel if you din't have such a butt-ugly face. Another car, this time with werewolves, then another with vampires. Goblins, ghouls, ghosts, clowns. Clutching the warehouse keys, I just keep on walkin – quickly, but tryin not to break into a batty-boy trot. Wanting to trot though cos that's what people fuckin do when it's raining this fuckin hard. That's also what people do when they're being chased by goblins, ghouls an ghosts. Stay away from me now, Arun, stay the fuckin fuck away from me with your pale green skin, bloodshot eyes, puke-covered mouth an complicated family-related shit drippin between your fingers. You keep it, I don't want your shit. Stay the fuck away. The next thing along this shitty road pulls up next to me. There's so much light inside it, it's almost glowing.

— You alright, mate? Hop on or you'll get pneumonia, says the bus driver.

There are five other people on the bus. Two kids, one old lady, some guy in a shellsuit an the driver. Somehow, even though they're ridin on a bus, they don't seem too plebby. Matter a fact, when I get off I feel like sayin Bye to all a them, but stead I just thank the driver. Dad's warehouse is at the end a this access road just before all the airport hotels. Looks more like an alley: gravel stead a tarmac, rust gates stead a automatic barriers, two street lamps sharing thirty yards. No parked cars, not at this time. They used to have a twenty-four-hour security guard lookin after all the warehouses an shit on this industrial estate. They used to have access cards an a café. Now they just got padlocks, dogs an a CCTV camera that in't even hooked up.

As I stumble through the alley, the memory a lending Dad a hand here when I was younger gives me an adrenalin rush that helps me walk an think straight. Real life slowly gettin back into focus. But real life sucks. In real life Samira dumps you. In real life all them fit ladies only let you into those nightclubs cos you were with Sanjay an they only flashed their skin through see-through dresses cos you were with Hardjit an he's fit. In real life Arun dies an everyone feels sorry for his fuckin mum. An in real life you never get that proper Bollywood showdown, the one where your father finally stops sulkin an kicks some ass.

I check behind me when I reach the warehouse entrance but I can't see shit for rain. Even with my bloody hand the guard dog knows my smell an knows I in't worth gettin wet over. I turn the padlock key, turn the shutter key, turn the front-door key an, once inside Dad's beloved warehouse, turn the two burglar-alarm keys.

I put my finger on the light switches but decide it'd be a bad idea to press. The industrial estate looks totally empty but you never know, one a the other units could have one a those fat, sleeping security guards. There could be some other guard dog that don't know my smell, some secretary stayin back late to fuck her boss, or some totally random waterproof muthafuckin passer-by out walkin their water-proof dog. Anyway, I was smart enough to bring a torch an I know where the boxes a new fones are kept. In between Dad's little office at the back an the shelves full a accessories, fone chargers an hands-free kits up front. All I need to do is take the fones out their card-board boxes, shove em into my suitcase an rucksack, then take the empty boxes out into the access road an burn em. No fuckin sweat.

The warehouse is bout as big as two basketball courts. It smells like a library even though I know Dad pays cleaners to vacuum the place every other day. There are, like, islands made a cardboard boxes in the middle a the warehouse, some a the islands stacked up way past your head. Each cardboard box has got twenty to thirty little boxes inside, each little box contains one brand new fone. No way I could do this wearin woollen gloves so Sanjay'd told me to burn the empty boxes an there'd be less things for me to wipe my fingerprints off. The door to Dad's office is locked an though I got a key for that place too, let's be honest, do I really need to nose around in there an find out he's got a secret stash a porn for when Mum in't puttin out? I can almost fuckin *hear* her ordering Dad around in the bedroom so I stop loading the suitcase with fones an slap myself: stop fuckin imagining this, Jas, Mum's fuckin granny knickers are fuckin with your head. But if your dad can't be the bad motherfucker a the house then it's up to you, innit. You gotta be the man a the house by being harder than your mum stead a being like your dad. All this shit'd be a lot easier if your dad was harder than your mum cos it's gotta be easier to be like your dad than it is to try an not be like your mum. If you try an not be like something, you might try too much, innit. An if you try an be harder than something stead a being as hard as something, there in't no limit to how hard you gotta be.

After zipping up the suitcase, I'm just bout to start fillin the ruck-sack when I think I hear footsteps in front a me. Then I'm fuckin positive I hear footsteps cos they're thumping on the ground, runnin towards me as if they're just jokers tryin to shit me up by pretendin like they're bout to rush me. Why don't they just come flyin on fuckin broomsticks? The footsteps reach me before I realise this shit's really happenin, one a them hittin me in the chest as I put down the rucksack an drop the fuckin torch. That's right, I drop the torch, fuckin force-fields-down-we're-under-attack style. I start coughin on the floor an think I see a grey or blue trainer turn black by stamp-ing on the torch. Stay the fuck away from me, I say. Stay the fuckin fuck away from me. But they can't hear me cos I forget to fuckin open my mouth or move my tongue. I can hear cackling, a broom-stick snapping, I can smell leather thongs an matchin whips. It's the black trainer in my face again. Then the trainers give me time an space to get the fuck back on my feet. I count three guys in total, wearin balaclavas under hoods or something so I can't make out their faces for shit. One a them's a big guy, bout six foot two, one is shortish, the other average. That metal bar or weapon or whatever that the Hollywood or Bollywood hero usually finds conveniently lyin around at times like this: it weren't fuckin there. I'm too scared shitless to ask the three hooded guys who they are an even if I weren't I'm still coughin an whimpering from the kick to my chest. No, please. No, please don't hurt me. Please. Please, no. Stay the fuck away from me. Take the fones, I groan. Take the fuckin fones. But they clearly want more than the fones, an the fuckin dickless pussy that I am, I slowly crouch down an start protecting my head even before they start kickin me again. An they *do* start kickin me. In the back an chest mostly, it's as if they avoid my head on purpose. After the first round a kickin, the big guy pulls me up an, like, throws me into the shelves. Then the other two hold me still while the big guy lays into me. Again, an again an again, avoiding my head until the last moment when he thumps me so hard in the mouth that my tongue an lower lip explode, bleedin in little bursts. My cheeks fillin up, thick gobfuls a the stuff droppin onto the warehouse floor like I was slowly puking up blood or someshit. It made me feel like puking up for real – the Scotch an stomach acid I had for lunch. I try an tell em to stop but can't say shit no more with my mouth all cut up an stead I just gurgle an splutter blood. There'd be no saving my black Kenzo suit now. So wet it was, my blood. I could feel it all mess up with the bits a ugly, straggling bumfluff on my face cos I still hadn't shaved since Arun's funeral. Samira'd been so disgusted with my beard I'd wanted to slice it off my face with an axe. Tryin not to think a her, tryin not to think a the drip-drip-drippin a blood from the messed-up end a my shirt collar an onto the floor. My head stirs an drags the rest a me down. I let my bloody, painted face roll onto the floor, slowly dragged by my mummy-it's-so-painful mouth.

The other two hooded guys now join in an suddenly I'm being gang-banged in the skull an chest by a pack a Rottweilers. When I was young, before I realised I was shit at sports, I used to love it when we played basketball during PE. I din't shoot hoops or nothin, I just loved listenin to the sound the ball made bouncing on the wooden basketball court. It was like popping bubble wrap, only louder, way fuckin louder. Listenin to myself being beaten around by the three guys reminds me a the sound a bouncing basketballs an makes me want it more. As if, like a basketball, my body was designed to make that noise, to be bounced around an banged up like some nympho ho. I am covered in bubble wrap. I am made outta the fuckin stuff. It feels like all my life I'd been deprived a proper air an now I'm being force-fed air bubbles directly through my skin. C'mon, guys, whoever the fuck you are, you can do better than that. C'mon, cut off my bollocks an stamp on em like you did with my torch. People say that sometimes when guys get raped by batty boys, they ejaculate too – even if they in't a batty boy them- selves. That leads to shame an shame leads to self-loathing. This here is the assault an battery version a that shit. Only my self-loathing is worse cos I'm wishin I'd been here before. I'm wishin that I'd got mugged a few times when I was younger, that maybe my dad had beaten me shitless stead a sulkin all the time cos then I could beat him back, tear his eyes out or crush his skull, say whatever the fuck we felt like sayin – even if we were only talkin over the fuckin fone.

There in't no stoppin the three hooded guys now. They're so fast with their moves that I hardly have time to scream before the next foot, fist or forehead makes that basketball sound against me, pops the bubble wrap, cures my headache, feeds me. Rapid-fire beatin, like how sometimes the PE teacher would lob three basketballs onto the court just for a laugh. It has a kind a rhythm bout it that I just can't block out. They hit a cymbal by stampin on my bloody right hand. Then I start ruining their rhythm by screamin an cryin. Howlin like a baby in fact. The basketballs in the warehouse only slow down for one last thud as my body hits the floor again. I watch the three guys pick up the suitcase an rucksack a fones without sayin a word. Then they leg it outta there just as quickly an loudly as they'd charged towards me in the first fuckin place. I got this cousin who's a dentist. I'll need to see him sometime. It's started bleedin again an my cheeks swell up with the blood. Mama, Mama, my mouth hurts, Mama.

I in't sure if I pass out or just fall asleep into another wet dream but suddenly I'm the badass gangsta takin on those three hooded guys for stealing my dad's fones. My turn to beat the shit outta them. Punchin their faces in, breakin their necks an crushing their skulls, slowly, so that bits a their flesh, sinuses an brains ooze out through their nostrils like the snot I'll smear over their eye sockets after pullin their eyeballs out an forcing em to eat em like two pakoras fried in sunflower oil an dipped in some aunty's napalm sauce. Even better, I'll take the three a them to the nearest public toilets to see if they really are as dickless as they been actin, to bang their skulls against the diarrhoea-stained toilet bowls, mash their heads against the vomit-blocked urinals, ripping their ears off with my teeth an stuffin em up their nostrils, before stickin their cracked heads back inside the diarrhoea-filled bowls an flushing. Wipe my blood on their hoods an dry my hands on the faces underneath. So, it was you three fuckers then. I thought you were . . . Fuck it. In't no point chattin to them cos they can't hear. They can't even smell cos you've cracked their noses, lettin them feel the pleasure a blood in their sinuses mixing an gurgling with blood in their throats. They should thank you cos the blood in their nasal passages will block out the smell a the diarrhoea an vomit-stained urinals. Then drag all three a them towards the sinks an smash their heads on them so that the taps push their left eyeballs in, leavin em hanging on the basins by their eye sockets, blood from their heads pouring into the sink faster than the water flowing in through their eye sockets an into their skulls. The water then being ooltied outta their mouths an the holes where their ears had been. But not outta their nostrils, a course, cos they were stuffed with their ears. In't nobody messes with me cos I'm a hard muthafucka, innit.

When I come round again I feel grateful for finally being able to get some sleep. The clock on the warehouse wall says 2am, which means I'd managed nearly four fuckin hours. Result. An without a pillow or a blanket or a fuckin book. Although I ache all over, somehow I know in't no bones been broken. It's like a new rudeboy rule for me: if you're gonna get the shit kicked outta you, make sure you pass out. Get some decent sleep an you'll feel fuckin great. But by the time I get the fuck back on my feet, the pain comes back with a final basketball bang. That thing bout none a my bones being broken: scrap that shit. But right now I'm more worried bout my blood – not on my face an body but on the floor. I've watched *CSI* enough times that soon as I see it I know I'm seriously fucked. Soaked into

327

the carpet, my DNA is like a fuckin mobile-fone security number that can't be unblocked.

Ignoring the pain the way they teach you to in martial arts, I spend ten minutes tryin to wash the shit out the warehouse carpet with water from the bathroom tap, only to see the lather go pink like some flesh-flavoured milk shake. I untie Mum's granny knickers to soak the shit up, but still no fuckin use. Like a fuckin pussy-cat I even try an slurp some up with my tongue but the carpet stains just keep on growin. So what I do is this: I cover the stains with all the empty cardboard boxes, find a matchbox from one a Sanjay's flash nightclubs in my jacket pocket an I fuckin torch em. First the boxes disappear, then the carpet starts smelling a burning hair, then my bloodstains evaporate an take my DNA code with em. The fire heats up the blood on my face an I stand there hoping that'll evaporate too before figuring it'd probly be a good idea to put the flames out. I'd been smart enough to grab a fire extinguisher from outside the warehouse bathroom. But how the fuck was I s'posed to know the whole place would start blowin up before I'd even pulled the pin out? Even as I leg it out the door with the flames suckin off my trainers an mini explosions from the electrics in the walls sending sparks flyin into my face, I din't know the whole place'd blow the fuck up. That shit only happens in films, right? I just thought the carpet would burn a little, maybe the fire brigade would put it out, call it arson an that'd be that. Stead I get a fuckin Bollywood-style fire, fuckin exploding explosions that throw me into the gravel an cremate everything except the two things I wanted to be cremated: me an my mum's fuckin granny knickers that are now somehow tangled up in my suit.

27

If you ever want to have some big Bollywood soap-opera showdown, get yourself wound up in hospital. Just watch any episode a *ER*, *Casualty* or *Holby City*. Soon as some unlucky fucker ends up in hospital, their wives or parents or whoever start doing some big, complicated family-related shit an that shit always ends up becoming a full-on showdown. People suddenly decide their parents never loved them, their wives never understood them or their husbands are havin affairs. Maybe it's them bright lights they got in here. Maybe it's cos so many a the doctors act like desi versions a the dad from *The Cosby Show*. Maybe it's just easier to cry when you're wearin nothin but your chuds an one a them hospital gowns that give you a freezing back.

When I was eight an had to get circumcised cos a some infection I'd got down there, me an Mum ended up havin some big showdown right here in Ealing Hospital over the way I kept askin for stuff. Batman toys, Transformers, a radio-controlled car. That kind a shit. Seems that I was turning into some spoilt brat cos all the other kids never cried when their mums led them out a Woolworths' toy section with the shopping basket still empty. Then there was this other time when I was bout fourteen years old an had to have an emergency appendix operation. A couple a days later an Mum suddenly decides to do her own impression a my appendix by, like, exploding right there in that exact same children's ward. Seems that I'd been a total khota an nearly died cos I din't speak up proply bout my stomach ache. — The doctors must think I'm not fit to be a mother, she'd screamed at me. — They must all think I'm some kind of Hitler woman that you were too afraid to tell me you had a tummy ache. She even threw down my lunch, which she'd just brought from home in one a them plastic containers cos I couldn't stand the tutty hospital food no more. Said she'd reached the decision that the real reason for all my too-scared-to-speak-up-stammerin problems was cos I was a wimp an weren't good at makin friends. I was readin some History book at the time while all the other kids in the children's ward were playin cos they'd already finished their tutty lunch. I even remember the book, *Making Modern History*, cos after she'd started her big Bollywood soap-opera showdown I folded down the page I was on, shut the thing an threw it at her. That's right. I threw the fuckin book at my mum. An then I even started arguing the fuck back with her. Honest to God. I was lyin there, cryin an tellin her she shouldn't be so embarrassed a me an so fuckin what if I stammered? I din't actually swear at her, a course, an I in't too sure she understood what the fuck I was sayin anyway cos I was cryin an stammerin so much. But the point is I argued the fuck back.

That's the best thing bout havin a showdown in hospital: you suddenly grow the balls to argue back. It makes sense, innit: there you are, laid up in a metal bed with all these doctors an nurses lookin after you, an so you just figure, Fuck it, I'm in hospital an I'm upset, don't fuckin mess with me. Even when I was just an outpatient here three years ago, gettin me a sling for a tendon I tore during PE, I fought the fuck back in a showdown with Dad. After not sayin jackshit for like a whole hour, he suddenly dropped one a his slimy let's-criticise-Jas shits, sayin I'd be less crap at sports if I took an interest in the cricket an football matches he liked to watch on TV on Saturdays.

When today's hospital showdown starts, I'm feelin so fucked up that being around Mum an Dad can't make me any more nauseous than I already am. Still, Dad's fuckin me off big time, layin into me, tellin me what's what. Pretendin like he knows anything bout me an he's therefore got some right to tell me I'll've fucked up my life if I get a criminal record or someshit cos a all this. I mean, c'mon, Dad. You know you more vexed that maybe I fucked up your life, your business, your reputation an social standin. At least Mum here's honest, tellin me how much I've shamed her name in the community an givin it the usual After-Everything-We've-Done-For-You shit.

The After-Everything-We've-Done-For-You shit has got to be the dirtiest, stinkiest, slimiest shit your parents can do on you. It's the same as sayin, We've fed you with food, toys an clothes an holidays, so now even if you don't like it you've got to eat complicated family-related shit for dessert. Eat it all up. Every last splodge. Lick the plate and then lick my butt-hole because of everything we've done for you. Soon as Mum drops that After-Everything-We've-Done-For-You shit from her mouth she starts remindin me a Amit an Arun's mum. Honest to God, the two a them could be bhainjis. Mum even looks like a fairer-skinned version a Amit's mum right now, staring at me like she reckons she knows what's what. Like she knows anyshit bout anything to do with the proper world. Sittin her butt down in the only comfy chair in the whole ward, which she nicked from the guy in the bed opposite me. He's an old man who keeps shoutin at the nurses, tellin em all how he expects to be treated with more respect. Tellin em how he fought in the war against Hitler an how they'd all be speakin German if it weren't for him. German stead a Gujarati, I guess. The old man's eyesight's obviously crap so he hasn't seen Mum nick his chair, otherwise she'd probly be havin showdowns on two fronts.

Dad's just got one a them little orange plastic chairs but he keeps gettin up to stroll around my bed or take another chai break. Matter a fact the whole a today's hospital showdown is stuffed full a, like, fuckin TV ads for Tetley, Typhoo an PG Tips, starring Mum an Dad sayin how they're the only good tea bags in the world each time they stop our soap opera to go get another cup a the vending machine's unbranded, mud-coloured, metallic-tasting diarrhoea in plastic cups that probly keep the hospital busy by givin people cancer or someshit. There're ads for private healthcare too, with Mum sayin in between each sip that it's high time Dad got BUPA medical insurance for us stead a relying on the tutty NHS. Seems that all her friends, sisters an cousins got BUPA. Then, to prove her point, she screws up her newly threaded eyebrows an looks round the ward at all the other patients as if they were, like, sick.

Ealing Hospital's just like every other NHS hospital I been to round London. Nurses havin to deal with the same sick walls, leaky furniture an diluted disinfectant. Some tutty children's art project on the walls next to crumpled-up Give Up Smoking leaflets. Just outside the ward, I'd seen the same boxes with the words 'Hazardous Waste' written on the side an the exact same 'Stop, wash hands before entering' signs next to the antibacterial soap dispensers that were stuck up like flaming torches on either side a the double doors. Only difference is, here in Ealing Hospital, the signs are translated into Panjabi as well as Hindi an Urdu cos we're just down the road from Southall, innit. Further down the corridor from the soap dispensers the same long-assed lifts that make you consider takin the stairs even if you in a fuckin wheelchair. I figure this must be why Ravi's dad don't like makin National Insurance contributions as well as payin taxes. Still, maybe he in't being fair. Just like I'd stopped slaggin off plebby public transport, maybe all that talk bout the tutty NHS an bed shortages an shit is bollocks too. At least, I couldn't see no bed shortages in this place. Matter a fact, I'd counted six empty beds, four in the ward an two in the corridor outside. What they in't got is mattresses.

After finishin his fifth cup a tea, Dad gives the plastic chair a rest an stays on his feet, walkin round the bed. Askin me again what was I thinkin? What was going through that mind of mine? Who did I think I was? Stealing from my own father. Blowing up his business. After-Everything-We've-Done-For-You-After-Everything-We've-Done-For-You. An every time I try an say something he just twists

it into something I din't mean before I can even finish sayin it. I in't
sure whether he's doing this on purpose or whether it's cos he's so
used to sulkin he actually don't know how to argue. What were you
thinking, son? After-Everything-We've-Done-For-You. But mostly
Mum an Dad want to tell me I been a bloody stupid fool for hangin
round with troublemakers like Hardjit an Ravi in the first place. We
told you they were different to you. We told you they were good-
for-nothing ruffians. Now see the trouble you're in. You're not like
those kind of boys. Always, always, you're not like those kind of
boys. After-Everything-We've-Done-For-You. Always, always, After-
Everything-We've-Done-For-You.

The showdown gets so loud that some nurse comes over an closes
the green curtain around my bed. Shame. She's fit, the nurse. Long,
black wavy hair, thin yet juicy lips an grey eyes that could even be
blue. As she pulls the curtains to the foot a my bed I notice how
shiny her white stockings are an how they don't match the black
hipster panties showin through her tight white uniform. She don't
even look like a real nurse, more like one a them porn stars or stri-
pagrams who dress up like nurses just so that they can undress like
one. For a moment I think I might even've got enough to impress
her: two cracked ribs, a broken nose, split lip, lots a bruises an a
mild concussion. She'd smiled at me earlier when she told me I might
be well enough to go home tomorrow. But who knows? Maybe you'll
have to stay with us a little longer, she'd said. Whatever happens, one
thing's for fuckin sure: I'll definitely be well enough tomorrow to
finally talk to the feds bout all this, give em a statement, that kind
a shit. But not today. That's the thing bout concussion: the A&E
doctor told the feds that they'd got to lay off me for a day. It's worth
remembering that if you ever decide to become a badass hard muthafucka.

Right now, the only thing the feds know is that I was tryin to rob
my dad's mobile-fone warehouse an burnt it down after gettin the
shit kicked outta me by three unidentified assailants. They don't
know why. I'd told em I'd got no fuckin idea who my attackers were,

I couldn't even take a guess. They'd questioned my dad bout everything when he first arrived. He said he din't have a clue what the
bloody hell was going on. We hadn't yet started our showdown by
that stage, you see, so all I'd said to Mum an Dad by then was, Ow,
Mummy, Mummy, my head hurts. I'd waited for the two feds to go
an for the A&E doctor to move me up to this ward before I told
Mum an Dad anything. But when I did, I'd decided to just oolti it
all out before it brewed into diarrhoea. I wanted someone to know,
I guess. An who else was there to tell? I in't good at makin friends,
remember. In't nobody else listenin to us anyway. The nurse was
too busy helpin patients, an when she weren't doing that she was too
busy being fit. The World War II vet was probly deaf as well as blind.
The guy next to him was playin some weird heavy metal shit on his
walkman an the guy next to me was unconscious. The other beds
in the ward were either empty or too far away an so I continued
oolting up everything that led to me burning down Dad's business.
But unlike the fights, the bunking, the daytime bhangra gigs, the
fone-unblocking business an Arun's complicated family-related shit,
I wanted Mum an Dad to know that rippin off the warehouse was
my gig. Mine an Sanjay's. Hardjit, Amit, Ravi an any a them other
guys I shouldn't be hangin round with had fuck all to do with it.
This was me. You should be proud a me. This is who I am. Pleased
to meet you.

After a while, both a them shut the fuck up for a bit an just start
lookin at me like they don't know me. Like I'm holdin a gun to their
head after raping the other with a strap-on lump a the complicated
family-related shit still brewing inside our butts. Actually, I really
need to take a shit myself now – a proper shit, I mean. Problem is
I'm wearin that hospital gown an no fuckin way am I lettin that fit
nurse know I'm takin a dump while, like, holdin up a fuckin dress.
So I just lie there in my gown, Dad just sits there in the plastic orange
chair an Mum gets even smaller in the comfy one she's stolen from
the World War II vet. She's lookin cold an pale an devastated while

Dad just looks like some alien's sucked his brain out his butt an left him with no mind, no thoughts, no nothin. But as I stare at him more closely, I could swear Dad's growin brand new bags under his eyes. They look more like fuckin suitcases given the amount a shit building up between us. An pretty soon it starts sprayin out again, onto my bed sheets, my gown an the curtains.

— I don't know what the bloody hell you're doing hanging round with these delinquent fools for anyway, Dad says again. — Wait one minute while I phone their parents, tell them what sort of trouble their sons have got you into.

— Dad, I warned you downstairs in A&E: if you call the other guys' parents things'll be ten times worse.

Suddenly Mum starts all her cryin shit bout how horrible her life is, how will she hold her head up, what will other people say when they find out I'd gone out with a Muslim girl. Honest to God, for a while it seems like that's what's upset her the most. Me snoggin a Muslim. She's a bit like Ravi's mum in that way. Aunty was always tellin Ravi she'd die if he ever went out with a BMW (by which she meant black, Muslim or white). Matter a fact, I reckon the only reason she gave Ravi her lilac Beemer was to make him feel too guilty to get his own BMW. Then Mum starts givin me grief again for hangin around with my ruffian friends, sayin how she'd always told me that Hardjit fellow was trouble. Apparently you could tell from his eyes.

Twenty minutes later an they're *still* shoutin this same shit at me. Hopefully the closed curtains will keep bits a my brain from splattering all over the ward when my fuckin head explodes. Every blood vessel up there rumbling my brain the way you can suddenly feel your guts churning around bout an hour after you've eaten some dodgy, undercooked kebab. The sound a your stomach makin a decision – will it be oolti or will it be diarrhoea? Will your brain explode or will it just melt an trickle out your eyes an ears? Or will the veins up there freeze like pipes cramping up under my cold an aching skull? Whatever the fuck's going on up there, I try an make it hurt less by tellin both Mum an Dad to just shut the fuck up.

It's Dad who breaks the silence by askin me one more time to explain the VAT fraud Sanjay'd got going on. What the fuck? Are you thinkin bout copyin it an addin it to all the other dodgy tax dodges that you call business? Maybe you should go work with Ravi's old man. This is serious shit, Dad. This is how I know that Sanjay's actually a big time G an not just some other desi kid tryin to act like a G. Dad looks at me like he can't understand what I'm sayin an so I explain that a G is a gangsta, a badass, a bad apple, Dad, a fuckin bad apple. He gets up, massages his forehead, opens the curtains an leaves.

— You see what you've done to your father? goes Mum. — You'll kill him with all the stress you've caused him.

Here we go again, I think to myself. That fucked-up rule that says the best way to respect your elders is to treat them as if they were fragile little four-year olds. When I try an explain this to her she decides not to understand me.

— You'll kill me with all the shame you've caused, she carries on. — You get a criminal record, I won't know what to do.

— I haven't got a criminal record yet, Mum. Who says I'm gonna get one anyway? Look, when the police come to talk to me tomorrow an take that statement or whatever I'll explain all bout Sanjay. I don't want to grass Hardjit an the others but I'll grass up Sanjay's whole VAT scam no probs. Maybe if I do they'll let me off lightly. The feds do that all the time if you grass people up.

— Yes, of course you would know this. You with those delinquent friends of yours.

Then she slaps me. Once. Twice. My face burns as if some alcoholic napalm chilli sauce is being rubbed into an open wound. She's cryin as she does this, an a course I just let her. She's my mum, my elder, an so I just lie there an let her carry on rubbin the chilli sauce into my wounds. What the fuck else can I do? Hit her back? After a couple a minutes Dad comes back in, holdin his mobile fone.

— I just spoke with your old teacher Mr Ashwood, Dad says to me. — I had his mobile number from when you did extra lessons after school. I asked him what the bloody hell this Sanjay friend of his has done. Bloody fool.

— Dad, this in't Mr Ashwood's fault. Why're you always lookin for someone else to blame? It's my fault. Not Mr Ashwood's, not Hardjit's, not Amit's or Ravi's. My fuckin fault.

— Don't be a bloody fool. Mr Ashwood is coming to visit you tomorrow to sort things out. But he says the most important thing now is not to let you get a criminal record. No jail, no boys' home. No more bad influences. No life of crime. So I'm telling you, son, tomorrow you will not tell the police about Sanjay.

— But Dad, I was just tellin Mum, maybe if I grass him they'll let me off.

— Don't be a bloody fool. What if he tries to blame all the stolen phones on you? Then what will you do? Say it was the other boys? Hardjit and these other boys won't get in much trouble, they didn't burn down my warehouse. So, I've decided: tomorrow there will be no telling the police about Sanjay. I wish I could tell them you were just picking up the phones for me.

— What, with a suitcase in the rain while you sat at home an watched TV? I don't think they'll believe you, Dad. An anyway, you already told em you din't know what I was doing there. They'll get sus if you change your mind.

— Of course I know this. I know this. I know they won't believe me.

— So let's just tell em the truth then. They might let me off lightly.

— No. No. Mr Ashwood is right. You must not get a criminal record. There are already too many bad influences on you. So, I've decided. I *did* send you to the warehouse. That's why you went there. I sent you. I asked you to steal some phones and burn the place down so that I could claim it from the insurance company. You pretended some people beat you up to make it look like a robbery but then you accidentally knocked yourself out. This way, the police will understand why before I told them I didn't know what happened.

Mum started protestin an cryin again. I guess she must've figured it'd be even more shameful if society thought she'd got a criminal husband rather than a criminal son. But truth is, even I thought Dad was being a bit crazy.

— Dad, I don't understand. I mean, I tried to rip you off. Why not just dob me in?

— You think there's something unusual about a father trying to protect his son?

— No. But this is a big deal. You could end up going to jail. Me, I'll probly just get community service or something. At worst a few months in Feltham Young Offenders Institute. You can come an visit if you go an see any Bollywood films at Feltham cinema. An who knows? Might even give me some street cred.

— You won't go to a young offenders' home, goes Dad. — Mr Ashwood explained it to me, you are not a boy any more.

— I'm just jokin, Dad, can't you tell? Why would you guys go to the cinema to see a Bollywood film?

— This is no time for jokes, son, we must, howdoyousay, get our story straight.

— You're serious, aren't you, Dad?

— Of course I'm bloody serious. This is a bloody serious matter.

— I know, Dad, I know. I just don't get why da fuck you'd do that for me.

— You watch your language, son. Why don't you think I'd do this for you? You think I'll let you go to jail? Is that what you think of me?

— No. Look, all I'm sayin is it's just a bit outta the fuckin blue.

Now it's Mum's turn to tell me not to swear at my dad. An in a weird, fucked-up way I'm glad. It's nice to hear her stick up for him, you get me? I wonder whether Amit's mum'd do the same for her husband.

— What do you mean, this is out of the blue? goes Dad. — You mean to say I never supported you when you've needed me before?

That the only people who ever helped you in life are Mr Ashwood, bloody Hardjit and this Sanjay fellow? Everything I've done, I've done for you but you act like I've never given you anything.

— No, Dad, I'm not sayin that.

— Yes you are. I know this is what you like to think. That your parents aren't there for you. But tell me, son, what about when you failed your A-levels? Who spent two weeks fighting with the examining boards? Who arranged your retakes?

— Yeh, but this is a bit different, Dad. I mean, you could go to jail for this. I'm just sayin, it's all a bit shocking that you would do that, that's all. I mean, we in't exactly best mates, Dad. I mean, let's be honest, do you really even know me? I mean, all that stuff I was just tellin you bout that Samira girl, that's the first time I ever told you bout a girl. An if she hadn't been part a why I ended up burnin down your business I probly never would've spoken to you bout her. We just never talk – you're too busy with your fones.

— You want to talk? Let's talk. I've given you everything you could want and all you do is look for reasons to pretend we don't even exist and behave like some delinquent rebel. But just as I can't bear to see my son in a hospital bed, I won't be able to bear seeing him in a jail either. What more do you want to talk about?

An so there I was, lyin in a gown covered in Mum an Dad's sobby shit. After everything Dad's just said an after everything they've done for me, all I can manage to do is wipe his shit from my eyes an say,

— I'm sorry, Dad.

— You say I don't know you. But you don't know me. All the time playing with those friends of yours. Remember how at one stage your mother and I even thought you were doing drugs because at least then your behaviour would make some sense. I ask you to come and watch football with me. You don't want it. What can I do?

— Dad, it's not that I don't want to, it's just that –

— What? Because you think you're one of them?

— What?

— One of those Hardjit, Amit boys. You're not like them. We keep telling you. You don't want to know us because we keep telling you. What's wrong with us, son? What's wrong with us that you spend more time with Hardjit's father and mother than you do with your own father and mother? I know for a fact Hardjit's father never wants to watch football with his son. I know him. I know this. I know these things. Those two, father and son, they *really* don't know each other. But why do you pretend it's the same with us? And while Hardjit's father is always saying how his son abuses his Sikh religion, I've respected your ways, your youngster's version of Indian culture. And we both tried. Your mother and I. We tried for your sake to be friends with them, to be like them, to get to know them. So that's how we know what we're talking about. Your mother here, she even tried to cook like their mothers. We tried. You're not like them, son. Now look at the trouble you're in.

— What're you tryin to say, Dad? Mum, what's Dad tryin to say?

— You know exactly what your father's saying, Jas.

— Yes. You know exactly what I'm saying, Jas. You think I'm being . . . what's that fancy word you always use? A bigot? You think I don't want you to hang around with these other boys because I'm a bigot? Why can't you just use the word racist, Jas? That's what you think, isn't it? That your mother and I are racist? Isn't that what you think, Jas? I don't even know why we agree to use this Jas nonsense nickname of yours anyway, I mean what kind of a name is that, Jason? You hear what your mother and I are trying to say to you, Jason?

I din't even look at him.

— What nonsense is this you don't even respond to your own name? Jason Bartholomew-Cliveden, do you hear what I'm saying?

Then Dad grabs the clipboard from the end a my bed an, like, shoves it in my face. — Look, he says. — It says your name here on your medical chart: Jason Bartholomew-Cliveden, aged nineteen, white, male.

*   *   *

After it's obvious that I in't gonna stop ignoring em, Mum an Dad head back to the tea machine for more diarrhoea, which they bring back an slurp at my bedside. I accuse them a being bigoted like I always do, but it don't help cos they say they din't mind my old desi friends, my coconut friends. So I just carry on ignoring em and they just carry on slurping their diarrhoea an there in't no more show-down. There in't even no more talkin till the fit nurse with the black hipster panties strides over an says, — Excuse me, Mr Cliveden?

— Bartholomew-Cliveden, goes my dad. — Why can't people get our surname right?

— Sorry, Mr Bartholomew. It's just that it's getting late and patients really aren't allowed visitors after nine.

— But our son, he's hurt and upset.

— I know, but Jason's not in a serious condition. I'm sorry, sir. But it *is* midnight.

Dad just grunts an doesn't even nod goodbye at me. But Mum leans over an strokes my head, gives me a kiss on the cheek, asks if I need anything. Why she does all this when I been ignoring em for twenty minutes I got no idea. Cos she's my mum probly.

When she an Dad have finally gone, the fit nurse comes back over an puts her own hand on my head. Her wrists smell more like peaches than hospital disinfectant. Then she shoves a thermometer in my mouth to double-check. It's while she's readin the thermometer that she realises I'm blatantly staring through her tight white uniform at her probly padded breasts.

— Where's that from then? I say before she can react. — Your name?

— Oh, my badge, she smiles, curling those thin juicy lips till dimples break in her cheeks. — Isn't it obvious? Then she holds the thermometer to her eyes. — You seem to have a slight fever, Jason. Let me get some paracetamol for you. I try not to check out her white stockings an perfect butt as she walks towards the nurses' station in the corner. From behind she looks skinnier an curvier all at the same time. She's taken my medical chart or whatever with her an stops to read it like it's the most important chart in the world. I'm thinkin, maybe cos she's a nurse she in't allowed to wear black stockings to match her underwear. Then I'm thinkin, maybe I should stop perving, when suddenly she turns an comes back.

— It looks like you've had enough paracetamol already, she gives it. — So I'll wake you up in two hours, and if you've still got a fever then, I'll call the doctor on duty – he can decide whether to start you on some antibiotics.

Then she notices me lookin at her breasts again an gives it, — Are you still trying to guess where my name is from?

— Hmmmmm, I give it, — Shilpa Mohan? Sounds Indian.

— Well done, she goes, makin sure my water jug is full an then hangin my chart back on the foot a my bed.

— Sounds Panjabi, I go, managing to bring out her dimples again. Then she walks back round to my bedside table, grabs the jug an pours me a fresh glass a water.

I wanna show her my good manners by sayin Thank you. But Jazzy Jas Man can do better than fuckin Thank you. I shoot her a look an give it, — Shukriya.

ACKNOWLEDGEMENTS

Thanks for turning my manuscript into a book:
Peter Straus and Nicholas Pearson;
Richard Bravery, Michelle Kane and all at 4th Estate;
Rowan Routh, Zoe Waldie, Lisa Baker and all at Rogers Coleridge &
White;
Inigo Thomas and Katherine Fry.

Thanks for suggestions, support and advice:
Monica Malkani, Bharat Malkani, Sushma Juneja, Graham Watts,
Lucy Kellaway, David Goodhart, Alex Linklater, Anup Chowdhry,
Omar Methar, Anisha Patel, James Pickford, Reena Bhardwaj and
Michael Skapinker.

Thanks for help with the research:
The late Dr Sue Benson and all those who agreed to be interviewed.

Thanks for making me read books:
Paul McLoughlin, Rosella Miles, the late James Ferguson and Meena
Malkani.